Praise for *Under Her Roof*

'Intense, intricate and packed with intrigue, *Under Her Roof* is a thrilling and addictive read.' B.A. Paris, author of *Behind Closed Doors* and *The Guest*

'The brilliant A.A. Chaudhuri with another thrilling read. This one is her best yet. **Taut and intricately plotted with such exquisite writing.** Characters that jump off the page. And **a smouldering read.** You know something is going to get you. You just don't know what.' Imran Mahmood, author of *You Don't Know Me*

'*Under Her Roof* is **a compulsive thriller that crackles with a sense of menace.** Tense, twisty, and gorgeously atmospheric, it **pairs a gripping plot with dark, intricate themes.** Money, class, sex and obsession are all used to expose the rot beneath the gloss of desirable London living.' Kia Abdullah, author of *Those People Next Door*

'*Under Her Roof* is **a spine-tingling, cerebral thriller** packed with real psychological depth and **a final twist that hits you like a gut-punch.**' Chris Merritt, author of *Committed*

'*Under Her Roof* is **a masterclass in suspense** – I couldn't put it down, and **the twists will absolutely floor the reader.**' Lisa Hall, author of *Between You And Me*

'A.A Chaudhuri's darkest novel yet. **Made me lock the door twice.**' Jacqueline Sutherland, author of *The Coffin Club*

'I should know better than try to predict A. A. Chaudhuri's endings. **This spine-tingling masterpiece of a thriller has a perpetual creeping death vibe with more twists than an Alpine road.** Chaudhuri's talent for hooking the reader with **ingenious plots and addictive characters** is only surpassed by her ability to craft **explosive, unguessable endings.**' Graham Bartlett, author of *City On Fire*

'*Under Her Roof* is **a gripping, voyeuristic page-turner with a chilling secret at its heart, from a hugely talented crime writer at the very top of their game.**' Howard Linskey, author of *The Inheritance*

'**A dark, twisty, unputdownable thriller** that will send your mind spinning. **Truly sublime.**' BP Walter, author of *The Dinner Guest*

'**Simmering with tension** and an underlying sense of danger, *Under Her Roof* is **an addictive thriller with a jaw-dropping twist.**' Michael Wood, author of *The DCI Matilda Darke thriller series*

'**A tense and atmospheric** slow-burn thriller, **perfectly plotted and with a brilliant twist** – A.A. Chaudhuri at her absolute best.' Catherine Cooper, author of *The Island*

'**Dark, gripping and smouldering** – all at the same time! **Intricately plotted and the twist flawed me.** *Under Her*

'A **darkly addictive** and **unputdownable** thriller, it kept me guessing, I loved it!' Jane Isaac, author of *One Fatal Secret*

'A **compelling psychological thriller** that kept me second guessing myself throughout. **And when the twists came – wow!** I had no idea! **Fantastic storytelling** from A.A. Chaudhuri.' Joy Kluver, author of *Last Seen*

'A. A. Chaudhuri has really pulled it out of the bag with her latest twisty & compelling psychological thriller, *Under Her Roof*! **I was gripped from the start to the explosive finish. The characters were fascinating, the writing flawless and the story was one that will stay with me for a long time to come!** Utterly fantastic! Everything I have come to expect from an A. A. Chaudhuri.' Christie J. Newport, author of *The Ordinary Man*.

Under Her Roof

A. A. Chaudhuri is a former City lawyer. After gaining a degree in History at University College London, she later trained as a solicitor and worked for several major London law firms before leaving law to pursue her passion for writing. She lives in Surrey with her family, and loves films, all things Italian and a good margarita!

Also by A. A. Chaudhuri

A.A. CHAUDHURI

Under Her Roof

hera

First published in the United Kingdom in 2024 by

Hera Books
Unit 9 (Canelo), 5th Floor
Cargo Works, 1–2 Hatfields
London SE1 9PG
United Kingdom

A CIP catalogue record for this book is available from the British Library.

Print ISBN 978 1 80436 295 2
Ebook ISBN 978 1 80436 294 5

This book is a work of fiction. Names, characters, businesses, organizations, places and events are either the product of the author's imagination or are used fictitiously. Any resemblance to actual persons, living or dead, events or locales is entirely coincidental.

Look for more great books at www.herabooks.com

Printed and bound in Great Britain by Clays Ltd, Elcograf S.p.A.

1

For Chris, Adam and Henry, with love.

Appearances are often deceiving

Aesop

Prologue

How is this even happening? How have I found myself on trial for murder?

Anyone who knows me will tell you I am not capable of murder. Yet the evidence laid out by the prosecution would suggest otherwise.

I keep my hands clasped tightly together on my lap while sitting silently in the dock waiting for the judge to enter the room. I do so partly to stop them from shaking, but also because it gives me something to focus on, as does looking straight ahead at nothing and no one in particular. I am fearful of making eye contact with anyone at this moment. I am under the microscope, my every move being watched, and it's hard to act naturally under such intense scrutiny.

Likewise, it requires every ounce of effort on my part to hold back the words on the tip of my tongue itching to get out but constrained by the court's strict contempt rules. Rules I am terrified of breaking, knowing the judge and jury already have the wrong impression of me. They doubtless consider me a monster, something I cannot blame them for, and so I daren't say anything to further augment that macabre image. Equally, I am too frightened to meet the jury's gaze, even though I so badly want to protest my innocence through earnest eyes. Make them see that I am not the monster here, but rather, the victim.

I worry that they will interpret my staring as a look of menace, a warning that they had better not reach the wrong verdict if they do not wish to become victims themselves. But then again, will my failure to meet their gaze cause them to believe I have something to hide? A sign of a guilty conscience perhaps? Even though I have nothing to feel guilty about, having done nothing wrong. I should have come forward sooner, should have trusted what my gut was telling me. But I suppose I didn't want to believe it. And by the time I had reconciled myself with the truth, it was too late.

My barrister is brilliant, but he is not a magician. There is only so much he can do in the face of insurmountable evidence planted against me. Despite me knowing the identity of the real culprit. Someone who is smart, devious and callous through and through. Someone who tricked me, tricked others, and who set me up for a fall from which I fear there'll be no picking myself up. Someone who, right now, is sitting in this very courtroom. Taunting me with their sheer presence, ramping up my suffering and the sense of injustice that courses through my veins and fuels a rage I can only contain by clenching my hands even tighter, the bones of my knuckles jutting through my pallid skin, my nails almost drawing blood.

There's only one more witness the defence hopes to call. One who, until now, has failed to come forward and give evidence. But who could hold the key to my salvation.

I pray to God that they come through for me. Can be made to talk, tell the truth. That they won't let pride or anger stand in the way of doing what is right. The fact is, right now I'm in a hole so deep, that without their testimony, I fear it's going to take a miracle from the Almighty to pull me out.

Chapter One

Seb

'It's a fantastic property, as I'm sure you could tell from the photos on the website,' Max, the guy I spoke with yesterday on the phone, assures me after we shake hands and engage in small talk about what a wonderful part of London Hampstead is. It's eleven a.m. on a bitingly cold Saturday in early January. Thankfully, the sun is shining brightly making the glacial weather more bearable, as does the thick woollen overcoat I'm wearing in a bid to stop the ice-pick wind from cutting through me, despite my naturally muscular frame. I tell Max that I couldn't agree more, both about the photos and Hampstead. As a struggling writer, I can't think of a better place to inspire me, the area a veritable breeding ground for literary greats, past and present. Although that's not the only reason I'm here in London. I don't mention this to Max, however. It's something I plan on keeping to myself for the time being. If, and until, I know more.

Max isn't an estate agent. He introduces himself as an assistant to the owner of the property we're about to see, assuring me that I personally won't owe him a penny should the tenancy be offered to me. Because I'm not exactly flush with cash, I'm reluctant to pay excessive estate agents' fees, and so decided to look on the Open-Rent website to see if I could find anything suitable to rent from a private landlord in the north London area. Cutting out the middleman enables me to save a ton of cash I cannot afford to fritter away, even though I have quite a bit of money in savings and have recently started working part-time in a swanky bar in Kensington that pays better than the East End dive I've been pulling pints in these past few months. Those savings won't last forever, though, and I'd rather keep them aside for a rainy day, or when I'm ready to put down roots. I'm also hoping that renting via a private landlord will be a less invasive process than going through an agent. The fewer questions asked the better, as far as I'm concerned. I don't need my past being dug up, having done my level best to bury it since my late teens.

When I started searching for rentals, I ideally wanted my own place, as opposed to renting a room in a house or flat shared by other tenants and where I'd be under constant surveillance, but I also realised that beggars can't be choosers and that it was highly unlikely I'd be able to find anything all to myself in Hampstead even remotely within my price range, the area famous for having more millionaires than any other zone of London. So I'd settled on the idea of renting a flat or studio somewhere close by – Kilburn, for example – which would still allow me easy access to Hampstead's literary scene, along with the ability to pursue another agenda I haven't told anyone about. Not even my closest friends. Including Jasper, my best mate from Edinburgh university, who moved to London after we graduated and with whom I'm currently staying in Camden. Jasper's the only person who knows everything about my past. The only one I've felt able to trust with my deepest, darkest secrets when Mum and I returned from Nigeria, the both of us having disappeared there for three years soon after my sixteenth birthday. After Jasper and I graduated in English literature, he found himself a job at a publishing house just off Charing Cross Road. I was happy for him, if not secretly a little envious. But despite my buried jealousy, the thought of applying for a similar position where potential employers were bound to ask questions, but more worryingly do their due diligence, was one that filled me with dread. University was bad enough, despite me changing my name before I enrolled and choosing to study as far away as possible from where I grew up in Brighton. But the working world isn't so forgiving, and I seriously doubted that a publisher would greet me as warmly into their fold as they did Jasper if they discovered my background. Bottom line – people are nosy, they ask questions. They want to know where you're from, about your family, your childhood. That's not for me, it can never be, because I'll never be able to eradicate the past. Who I am. All that despite my burning desire to write, and having been told by my careers advisor that getting a job in publishing might be the first step on the ladder to writing success in an industry where striking a book deal was akin to winning the lottery, and therefore a touch of nepotism wouldn't go amiss. Still, I'd avoided the inevitable questions by going travelling for two years after graduating at twenty-two. Despite feeling guilty about leaving Mum alone, having persuaded her to come back from Nigeria with me when I started university. I guess, having lost Dad unexpectedly in my mid-teens, I wanted to keep her close by for fear of losing her too, and she'd reluctantly agreed to move to Scotland, finding a decent two-bedroom flat in Edinburgh where I could check on her and stay during the holidays. Anyway, after finishing my degree and unable to summon the nerve to apply for a proper job, I'd visited far-flung countries like Australia, New Zealand and Singapore, where no one knew me from Adam, and where I could be free, get lost in the crowds, immerse myself in a different culture and forget about the scandal back home that continued to stalk me like my own shadow.

Coming back to English soil aged twenty-four after such a long break, I had hoped to feel different. Reborn. That enough time would have elapsed for me to feel more optimistic about the future; certain that I could fit into normal society and feel proud of who I was. But I didn't feel different. And I didn't feel proud. And then, when Mum took her own life six months after my return, I knew that I could never be free. Never live a normal life. Just as she hadn't felt able to, broken by what happened to us, neither the crossing of oceans nor the passage of time a cure for the wounds that would never heal. Mum's suicide is something that haunts me day and night. A suffocating black cloud that looms over me wherever I go, and one I feel sure I'll never be free from. Not until I take my last breath. I guess it's partly why I write. It's an escape, a fleeting release from the pain and regret I feel.

As a writer, I can be anyone, switch personas, enter and abandon any world, but more importantly leave the crappy one we're born into to those able to walk about it freely. No one need know my real name, the baggage I've carried like a millstone around my neck since my life changed forever. And so, I have no choice but to survive on my inheritance and part-time stints that pay the rent and allow me to write until one day that big break might come.

Despite knowing there was zero chance of me finding somewhere affordable to rent in Hampstead, I still had a browse on OpenRent out of pure nosiness more than anything, I suppose. And that's when I saw the listing for Number 8 East Heath Road. Described as being a contemporary, minimalist six-bedroom house and covering an incredible 7,000 square feet, but even more astoundingly within my budget, despite it looking like something out of *Tatler* which the likes of me should never set foot in, let alone live in. It was too good to be true, and when I looked more closely at the small print I realised why. What was being offered to me was, in fact, a room, rather than the whole property, and so I'd effectively be a lodger in the house rather than a tenant. This was why it was so cheap. Also, in exchange for the moderately priced rent, the owner of the property – also resident there – required his prospective lodger to carry out certain jobs for him on an ad hoc basis. Such jobs were not specifically listed but all interested parties were instructed to make further enquiries via the named contact – Max – on the mobile number provided.

It seemed a bit cheeky to me, to have advertised on a private rental website rather than a site more suited to spare room vacancies like Gumtree or SpareRoom. And given my desire for privacy, I'm not sure why I made the call knowing I'd be living with the landlord – surely, an even worse prospect than sharing with a fellow tenant? As a lodger at the property, I'd potentially have far fewer rights than that of a conventional tenant under an assured tenancy, the landlord fully justified in entering my room unless agreed otherwise, while also free to draw up his own set of rules however he saw fit. Perhaps sheer curiosity got the better of me. The excitement of seeing the property in the flesh, having been wowed by the photos. Because there's no denying, the place looks out of this world from what I saw on the website. Heaven compared to the pretty ropey flat Jasper is renting in an equally dodgy area of Camden, and where every night coming home from the Tube station I spend much of the time looking over my shoulder, wondering who might pounce from the shadows and do God only knows what to me. Plus, I suppose I was curious to learn what jobs would be required of me. Logic dictated that they must be fairly onerous – the price of living in such luxury. Even so, I felt the urge to find out for myself. I had nothing to lose and was under no obligation to take things further.

I follow Max's lead through the property's impressive automatic wrought-iron gates, which he opens by pressing a stylish metallic key fob. He may not be an estate agent, but he certainly looks and acts like one. Pearly-white smile. Sharp pinstripe suit, black brogues polished to perfection, immaculately gelled hair with not a strand out of place. That, along with his public-school accent, natural gift of the gab and peacock-like strut, makes me wonder why he's not making millions punching numbers at a trading desk in the City, rather than showing the likes of me around a property in north-west London. He reminds me in some ways of Dad. Everything about him radiated confidence. It was instinctive. From the way he walked and gesticulated with his hands, to how he spoke with clear yet animated diction. Always the charmer, but without being sleazy, and with an innate ability to make anyone he was with feel at ease. The kind of guy you'd want to be stuck in a lift with. Effortlessly effusive, a born showman. But not in an arrogant way. I'm more like Mum, I guess – naturally quiet, self-effacing. Cautious.

9

I'd been standing in front of the gates no more than five minutes trying my best not to freeze to death before Max pulled up in his cobalt-blue BMW. Whoever the landlord was, he must pay his assistants well, I thought to myself. Unlike Max, I'd taken the Northern line from Camden, having nearly missed the Tube I was aiming for. At least with it being relatively early for a Saturday, the capital having not quite come alive after the first night of the weekend's partying, I managed to find a seat, in contrast to weekdays when it's all I can do to stop myself from being elbowed in the face or throw up while squashed inside an airless carriage that reeks of bad breath and body odour.

I've never liked confined spaces. Not since a classmate at school thought it would be hilarious to lock me in his parents' cupboard under the stairs during a sleepover. I was only six and terrified. I prefer the fresh air, being out in the open. It's why I loved Australia and New Zealand, with their vast open plains, the outdoor way of life. Likewise, I know I would have happily stayed in Brighton had circumstances beyond Mum's control not driven us away to Nigeria, and then later to the big city on my return to the UK. First Edinburgh and, in the last few months, London, where I can feel anonymous, get swallowed up in the crowds.

Max continues to guide me along a gravel pathway up to the front of the property, a vast brick and glass-fronted building, unique in its design and set on a slight slope allowing for greater seclusion from the street, while the imposing leafy-green shrubbery either side of it only enhances that sense of isolation. It also appears to have a name etched on a slate plaque pinned to one side of the door:

I'm instantly intrigued, thinking how apt it feels for the property's secluded position. *Perhaps living here will bring me the peace I desire?*

'Can I ask why the room wasn't listed on a website like Gumtree?' I ask. 'It's a bit misleading advertising on a private landlord website, don't you think? I was initially looking for somewhere to rent to myself, not just a room.'

Max gives me a slightly irritated look. I get the feeling I'm not the first person he's shown around who's asked this. 'My boss is a very cautious person. Doesn't trust those types of websites. Sites that only advertise single rooms, I mean. Thinks it might attract the wrong sort, if you follow me. You can never be too careful as to who you let into your house these days. I mean, you hear all sorts of nightmare stories about lodgers from hell, don't you?'

It feels like a bit of a pretentious answer to me. Then again, he has a point. You *can* never be too careful, and casting my eye around the lavish surroundings, I suppose I get where Max's boss is coming from. 'Is the landlord home?' I ask as Max runs his finger down the keypad of what appears to be some kind of fingerprint smart lock. He then removes a key from his pocket and uses it to unbolt a standard chrome five-lever deadlock fitted at the top of the door. Clearly, he wasn't kidding about the landlord being vigilant.

'No,' Max replies, looking back over his shoulder, 'not right now.'

We step into a spacious hallway. An alarm immediately sounds, and I watch in amazement as Max opens a trapdoor picture frame bordering a stormy ocean scene to reveal a keypad alarm. Very slick. Glancing around,

I'm also struck by the elegant parquet wood flooring and pristine off-white walls, as well as the natural light flooding in. What an awesome place this would be to write in, I think.

'She thought you'd be more comfortable seeing the place on your own first,' Max continues.

'She?' I repeat with surprise. I guess it's pretty clichéd of me to have assumed the landlord was male, but the fact is I did, and it's somewhat floored me to learn otherwise. After all, this isn't a normal arrangement where I'll be living on my own. She'll be living under the same roof with me. Not only that, I'll apparently be doing random jobs for her. Not that I have anything against working for a woman. I'm one of the most liberal-minded guys I know. It's something I've consciously tried to be over the last few years. A mindset my beloved mum instilled in me. I guess it's more the thought of cohabiting with her that makes me uneasy. It won't be so bad if she's elderly, I suppose. Some sweet grandmotherly type I can hang up the washing for or offer to carry the groceries inside. But looking around, it doesn't feel like your typical 'grandma' pad. What if she's much younger, attractive? That would be a whole other ball game and it makes me feel uneasy. I like women, I enjoy their company, but I've never been that relaxed around them. It takes time for me to feel comfortable in their presence. Unlike Jasper, the campus Casanova at university, hooking up with a different girl every month, it had seemed.

'Yes,' Max says with a knowing grin. Clearly, he's read my thoughts, his mind perhaps wandering to places it shouldn't.

Maybe that's why the listing didn't say 'Landlady'. Thinking it might put off prospective male lodgers like me. Equally, perhaps it explains why the landlady chose not to advertise the room on a site like Gumtree. Because she needed to ensure she'll be safe with whomever she lets the room out to, not wanting to attract the wrong sort as Max suggested.

'Don't worry, she won't bite; she's very nice, very easy-going,' Max tries to reassure me. 'I think you'd get on well.'

'I, I wasn't suggesting she wasn't,' I protest. 'It's just that, well, I…'

'Hadn't expected her to be a woman?'

'Well, er, yes, that's right,' I stammer.

'I assure you, she won't be in your way, or invade your space. She does a lot of charity work, which keeps her occupied. And with the property being so huge, and having two reception rooms, you'll have plenty of privacy. I know she's not one for watching a lot of TV either. She tends to sit in her study and read. Or spend time in her art studio. She's a very keen artist. All in all, I doubt you'll cross paths much, except when she needs help with something.'

'Which involves what exactly?' I ask. 'Fixing a leak, doing the laundry?'

Max smiles. 'That's not for me to say. If you decide you like the place, you'll need to come back and meet with her. Ask all the questions you may have then. She'll tell you all you need to know. For now, relax, and let me show you round.'

Christ, it sounds like a full-on job interview. A part of me is saying I should tell Max no thanks and get the hell out of here, but I can't help being curious to find out more. If anything, having come this far, I'm eager to see inside.

Before showing me around, Max gives me an overview of the property's main features including two reception rooms, one with a dining area and glass-balustrade balcony, a study with an extensive library, a kitchen/breakfast room, six bedrooms with two en-suite bathrooms, the master having a private balcony, as well as a lower ground floor swimming pool and gym and rooftop garden accessed from the second floor. Clearly, this woman is loaded, but how did she come to have so much money, I wonder. Max also explains that several years ago the landlady spent a fortune remodelling with sustainable materials. 'My boss is very environmentally aware, and from what I understand she was keen to modernise the place in as eco-friendly a way as possible. The inclined site on which the house is built ensures maximum privacy from the street while allowing for vast amounts of natural light to pass through the rear elevation into the main space, as you can see.'

I can. Right now, the dazzling light streaming through almost blinds me. So much so I could do with some sunglasses.

Max guides me around the ground floor. There's so much space, the cream and fawn walls and minimalist décor enhancing the vastness of each room. Everything is spotless, from the larger living room adorned with immaculate cream leather sofas, elegant brass lamps and polished glass and gold-rimmed side tables, to the kitchen with its huge white marble-topped central island and swish handle-free fittings, to the dining area decorated with eye-catching pieces of modern art and understated yet striking sculptures. Both living rooms have fancy Bose sound systems, while I notice speakers in the kitchen too. Max continues the tour upstairs – again mostly tiled or parquet flooring with the odd silver-grey chenille rug breaking up the space, as well as strategically placed vases and various pieces of artwork similar to downstairs. We view each of the six bedrooms, including the one I'd be staying in, all with the same minimalist décor, the bathrooms sporting similar neutral tones, before venturing up to the second-floor rooftop garden which offers stunning views of the Heath and beyond. We linger there a while admiring the panorama, inhaling the cold, crisp air, my mind speculating whether I'll ever find what I've come looking for here in London, having so far drawn a blank. The thing is, I have so little to go on. What's more, so much time has passed, and a lot can change in a matter of months, let alone years.

'Phenomenal, isn't it?' Max stirs me from my thoughts.

'It is,' I agree, while again wondering how the landlady came to be so rich. It brings me to another point – why have a lodger? Clearly, it's not for the money.

I'm about to raise this when Max says: 'I hope you don't mind me asking, but what do you do for a living?'

I hate that question. Because, unless you're John Grisham, people expect writing to be a hobby on the side and inevitably follow it up with, 'Yes, but what's your real job?'

But to my surprise, when I tell Max I'm an author he doesn't patronise me. 'How interesting. Had anything published I might have heard of?'

I smile awkwardly. 'More of a struggling author, I'm afraid. But it's been my dream to write since I was little and I'm hoping I'll make it one of these days. For now, I work nights in a bar, if you were wondering how I manage to make ends meet. I also have a good chunk of savings.'

Max nods. 'Great. What genre do you write?'

'Horror slash thriller I guess you could call it.'

Max shivers. 'Ah, not for me then, I'm far too squeamish.'

'Horror's not for everyone,' I say. 'I find it surprisingly cathartic, though. Helps me confront my own fears.' It's true. Choosing to write horror in my late teens was partly a reaction to my phobia of closed spaces, along with rats and death. It helped me deal with Dad's passing. A bolt from the blue that crushed me. Although I don't tell Max this last detail.

Max looks slightly awkward as I explain my reasoning. He probably thinks I'm some weirdo now. Maybe he'll tell the owner as such, and I'll get a call tomorrow saying the room's been taken. Not that I'm sure I want to take things further. Obviously, it's tempting, just because the property is so incredible, but I'm still wary of living with the landlady, much less potentially being at her beck and call doing who knows what jobs.

Max takes me back downstairs to the more informal of the two reception rooms where he opens a set of sliding doors leading out to another garden, although it's considerably smaller than the main roof garden. He recites the details parrot-fashion. 'The mature gardens here on the ground floor were designed by an RHS Chelsea Flower Show gold-prize-winning gardener, would you believe. While the terrace on the lower ground floor, where I'll take you now, is used for private entertaining. There's also a pool and a gym down there as I mentioned. Plus, the landlady has her own art studio which I'm afraid is strictly out of bounds to her lodgers. Although she did do me the honour of a quick peek when I first took the job. I'm a keen artist myself, you see, and she kindly showed me some of her work. Generally, though, it's her private space, where she likes to sculpt or paint.'

Fair enough, I think to myself, while wondering if some of the artwork I've seen around the house is hers. Impressive yet noticeably dark pieces ranging from rugged landscapes to haunting portraits.

'You mentioned the lower ground level is used for private entertaining. Does the landlady do much of that?' I ask as Max guides me down a set of grey granite stairs.

I do hope not. Parties aren't really my scene. Too much small talk, fake smiling and pretending to look interested. It's exhausting. And there's always the fear I'll say too much under the influence. Or worse, blow my cover by a simple slip of the tongue. It's easily done, sober or drunk. Although I suppose I can hide myself away when she has people over. I mean, the house is big enough. Or I could go to Jasper's. Jasper says I need to get a life, get laid. Find a girl I can have a meaningful relationship with. But getting close to a woman always worries me. It somehow feels wrong. I want to be honest with someone I care about. After all, what value is there in a relationship based on lies? It always ends in tears. I, more than anyone, should know that. But it's also a massive risk telling them about my past, because there's every chance they'd want nothing more to do with me. Equally, if I lie and say nothing, I'm not sure I could live with the deception. My heart has been broken once, and I fear I'm not strong enough for it to be broken again.

'The landlady is involved with several charities, as I mentioned,' Max says as we enter a sizeable room. It's virtually empty save for a fully stocked bar at one end. 'So, she'll sometimes hold gatherings in here, particularly when the weather is iffy or it's not warm enough to entertain outside. But it's rare, and it didn't bother her

17

last lodger. He never complained, as far as I know. He worked long hours, had a busy social life himself. Too busy, it seems.'

Another 'he', I think to myself, while not failing to note the ominous tone of Max's last sentence.

'Too busy? What do you mean?'

Max sighs, then shakes his head. 'He was a trainee at some hotshot City law firm. I'm sure you've heard the hours at such places can be brutal. Not just the work, but the partying. Drugs, booze, anything to take the edge off the long days, but also to fit in with the *work hard, party hard* culture. From what I heard, Ethan was into coke, ecstasy, the hard stuff. One night he came home high, went up to the rooftop garden and threw himself off the building. Thought he could fly. That's what they presume anyway, only because he'd shown no signs of being suicidal.'

I visibly flinch. 'Christ, that's awful.' At the same time, I'm surprised how indiscreet Max is being. Then again, I suppose it's better to be upfront about these things.

Another shake of the head. 'Yes, it's dreadful. It was the middle of the night, and the landlady was sleeping. She found his body the next morning. It wasn't a pretty sight as you can imagine and she was extremely shaken, having become very fond of Ethan, and despite him not being the easiest of lodgers from the little she's told me. This was early December of last year. The start of the party season. Poor thing was distraught. Almost felt responsible even though, let's face it, he was a grown man and there was nothing she could have done to stop it from happening. When she employed me as her assistant she explained that she was worried about taking on another lodger so soon. But on balance, I think she feels safer in the house with someone else here. It's so big, in such an affluent area, which we all know can attract the wrong types.'

'Yes, of course, I can understand that.' I nod.

I wonder why she isn't married. Perhaps she's divorced or a widow.

'Ethan's firm was quick to put a lid on the whole tragedy,' Max goes on. 'I'm guessing they didn't want people thinking it was the pressure of working long hours that caused him to drink and take drugs and consequently fall.'

'What about Ethan's family? They must have been devastated.'

'Yes, of course. I suppose it's possible they were heavily compensated by Ethan's firm to keep quiet.'

He's probably right. It's sad, though. 'So has the land-lady had a lodger living with her for long?' I ask. 'Who even is she? There was no mention of a name on the website.'

'I believe Ethan was her first lodger. He was with her for nearly two years. Her husband passed away seven years ago, and it took her a long time to come to terms with his death.'

Widow. Ahh. That makes more sense. Perhaps she is quite old, after all. It still seems like a strange place for an elderly woman to live, though. And five years living alone in such a vast house is a long time. Why not move somewhere smaller?

'I'm sorry to hear that. I'm guessing he was very successful to be able to afford a house like this.'

'Yes, he was an extremely wealthy man. But again, I hope you don't mind if I leave it at that. The land-lady doesn't like me disclosing his identity unless the prospective lodger wishes to take the application further. She's a very private person, as I said. And with this being such a desirable property, and her being a woman of considerable wealth, I am sure you can understand her need for discretion.'

It's all a bit cloak-and-dagger. I feel like I'm applying for a job at MI5. Still, I guess I can empathise with her desire for privacy. It's exactly how I've lived my life since returning to the UK.

Looking around me, and thinking about the rest of the house, I'd be a fool not to take the room. OK, so it's not the arrangement I was hoping for, but there's no denying the place is incredible – the light, the spaciousness, the location, it's all so perfect, so liberating, and might just be the calming influence I need to help me deal with my grief over Mum and make a difference to my writing. Plus, Jasper has a steady girlfriend now and although Rochelle is nice enough, it's clear she'd prefer me not to outstay my welcome.

Even so, there's something about the whole arrangement here at Serenity House that niggles me. Something shadowy about the landlady and the property that makes me question whether I'd be doing the right thing in moving in.

It's not enough to sway my decision, though. Because once we're back on the ground floor, and I'm struck by the quiet, peaceful surroundings, the sense of privacy, the apparent safety of the area in contrast to the constant shouting, swearing and blaring of sirens I've put up with these last six months in Camden, when Max asks me if I'm thinking of taking the room, I don't even hesitate to reply.

'Yes, I am. When can I meet the landlady?'

Chapter Two

I press play on the recording and watch you closely, Sebastian, as you obediently follow her lackey from room to room. Upstairs, downstairs, my eyes never leave you, although of course you are oblivious to this. You have no idea that your every move is being watched. Studied. Digested. Recorded. Just as she has no idea. Some people might argue that what I am doing is creepy. Voyeuristic, even. But the thing is, I have to be sure you are a good choice, and that you won't cause her trouble like the last one.

I always knew her taking in a lodger would be a bad idea, especially one so young. She was doing so well on her own but I suppose that, aside from making threats of a certain kind, there was nothing I could do to stop her, short of revealing myself to her. Something that was far too risky. It would upset the balance of power which for now weighs heavily in my favour. It's true that sometimes I yearn to show myself to her, to reignite the closeness we once shared. But she turned her back on me all those years ago, and I cannot be sure she won't do it again. This way, with me hiding in the shadows, I remain in control. Able to watch over her.

And so, despite my misgivings, I gave her the benefit of the doubt with Ethan. And for a while, to my surprise it seemed to work, and I thought perhaps I'd been wrong in being so cynical about the whole arrangement. Perhaps allowing jealousy to cloud my judgement. But in the end, as usual, I was proved right. He caused her undue stress, betrayed her, just as I predicted he would.

I've been watching her and this place for some time now. Long before her husband – Charles – died, in fact. It took me years to find her, quite by chance as it happens, after she moved away, changed her name and became someone I hardly recognised. Different hair colour, her body no longer round and soft but lithe and toned, her mannerisms as polished as her nails, as if she had done her utmost to become a different person. To hide from her past. Something I can hardly blame her for, considering all that she went through. I had to do a double take when I first saw her in the bathroom of the restaurant we both happened to be dining in that sultry summer's evening. I couldn't believe my eyes, thought perhaps I was seeing things, having spent years trying to find her. It was her and Charles's wedding anniversary, I came to understand, having overheard the waiter allude to the happy occasion when she sat back down at the table and he poured them both a glass of Bollinger. The bathroom was one of those modern quirky set-ups, where although the individual cubicles were marked ladies and gents respectively, the general washing area was unisex. She didn't appear to recognise me as we both happened to look up at the same time and check ourselves out in the washroom mirror. Although she looked very different, there was no mistaking her eyes, as lovely and dark as a clear night's sky. I was a little hurt at first that despite making eye contact she didn't twig it was me. In fact, she seemed to look right through me, as if I was a ghost. Then again, we were just kids when we last saw one another. Also, when I peered a little closer and saw the distress in her eyes which were red-rimmed from crying, I realised something terrible must have happened and that she wasn't thinking straight. For the rest of the evening I sensed she was trying her best to put on a happy face for her husband's sake. But she didn't fool me. Because I knew her better than anyone despite our having not been in each other's lives for years. And I guess I always knew that, some day, she would need me again.

I could feel her pain, her tension, her struggle to act normally. And then, when I scanned the room, I realised the cause of her distress and it was hard not to explode with rage.

I made up my mind then and there that I wasn't going to lose her again. Especially having seen how upset she was. Not to mention the reason why. I knew I had to take control before things got out of hand. I stayed close and followed them home, discovered where she lived. It was so easy for me to gain access to Serenity House, despite its ultra-modern alarm system they believed to be foolproof. After that, it was a piece of cake. Spy cameras are so easy to buy and install these days. So tiny and discreet no one need ever know or guess they are there. Especially when concealed in the least obvious of places. That's the beauty of the modern age, Sebastian. I can watch her whenever I like. On my laptop, when I am out and about on my phone; so easy, so convenient. I use whatever medium suits me best at any given time.

Granted, she would be shocked if she knew. She's always been such a private person. Deeply insecure and fiercely self-protective, the thought of someone invading her personal space, watching her comings and goings, monitoring her every step, would horrify her. But I find it so insightful watching what goes on in this house. Observing her go about her daily humdrum life. Watching her undress, shower, eat, sleep, drink. Work out. Guard her precious art studio like a hawk. She prays every day that her secret is safe. And it is. Unless I decide to tell on her, that is. Which I would never do. Unless she does something to make me really mad.

I watched her fuck that lodger too. Not once, but several times. I hated it when she did that. Going on top, sucking his dick, letting him go down on her until she moaned like a whore. It sickened me that she seemed to enjoy screwing a much younger man. The very notion that he turned her on was revolting, and it made me realise how screwed up she is. How desperate for affection. Charles I could tolerate, but Ethan? He turned her into a promiscuous hussy, and it was shameful to behold. Thankfully, there's been nothing of that nature lately. Aside from the times I've watched her hands disappear underneath the duvet or sink down into the hot bathwater. On those occasions I've wondered who she thinks about to make her come so hard. Sometimes I kid myself that it might be me. I just hope I can trust you, Sebastian, to keep it in your pants. Because if you disappoint me there, there's no telling what I might do.

After the whole ugly business with Ethan, deciding on a new lodger at Serenity House isn't a decision she takes lightly any more, I can see that. And I'm glad of it. She's rejected a plethora of candidates in recent weeks, and I must give her credit for that. She realises she must choose more wisely this time. There are rules to be followed, hoops you must jump through, Sebastian, before a firm decision can be made as to whether you are a suitable candidate in her eyes. Of course, money is not the issue. That was never the reason she took in a lodger five years after Charles died. She stuck it out on her own for as long as she could bear because she was afraid of the truth coming out. But in the end the isolation got to her. She needed the company, to feel safe. Something I understood. She's never been good on her own, and with the house being so vast, so isolated, and a spate of burglaries having occurred in the area, I'm guessing she felt vulnerable without Charles around to protect her. Hence the tightened security. But what she doesn't realise is that I've been protecting her for a long time now. I would never allow any harm to come to her. Really, she doesn't need anyone else.

A new friendly and compliant lodger will take her mind off things. That's what Dr Martin told her. I'm guessing her old friend – Dr Adams – has said the same. It's not a bad way of *looking at things, I suppose. Someone to distract her from the secret that is steadily driving her insane. The way Charles had distracted her. For a time, at least. Someone who, if need be, can be her knight in shining armour – the hero she's always fantasised about since she was a little girl – despite me having warned her so many times when we were kids to be wary of strangers who seem too good to be true. She's not a child any more and you would think she'd be smarter about things. Know better than to trust handsome, seemingly pleasant types, so appealing and harmless on the outside, but who can be capable of unimaginable evil!*

Not only do I study your movements, Sebastian – your every expression, glance, gesture – like a psychiatrist forming a first impression of a new patient, I also listen to what you say and how you say it. I take in the sound of your voice. You are articulate, well educated, but you also have a calm and quiet inflection. Not in the least bit arrogant or affected. Although this may be a ruse, of course. Because I don't always trust what I hear or see on the outside. After all, it's what's on the inside that counts, but the soul is so much harder to penetrate. I note with interest the questions you ask of Max, along with your reaction to his explanations and the additional pieces of information he gives you on the house. You interest me, Sebastian, because I am not quite sure what to make of you. Ethan was an open book. Charming but conceited. And yet despite his blatant arrogance, I think she hoped he could be tamed. But she should have known better than to take in a lawyer. They're meddlesome types. Arrogant, selfish and not to be trusted. I knew he'd start asking questions he had no business asking, sticking his nose in where it wasn't wanted. Snooping around. Finding things he shouldn't have gone looking for. I suppose I am partly to blame. Having let jealousy get the better of me. I couldn't help getting involved. It's her fault mainly, though. She allowed herself to get too close, to become emotionally attached. And when that happens it never ends well for anyone.

You certainly don't seem like the prying type, Sebastian, despite your questions. Questions I suppose I can't blame you for asking. Of course, writers are inquisitive sorts too, but in a different way to lawyers. They study people, human nature, assimilate in minute detail life going on around them. All for the sake of their art. And unlike lawyers who devour facts, who feed on reality, writers prefer to live in a make-believe world, motivated by their desire to escape real life. It's something I applaud. Because the worlds we find in books are often so much more inviting than the grim existence we're forced to endure. Your future landlady knows that, Sebastian. She's a classic example of someone who prefers the world of books to the one she was born into. Simply because the latter failed her so badly in her formative years. I wonder — did it fail you too?

You're quite exquisite, Sebastian. With those high cheekbones, that striking tint to your skin, which tells me one of your parents must be of colour. There was a boy like you at school; his mother was Ghanaian, his father English, and I am guessing you have similar roots. Unique. And so very beautiful, with your razor-sharp jaw and graceful demeanour. I see the way your eyes furtively survey your surroundings as if you do not believe yourself worthy of them. So humble. Humility is a quality deficient in so many these days. I know it's something I lack, but I can see that you have it, and she'll like that. Because it's how Charles was. I note the way your cheeks flushed on being told the landlord was female. Ethan hadn't been fazed by this. In fact, he got a thrill from it — the perverted bastard. But I see that the prospect worries you, which tells me you're a timid sort. Naturally introverted, like her. I'm guessing you prefer to live your life in the shadows, rather than be the life and soul of a party the way Ethan did. And that bodes well.

Then again, I never take things at face value. Something tells me there's a darkness buried within you, Sebastian, even though you try so hard to conceal it. Because when I zoom in on the camera and look into those big chocolate-brown eyes of yours, I can see that your load is a heavy one. It takes one to know one, I guess.

What is your secret, Sebastian? What darkness are you hiding? I am going to find out for her sake, you mark my words. I always do.

And if I don't like what I find, the best thing you can do is run.

Chapter Three

Adriana

I wake with a start to the sound of rain ricocheting off my bedroom windows. At least it was bright and dry earlier, despite the icy temperatures. But when the morning sun swiftly disappeared behind ominous clouds that seemed to appear from nowhere, the weather turned even chillier, with a punishing wind that lasered through my slender frame. I turn my head towards the windows, grateful to be inside, despite feeling lonely in this house all by myself. The force of the rain is quite alarming. Brutal. Invasive. As if strong enough to break through the glass and attack me in my bed, even though I know the panes are impenetrable. The fitter who installed them assured me of this when I had all the windows in the building replaced as part of the house refurbishment. Fulfilling Charles's long-held dream of going eco-friendly, in line with his company's policy and the values it promoted. I'll admit that replacing all the windows was also partly psychological. When Charles died unexpectedly seven years ago of a heart attack, I instantly felt so vulnerable, despite the high-tech alarm system he had fitted before we moved into our dream house twelve years ago. One of the happiest days of my life. Aside from our wedding day, of course. He was the best of men. Kind and true and generous. He took care of me, and I always felt safe here with him to protect me. I was the best version of myself with Charles. He, who broke through my emotional walls and made me feel good about myself, about being able to love and be loved back. Until that fateful day occurred. When something happened to shatter my new-found confidence. Putting a strain on my marriage and making me wonder, even now looking back, whether the stress I put Charles under with my mood swings and heavy drinking led to him being taken from me too soon. I hate to think that's the case, but whatever the cause, his sudden death hit me like a stray bullet that pierced my heart and splintered my soul. A shock so devastating I didn't leave the house for six months.

My aunt and uncle came to stay with me in the immediate aftermath. Concerned for my well-being. Frightened I might do something stupid in my low condition and revert to how I was in my early teenage years, anxious and depressed, experiencing frequent panic attacks that had me thinking I was dying. Back then, I sometimes felt that death might be preferable to the tidal wave of utter helplessness that overwhelmed me. They became surrogate parents to me after my real mother and father passed away a few months shy of my fifteenth birthday – that sensitive age, when my hormones were raging, my body going through all sorts of changes. Anger, grief, confusion shooting through me. A time when I needed a mother more than ever. Not that my real mother had ever been great at the role. Far from it, it pains me to say. Thanks to Aunt Georgie and Uncle Philip, I got through that time, got a handle on my drinking, and they left only when they felt it was safe to do so.

I yawn loudly, my head still foggy from having been locked in a deep sleep. Looking at the time, I'm startled to realise I must have dozed off for a few hours, yet I don't feel as refreshed as I should do. That's been happening a lot lately. It's frustrating. But I guess I did go hard at the gym. I've really been pushing myself on the cardio, but perhaps I need to ease up. They say exercise is good for sleep, but too much can have the opposite effect. Can make you restless, drained. Anxious. It's just that, since the whole business with Ethan, exercise has been a lifesaver, the only way I've managed to blank out the image of him lying dead on the ground. Blood everywhere. His neck broken, his vertebrae shattered, such was the force of the fall. An image that always seems to appear in my head as soon as I get under the covers and have nothing else to distract me. Ramping up my stress levels. To be honest, my sleep patterns have been all over the place since Charles died. Before that, even. My mind beset by fear and anxiety, along with an overwhelming grief and guilt I know I'll never be free from. Dr Martin says it's natural to sleep when you're depressed, when the joy has gone out of your world. He said he treats lots of patients in the same position. Unable to drop off at normal times because their minds are too wired, but who eventually give in to the rest their bodies are craving. Be that at two in the morning or in the middle of the afternoon. He says that's why I need a companion, a form of distraction other than my charity work to release my mind from the gloom that holds it so tightly within its grasp. And he agreed that taking in a new lodger, despite the unfortunate business with Ethan, might help with that. Someone who can help out around the house, do the little jobs Charles used to take care of, despite the debilitating knee pain that marred his life since getting injured on the rugby field aged eighteen. Ethan wasn't so great at those, but he had other qualities and it makes me sad when I think about the good times we shared. The fact that he had his whole life ahead of him.

Night-time is the worst, when every creak, every sound seems to be accentuated a thousand-fold. It's not so bad when I have work to do. And I'm sure, if it were summer and I could sit outside with friends on the roof terrace in the balmy evening air, chatting and drinking wine, I'd feel less isolated. Less trapped. But at this time of the year, when everything is so bleak and desolate, I feel especially cut off. Vulnerable. Exposed.

I tell myself the antidepressants Dr Martin prescribed twice daily can't help with my erratic sleeping patterns, causing me to nod off at odd times, but still wake feeling thick-headed, like I've got the worst hangover. But perhaps that's wishful thinking. Me wanting to bury the real issue here. That for some time now I've had the feeling I'm being watched, causing my sleep to be restless because I'm too afraid to drop off. I lie wide awake in this vast bed of mine, my heart beating rapidly, my ears pricked for the faintest noise or movement. My gaze fixed on my closed bedroom door, terrified that any minute an intruder is going to creep in and murder me in my sleep. It's just a sixth sense I have, that I am not always alone, and it's something that scares the hell out of me even though I know how secure the house is and that it's probably pure paranoia. Like a child afraid of the monsters that only emerge at night.

I enjoyed my workout earlier at my local gym. I didn't need to go there. I've got my own fitness room here. After we bought the property, Charles had it installed for me on the lower ground floor, along with my art studio. As well as being able to paint, he knew how much I loved to exercise. And that our home was where I was happiest. I'd like to say that's still the case. That I spend so much time here at Serenity House because it brings me joy. But the truth is, I can't afford to stay away for long. It's too dangerous.

My home gym is equipped with all the cardio machines and weights I could possibly ask for, and I'll often spend over an hour in there, sweating out my stress, centring my mind. It's why I'm so slender, I suppose, although that's also partly down to genetics, my mother having been a model in her twenties. But today, I needed to make myself scarce to give Max time to show my prospective new lodger around. I don't like being in the house when they're looking. Can't bear for them to feel uncomfortable or fear that their every move is being watched. I know that feeling. It's unnerving. Makes you feel tense, claustrophobic. Unsafe. Above all else I want my new lodger to feel at ease living here. To trust that I'll respect their privacy as much as I hope they'll respect mine.

Despite being a private person, I've never been good on my own. Not since I was a little girl. Being an only child, you'd think I would be, but it wasn't the case. My parents socialised a lot, with my mother mixing in the circles she did, and my father a successful property developer. Because of this, they made little effort to spend time with me. My mother was more interested in living the high life, in keeping up with the Joneses, along with other things she kept from my father. While he was a workaholic. The various childminders and babysitters I had from the moment I could crawl knew me better than my own parents. I guess that's why I buried my head in books. It was an escape from the loneliness. But when my parents died, and I moved far away from my childhood home in Devon to live with my aunt and uncle in Guild-ford, things were different, and for the first time in my life I felt truly happy. I became a new person and never looked back. Before long, I took my aunt and uncle's surname of Carter, going on to study sociology at Royal Holloway aged nineteen and then, shortly after graduating, meeting Charles by sheer chance in a bar while out for a friend's birthday. It was love at first sight for the both of us. We married after a year of dating and that's when I got involved in charity work. I had no idea what else I wanted to do with my life, and with money not being an issue, I was extremely fortunate to be in a position to throw myself into good causes. Everything was perfect for six whole years, until that dreaded day. When my past came back to haunt me, and the perfect life I had built rapidly began to fall apart.

I'm looking forward to having a new lodger, so I can feel safer in this house, breathe easier at night. The reality is, I'm a rich widow, a sitting target for some crazed stalker or canny criminal looking to take advantage, and so I need to be careful despite having gone to excessive lengths to make the house secure. CCTV-controlled gates and a fingerprint-recognition door lock, for example. Both of which I wish we'd had when Charles was alive. It's the quiet moments especially, like the other night when I was opening my front door, and I could have sworn I heard something behind me. OK, so it may have been the wind, the rustling of the leaves that sounded like a whisper in my ear, but what if it wasn't? What if it was someone who means me harm? Someone who knows I no longer have Ethan around to protect me?

I had the same feeling walking home from the Tube station the other night. I tend to avoid the Tube, but I couldn't get a cab for love or money when I left a fundraising event in Chelsea. Again, I may have been imagining it. I have been especially jittery since Ethan fell. But there's something called instinct, and my instincts are usually spot on, even though Dr Martin would perhaps suggest otherwise. He admitted the antidepressants I've been on since Charles died can cause hallucinations, especially when combined with the additional sleeping pills I take on and off, and I'd like to think, or rather hope, that he's right. It would make sense, even comfort me, knowing the pills are to blame, as strange as that might sound.

But what if they aren't? What if I am being watched?

What if there's someone out there who knows what I've done and is looking to punish me? Expose me. Even though I am not to blame for what happened.

I showered at the gym to give Max more time to show my potential new lodger around, so when I unwrap myself from the duvet, I don't have to worry about changing into fresh clothes. I do realise I need more layers, though. Currently, I'm dressed in a vest top and pair of knickers, having been warm and toasty under the covers. But now I feel chilly as I sit on the side of the bed, my bare feet planted on the floor, before raising myself up and going over to the chest of drawers where I keep my thicker jumpers. I pull out a powder-blue zip-up fleece, fling it on, before grabbing a pair of fleecy jogging bottoms I left draped over my dressing table chair and slinging them on too. Then lastly, my slippers.

I look around for my phone, but then remember I consciously left it downstairs in the study on Aunt

Georgie's advice. She read in a magazine that it's bad to have any kind of electronic gadget in the bedroom. Said I'll sleep much better if I keep my devices downstairs: out of sight, out of mind. I suppose I've always felt safer keeping my phone with me, particularly since Charles died. In case I need to make an emergency call. But it's not like I don't have a landline up here, so a few weeks ago I decided to give Aunt Georgie's advice a shot. If banning my mobile from the bedroom is one step towards sleeping naturally without the aid of pills, then I'm all for it. Even though I feel I have a long way to go on that front.

I leave the bedroom and pad down the stairs to the kitchen, realising that my mouth is parched and I'm in need of refreshment. The door is wide open, which is slightly odd, because I'm almost certain I shut it before going for a lie-down. I don't like leaving the door of any room in the house I'm not currently occupying open. It comforts me to keep the doors shut, even though I know how completely illogical that sounds and won't stop a burglar from intruding. Oh well, I must have been so tired I forgot to close it, I think to myself. A shiver runs up my spine when I think about the alternative. Glancing at my watch, I see that it's just on 5:45 p.m. A little early for wine, and really, I could probably do with more water to replace the fluids I lost earlier on the treadmill – dehydration perhaps explains me failing to shut the door – but it's a Saturday and I didn't have any booze last night so I think what the heck and decide to treat myself to a glass or two from the bottle of Chablis I got on my last Waitrose order. It's not like I drink nearly as much as I used to; there was a stage when I couldn't go a day without reaching for the bottle. I grab a tall stem wine glass from an overhead cupboard, pull out the wine from the chiller cabinet and unscrew the top. Then pour myself a generous measure and take it through to the study where I find my phone on the desk, the charger plugged into one of the sockets on the wall behind, although not the one I remember slotting it into. I tell myself not to worry, that it's no big deal, while ignoring the uneasy sensation kneading my insides. My eyes dart around the room as I sit down on the leather swivel chair, disconnect the phone from the charger lead, and immediately see that I have two missed calls. The first is from Max, who appears to have called shortly after I got home from the gym and went upstairs for a nap. There's also an email from him sent a few minutes after that, so I'm guessing he decided to message me after I didn't pick up.

Hi Adriana,

Hope all's well with you? Couldn't reach you on the phone, so just dropping you a line to let you know how I got on showing Sebastian Walker around the house today. Well, the answer to that is very well! I think we might finally have struck gold! He seemed like a really nice, down-to-earth bloke. Quite different to your last lodger from what you told me. Not the showy loud type at all. He's a struggling writer, and loves the area for obvious reasons. Hopes it'll inspire him! He said he works in a bar part-time plus he has some savings put away that'll cover the rent, although I know having a lodger is more about giving you a feeling of security than the money. He seemed to understand your need for privacy, didn't pry too much once I explained it all. Sadly, both his parents have passed away. I'm guessing he inherited all the money – unless he has a sibling of course – so that's also how he's able to make ends meet. He said he doesn't have a girlfriend, so you won't have any complications on that front. Not at the moment anyway! The only thing I found a bit odd, when I did a quick search back at the office, is that he doesn't appear to be on any social media. Seemed a bit unusual for a single bloke of 25 who's been to uni and gone travelling but I guess it's not compulsory, and in some ways quite refreshing! Anyway, just wanted to flag that up with you for the sake of transparency.

Lastly, I think he was a bit surprised to hear you were female. Like I said, he seems quite shy, and had been after a flat to rent to himself, but couldn't resist enquiring about your room because, let's face it, it's a stunning property most of us can only dream about living in! Hope you don't mind, but I said I knew for a fact you weren't the type to get in his way, so fingers crossed I assured him on that score.

I did take the liberty of checking your diary and you don't appear to have any other engagements on Monday morning, so I tentatively suggested 10 a.m. assuming you're happy to meet with him?

Let me know,

Best,

Max

Lovely Max. I knew the moment I met him he was a good choice. Thorough, conscientious. He's only been in my employment since mid-December, but I can tell he's a keeper. Ambitious for sure, but there's nothing wrong in that, plus his heart's in the right place and I appreciate the extra mile he goes in vetting potential lodgers.

He made a point of getting to know the house inside out in his first couple of days before showing a carefully selected few around over the last fortnight but didn't think they were suitable. Which I agreed with, having digested his feedback. After Ethan turned out to be so wild and unpredictable, I emphasised to Max how important it was for me to take on someone with a calmer disposition. Someone who keeps himself to himself, and doesn't cause me undue stress. I've had enough of that to last me a lifetime. And from the way he's just described Sebastian it sounds like he fits the bill. Plus we appear to have a few things in common. For one, our love of books, and two, both his parents are dead like mine. Obviously, I won't bring that up unless he volunteers the information himself, but just learning this makes me feel drawn to him.

I set down my wine on Charles's beloved bespoke walnut-finished desk and type a response to Max, thanking him for the information and confirming I'd be happy to meet with Sebastian at ten a.m. on Monday.

I press send before shifting to the kitchen and topping up my wine, conscious that the second missed call was from Dr Adams, the child psychologist my aunt and uncle took me to see after my parents died and I moved to Guildford. He's also sent a follow-up email. If it wasn't for Dr Adams, I'm not sure I'd be sitting here today, having contemplated suicide a month or so after my mother and father passed away. Life had seemed so cruel, so futile at the time, I didn't see any point to my existence. But he turned my life around, helped me deal with my grief, and for that I'll always be thankful. I hadn't expected him to be in touch so soon. I only saw him on Thursday, just two days ago. I was still feeling shaken by Ethan's death and needed to see a friendly face. I'm ashamed to say I broke down in front of him, got a bit hysterical, in fact. Told him things I've not told anyone. Let him into my deepest fears. But he was as patient as ever with me, and I left feeling somewhat lighter. Despite me moving away from Guildford to London some twenty years ago now, we've kept in touch in all that time. He even came to visit me after Charles died, when I was feeling so low, and it was then that he recommended I see Dr Martin, more local to me, on a regular basis, with whom he went to medical school. Dr Adams is a gem of a man, someone who'll always hold a special place in my heart and who I trust unreservedly.

I sit down at the kitchen table and read the email.

> Adriana, I hope you're managing OK after the awful business with your lodger. It was good to see you on Thursday and I hope our chat helped. Listen, I wondered if you might be able to come and see me again? There's something urgent I need to discuss with you, and it's best we do so in person. Can you give me a call back, so we can arrange a time? Or I can come and see you. It's no problem for me to hop on a train. Thanks, take care. Dr Adams.

I'm not sure what to think. His message is rather cryptic, and I wonder what can be so important that he can't tell me over the phone or in the same email. Also, that he's prepared to come and see me here at home. When I left on Thursday, he told me to take it easy, that we'd chat again soon, and that I should try not to worry too much in the meantime. But there's no mistaking the anxious tone of his email, despite the sweet man clearly trying his best not to alarm me. I don't waste a second in calling him back. He seems pleased to hear from me, if not a little agitated, and we settle on Monday afternoon at 3:30 p.m., giving me ample opportunity to meet with Sebastian in the morning before getting a train to Guildford.

I sip my wine, then go to the fridge and fish out the tub of olives I picked up at a local deli, conscious of my rumbling stomach, but even more so of my solitude. All my friends are married or attached, and I don't have any charity events planned until next week, so for now I feel somewhat at a loss. In truth, since losing Ethan, it's been hard knowing what to do with myself. And my isolation makes me dwell on the fact that I miss him being around. Even now, I keep picturing his lifeless body. It haunts my dreams, almost drives me mad wondering what had possessed him to go up to the roof at that time of the morning even though the coroner ruled that the drugs were to blame. That he was out of his mind when he went up there. Despite what *her* next door claimed to have seen.

Of course, I have my charities, my gym sessions, my occasional meals out with friends to keep me occupied. My art. Something I've done religiously since my teens to manage my anxiety. But the fact is, there's nothing like having another human being in the house for company. And although I know I can never marry again, not just because there'll never be another Charles but for other reasons too, it'll be good to have someone close by to talk to, fill the void.

Being alone stokes the bad memories. Memories I'd tried to convince myself were just my imagination until that day when reality hit me like a smack in the face and it all came flooding back. Alone, my mind dwells on that time, on the terrible secrets that grate at my soul. Secrets that are buried in this house.

A part of me yearns to confess them, to finally be free of the guilt that weighs me down. But I know I cannot if I value my freedom.

What I need is a new focus. To take my mind off things and allow me to feel safer going to bed at night.

And I'm hoping that new focus will be Sebastian.

Chapter Four

'*Hi, I'm Xavier, I'm new here, just started this week. Are you OK? You look bummed out.*'

Scarlett had been sitting by herself under the big oak tree in the playground for most of break time clutching Bert, her beloved teddy bear, her mind replaying the hellish events of last night when Mummy had gone ballistic at her. At eleven, she knew she was probably a bit old to be carrying her teddy around, and it gave Jasmine and her nasty friends added cause to pick on her, but lately things had got so bad at home she felt safer with him in her arms. She loved Bert like a member of the family. Who was she kidding? He was more precious to her than any member of her family, having been by her side since the day she was born. He'd never abandoned her, never neglected her, not the way her parents did. She never went anywhere without Bert. Most importantly, he cuddled up in bed with her. That dark time when she was most scared, when she heard creepy noises when Daddy was away, and she needed him more than ever to keep the nightmares at bay. Even though Mummy said she was too fucking old for soft toys and needed to grow the fuck up! What did she know? She was hardly ever around, and when she was at home, she wasn't really 'there' with her, didn't spend any quality mummy-and-daughter time with her. She was either too busy on the phone talking to her annoying friends, or arguing with Daddy or kissing the babysitter behind Daddy's back. Mummy had no idea she'd seen them kissing as she'd peered through the crack of the sitting room door. She'd seen him and Mummy do other stuff too. Disgusting things. Things that frightened her. Haunted her dreams. Mummy thought she was in bed, but she wasn't. Because she never slept well these days. Mummy only cared about herself, about her happiness and not Scarlett's. Whether it was her face, her figure, her friends, her parties. She was obsessed about her weight too. Daddy said so. He said she had starved herself when she was pregnant with Scarlett because she didn't want to get fat. Which probably explained why Scarlett weighed less than six pounds at birth, despite being a week late. It was a marvel Scarlett had been born alive. She wondered why Mummy had a child in the first place if she was such a burden. But then Mummy told her she hadn't wanted kids at all, and that Scarlett had, in fact, been an accident, a huge mistake, and that had made Scarlett feel really sad; more unwanted than ever. Scarlett preferred Daddy. He was kinder to her, less selfish, but he was always working, always so stressed with his job, and so never had time for Scarlett either. Scarlett badly wanted to tell him about everything that went on at home, the awful things she'd seen. But she was too afraid because she'd been warned that if she did, bad things would happen. To her and to Daddy. She also didn't want to make Daddy more stressed. She heard that Betsy David's daddy died of a heart attack because of stress and that was the last thing she wanted for her own daddy. She couldn't bear the idea of it being just her and Mummy, who would no doubt take it out on her. And not just by shouting, but in other ways too. She had burn marks on her arms and thighs to prove it. Even worse, Mummy might get married again. To someone as horrid as her.

So thank goodness for Bert, who loved her unconditionally. Unlike the selfish grown-ups who should know better. He cheered her up when she felt blue, laughed with her when she felt happy. Although that was rare, it had to be said. Except when she played with Eve, who lived next door, and who she'd known since she was seven. The sister she'd always wanted, but never got because Mummy was too selfish to get fat again. Eve was kind, clever and pretty. Everything Mummy told Scarlett she wasn't. Scarlett wished Eve went to the same school as her, but she didn't; she attended some posh private school Mummy claimed would be wasted on Scarlett. Mummy didn't care about Scarlett's education, all she cared about was spending all the money Daddy earned on herself. On things like Botox and massages. And Brazilian waxes, whatever they were. Scarlett wanted to hate Eve because she was so perfect and had such a perfect life but mostly she was jealous of the loving relationship Eve had with her mummy. But Scarlett couldn't hate her, because Eve was always there for her, and she would come round and play when Scarlett's parents were out or too caught up in their own worlds to be bothered with her.

Startled by the voice, and having been dwelling on her miserable home life and how she wished she could run away with Bert (and possibly Eve although she knew Eve's mummy would never allow it) and never come back, Scarlett looked up. And that's when she saw him. Xavier. She'd never seen him before but he just said he was new to the school so that explained things. Unlike her tiny infant school, Holyfield Primary, where there was only one class of twenty-five per year group, Barrenclough Senior School was massive, with four forms of thirty per year group so it was no wonder she hadn't noticed him.

'Hi, I'm Scarlett,' she said, wondering why he was being so friendly. What the catch was. She suspected it wasn't normal to be so suspicious of people, but she couldn't help it. It had become ingrained in her. 'What form are you in?'

'AF7. You?'

'KT7,' she replied. 'I hear Mr Freeman can be strict. I'm glad I have Miss Truman.'

He sniggered. 'Yeah, he can be, but I've figured out a way to get around him. The thing is, with grown-ups, they think they know it all, but they don't. They can be pretty dumb, pretty blind actually.'

Scarlett was suddenly all ears. This boy interested her. He seemed smart, a bit too full of himself perhaps, plus there was something a bit sneaky about him, an almost devious look in his eyes. But he also amused her. Distracting her at this moment from her problems at home. And when she thought about it, she realised he was right: adults could be dumb. Take Mummy, for example. She was unbelievably dumb. Despite thinking she was so clever. While Daddy was blind. Blind to what was staring him in the face. The hideous things happening right under his nose. Things that made her shudder at the thought.

'I think you're probably right. Do you live with your parents?'

'Just my dad. Mum died last year.'

'I'm sorry.'

'I'm not, she was mean to me, mean to Dad. I hated her if I'm being honest.'

Scarlett didn't know what to say to this, but she felt an immediate empathy with the new boy. Like her own mummy, his mummy had treated him badly, and he no doubt knew exactly how she felt. The difference was, he seemed more resilient, accepting of the fate that had been handed to him. She wished she was more like that. Less emotional. She wished she didn't take it so badly when Mummy constantly put her down. Forever dismissing or rejecting her feelings, making her feel that she was wrong to have feelings at all, that they were of no consequence. She didn't want it to hurt, but it did. Badly. Made her feel worthless, unimportant. As did the constant eye-rolling whenever Scarlett tried to talk to Mummy about how she felt. Her mummy's constant put-downs made Scarlett question whether she was right to feel the things she did, whether there was something wrong with her. And that in turn made her feel anxious. She wondered if this boy was autistic, just because he didn't seem bothered by his own mummy's neglect. There was a girl in her class who was on the spectrum. She didn't show much emotion either. But then again, Xavier probably hadn't had to deal with the other stuff Scarlett did.

'Anyway, do you want to hang out?' Xavier asked. 'There are some right twats in my class, not my type at all. You seem OK, though, and you look like you could do with a friend. Other than your bear there.'

He smiled. She didn't think he was being rude or making fun of her when he said this. He was trying to be funny, make her laugh, and it worked. Because she found herself giggling almost hysterically, something she hadn't done in a long time. It was nice to have made another friend, besides Eve. As much as she loved Bert, the conversations were always so one-sided.

'Sure,' she said. 'Maybe you can come over to my house one day.' She thought how nice that would be. To have another friend over to play. Someone other than Eve. Who could be quite bossy, come to think of it. In the best kind of way. Maybe she could have her round at the same time, introduce them. Hopefully, Eve wouldn't be jealous. They could be like the Three Musketeers.

'Great, I'd love that. I've got Dad wrapped around my finger, so it won't be a problem. How about today after school?'

Scarlett smiled. 'Sure, that'd be great. Perhaps we can watch TV or do homework together?'

Xavier wrinkled his nose. 'Homework? Pah, dull! TV sounds good, or something a bit more adventurous.'

Scarlett's heart juddered. Both with fear and excitement. 'How do you mean?'

Xavier grinned broadly. Had that same mischievous glint in his eye. 'I'm not sure yet, but I'll think of something. I'll surprise you.'

Just then the bell rang, signalling the end of break time. 'I'll meet you at the gates after school then?' Scarlett said. 'It's about a fifteen-minute walk to my house.'

'Sure, sounds good.'

Scarlett watched her new friend run off, buoyed by the lighter feeling in her chest, last night's horrific events for now put out of her mind.

Life was looking up. She only hoped she was right to place her trust in this boy. That there wasn't something more sinister to that broad grin and cheeky face she found so instantly appealing. After all, appearances could be so deceptive. She knew that only too well.

Chapter Five

Seb

This is it. Here goes nothing. It's Monday morning and once again I find myself standing in front of the imposing gates of Serenity House, ready to press the buzzer. Unlike on Saturday when the weather was dry and sunny, it's a miserable morning despite being a touch warmer, the rain sheeting down in bucketloads, and stupidly I didn't bring an umbrella with me. Neither do I have a hood, being dressed in the same smart brown wool overcoat I wore on Saturday wanting to make a good impression. That being so, I really hope the mysterious landlady I'm here to meet doesn't keep me waiting too long. Else I'll look like a drowned rat by the time she opens the door.

Looking around me I can't see anyone about, despite it being a residential street and only a few minutes' walk from the Heath. I guess it's not surprising given the rubbish weather and with it being a Monday. Plus, all the houses along East Heath Road appear to be set apart from each other by grandiose gates and towering hedges. The author in me wonders who occupies them, and what secrets they might keep.

I take a deep breath and ring the buzzer attached to the intercom system, butterflies skimming my insides as I do. I don't know why I'm feeling so bloody nervous.

It's not like I'm applying for some high-flying job in the City, or about to take a life-changing exam, but the covertness of the whole thing has somewhat unsettled me. I was tempted to do a title search on the Land Registry website to see if I could find out the landlady's name. Jasper said I should. He said it was pretty weird how secretive she was being, and that he'd want to know who she was before meeting with her. He had a good point. It made me wonder if she was hiding something dodgy. Something she worried might put prospective lodgers off. Other than the fact that her last lodger fell from the roof of her property, of course. Now *that* I couldn't resist looking up on the internet. But I found nothing that told me any more than I already knew. Just a heartfelt mention in the obituaries section of *The Daily Telegraph* referring to *the tragic and sudden loss of a beloved son and brother, Ethan, 24, taken all too soon from his devoted parents and ever-loving sister, Sara.*

Like Max said, Ethan's firm must have found a way to bury the incident, not wanting to dissuade prospective trainees from applying for fear of being worked to the ground and meeting a similar fate. A tactic which I'm sure met the wholehearted approval of the owner of Serenity House, who would understandably have been concerned about its value plummeting overnight despite it being nothing more than a dreadful accident. Anyway, when I thought about it, and considered my own need for privacy, I decided it would be wrong to snoop. Hopefully, the landlady will be transparent with me when we meet face to face. It's only natural for her to be cagey about whom she lets into her house. A sitting duck for wily criminals looking to exploit a wealthy widow living alone. Besides, Max could have glossed over Ethan's death knowing it might put me off. But he didn't. Rather, he was honest from the start, presumably at the landlady's request. I've therefore convinced myself there's nothing for me to feel concerned or suspicious about. And that, before long, everything I need to know will be revealed.

Luckily, she doesn't keep me waiting long. No sooner have I pressed the buzzer and confirmed my name than the gates open. Albeit at a snail's pace. From the corner of my eye, I notice the tiny camera positioned above the buzzer to the side of the right-hand gate, and instantly feel a little self-conscious, wondering if she might have been watching me these last few minutes, sizing me up. I wouldn't blame her; I'd probably do the same in her position. Aside from the mystery of it all, I suppose I feel particularly anxious because I've never been some random person's lodger before. I've either lived with both my parents (before it became just me and Mum), or shacked up with friends like Jasper. Even when I travelled, I stayed in cheap studios or hostels. It was never a one-on-one set-up with a perfect stranger.

I stride quickly through the gates and up to the silver-grey stainless-steel front door – an indestructible choice of material and again perhaps indicative of the owner's cautious nature – conscious that my coat is pretty much soaked by now, my hair wet through. Before I've even had the chance to knock or press the bell, the door opens and there she is.

And *nothing* like your typical gran. In fact, she looks much younger than I expected. Not to mention stunningly attractive. Exactly what I was dreading. I hadn't thought it possible, but I suddenly feel more nervous than ever.

'You poor thing, do come in,' she says, ushering me inside with an outstretched palm. I notice the glimmering diamond on her left ring finger, the simple platinum band complementing it tastefully. She may be a widow but clearly her husband is still very much in her thoughts. I say thank you and hurry inside before she closes the door behind me with something of a thud. The central heating must be on fairly high because it feels warm and cosy in the hallway, despite it being a large house to heat. But I'm guessing heating bills aren't an issue for her. Looking down, I feel embarrassed by my sodden shoes staining the immaculate parquet floor, the water dripping off my coat and jeans and adding to the unpleasant mess I'm making. *Good start, Seb.*

'Sorry, I'm such an idiot not bringing an umbrella,' I apologise, feeling my face grow hot, although thankfully my darker hue doesn't colour the way pure Caucasian skin does.

'Oh, don't be silly, it's just a bit of water, no harm done,' she says soothingly with a flick of her wrist, causing the silver charm bracelet she's wearing to jangle. 'Let me get you a towel for your hair.'

'Really there's no need,' I protest, feeling embarrassed again.

'Don't be silly,' she repeats, 'it's no bother. Just wait there a second.'

I watch her dash up the stairs and in no time at all she's back with a towel. I take it from her with a grateful smile and proceed to dry my hair.

'The weather is so unpredictable these days, don't you find?' she says. 'What with climate change and all that. I never know what to wear. Plus, I always find it's such a faff carrying around an umbrella, especially on the Tube. I'm guessing that's how you got here? Max mentioned you're currently living in Camden with a friend.'

'Yes, that's right,' I say. Her voice is soft and velvety, with a warmth that instantly puts me at ease. 'It's only three stops, so I didn't have far to come,' I explain further. I bend down and unlace my shoes, then remove them, at which point she instructs me to leave them on the mat by the door.

I do as she says, our eyes settling on one another a fraction longer than necessary as I stand and meet her gaze, an exhilarating feeling I've not experienced in some time rushing through me in those few seconds, before she breaks the awkward hush by offering to take my coat. I say thank you, then strip it off and pass it to her. 'I'll hang it up in front of the heated rail in the kitchen. Should dry in no time,' she assures me with a radiant smile that takes my breath away. 'I'm Adriana Wentworth by the way.' *Finally, a name.* 'Come through and I'll make us something hot to drink.'

I follow her lead to the kitchen, my eyes taking in her lithe, slender frame from behind, the light and graceful way she moves. The way a trained dancer might. Unlike me, she hasn't dressed up for the occasion. She's wearing pale cream jogging bottoms and a matching sweatshirt, her bare feet revealing dark red painted toenails, her brunette tresses tumbling down her back in loose waves. There's an elfin beauty to her, her dressed-down appearance and lack of make-up save for the dab of lip gloss and black mascara I noticed when we first made eye contact only accentuating this. I wonder how she came to be a widow so young. She can't be more than thirty-five. Unless she appears younger than she is, of course.

I watch her hang up my coat on the rail, then remove two mugs from an overhead corner cupboard, before flicking the switch on a chic white and silver-grey patterned De'Longhi kettle lying beneath it. Everything in the kitchen radiates effortless style, while the scented reed diffuser lying in the middle of the central island adds to the warm, classy feel. As do the cream leather-cushioned bar stools tucked underneath it. Again I wonder what her husband did for a living that enables her to live in such luxury. Also, how often she has a cleaner, because the place is spotless. Such a contrast to the mess Jasper exists in. Although, it's true his place has a certain lived-in charm about it.

'So, Max tells me you're a writer?' she says. 'That's exciting! I'd love to be able to write a book, but I'm not sure I have the patience, or the talent.'

'Er, yes, that's right,' I say. 'A struggling one, I should add. Although I'm just in the middle of finishing a second novel. Didn't have much luck with the first one, got rejected left, right and centre.'

It's true. Having thought I'd written the best thing since sliced bread, it appeared that the sixty or so literary agents I applied to didn't agree. It was disappointing to say the least, and a real wake-up call.

'Don't worry, I'm sure if you're good and you work hard, you'll get there. I don't know much about the industry but Charles, my late husband, had a good friend who worked in publishing, and he said it's one of the toughest industries to crack. Like any entertainment field, I suppose.' She pats the side of her nose. 'Plus, not so much *what* you know but *who* you know.'

I grimace inside. Because if that's the case I'm screwed. I don't know anyone with any useful connections. Besides

Jasper, of course, but right now he's more tea-room boy than high-flying editor capable of pulling a few strings for me. Still, from the research I've done, I know writers scrabble for years before getting their big break, or even managing to have anything remotely respectable published. And that's something that gives me hope, knowing I am by no means alone. If only I had the balls to apply for a proper job to pay the bills until that day comes. But I'm too chicken. Too afraid of my past being dragged up. At least I have the money I inherited from my parents to live off in the meantime. Not that that's ideal. Because at some point it's going to run out.

'Yes, I'm sure you're right.' I nod. 'I'll just have to plug away and hope for the best.'

The kettle comes to the boil. 'Sorry, I should have asked,' Adriana says, 'coffee or tea? Or something herbal?' I opt for a white coffee while she has mint tea and, before long, we're seated on a plush cream leather sofa in the smaller of the two reception rooms. I say smaller, but it could practically fit Jasper's entire flat in it. Again, I feel nervous sitting here alone with this woman I know nothing about. It doesn't help that she's so attractive. As well as being smart and well spoken. Beautiful, intelligent women always make me tongue-tied, even though I know I'm not stupid or bad-looking myself. Jasper says if I made more of an effort, I'd have women queuing up to go out with me. But that my sullen expression puts them off. He's probably right. But I just don't have the energy or the inclination to change my ways.

'Max tells me you're a keen artist,' I say. 'Is that one of yours?' I motion to an oil painting on the wall opposite. A little girl wearing a pink dress takes centre stage. She's walking along a dark gravel path, a canopy of lofty trees, their branches gnarled and twisty, shrouding her. It's creepy, yet captivating.

Adriana's eyes travel to the painting, her gaze wistful. I can't help wondering what she's thinking, or what the deeper meaning is behind the piece. 'Yes, that's mine. It's not very good, but art is my passion, I find it so restorative.'

'You're too modest,' I say. 'I think it's stunning.' She lowers her eyes, her cheeks suddenly flushed, as if she finds it hard to accept a compliment. 'And I know exactly what you mean about finding your art therapeutic,' I continue, 'it's the same for me with my writing.'

We share a knowing smile, as if to reinforce our mutual understanding. Then Adriana changes topic. 'So, do you know Hampstead well?'

I watch her take a sip of her mint tea, the smell of it infusing the air around us, her luminous eyes peeping over the rim of her mug as she waits for me to respond. At the same time, I hear the faint ticking of the large chrome sun-shaped wall clock above the fireplace. There's something so enigmatic, so enchanting about Adriana and this house. Intuition tells me there's a lot more to her than meets the eye. But I try not to dwell on this. I'm hoping she'll reveal more about herself and her late husband once she's asked everything she wants to know about me. After all, she's the one in the driving seat here, with undoubtedly a whole host of candidates queuing up to rent a room in a place like this. Even so, it cuts both ways. And naturally, like Jasper said, it would be good to learn a bit more about the person I'm to live with. Because she is as much a stranger to me as I am to her. Something that both excites and unnerves me.

'Not intimately,' I say. 'I mean, I've visited before; it's such a beautiful historical part of London and it would be my dream to have a place of my own here one day. But right now, that's all it is. A dream.'

'But you get by OK with bar work and some savings, Max mentioned?'

'Yep, I'm very fortunate in that sense. Plus, it's not like I spend a lot. I don't have a girlfriend or a family to provide for. I don't even have brothers or sisters. And I'm not a big partygoer.'

Fucking hell, saying all that out loud I sound so dull. No wonder Jasper's always taking the mick. He calls me a boring old fart constantly.

'But I hear you went travelling?' Adriana says.

'Yes, but that was before Mum died. Until then, apart from my three years at uni, I still lived with her.'

Her expression clouds over at the mention of Mum's passing, and I get the same look of pity I always receive from people when I tell them my parents are dead. It's because I'm so young. They don't expect it, and I get that. It's much easier to accept the death of elderly parents who've lived a long and full life. But Mum was only fifty. 'I'm so sorry for your loss,' Adriana says, her voice full of empathy. 'Max told me your father also passed away. You seem so young to have lost both parents. Do you mind me asking how they died? Of course, you don't have to tell me, it's really none of my business, and I don't mean to make you feel uncomfortable.'

I swallow hard. It isn't any of her business, but I don't blame her for being curious. I would be too. It's natural. 'My dad had cancer,' I lie. 'He passed away just before my sixteenth birthday. Hadn't long turned forty-one.'

'Oh my God, that's tragic,' she says. There's genuine sympathy in her tone and gaze. It reassures me she's a decent person.

'And Mum, well, she never really got over his death.' *In so many ways.* 'She suffered from bouts of depression on and off after he died. He was everything to her, and it was as if she lost her zest for life. She tried to put on a brave face for me. But eventually, I guess it all got too much.' I feel my eyes well up and will the tears not to escape and betray my pain.

The fact is, it wasn't just Mum's love for my dad that caused her to swallow a bottle of pills. It went much deeper than that. We should have stayed in Nigeria. Coming back home, at my insistence – something that fuels the guilt in me every time I think about it – brought it all back for her. I should never have forced her. She should have remained with her brothers and sisters, who looked after her. Distracted her. But Nigeria wasn't for me long-term. Yes, I loved the people, the culture, but I was born and raised in the UK, and I longed to return. Despite everything that happened here. Besides, it wasn't just missing home that drew me back. It was fate. Because if I hadn't returned, I may never have discovered what I did. The reason I came to London, despite me telling Jasper I just fancied a change of scene.

Adriana sets her mug down on the stylish white gloss coffee table, then edges closer to me on the sofa. She places her hand on my arm, and a surge of electricity shoots through me as she does. She's so beautiful, so charismatic, her soulful eyes full of understanding as if she herself has been through a similar pain, and I can't help feeling an instant connection with her, along with a chemistry that thrills me, yet at the same time makes me feel incredibly awkward. I so long for a woman's touch, for the feel of her bare flesh against mine. To lose myself in her, blank out my torment, my grief, if only for a night.

It seems like forever since I was intimate with anyone, but I'm too scared of getting close to them, too frightened of feeling something. For fear of being hurt, but also laying myself bare.

'It's hard losing your parents so young. And I can fully empathise,' Adriana says. 'I lost mine at a similar age to you when your father died. I was fourteen.' She removes her hand from my arm, and I feel both relief and disappointment. What's wrong with me? Why is she having this effect on me? I can't go falling in love with my landlady, that would be a recipe for disaster. I tell myself to get a grip, but there's just something about her.

'I'm so sorry to hear that,' I say, before draining the last of my coffee, feeling much warmer than I did an hour ago. I want to ask how they died but unlike her I'm too shy. I don't want to offend her. But I needn't worry. She tells me of her own accord.

'It's fine,' she says. 'It was a long time ago now, twenty-five years to be precise.'

So she's thirty-nine, slightly older than I thought, and four-teen years older than me. Why am I even making that calcula-tion? I ask myself. I'll admit I've always had a bit of a thing for older women. Perhaps it's because they seem more self-assured, more honest and emotionally stable than girls my own age; past the playing-head-games stage or getting trashed every weekend at some seedy nightclub which smells of sweat and has sticky floors and where I can't even hear myself speak. Some guys like that, find it a turn-on, but I never have. I'm not sure if it's the trauma I suffered so young that caused me to bypass the normal teenager stage, but whatever the case I know that being able to have a deeper conversation with someone, to talk about stuff that matters, means more to me than meaningless sex.

'There was a fire,' she explains, her gaze all at once pensive, seemingly transported back to a dark time. 'I was in my bedroom, having gone to bed perhaps a couple of hours before my parents. They never went to bed early. Midnight was normal for them. It was unusual for me to be sleeping because I never slept well as a child. I still don't. Mother loved her candles, she would have them all over the house but was usually so careful to blow them out before going up to bed. But it seems she missed one in the living room that night. Or forgot, who knows. They thought our cat, Molly, probably knocked it over. My room was on the second floor, but we also had a loft conversion, where my parents slept.' She pauses for a second, lost in that moment. 'My mother had been on at Father for some time to get the smoke alarm fixed. It had been playing up for months, but he was always so busy with work and hadn't got around to it. If only he had, they might have woken up in time and got us all out. I remember waking up, smelling the smoke, a feeling of sheer terror running through me. Frozen in my bed. And then I started screaming, crying out for my parents to wake up and come downstairs to get me. By the time the fire brigade arrived, our neighbour having rung nine-nine-nine, it was too late. They managed to get me out, but Mother and Father were trapped, and never made it.'

She stops talking, her gaze still with that vacant look, the silence deafening, the ticking of the clock suddenly that much louder. I hadn't expected such a tragic story. I can't even begin to imagine what she went through. How frightened she must have been. And what makes her story so heartbreaking is that, unlike mine, her parents' deaths were an accident. A cruel twist of fate.

'I'm so sorry,' I say, while at the same time thinking how trite my words sound. Although, really, what else is there to say? No words can ever do such a tragedy justice.

'That's OK.' She gives a sad smile. 'As I said, it was years ago now. You're the first person I've gone into detail with since Charles. I just tell people my parents died in an accident and leave it at that. It's easier. I went to live with my aunt and uncle after they died. A hundred and fifty miles away in Guildford. They were very good to me, kind and patient. They helped me deal with my grief, as did the child psychologist I saw, and I suppose, over time I became somewhat numb to the whole episode. I occasionally think back to that night, though. How I thought I was perhaps still asleep, having a nightmare. But then, when I opened my bedroom door and saw the flames rushing up the stairs, I knew it was all too real. When the fireman carried me out, our next-door neighbour instantly came racing towards me, on the one hand relieved to see me, but on the other sensing it would fall on her to explain that I became an orphan that night. When I asked about my parents and saw the pained look in her eyes, a look of dread, of pity, I knew it was bad.' Silence once more. A silence that seems to rebound against the walls and echo in my head. Then she says more abruptly, 'Christ alive, I need to get a grip. I can't think why I told you all that, you barely know me! I'm sure you don't know what to make of me laying my sob story on you, but I suppose learning you also lost your parents brought it all back. Our sharing some common ground. Do forgive me, I promise our conversations won't always be so heavy. I hope I haven't put you off taking the room?'

I give a light chuckle, touched by her thoughtfulness, despite the personal tragedy she's just described. 'Don't apologise, I understand. And again, I really am very sorry. I promise I'll keep the details to myself.'

She smiles gratefully, then moves the conversation on, her tone more upbeat. 'So, you're obviously interested in the room, else you wouldn't be here. I assume Max showed you the bedroom you'd be staying in? I must admit, I never go into any of the bedrooms aside from my own. If it wasn't for Maria, my cleaner, they'd be gathering dust. You're welcome to any of them.'

'Yes, Max did show me. It's a great room, and it's a fabulous house, I'd be a fool not to be interested, anyone would be. Forgive me for asking, though, but I was a little surprised at the price. I mean, you could ask for a lot more.'

She sinks back into the sofa, then turns to face me sideways on, sliding her hands through her hair as she props her head against the palm of her hand and crosses one leg over the other, her painted toenails on full display. So relaxed, so effortlessly poised. And apparently so at ease in my company, despite me being a complete stranger. I'm not sure I've ever met a woman quite like her, and I wonder if she's like this with every stranger she meets. Perhaps so, and it's just her way, meaning I shouldn't flatter myself in thinking I'm special.

'I could ask for more, it's true, but it's not really about the money, it's about having company. Feeling secure.' She laughs. 'Don't worry, I'm not asking you to be my bodyguard or anything.' I can't help laughing too as our eyes linger on each other once more and she coquettishly tucks away a loose strand of hair behind her ear. 'But I'm a widow living alone in a big house and it can feel a bit isolated at times. It's nice having someone around, especially when it's dark and you tend to hear all those strange noises that are perfectly harmless but sound so ghoulish in the dead of night. It sounds very un-PC, but it's why I like having a male lodger. I just feel safer.' She pauses, her eyes delving into me again, making my insides burn. 'You must think me a little pathetic?' She raises an eyebrow, her lips curling up at the sides.

'Not at all, it's entirely understandable,' I say. 'When Dad died, the house somehow felt less safe without him in it.' I don't mention that the invasion of reporters outside our front door didn't help that feeling of vulnerability. Nor did the obscene graffiti sprayed across it. 'We relied on him so much, and suddenly felt exposed.'

She nods. 'Yes – exposed. That's the best way to describe it.'

Just as she says this, I see a look of fear in her eyes. Making me wonder if something's happened recently to scare her. Other than the strange noises we all hear at night she just referred to. *Is she afraid of something or someone?* Or is it merely the shock of how her last lodger died? If so, why doesn't she just sell the house, move somewhere smaller, perhaps closer to her aunt and uncle? It's obvious she cares for them deeply, and there's nothing like being around family to make you feel more secure. But it's not my place to ask. She must have her reasons for staying, or I wouldn't be sitting here. 'The listing mentioned some jobs you might need help with?'

She swats the air with the back of her hand. 'Ah, that's nothing really. To be honest, I can afford to employ a professional to fix a tap or mow the grass. I just say that on the listing to ensure I don't attract the lazy type, the sort who treats his room like a pigsty. It's important to me to have a lodger who respects the house, and appreciates it. I have a friend who rented a room out once and, my

God, it was horrific. Pizza boxes, dirty clothes all over his bedroom floor. Even used condoms. Plus, he had the cheek to ask her to do his washing for him. It put her off for life.'

'Christ,' I chuckle. Then quickly check myself. 'Sorry, it's not funny.'

She laughs too. 'No, it wasn't at the time for poor Charlotte. We can look back and have a giggle about it now, though.' She pauses, and once again I feel the heat of her gaze on me. 'Anyway, I think my ploy worked because you seem like the conscientious sort. Not a slouch by any stretch of the imagination.' There's that tantalising yet clumsy silence again, and I'm desperately trying to think of something to say to fill it when she says jokily: 'But I may call on you to do the odd quick-fix job at some point, if I'm really in a bind. Assuming that's OK?'

'Of course,' I say, 'I'd be happy to help. Not that I'm that great at DIY, I should point out.'

'I'm sure you're better than I am. My husband did all those jobs before I relied on handymen for years.'

Is this my cue to ask who her husband was and what happened to him? Again, I don't have to because she offers the information up herself. She must suspect it's something that's running through my mind.

'Charles was a highly successful businessman. He started out in IT but diversified into real estate, aviation and developing clean energy products.' She pauses, looks around her. 'It's why I had this place remodelled after he died of a heart attack seven years ago, to honour his dream of contributing towards a greener environment.'

'That's a lovely tribute to him. I'm so sorry to hear of his passing,' I say.

'Thank you. It was a shock, as you can imagine. He was fifteen years my senior, but I thought we'd have a lot more time. But life is cruel. As you know only too well.'

She stops talking, her gaze fixing on me once more, her eyes glistening with tears. Cruel doesn't begin to cut it, I think to myself.

'I've not had much luck in recent years.' She dabs her eyes, gives a bitter laugh. 'And I worry people might think this house is jinxed. I wonder myself sometimes. If someone up there is playing a wicked game with me. I take it Max told you about my previous lodger, Ethan?'

'Yes.' I nod.

'Good. It pays to be open about these things, I feel. Ethan was a wonderful young man, bright and funny. But a little on the wild side. I was constantly on at him to cut down on the drink and the drugs, but he was under a lot of stress at work and the night he died he was high on both, having been to a work Christmas party. I guess we'll never know for sure if it was the drugs that caused him to fall off the roof by accident or because he was hallucinating – that's what the coroner concluded. Or if he was depressed about something. Perhaps it was a bit of both, I only wish he'd opened up to me if he was feeling low or overworked. Having said that, I guess men tend to be less forthcoming about these things, don't they?'

I nod. 'Yes, I suppose that's true.'

Watching Adriana reminisce about Ethan, it's clear how genuinely sad and upset she is about what happened to him. She's had to endure so much pain and loss for someone who's not yet hit forty, and I can't help feeling for her and what she's been through. But more so a keen affinity when I think about the various tragedies that have affected my own short life.

'Anyway,' she continues, 'I suppose the last thing for me to tell you is that being married to Charles allowed me to get involved in charity work. Perhaps Max mentioned that?' I nod and she continues. 'Although Charles left the business to me, I'm not cut out for the corporate world the way he was, so I handed over the reins to his brother, Stuart, who was Charles's right-hand man. I'm on the board, and Stuart's very good at keeping me apprised, but I have to say it's a relief not to be involved in the day-to-day management.'

'What charities do you work with?' I ask.

Adriana smiles. 'Mainly women's and children's charities. I'm patron of a couple, on the board of trustees for another. Help out with campaigns, raising awareness and so on. I do what I can, and I like to believe it makes a difference.' She sighs. Pulls herself off the sofa. Perhaps indicating the meeting is over. 'So, what do you think? From my end, I'd be very happy to take you on as my lodger, if you think you can put up with me?'

I smile. Say a little too cheekily, 'I think I can manage that.'

'Great,' she says with something of a flirtatious smile in return. 'Ah, almost forgot, there is one final thing.' I watch her go over to a bureau in the corner of the room, open the top drawer and pull out a sheet of paper. She closes the drawer then comes back over and hands it to me.

'What's this?' I ask.

'It's just a few rules I like my lodgers to abide by. Nothing too onerous, so don't worry. Obviously, we'll both need to sign a standard lodger agreement, but these are things I especially want to draw your attention to. You can put your signature on the dotted line at the bottom assuming you're happy.'

I scan the sheet:

1. No overnight guests, male or female;

2. No swimming in the pool while under the influence of alcohol or heavy medication;

3. No shoes inside the house aside from slippers, with the exception of the lower ground floor entertainment space;

4. No furnishings to be brought into the lodger's bedroom without the owner's express permission;

5. No candles permitted anywhere inside the house;

6. Access to the owner's art studio on the lower ground floor without her prior permission is strictly forbidden and will result in automatic eviction of the lodger and a £5,000 fine;

7. Do not under any circumstances speak to the neighbours at number 6.

Most of it seems reasonable, as I would expect. Adriana's dislike of candles is understandable given what happened to her parents. And it's fair enough her not wanting people snooping around her art studio without her approval. It's her personal space, and I respect that. Clearly, she values her privacy, and it perhaps explains rule 1 even though at first glance it seems a little harsh. I also get the feeling she likes things just so and to her taste, so perhaps rule 4 shouldn't be a surprise. But the last condition strikes me as heavy-handed, if not a little disturbing.

'All OK?' Adriana says.

Does she really think I won't wonder what rule seven is all about? I hesitate. The last thing I want to do is upset her. But equally, I can't say nothing. It would bug me too much. I need to know the reasoning behind it before I agree to move in.

'Erm, it's just the last rule. Number seven. It just seems a little…' – odd, creepy, autocratic all come to mind, but I will myself to think of something better, more diplomatic – '…*unusual*,' I say.

I hold her gaze and think I see a flash of anger in her eyes. But then she smiles, her features softening. 'I don't blame you for thinking that. All I can say is that I have my reasons. Reasons which are personal to me. Thus far I've been very open with you, said more than I'd normally dream of revealing to a stranger – I guess because I can empathise with the loss and pain you've suffered and I feel it's important we start off on an honest footing. But you can probably tell by now that, fundamentally, I'm an extremely private person, and I get the sense that you are too. So I'm hoping you'll understand why I'm keen to keep those reasons to myself. But I want to reassure you that they are in no way a reflection on you or your staying here comfortably as my lodger. I just need you to respect the rules of my house.' She pauses. 'Of course, if you don't feel comfortable agreeing to them, I can't force you to. It does mean, however, that this will be our last meeting and I shall have to wish you the best looking for another room to rent.'

I stand there mute. A little stunned and unsure of what to say. There's a voice in my head telling me to pass. That there's something menacing about Adriana's last rule that should tell me to run for the hills. Clearly, she's got it in for the neighbours at number 6. But why? What is it about them? What could possibly be so bad that she's taken it upon herself to forbid her lodgers from speaking to them? The curious part of me is desperate for an explanation. Because I'm wary of secrets. Secrets destroyed my mum, our family. But I'm also aware that I'm being something of a hypocrite, because I also have secrets of my own. Secrets I'll never share with Adriana.

And so, when I look around, when I think about giving up the chance to live at an affordable rent in a palace like this, as opposed to slumming it in some dive that might cost me more, I realise that I can't say no. I can live with a few strange rules. After all, and as Adriana said, they don't reflect on me, they reflect her own private reasons.

So long as I abide by them, there's nothing for me to fear.

Chapter Six

Seb

It's Wednesday, two days on from my meeting with Adriana and I'm just in the middle of packing all my belongings into boxes and a couple of old trolley suitcases that have seen better days. I don't have masses of clothes, to be fair, I've never been into designer gear the way Jasper is. I'm more about comfort. More of a jeans, jumper and trainers kind of guy.

What I do have a lot of, though, and which take up most of the boxes I got from a local Big Yellow Storage branch, are books. Plus Mum's old CDs, which I can't bear to part with. Living in the digital age, the era of Kindles and Spotify, I should probably shelve some. Or at least give half away to charity or some other worthy cause. And I definitely shouldn't buy any more books. It would be friendlier to the environment and way more cost-effective. But I guess I'm the old-fashioned type. I love the feel of a book – the cover, the pages – turning them, inhaling their unique scent. Books and music have always been a sort of addiction for me. Which I tell myself is far healthier than relying on drugs and alcohol to give me my kicks. I like the way I can get lost in both. The way they soothe my soul when I'm stressed or feeling particularly worried about something. More importantly, books remind me of my mum, who read to me as a boy, teaching me the magic of stories and the worlds they could transport me to. After everything that happened to me as a teenager, I needed that more than ever. The ability to lose myself in another world, a world that helped me escape the hideousness of what was happening in my own reality.

There's a knock on the door. 'Mate, can I come in?'

It's Jasper. I heard the front door slam a few minutes ago, surprised he was home this early. It's just on six and normally he's not back before seven. The editor he works for is a bit of a tyrant from what I can gather, and what with Jasper being ambitious and keen to make his mark on the publishing world, he knows he can extract his pound of flesh from his obliging rookie.

'How's it going?' Jasper asks on entering the room, his eyes taking in the scene. He's removed his tie, his blue checked shirt open at the collar, his floppy red hair as crazy as ever. I love Jasper like a brother, he's been so good to me since we bonded on the football pitch at uni, and I'll miss our chats, our vocal Xbox sessions on the sofa, watching footie on the telly with a beer and a curry on the weekend. But despite all that, and although I'm grateful to him for putting me up for a pittance, I'll be glad to have more space. There's barely room to swing a cat in his spare bedroom.

'Not too bad,' I say, taping up the last of the boxes. Moving house is always exhausting, and right now, having been at it for a few hours, I feel done in. 'That's it, last one boxed up and ready to go.'

Jasper grins. 'Looks like you're in need of a beer?'

I grin back. 'You got that right. Listen, are you sure you're OK to help me move on Friday? I feel guilty you having to take a day off work.'

It's all been a bit of a whirlwind since meeting Max last Saturday. After I somewhat cagily signed on the dotted line agreeing to Adriana's special set of rules on Monday, Max emailed me the standard lodger's agreement yesterday which I duly initialled and emailed back. He said Adriana had a fairly busy schedule next week with various appointments and her charity work occupying her time and therefore it would suit her better for me to move in by the end of this week so she could be around to help me settle in. I did wonder, though, if this was code for keeping an eye on me. Something I don't begrudge her for. She doesn't know me well enough yet to trust me. But hopefully, with time, I'll earn her trust.

Jasper shakes his head, then runs his hands through his unruly mane. 'Mate, it's fine. I couldn't have helped out on Saturday as you know, what with Rochelle and I having lunch with her sister and fiancé. So, it had to be Friday.' He comes up and places a hand on my shoulder. 'You're my best friend, and I want to help. I know you'd do the same for me.'

I smile appreciatively. 'Course I would.'

'Besides,' Jasper says with a grin, 'I'm keen to meet this mysterious landlady of yours.'

At this, I feel my cheeks burn. 'Oh God, please don't say anything to embarrass me.' Unlike me, the one thing Jasper isn't, is shy. Head of the debating society at uni he was never backwards about coming forwards and would always speak his mind if he believed there was something that needed to be said. I tell him constantly that publishing is wasted on him, and that he should have gone into law or politics. For this reason I've not had the nerve to tell him how stunning Adriana is, let alone admit I'm attracted to her. He'd only give me grief. Try and convince me it's a bad idea moving in with her. Which it may well be, but I'm trying not to think about that. His outspokenness is why I've not mentioned the other reason I came to London. He'd only say I was asking for trouble in dredging up the past, a potentially futile exercise that may only cause me further grief rather than provide me with the peace I seek. He may be right, but I have to try.

'Calm down, I won't,' Jasper says as I usher him out of my bedroom and close the door behind me. We head for the kitchen where Jasper grabs two beers from the fridge. 'But you can't blame me for being a little curious. What with those weird rules she's set. I mean, what the fuck is number seven all about? You have to admit it's kind of creepy.'

'I don't know.' I shake my head. 'And it's not my place to ask. When you think about it, none of her rules directly affect me or my ability to live in her house comfortably. Including the last one.'

'Not that you know of,' Jasper says while handing me a beer. He gives me a long, lingering stare, as if to make a point.

'What the hell's that supposed to mean?' I say.

He looks away briefly, shaking his head. 'Nothing, really. Look, don't get freaked out. I know what a stressor you are. All I'm saying is – be careful. Fact is, this woman is a total stranger to you. Even if she's loaded and her husband was some big-shot businessman, it doesn't mean you should be any less wary. I don't blame you for taking up the offer, the place is frigging awesome from the photos you showed me, bloody perfect, in fact, and really, you'd be mad to pass it up. But, and forgive me for sounding so cynical, I've never trusted perfect. Perfect scares me because there's no such thing. In my experience, there's always a catch.'

Chapter Seven

Adriana

'How have things been, Adriana?'

It's Thursday, two p.m., and I'm sitting across from Dr Martin in his office on the King's Road. It's a bit of a trek in an Uber from Hampstead, but I don't mind. It gets me out of the house, to a different part of London I've always loved. It also gives me the chance to do a spot of shopping then have lunch at Bluebird – one of my favourite haunts and where Charles took me on our first date. Unlike Oxford Street, a chaotic hubbub of traffic, people and shops I don't much care for, the King's Road is more intimate, less frenetic. I don't have to battle marauding crowds that stress me out or worry as much about getting pickpocketed or accosted along the way. I know it sounds a touch snobby, and that if it wasn't for my marrying Charles, I may well have found myself working in a shop on Oxford Street, let alone being able to afford to go shopping along it – I didn't exactly shine in my degree and hadn't a clue what to do with myself after graduating with a 2:2 so I hardly had a glittering career ahead. But I can't help who I've become, nor my naturally wary disposition. It's always been crucial for me to feel safe. To not feel frightened or intimidated by my surroundings or put myself in a situation that might induce the panic attacks I suffered in my teens. Frightening episodes that made a comeback fifteen years later, after I thought I'd seen the back of them. And so, I do whatever I can to maintain a calm state of mind. And that includes having routine and set places I restrict myself to. It's also why I see Dr Martin privately every other week on Dr Adams's recommendation. Not because I'm some rich, pampered widow who can afford to see him. But because he makes me feel safe. Secure. Since Charles died that's something I've craved more than ever. While I'm here I also intend to ask him about Dr Adams. I was all set to visit him on Monday afternoon, keen to know what it was that was so important he couldn't discuss it over the phone, but when I checked my inbox on Monday morning there was an email from him sent late Sunday evening saying something urgent had come up and he therefore needed to rearrange but would be in touch ASAP. It seemed a slightly odd time to be emailing, and I did wonder why he didn't just try calling or leave me a voicemail, particularly after he'd sounded so eager to speak to me. But in any case, I wrote back telling him not to worry, that I understood completely and would be happy to rearrange whenever was convenient to him. But I've not heard anything since, which is unusual for Dr Adams as he's normally so prompt to respond. I just hope he's OK. That nothing bad has happened to him.

'OK, I guess,' I say in response to Dr Martin's question as to how things have been. I could lie down on the couch if I wanted to, rather than sit facing him across his desk. Dr Martin told me the first time I came to see him that many of his patients prefer to lie down. To close their eyes as they unburden themselves. That they find this less intimidating than having to make eye contact with the professional assessing them. But I am not like other patients, and lying down is the last thing I want to do. Not without the aid of sleeping pills that is, despite my pie-in-the-sky desire to wean myself off them and sleep naturally. The truth is, lying down induces painful flashbacks of my childhood. Memories I repressed for so long until Dr Adams got me to confront and overcome them. Before that terrifying night happened fifteen years later, when they all came flooding back, and I found myself yielding to their vice-like grip once again. And so, when I sit up and see Dr Martin across from me – a safe and friendly face who I know only has good intentions – it calms me, gives me someone solid and reliable to focus on. Someone I can trust. There are very few people I've felt able to trust in this world. I can count them on one hand, and Dr Martin is one of them.

He sits back in his chair, rests his elbows on either armrest then steeples his hands beneath his chin, waiting for me to continue. He always appears so composed and together, but today there's a brooding look in his eyes. As if something weighty is troubling him.

'I've been tired, lacking in energy, sleeping a lot more than usual since Ethan died,' I say. 'I was exhausted on Sunday. Spent most of the afternoon in a daze.'

It's true. Sunday afternoon passed in something of a blur. I'm not sure why, but I felt completely shattered and must have drifted off after lunch. I didn't come to until around five. Then went to bed at ten.

'It's understandable, you went through quite an ordeal. Finding his body on the ground like that, it would have been a shock for anyone.'

I think back to my conversation with Seb on Monday morning and feel a twinge of guilt for not being entirely honest with him about Ethan. Alluding to his possible depression but failing to mention our argument the night before he fell.

The thing is, and what continues to bother me, is that Ethan had come home high before and never gone up to the roof. Not in the entire two years he lived with me. And so I can't help wondering if he was still upset about our row. I had every right to be mad with him after what he did. To be honest, he'd been acting strangely for some time. He'd seemed distant, preoccupied, which was so unlike him. As if something was playing on his mind. I asked him what was wrong – up until then we'd had such a solid, honest relationship, or so I thought – and he'd admitted to speaking to *her* next door at number 6. She put ideas into his head. Ideas about things that were no concern of his, or hers. Not only that, he told me he'd found something; something private of mine he shouldn't have gone looking for. I felt so furious, so violated, when I discovered what it was, that I told him I wanted him out of the house by the end of the month. But now, looking back, I realise I may have been too harsh on Ethan. The firm he worked for was known for running its trainees into the ground, and he'd mentioned to me on several occasions that he wasn't sure if he could hack the pace. It breaks my heart to think that our row – my casting him out – could have pushed him over the edge. That he went up to the roof with the intention of taking his own life. Even though the autopsy confirmed that the copious amounts of alcohol and drugs found in his system were almost conclusively to blame, and so it was likely he wouldn't have known what he was doing when he fell. That it was, most probably, the cruellest of accidents. I guess we'll never know the truth for certain. But that in itself is driving me crazy.

Dr Adams is the only one I've mentioned the argument to. That, amongst other things. I told him last Thursday because the guilt was eating away at me. I felt I'd known him long enough to trust he wouldn't think any less of me or assume my sharp tongue drove Ethan to his death. Which he didn't. In fact, he was as understanding as ever. Despite asking some questions that threw me a little. I feel bad for keeping Dr Martin in the dark. But the truth is, he doesn't know me as well as Dr Adams and the last thing I need is to draw attention to myself, or give him the impression that I may have inadvertently caused Ethan's death. I can't bear the thought of him deeming my actions cruel or unfeeling. It's a self-esteem thing, I suppose. I've never had a lot of it, and in many ways it's held me back in life. Even so, I give a faint nod in response to Dr Martin's comment, grateful for his empathy. It's something I've always craved: the empathy of others. Kindness. It's why I think Seb will be good for me. I can see it in his eyes, hear it in his voice. There's something so familiar about him. He reminds me of a younger Charles, I guess. Calm, understated, level-headed. Not in the least bit full of himself the way Ethan could be, even though his confidence was partly what attracted me to him. Ethan was exciting, charismatic. And after five years of living alone I found his energy and exuberance refreshing. He reminded me of an old friend of mine. Someone who had been the opposite of me – confident through and through, full of life, of get-up-and-go. Someone a bit naughty, prepared to take risks, notwithstanding the costs. Looking back, I realise what a bad influence he was on me, but at the time I thought he was the bee's knees. Because I was a child, and children can be so naïve. They only see what they want to see.

'Yes, thank you, it was a shock. And I suppose that's why I still find myself having nightmares about it.'

Dr Martin frowns. 'And you're taking the antidepressants I prescribed?'

'Yes.' I hesitate.

Dr Martin frowns again, the way a teacher might when confronted with a disobedient child. 'What is it?'

'I just want to feel in control again. Like I did when Charles was alive. Before that, even, after I went to stay with my aunt and uncle and Dr Adams helped me get a handle on my depression, with occupational therapy and weekly art classes. I'm frightened of going back to how I was in my teens and had all those panic attacks. Recently, I've, I've just felt a bit off-kilter, a bit out of it, as it were. And so, I'm wondering if now's the time to come off the medication, so I can clear my head, make a fresh start. You said yourself the antidepressants can have an adverse effect after a time. Can even cause hallucinations and so forth. Maybe if I try and wean myself off them, the nightmares will stop. And I'll feel clearer-headed.'

I'm such a hypocrite for saying all this. For trying to blame everything on the medication Dr Martin prescribed. The fact is, I haven't been totally upfront with him. Not just about Ethan and our argument, but about the one glaringly obvious factor I know in my heart is impeding my recovery. That horrific night a decade ago. Something I shall never be able to tell anyone about. Not while I live and breathe. Not even Dr Adams. I almost told Ethan one night, when we'd drunk a bit too much wine, and started exchanging stories. He opened up about his childhood, how his father could be a bit pushy, how he always expected him to shine at everything and that the pressure was sometimes so great he felt suffocated, like he wanted to run away from it all. I'm sure that's why Ethan drank, took drugs. It was an escape. And having shown me his vulnerable side, a side he rarely let anyone into, I guess he felt entitled to ask about my own childhood. I was almost on the verge of unburdening myself to him. But then I stopped myself in time, thank God. Managed to distract him in other ways…

But he wasn't stupid. And I'm guessing he clued up on my reluctance to talk about my past, got the bit between his teeth and started asking questions. Questions I didn't feel comfortable answering. Because I knew it had the potential to open up a can of worms I'd be unable to contain.

'It's possible,' he says. 'But I'm not sure you're strong enough to come off them yet. We can certainly halve the dose. What do you think? Perhaps take one early evening, rather than just before bed. Just to settle your nerves, help you drift off later. That might stop the daytime sleepiness. Although I'm not convinced the medication is causing that. I specifically prescribed a low dose, just enough to take the edge off. To be honest, I think it's more the depression that's making you tired.'

'Yes,' I nod, 'yes, of course, you're probably right. OK, let's do that.'

He nods, makes a note. 'And how is the hunt for a new lodger going?'

I smile. 'Good, actually. I've found someone. He's moving in on Friday.'

Dr Martin suddenly looks concerned. Not the reaction I expected.

'What's wrong? Aren't you pleased for me?'

He hesitates, then says, 'Yes, yes, of course, that's wonderful news. You seem happy. Relieved.'

'Yes, I am,' I say. I describe Seb to him and again feel a tug of shame that I can never be entirely honest with my new lodger. Particularly as he seems like such a kind soul. He has no idea how fragile I am inside, because I'm good at putting on a face with strangers, making myself out to be this confident, poised woman in my late thirties, when much of the time I feel like a frightened child. So many of my relationships have been built on lies. So many tarnished by guilt. It's something that grates at my conscience, but I don't see that I have any other option but to carry on the charade.

'Sounds like the perfect choice,' Dr Martin says.

'I hope so,' I say. 'When I took Ethan in, I never imagined he'd be so volatile. That things could have ended up the way they did.'

Dr Martin has no idea that my and Ethan's relationship became sexual a year after he moved in. We were never exclusive. He slept with other women, and I was OK with that. Sex wasn't something I was seeking when I took him in as my lodger, and it wasn't as if I was completely starved of sex and therefore desperate to get laid, because I did go on dates after Charles died; dates that ended up in the bedroom several times. But I guess with our living in such close proximity to one another, and him being so sexy and smart, as well as an incorrigible flirt, in some ways it was inevitable. He wasn't timid about telling me that he found me incredibly attractive. That he couldn't stop thinking about me when he was lying in bed, and would imagine doing all sorts of dirty things to me. Similar to the drink and the drugs, sex for Ethan was an escape from the pressures of daily life, a means to offload all the stress and high expectations weighing heavy on his young shoulders. I can't ever imagine Seb saying such things to me. He seems too shy. Even though I'm also certain I didn't imagine the chemistry between us on Monday. I've always had that effect on younger men, through no conscious effort on my part, I might add. It seems to radiate off me. Charles used to joke about it when we'd be out somewhere fancy, and he'd notice men's eyes latch on to me the minute we entered a room. He never felt threatened, though. Because he knew that my heart belonged to him, and him only.

It wasn't love with Ethan, at least not on my part, although I did come to care for him. It was lust, pure and simple, and I allowed myself to get caught up in the throes of physical attraction, flattered that he wanted me. The thing is, I've always had a complicated relationship with sex. It's something that both disgusts and excites me. Something I resent and yet crave.

I often wonder if Dr Martin suspects there was more to my relationship with Ethan than friendship, though. Just because of how cut up I was about his death. How stressed I've been ever since. Neither he nor Dr Adams have any idea that Ethan's father came to the house shouting abuse at me a few days after he died. Accusing me of toying with his son's emotions. Of being a lying cut-throat whore rather than the virtuous grieving widow I made myself out to be. At first, I was both shocked and confused by his behaviour, but then I realised Ethan must have told him about his conversation with Stella at number 6. Despite my having tried my best to convince Ethan that what she said couldn't be believed. And that she was very much mistaken in what she thought she'd seen all those years ago. She was wrong about other stuff too. Things she had no business speculating on. I said all this to Ethan's father, told him that she was nothing but a sad, divorced lush who never slept, who thought she knew it all, but who really knew nothing and had nothing better to do than snipe and spread malicious lies. But I'm not sure he believed me. He was a grieving father looking for someone to blame and I was the obvious target.

I'm not sure what Stella's endgame was with Ethan. Perhaps she wanted to impress him, get him on side with her lies. She was always jealous of me, jealous of how in love Charles and I were after her own husband left her for a younger woman. And then later, envious of the fact I had taken in a young, handsome lodger, perhaps even suspecting we were sleeping together. She couldn't stand me finding happiness again because for the five years I lived alone we were equals in her eyes. We even had coffee together occasionally, despite having nothing much in common other than the fact we were both single. And it's perhaps why she invented stories about me, stories that gave Ethan the wrong impression because, like I said, she'd seen what she wanted to see and not what was true. Both the green-eyed monster and the booze talking. I tried to convince Ethan of that. Urged Stella to get help for her addiction. But she didn't want to hear it. Wouldn't admit she had a problem. And so now we don't speak any more. And I suspect it's another reason why she's tried to create more trouble for me recently. Wasting the police's time with her delusions about how Ethan really died. Even though there's still something about him going up to the roof so late at night that feels wrong. But I push the thought aside, because drawing attention to this house is the last thing I need. And it's why I was grateful to Ethan's firm for using their influence to clamp down on the whole sorry affair.

'No, of course you could never have known he'd be so temperamental,' Dr Martin says softly. 'And that must have been hard for you. After all, getting a lodger was supposed to bring you comfort and stability, not more anguish.'

I nod. 'Yes, that's true. And I think things will be different with Seb. He has a completely different temperament. I already feel brighter, more optimistic.'

'That's good.' He hesitates, and I notice that same preoccupied, almost sad, look in his eyes I saw earlier. I have a feeling he wants to tell me something but for some reason is holding back. Perhaps fearful of my reaction. It scares me.

'What is it, doctor?' I ask tentatively.

'There's something I need to tell you. Something that's going to be difficult for you to hear.'

My heart kicks. 'What is it? Please tell me,' I say anxiously, despite being afraid of his response.

He lowers his eyes, then looks back up, his expression grave. 'I'm afraid Dr Adams was found dead at his home in Guildford yesterday.'

Chapter Eight

Before

Scarlett and Xavier hid behind the wall in the playground watching Jasmine and her groupies giggling away at whatever they were reading in their girly magazine. Jasmine was the most popular girl in Scarlett's year. Smart, confident and pretty, she got straight As in every subject, was in the top teams for both hockey and netball, and not only that, she'd just been given the lead in her class's end-of-year summer play – Alice in Wonderland. Scarlett was in the D team for both sports and did her level best to hide whenever drama roles were being allocated. It wasn't that she was shockingly bad at sport or drama, she just didn't enjoy either much. Sport was too rough for her. Plus, she didn't feel comfortable being in a team. She couldn't stand all the pre- and post-match huddling, the tedious overdramatic fighting talk, the pushing, shoving and shouting that went with it. The touching. As for drama, she hated being the centre of attention. Rather than flaunt herself onstage, she preferred to hide in the background, have a bit part with a single line or preferably no lines at all. In her heart she knew it was because she lacked confidence, felt vulnerable in front of a big crowd who would potentially make fun of her if she messed things up. She didn't need that added stress in her life. She got enough ridicule at home.

Unlike her, Xavier excelled at everything. At least, that's what he told her. Not because he was a team player and enjoyed being part of something bigger, but because he was a show-off. He enjoyed being the best. Also, unlike Scarlett, confidence wasn't something he lacked, and Scarlett supposed he might be considered too confident, forever wielding his superiority over others and doing whatever it took to be the best and make sure everyone knew it. Such a contrast to Eve, who was quietly assertive. Confident in her own skin, without feeling the need to brag about it to others. Still, Scarlett found Xavier's gung-ho attitude refreshing, exciting even. And excitement was definitely something she could do with in her lonely life.

Right now, Jasmine and her friends were flipping through a copy of More, tittering at some article or other. It was probably about some cute actor or pop star, Scarlett thought, or perhaps they were reading yet another quiz about sex. They thought they were so grown-up but really they had no idea what they were talking about.

'Let's do it now,' Xavier whispered into Scarlett's right ear.

'No, we can't,' Scarlett whispered back. She looked around cagily, hoping no one could overhear them, even though there was nobody in their immediate vicinity. 'We'll get caught.'

'Rubbish. There's still fifteen minutes to go before break ends, we have plenty of time. It's a sunny day, so no one's going to be stuck inside and see us. Come on, you want to get your own back at them, don't you? Especially Jasmine. She's such a cow.'

Scarlett thought about this for a while. Thought about the other day when Jasmine called her a loser because she'd messed up a presentation on William the Conqueror in history class. It was so humiliating. And galling because she'd prepared for it thoroughly. But when she'd stood up to face everyone in the class, she froze; the words just wouldn't come out of her mouth and she'd ended up running out of the room and getting a detention which she felt was very unfair.

Later, Jasmine and her posse had made snipey comments in front of everyone in the class. Xavier hadn't been there at the time, he was in another form, of course, but when she told him later after school he was livid. Told her she had to get her own back. That she had six more years at this school and she'd never survive if she didn't make a stand now.

'So, tell me again what you want to do?' Scarlett said while enviously watching the girls continue to giggle. She wondered what it must feel like to be popular. She imagined her mother would have been one of those girls, possibly even the ringleader. So full of herself and oblivious to others who she considered beneath her. That's how she behaved now. Even towards her own daughter. Whom she regarded as nothing but a scourge on her own life. Even though Scarlett thought her mother was a bit washed-up now. Too much drinking and too many late nights to blame for her fading beauty.

'Jasmine's allergic to pollen, right?' Xavier said.

'Yes, she has all sorts of allergies, constantly goes on about it in class.'

'Well, what do you know... I have a whole bag full of grass here.'

Scarlett looked down to see a plastic Tesco bag full of grass cuttings.

'Dad was mowing the lawn yesterday, so I seized the opportunity to bring some in for you, after remembering how upset you were.'

Scarlett smiled, grateful for her friend's thoughtfulness. She also felt a tingle of excitement at the prospect of perfect Jasmine breaking out into hives even though she knew how wrong it was. The thing was, no one cared about her. About the wrongs she had suffered. So it was high time she stopped worrying about others. High time that evil Jasmine was brought down a peg or two.

Scarlett grinned. 'OK, yes, let's do it. Let's get our own back on the bitch.'

Chapter Nine

Adriana

Bile creeps up my throat as I look at Dr Martin, unable to comprehend what he's just told me. *Dr Adams is dead?* It's a miracle I manage to speak. 'What?' I say faintly. Praying I misheard. 'Are you sure?'

He nods. 'I'm sorry, but it's true. Poor man. Were you aware he'd been suffering from breathing problems?'

I cast my mind back to last Thursday when I went to see him. It's true I noticed how he'd seemed to have gained a lot of weight, and at times appeared breathless. But I'm also ashamed to admit I hadn't thought a lot of it. Too busy caught up in my own problems. Problems he listened to as patiently as ever.

'It seems he was suffering from pulmonary edema, something only his ex-wife and daughter knew about, although the post-mortem will confirm the exact cause and time of death.'

'I, I had no idea,' I say vaguely, still unable to believe that someone who had become like a father to me is dead. He was always so kind, so patient and understanding. It's why I felt able to confide in him about the nature of my relationship with Ethan. About our argument the night before Ethan died. About my other fears too. But now he's gone, and it's like a piece of me has died with him. I try to blink back the tears but it's no use. They're suddenly falling fast and furiously.

Dr Martin grabs the box of tissues lying on the desk to his right and offers it up to me.

'Take a few,' he says kindly.

I waste no time in accepting his offer with a grateful nod.

'I know you were extremely fond of him, as he was of you.'

I wipe away my tears and manage a faint smile. 'Thank you. I was. It's ironic, because I was actually about to ask if you'd heard from him recently.'

He cocks his head. 'Oh, why's that?'

'He emailed me on Saturday afternoon, saying he needed to speak with me urgently about something, but didn't want to discuss it over the phone. It was a little unexpected as I'd only just seen him two days before.'

Dr Martin frowns. 'Really? That is odd. Just out of interest, did you talk about anything in particular?'

I'm tempted to tell him, but in the end decide against it. It's too messy. Instead, I just say I craved seeing Dr Adams's friendly face after all the stress with Ethan.

'I see. And how did he sound in the email?'

'He, he sounded a little anxious.'

Another frown. 'And he gave you no indication what it was he wanted to talk to you about?'

'No. I rang him back that same afternoon, and we arranged for me to visit him at his clinic on Monday afternoon. But on Monday morning I woke up to an email from him saying something urgent had come up and he would have to postpone our meeting, but that he'd be in touch in due course.'

'Hmm. What time did he send the email?'

I think for a moment. 'Well, it was after I'd gone to bed on Sunday evening. Around eleven p.m. maybe. Let me check.'

I fish out my phone from my handbag, my fingers quivering just because I feel so upset. I check my inbox which confirms that the email was sent at 11:02 p.m. I show it to Dr Martin, and note the puzzled expression on his face.

'What's wrong?' I say.

'Dr Adams's secretary found his body at home yesterday, around mid-morning, after he failed to turn up to work. Apparently, he emailed her on Sunday afternoon saying he'd decided to take Monday and Tuesday off and would be in as usual first thing on Wednesday. However, the body had already well surpassed the stage of rigor mortis. Forensics estimated he'd been dead at least seventy-two hours.'

I furrow my brow. 'So that means he died on Sunday?'

'It would seem so. Obviously, we don't know the exact time; it could well be the case that he fell ill shortly after emailing you. Perhaps that's why he was postponing, because he was concerned for his health.'

'Yes, perhaps,' I say. 'But then again, you said he'd already told his secretary he wouldn't be coming in until Wednesday. Perhaps he was having urgent tests on the Monday and forgot about our meeting until late Sunday evening?'

'It's possible,' Dr Martin acknowledges with a nod. 'I'm sure his reasons for not going into work are being looked into.'

There's a moment of silence as Dr Martin's remark hangs in the air. It's perfectly feasible Dr Adams cancelled our meeting because he wasn't feeling well, considering his poor health. But why didn't he just say so in his email? Or leave me a voicemail to say as much? Why does it feel like there's something more sinister at play here?

Lost in my thoughts, Dr Martin's next comment brings me back to reality with a start. 'Adriana, I'm sorry to bring this on you at such a bad time, but there's something else I need to speak with you about. I don't want to alarm you, or cause you further anxiety, but neither can I ignore it.'

Alarm me? What on earth is he about to say now? As if I'm not feeling shaken enough. 'Excuse me for saying this, and I don't want to appear rude, but you just saying that alarms me,' I reply. 'As you correctly inferred, I'm not exactly in the best frame of mind right now.'

I'm slightly embarrassed by my terseness but the words just kind of fell out before I had time to stop myself. After all, I come here to feel calmer, not more wound up. But so far, it's been anything but the case.

Dr Martin's face is suddenly cloaked in guilt, and I feel bad about making whatever he's about to say more difficult for him.

'Sorry, Dr Martin,' I'm quick to apologise, 'I shouldn't be such a drama queen. It's obviously important, so please say what's on your mind.'

He nods and I wait on tenterhooks as he reaches inside the drawer to his right and pulls out a sheet of paper. 'I received a rather troubling email late on Tuesday from an address I don't recognise. I got someone I trust who's a bit of a whizz with computers to try and trace the IP address, but they had no luck. He said they must have used a virtual private network. I wanted to wait until I saw you in person to tell you about it.' He turns the sheet around and places it in front of me. 'Does this mean anything to you?'

Anxiety racing through me, I lean forward and read the email:

Dear Dr Martin,

I understand Adriana Wentworth is a patient of yours. You need to warn her to be careful because I'm certain the new lodger she intends to take on is hiding something. I can see it in his eyes. Tell her to be on her guard. He's not as innocent as he seems, I'm sure of it.

Protego@vistamail.com. The address means nothing to me. But I know from my Latin A level that '*protego*' means to guard or protect. I look at Dr Martin, aghast, his less than enthusiastic reaction when I told him I'd found a new lodger now making more sense, my insides churning as I realise the implications of what I've just read. I had wanted to believe it was the pills, my imagination, running wild with me, but now I know that's not the case. And that my instincts were right. I am being watched. But by whom? And how do they know about Seb? The only people who know he's my new lodger are the friend he mentioned is helping him move in – Jasper, I think his name was – along with my aunt and uncle and Max. And it can't be any of them. *Can it?*

Whoever sent Dr Martin the email must have watched Seb come to the house, perhaps first to see Max, and then me. Might they also have hacked into my emails? It's so easy to do these days, you hear of such stories all the time. Is that how they know I've been seeing Dr Martin, or have they been following me here? So much for feeling safer in this part of town. I suddenly feel that my life is not my own. That my every move is being watched.

I seek solace in the fact that it doesn't sound like this person means me any harm. Rather, they appear to be looking out for me. Even though I can't imagine I have anything to fear from Seb because he seems like such a gentle soul. Unless it's a bluff, of course, and the email is designed to mess with my head. In which case, could Stella have sent it? Is this her attempt to spite me after our falling-out? She has a prime viewing spot from her window, and could well have spotted Seb meeting Max. She hardly ever leaves her house as far as I know and is doubtless aware I've been interviewing prospective lodgers. Seeing Seb turn up for the second time perhaps she put two and two together?

I mustn't get ahead of myself. There are so many ifs and buts and I can't go accusing people without solid evidence. I'll lay myself open to a slander suit. It's what I threatened Stella with, for goodness' sake. Plus, there are a lot of sick people out there, people who get a kick out of making trouble for others, I should know. Charles used to get all kinds of threats and crazy messages, being the wealthy man of influence he was, but it was something he learned to deal with and mostly ignore.

But, on the flip side, what if this person is genuine, and there is some truth to what they're saying about Seb?

What if I need to be on my guard with my new lodger?

What if he's hiding something bad and I'm going to regret letting him into my house?

Chapter Ten

Seb

Jasper pulls up in front of the gates of Serenity House, then kills the engine of the van we drove here in. Neither of us have cars – it's not worth it living in Central London what with public transport being so accessible – so I hired a small van for the day to shift my stuff.

'Well, mate, this is it, no turning back now.'

I laugh. 'No need to be so dramatic, I'm only renting a room in north London, I'm not skydiving off Ayers Rock.'

Jasper shakes his head. 'I can't understand why you don't apply for a job at my publishers. I'd put in a good word, you know that. That way you'd be able to afford to rent your own flat in a decent neck of the woods. They're crying out for smart graduates like you. Quite frankly, they'd be lucky to have you. People aren't as nosy as you think. And it could be your way in to getting a publishing deal.'

'You know precisely why I don't want to go down that route, mate. No matter what you say, people *are* nosy. Besides, an office job's not really my bag. I like being my own boss, not beholden to anyone else's rules or restrictions. Plus I'm serious about my writing. I want to give it a proper shot.'

'You could have done that in Scotland, though.' Jasper's right. But he doesn't know the other reason I'm in London.

'That's true.' I nod. 'But I needed a change of scene. And what better place to inspire me than Hampstead?' I give a laboured sigh. 'After the shit I've been through, I think I deserve to be cut a little slack.' I look at Jasper with heartfelt eyes, willing him to see my point of view.

He gives me something of a sad smile in return, and I feel reassured by the understanding in his eyes. I know he only means well and wants the best for me. But sometimes he forgets that my life hasn't been anywhere near as smooth sailing as his. Quite the reverse, in fact. 'I do, mate, and I'm truly sorry for what you went through.' He grins mischievously. 'I'll be eating my words when you write that bestseller, I know it. But make sure you give my publisher first refusal, else I'll never forgive you.'

He wags his finger at me and I chuckle. Give him a friendly slap on the shoulder. 'Absolutely, goes without saying, Jaz.'

I clamber out of the van, go up to the side of the gate and press the buzzer. 'Adriana, it's Seb, we've arrived.'

Within a few seconds, Adriana's friendly voice comes on the line. 'Hi, Seb, I'm opening the gates now.'

I hop back inside the van as the gates open, but just as I do, I notice someone hovering a little way down the road. Far enough away so I can't decipher a face, but near enough to make me almost certain from their stance and physique that it's a man. He's wearing a black cap, dark joggers and a black anorak, almost as if he's trying not to be seen or, at least, be easily identifiable. He also seems to be looking my way. Staring right at me, in fact. A part of me feels like getting out of the van and investigating further, because it's a little creepy. But then I tell myself I'm probably reading too much into things. I'm in London after all, the place is full of weirdos hovering on street corners, no matter how wealthy the area, just like Max said. It's no wonder Adriana feels safer having a male lodger staying in the house with her.

'Everything OK?' Jasper asks.

'Yeah, it's nothing, let's go.'

I glance left through the passenger seat window as Jasper drives on and see that the suspicious-looking man is still standing there. Good job Adriana has CCTV-controlled gates and a high-tech alarm system, I think to myself. Not to mention a sturdy front door with more bolts than Fort Knox. Nothing and no one is getting through that thing. I couldn't be safer once I'm inside.

Once the gates have shut behind us, I push the dodgy bloke to the back of my mind and focus on the house and Adriana who's standing in the open doorway. She looks as lovely as she did on Monday. Perhaps more so, dressed in skinny jeans and a mint-green V-neck jumper, her hair fastened in a low ponytail. She greets us with a warm smile as Jasper and I step out of the van. 'You must be Jasper?' She extends her hand towards Jasper who takes it with a friendly grin, while cutting me a sly look as if to say *you said nothing about her being seriously hot*. I do my best to ignore him and say a silent prayer that he doesn't go and embarrass the hell out of me.

Thankfully, he doesn't. Although it's early days. You never know with Jasper, because diplomacy has never been his strong point. 'Yes, it's lovely to meet you,' he says. 'And thanks for taking this troublemaker off my hands, I thought I'd never be rid of him.' He looks at me and grins, then somewhat cheekily raises his eyebrows at Adriana, as if amused by his own wit. *What was I saying, I knew I shouldn't have spoken so soon*. She laughs along with the joke, although I'm guessing out of politeness rather than genuine amusement. And although I may be reading too much into things, I'm also certain I see a flicker of apprehension in her eyes when she glances my way. *Surely, she's not having doubts about me?* I can't imagine why. Can't think what could have happened between Monday and now to cause her to have second thoughts about my moving in. Unless she's been looking into my background and discovered something? Or perhaps Max has? God only knows how, though, I've been so careful. It's why I'm not on any social media. A recipe for disaster for someone like me. I tell myself I'm overthinking things, that it's probably my own paranoia getting the better of me.

She props the front door open against the wall with a doorstop, at which point Jasper and I start bringing all my stuff through. Thankfully, it's a dry day making the job less painful. Within thirty minutes everything is stacked up in the hallway, both Jasper and I feeling somewhat hot and sweaty from our labours despite the glacial outside temperatures. I also couldn't help noticing how quick Adriana was to lock the front door as soon as we were done unloading the van. It makes me wonder if she also spotted the strange man hovering at the end of the road earlier. Perhaps she's seen him loitering there before? I chalk it up as something to ask her later once I've settled in. Living here, I have a right to know if there's anything or anyone I need to be concerned about.

As Jasper and I both stand in the hallway catching our breaths, I watch my friend look around, his eyes agog as he takes in my new lodgings. 'Wow, it's some house you have here,' he says to Adriana. 'I don't blame you for being careful about vetting who you take on as a lodger.'

'Thank you,' Adriana says. 'My husband, Charles, loved this house, and it's why I could never live anywhere else. It holds so many special memories for me, and I like to think that he's still here, watching over me.'

'I'm so sorry to hear of his passing,' Jasper says. 'Heart attack, wasn't it? Quite unexpected.'

'Aren't they all, Jaz,' I mutter through clenched teeth. Jasper has a heart of gold, but he can be a bit tactless at times.

'Sorry,' Jasper says, holding up both hands, 'it's none of my business.'

'It's OK,' Adriana assures him, despite looking a little uncomfortable. 'Yes, that's correct. It was a heart attack and a massive shock. Charles was my world, but life can be so unpredictable. One minute everything's perfect, the next your whole life is turned upside down.' She gives me a knowing look as an awkward hush ensues. I take the opportunity to shoot daggers at Jasper, a warning not to stick his nose in where it's not wanted or do anything to embarrass me further. He gives me a sheepish look in return.

'Anyway,' Adriana breaks the uneasy silence, 'if you boys want to make a start on taking those boxes upstairs, I have a couple of emails to send. Once you're done, we can all have a cup of tea in the kitchen. How does that sound?' As her eyes flit back and forth between Jasper and me, we both find ourselves nodding like obedient schoolboys.

She walks away in the direction of the study at which point Jasper and I start hauling the boxes up to my bedroom two at a time. Twenty minutes later, we're both sat at the foot of my new king-size bed, three times the size of the single bed my six-foot frame has been squished into for the last six months. I lay back and stare up at the ceiling, exhausted, but thinking how I'm sure to sleep well later. Looking around me – everything is so elegant and uncluttered, from the sleek contemporary furnishings to the room's neutral tones and statement wall lighting – I can hardly believe I'm going to be living in such style. I tell myself I'd better not fuck it up.

'So you like the place?' I ask Jasper, raising myself up again on my elbows.

Jasper nods. 'Yes, it's amazing, obviously. Even more impressive in the flesh than in the photos you showed me.' He looks around. 'A little cold, though. What with all the white, minimalist décor. Sterile is the word that comes to mind.'

I sit up, feeling slightly irritated with my friend for putting such a dampener on things. He's always been a bit of a cynic. I'm not sure why. If anyone has reason to be cynical in this world, it's me, not Jasper. Who's had it pretty easy his whole life as far as I can tell. I mean, his parents are alive and together, he has a great relationship with his siblings, he's in a job that's going places and more recently he's found himself settled in a relationship with a girl who adores him. Quite honestly, I'd do anything to trade places with him. 'I wouldn't say that,' I say with a frown. 'I rather like it. You're just not used to being somewhere so clean.'

'Fair point.' He nods. Before a wide grin spreads across his face.

'What?'

'You know what. She's bloody stunning. And you're not exactly relaxed around women at the best of times.

How the hell are you going to manage being around Adriana? I saw the way you looked at her.'

I feign ignorance. 'How do you mean?'

'You looked like a teenage boy with a crush on his hot teacher.'

'Don't talk rubbish.'

He shakes his head. 'Don't pretend you don't know what I'm talking about. I know you, mate. You don't fall for women easily, but when you do, you fall hard. And I can't say I blame you in Adriana's case. She's gorgeous, intelligent, and not *that* much older than you to make the age gap a big deal.'

I shoot up from the bed, Jasper's remark making me feel decidedly uncomfortable even though a voice in my head is saying I wouldn't be acting so defensively if there was no truth to it. 'Again, you're talking rubbish.'

'Am I?' His eyes linger on me, but I don't succumb.

'Look, can we just change the subject?' I say. 'I'll be fine, I'll manage. She's busy with her own friends and charity work, and I'll be tucked up in here most of the day writing.'

'And what about in the evenings? You going to stay in this room twenty-four-seven?'

'No, of course not. Don't forget I'll be out three nights a week working shifts at the bar.'

He nods. 'Good point. And you're always welcome at mine, you know that, don't you?'

'Not sure Rochelle would second that.'

'Ahh, don't be so hard on her. She likes you, she just doesn't want you living with me permanently.'

I shrug my shoulders. 'That's fair enough. Three's a crowd and all.'

Jasper smiles then holds my gaze, as if he has more to say, but for some reason hesitates.

'What?' I probe. 'And don't say nothing, I know you too well and I can tell you're itching to say something. So spit it out whatever it is.'

His gaze becomes uncharacteristically serious. 'OK, but don't get cross.' He keeps his voice low, as if he fears being overheard, despite the closed door and the distinct clatter of crockery coming from the kitchen making it clear Adriana's otherwise occupied.

I roll my eyes. 'Christ, why all the whispering? She can't hear us from down there. What have you done now?'

'Nothing, it's just… well, I did a little searching on the internet.'

I raise my brow. 'Searching? For what?'

'I looked up Charles Wentworth, just because I was interested to know more about the guy.'

'Jaz, honestly.'

'What? Like I said, I was interested. You're my best mate, you've been through so much, and I feel it's my duty to look out for you. Let's face it, nobody else will.'

I sigh, thinking he has a point, and that I should be grateful that someone gives a toss about me. 'OK. And? What did you find out, Inspector Morse?'

My sarcasm is lost on him. His eyes still unusually solemn. 'I found out that his death came as a total shock to those who knew and loved him well. His brother, Stuart, for instance. Their parents passed away fifteen years ago, but Charles and Stuart were very close according to the newspaper article I read.'

I frown. 'Well, of course it would come as a shock. Heart attacks are a shock, generally. Unless there's a history of heart disease. Stuart was his brother, and

Adriana already mentioned he was Charles's right-hand man at work. They would have seen each other day in, day out. So naturally they were close.'

Jasper shakes his head. His voice becomes lower still. 'No, you're not getting my drift.'

I frown again. 'How do you mean?'

'Apparently, other than Charles being a bit of a work-aholic and having an old rugby injury, he was in tip-top condition health-wise. He'd only just had his annual BUPA check, in fact. Passed it with flying colours.'

I start to get an uneasy feeling in my gut. 'OK, but still, these things happen. Maybe it was stress.'

'It wasn't. Well, they didn't mention stress as a cause. The article said he died of a morphine overdose.'

'Morphine?'

'Yes. Adriana claimed he took it for the pain in his knee. But always in controlled amounts. The coroner ruled an overdose of morphine caused him to go into cardiac arrest.'

I shrug my shoulders. 'It can happen, I guess. Over-dosing on pain meds. You hear all the time about pro athletes getting addicted. And someone as rich as him would have access to all sorts of stuff.'

'But why go swimming after taking morphine?'

'Swimming?'

'Yep, that's where Adriana found him. Floating face down in their pool. Clearly, the added exertion on top of the opiates put too much strain on his heart. It seems like a dangerous thing to be doing when you've just taken morphine, wouldn't you say? Plus, you'd have thought he'd have been too out of it to even think about going swimming.'

The same uneasy feeling swishes in my belly as Jasper's words sink in.

'What are you saying, Jaz? Why are you telling me this now?'

'Seb, Jasper, I've made some tea!' Adriana's voice calls, presumably from halfway up the stairs so that we can hear her. I almost jump in fright, and immediately feel guilty for talking about my landlady's late husband behind her back, worse still speculating on the truth behind his death. Even so, based on what Jasper just told me, it does all feel a bit iffy.

'All I'm saying is that you need to be careful,' Jasper whispers. 'Enjoy living in luxury for a bit, but don't get too cosy with the landlady, no matter how hot she is. Rich people aren't like us. They're a law unto themselves. I'm not saying Adriana had anything to do with her husband's death, I'm just saying don't allow yourself to get too close to her. There's a reason why beautiful women who've lost their husbands in mysterious circumstances get labelled "Black Widow", but so long as you maintain your distance, keep things professional, there'll be no danger of you getting caught up in her web.'

Chapter Eleven

Adriana

It's just gone four p.m. as Seb and I stand on the front doorstep watching Jasper drive out through the gates.

I'm pleased he's finally left us in peace. Although it's clear he's a good friend to Seb and only has his best interests at heart, I hadn't failed to notice the way his eyes scanned the premises like a hawk after they'd shifted Seb's boxes upstairs and we all had tea and cake in the kitchen. He asked about Ethan too, said what a shock it must have been for me to find him lying there on the ground, which I obviously agreed it was. But it felt like he was fishing for more. In the same way it did when he asked about Charles. Almost as if he suspected there was something untoward about their deaths. And then, although I wasn't keen, I couldn't exactly refuse when he said he'd love to be given the guided tour of my *stunning* home. He certainly knows how to turn on the charm when it suits him and I expect he's quite a hit with the ladies, despite not being my type. There's a pushiness about him I don't much care for. And I didn't appreciate the way he hovered outside my art studio, presumably because Seb told him about it being out of bounds. 'So, this is the famous secret room, where the magic happens?' he said with a twinkle in his eye. It almost felt like he was goading me to explain why it was off limits, even though I'd already mentioned it was my private space, something even my husband had respected.

The questions he asked about Charles and how he died made me suspect he'd been doing some digging on the internet and had perhaps found the article about Charles having overdosed on the morphine he took for his chronic knee pain. Charles's lawyer, at my request, tried his best to keep my husband's morphine dependency out of the papers, but a week or so after he died, someone leaked it – we suspect either the pathologist or the coroner had talked for a price – and that was that. The thing I had dreaded most – my kind and brilliant husband being branded a drug addict – occurred, overshadowing all his personal successes, his constant championing of the environment, not to mention his involvement in charitable causes. I had so wanted to protect his reputation, his legacy, but I failed him, something I feel guilty about every day. That amongst other things.

We watch the gates close after Jasper then go back inside the house. Alone at last.

Although I'm trying my best to act all bright and breezy, I'm still feeling devastated about Dr Adams's death. The funeral is in ten days, so his secretary informed me when we spoke yesterday on the phone. She's asked me to say a few words, to which I agreed without a second's thought. My aunt and uncle said they'll be going too. They were as shocked as me to learn the news, and I can hardly believe I'll never see his kind face or hear his reassuring voice again. I just hope I won't crumble without his steadying influence.

I'm also trying not to let the email Dr Martin received get to me. I keep telling myself it could be a one-off, and that I need to keep things in perspective until I know what and whom I am dealing with. It could also be some elaborate hoax, even though that doesn't make the fact that I am clearly being watched any easier to bear. It's terrifying, if I'm being honest. Neither can I ignore the fact that there are various people out there who bear a grudge against me. Ethan's father and Stella, for example. Perhaps this is their attempt at revenge, as petty as it feels. Them wanting to scare me, bring me down a peg or two. After all, there was no mention of what Seb might be hiding, just mere speculation, and I had reassured myself with the fact that the credit checks on Seb came back fine, nothing even remotely suspicious in them.

But, like I said, it doesn't feel good being watched, whoever the culprit is. And it brings back memories of that night years ago now, but which I can still remember in chilling detail. A frightening episode I've tried so hard to forget, yet still haunts my dreams. I can only pray they aren't related. Because if they are, I'm in trouble.

When I got home from seeing Dr Martin, I felt so on edge. Glancing over my shoulder as I entered the gates, half thinking that whoever sent the email might jump out of the shadows and confront me. It's why I was so quick to shut the front door earlier after Seb and Jasper unloaded the van, in case whoever sent the email was spying on us. I also ran a virus check on my laptop, changed my login and security details, using the strongest password I could think of in the hope of making it as hacker-proof as possible. I even got up on a ladder and scoured the house for any evidence of a hidden camera but found nothing. Not that I'm an expert in such matters.

Of course, Dr Martin asked me if I had any idea who may have sent the email, or why they might have concerns about Seb. I told him I hadn't a clue on either score and was just as puzzled as him. Which obviously wasn't strictly true where the former was concerned, but I didn't want to get into my run-ins with Stella and Ethan's father before I have any solid proof, because he's bound to ask me why things are so acrimonious between us. That being so, he urged me to call the police, saying the whole thing screamed 'stalker'. He questioned why they hadn't contacted me directly and revealed their identity if there was any truth to their suspicions. 'Why all the secrecy?' he said. 'Surely, someone genuinely concerned for your well-being, who had good reason to feel wary of Seb, would have told you so to your face?' It was a fair point. A very good one. That, and the fact that the sender had chosen to remain anonymous and contact me through him surely cast serious doubts as to their own character and motives, he further pointed out. His concern was touching, and I guess, as my doctor, he was only fulfilling his duty of care to me. He suggested we call the police and show them the email, see if they'd be able to trace the source. I'd been tempted to do as he said, partly to confirm I wasn't going mad and had imagined someone had been watching me all this time. But also, to put a stop to this nonsense before it gains any traction. But in the end, I knew it was too risky; the last thing I want is the police snooping around the house. Plus, it didn't seem fair to go casting aspersions on Seb's character, however unfounded they might be, when as yet I had no real reason to be suspicious of him. And so, I told Dr Martin that for now I'd prefer to keep the whole thing between us. 'With any luck it's a one-off,' I said, trying to sound as blasé as possible. 'Just some troublemaker having his fifteen minutes of fame. Charles got similar messages all the time, but nothing ever came of them.' He hadn't looked too convinced when I said this.

And why would he? He's an intelligent man. But in the end, he reluctantly agreed when I explained I'd had my fill of the police after the whole business with Ethan and couldn't bear further intrusion when I was finally starting to get my life back in order. He seemed to understand where I was coming from. Had no idea that the real reason behind my reluctance was that I couldn't risk bringing the police into my home again. It couldn't be avoided after Ethan's tragic fall. But in this instance, I have a choice, and so I'd rather not tempt fate even though I know I may live to regret it.

For now, I tell myself to be careful, to keep my eye out for anyone suspicious, and pray that whoever this person is, they don't mean me any harm. And, more importantly, that they're wrong about Seb.

'So, I expect you have some unpacking to do?' I say to Seb as I close the front door, being sure to double-lock it once more. Something I normally only do before bed, but for now, in light of the email, feel safer doing at all times of the day.

'Yes, I'd best get on with it,' Seb replies. I notice the curious look in his eye, perhaps wondering why I'm so security-conscious. But he's too polite to say anything. Thank goodness. 'So I can relax over the weekend,' he adds.

I smile. 'Good idea. Do you have plans for tomorrow?'

'Well, I definitely need to crack on with my writing. But first, I thought I might go for an early morning jog around the Heath. Maybe grab breakfast in a cafe afterwards. I used to run outside a lot, but I've barely done any exercise since moving in with Jaz. No excuse now with all that green open space on my doorstep.'

'Absolutely. Sounds like a wonderful idea,' I say. 'I wish I was more of an outdoor person, but I always feel too exposed running outside. Anyway, it's meant to be dry all weekend, so I'd make the most of it if I were you. Still, you're most welcome to use the pool and gym whenever you like.'

He smiles. It's a warm, open smile. His eyes equally sincere. Reassuring me that my instincts are right about Seb and that the sender of the email is either playing with me or has got it all wrong. We all have our secrets, but it doesn't make us bad people. Sometimes we're forced to keep secrets through no fault of our own. I above all people know that.

'Cheers,' Seb says, 'that's kind of you. I'd definitely love to make use of the pool. After Dad died, I was a bit of a mess and found swimming very therapeutic. Not so keen on gyms, though. A bit stifling for me. I'm more of an outdoor type when it comes to exercise. Guess it stems from my childhood. Dad was very much the same, growing up by the sea. He instilled in me a love of the open air; we'd go cycling for miles on weekends. Around the Downs, all the way from Brighton to Eastbourne sometimes.'

'You must miss him very much?' I say as we start walking away from the hallway in the direction of the stairs. I can't help feeling a little jealous of how hands-on Seb's father appears to have been compared to mine. My father never did anything with me, he was always too busy working or trying to please my mother. He was good at the former, but failed miserably at the latter.

'Yeah, I do,' he replies. 'I miss Mum more, though. She was the best. The most selfless woman I've ever known.'

Again, the disparity between my and Seb's parents couldn't be starker. How I envy Seb for that. To have had such devoted, loving parents. Memories to cherish rather than repress because they hurt too much.

'Do you still miss your parents?' He looks at me with searching eyes, and I can't bear to lie and tell him that I do. But neither can I admit the truth – that I don't miss them one bit.

I end up fudging my answer. 'Well, I'm much older than you, I've had a lot more time to adjust. I don't really think about it any more.'

He gives me a strange look, as if he considers my answer odd. I can't blame him for that. Because it is.

We start walking up the stairs, barely a couple of inches separating us. I feel calmer having him near, less vulnerable with a young man in the house to protect me. And because of this, I can't help what I say next, the words just tumble out of me. 'Listen, as it's your first night, let me cook for you this evening.'

A part of me knows it's a bad idea. That I can't allow myself to get close to Seb the way I did with Ethan. It's too dangerous, for both him and for me. But I've had dinner on my own seven nights on the trot, and it would be nice to see a friendly face across the table for once, rather than my blank kitchen wall. It's only dinner, there's no harm in it. Even so, he looks slightly uncomfortable when I make the suggestion and it hits me again how he couldn't be more different to Ethan, who wouldn't have batted an eyelid.

'Don't worry, I won't make a habit of it,' I say. 'But you've had a tiring week with all the packing and moving, et cetera. Let me take a load off tonight.'

His face relaxes. 'Sure. That would be nice. I am pretty whacked. Hadn't really thought about dinner.'

I smile, relieved to have dispelled the momentary awkwardness. 'Great, anything I should steer clear of?'

'Nah,' he says with a grin. 'I eat anything and everything.'

'Perfect. Makes my life simple. I'll do salmon risotto.'

Just then our eyes linger on one another, and a rush of electricity charges through me. It was there on Monday when we first met, and I can tell by his expression that he feels it too. I'd be lying if I said I didn't enjoy the feeling, along with the power I yield over men. The feeling of being in control. It's exhilarating. The opposite to how I felt as a child. And yet, somehow with Seb it feels more than that, despite our being relative strangers. As if we share a bond nurtured from the loss and sadness that's marred both our lives. Still, I tell myself I cannot go there with him. He's too good a person. I can see that, can feel it, and given what he's been through, he deserves to be loved by a good woman.

A woman far less complicated than me.

Chapter Twelve

Before

I'm hiding out in Scarlett's house listening to every word that's being said, and it's all I can do to bite my lip and stop myself from lashing out at her parents and giving them an earful. I'm desperate to come to her rescue but fear making things worse for her. Better I stay concealed. Scarlett's dad has recently got home from work, to be greeted by the sound of Scarlett's mum, Steph, ranting at her in the kitchen. She, who herself has only just returned from a spa day. Her third this month.

Looking around the room, it's all such a joke, so fucking fake. Everything so clean, open and inviting. Much like the rest of the house. From the spotless porcelain gloss units to the elegant white orchid gracing the sprawling worktop, to the charming print of idyllic St Ives mounted on the wall. A seemingly soothing sanctuary of calm, but which couldn't be further from the truth. No outsider would be able to guess at the rottenness embedded within its walls, infesting the air like a putrid fungus. It's all a big, fat, ugly lie, and I want to scream it from the rooftops.

'Shut your mouth, you disgusting little tramp, how dare you tell such vile lies. I cannot believe I conceived a child as horrid as you. Is it that freakish so-called friend of yours putting you up to mischief again? Is he the one who's been putting such abhorrent thoughts into your sick little brain? Come on, girl, speak up, tell me, you little weirdo.'

The cow grabs Scarlett's shoulders and shakes her violently. My poor friend remains mute, and I can sense her pain. Both emotional and physical.

'Steph, stop it, that's enough,' Scarlett's dad, Brian, says. In something of a half-hearted fashion, though, it has to be said. Like he feels he needs to say something, but is also scared of his wife's reaction. It's clear who wears the trousers in this house. Steph dominates Brian. He never dares to disagree with her because he knows he's out of her league in the looks department and is petrified she might leave him. He's so weak. So pathetic. Despite Scarlett always defending him. A real man wouldn't take that, a real man would stand up to Steph, put her in her place, lay down the law and protect his only child. He has no idea that his slutty wife has been shagging the babysitter on and off for the last eight years. The son of his boss, for God's sake, the ultimate humiliation. And not just shagging him. He does vile things to her. Things that aren't legal. But the whore takes it without complaint. Seems to enjoy it. They make recordings too. Watch them on repeat.

Or maybe Brian does know. But is too chicken to point the finger in case he gets the sack. Scarlett has been desperate to tell him the truth, but she's too kind, and she doesn't want to hurt him. Even though she's been hurting inside herself for so many years now, having witnessed things no kid should ever see. She's also been too afraid to tell him for fear of the horrible things that might happen to her and to Brian if she does and gets found out.

Until now, that is.

I'm so proud of her for finally having the guts to speak up, having suffered in silence for so long. But I also suspect her efforts are a waste of time.

Steph glowers at Brian. 'It's all your fault. You're too soft on her. You let her get away with murder. Jason has been nothing but kind to her. Nothing but good to us. Babysitting at the drop of a hat when she was younger, staying later than planned when we've overrun. He's fetched her from school, made her meals, read with her at bedtime. And how does the little minx repay him? Repay us? By fabricating some dirty story. All to get him into trouble. He's your boss's son, for God's sake. A respected member of our community. Do you really think him capable of such things?'

Steph is such a bitch. She knows full well that Scarlett caught her and the babysitter going at it through the slit in the bedroom door. But she doesn't know the rest. Is so utterly clueless about the other stuff that goes on. What happens to Scarlett when she's not there. Poor Scarlett is trying to tell her, get her parents to listen. But Steph is screaming the house down, accusing Scarlett of cooking up stories to make Steph stop. Because she feels bad about Steph cheating on her dad, feels sorry for him. But Steph is wrong. So wrong. She doesn't know what's happening to her daughter right under her own roof. And that makes her an even worse mum than ever in my eyes. For not seeing it. For not protecting her daughter.

Right now, I feel so angry for Scarlett. So angry with the world, about the injustice of it all. I can see how much pain she's in; she can't take much more. This was her one shot at telling the truth, but I knew it would come to nothing.

Things can't go on like this. I have to do something. I need to protect Scarlett even if others are too scared to.

'Go to your room!' Steph commands with eyes like the devil. 'You are nothing but a lying, sick-headed, evil piece of filth, who gets off on concocting these disgusting stories for no other purpose than the sake of your own twisted enjoyment. I feel ashamed to call you my daughter.' Still not a word from Scarlett. It's like she's blanked out the world around her. Wrapped herself in an invisible cocoon so as not to let the bad stuff affect her any more.

But it's not enough. I can see how Steph's cruel words are affecting her. Along with Brian's failure to protect her. I cannot let the adults hurt the person I love most in this world any more.

Tonight, Scarlett's suffering will end.

Chapter Thirteen

Seb

It's 6:15 p.m. and I've just unpacked the last of my boxes, having been at it for two hours. Unpacking is a lot less painful than packing, I've realised, although that's perhaps because I've got masses more room to move about here at Adriana's than I did at Jasper's. I'm still trying to get my head around having so much space. Along with how clean and immaculate everything is. Jasper called it clinical, but I disagree. It's nice not living in a mess for once. After what happened in my teens, I became obsessed with hygiene. Would find myself scrubbing the kitchen floor, wiping the surfaces incessantly, showering twice, sometimes three times, a day. Mum was worried about me, almost sent me to see a child psychologist. It's another reason why we left England for Nigeria. Not just because she craved anonymity, but because she was scared of me being fucked up for life.

Anyway, I just hope I can meet Adriana's expectations while I live under her roof. It's obvious how being in this house allows her to feel close to her late husband. Such a contrast to Mum, who couldn't wait to escape the only home I'd ever known, its walls a hellish reminder of all that went on.

I fish out my laptop and set it down on the desk opposite my bed. Along with an in-tray of loose research papers and a framed photo of Mum, taken last June. When we'd gone to Portobello Beach one hot summer's day, four months after I got back from travelling. It's the last photo I took of her. She'd seemed so happy that afternoon. We walked barefooted along the sand, ate Mr Whippys on a bench while watching the world go by and I truly believed she'd turned a corner. Was even hopeful she might find love again. She deserved that more than anyone. But I realise now she was just being brave for my benefit. Putting on a face for the sake of her child even though I was a grown man, the way any good mum would. But beneath the happy exterior was a pain that continued to gnaw away at her until it eventually ate her up. I blink back the tears as I reflect on this, think about how broken she must have been. How stupid she must have felt not to have seen what was right before her eyes. It's the duplicity of it all that got to her, I know that now. I sometimes resent her for leaving me, but I can also understand why she did what she did; that she just didn't want to be in pain any more.

I glance left, admiring all my books lined up on Adriana's quirky zigzag-design shelf. I had no option but to keep most of them boxed up at Jasper's, and so it's nice to be able to admire them again. Mostly crime and psychological thrillers, interspersed with a few historical titles and the odd autobiography.

I walk over to the window and open the blinds. Unlike Adriana's bedroom, mine looks out over the road and Hampstead Heath beyond it. It's so dark out there now, meaning I can't make out much to speak of, save the odd passer-by. Hopefully, the weirdo from earlier has long made tracks. I still plan on asking Adriana about him when the moment feels right. Just to make sure he's not a real threat. It's crazy how different a place feels when the sun goes down and darkness descends. Earlier, when Jasper helped carry my boxes upstairs and I looked out, I saw children playing, dogs racing around, letting off steam and energy, much to their parents' and owners' relief and delight. I figure it's a normal scene most weekends in this part of London. More so in the height of summer when it's light until gone nine. Right now everything feels so bleak and wearying, whereas there's always such a feeling of hope and vitality in the summer months. I wonder if I'll still be here then. The tenancy runs for six months, which takes me up to mid-July. As Adriana doesn't really need the money she said she prefers to keep her tenancies short, with the option to renew at the five-month stage if we both agree. I can't blame her for being cautious, and I don't want to be tied down either. I'm to pay her at the beginning of each month, having already put down a deposit up front which I get back when I leave, an arrangement that suits me fine.

It's pin-drop quiet in my room, the benefit of the house's secluded position on a slight incline plus the windows being double-glazed. Hampstead's a busy residential area, brimming with boutiques, restaurants and cafes that come alive particularly on weekends, but the design and situation of Serenity House means I can barely hear any passing traffic. There should be no excuses now for not finishing my novel, I tell myself. It's my darkest yet. Centring on friends playing truth or dare in the basement of a remote Highlands cottage. When all the lights go out one of them is killed in those fleeting seconds and it quickly becomes clear they're not alone. Jasper calls me warped. Jokes that 'it's always the quiet ones'. I'm not sure how the ideas come to me, and I'm certain a shrink would say it all stems from my childhood. And maybe that's true. But I couldn't care less. I don't need therapy to help me confront my fears, that's what I have my writing for. It's all the therapy I need. A bit like Adriana with her art, I suppose. I still have around 30,000 words to go, and plan on getting stuck in tomorrow after my run.

Just then, my phone pings. A text. I rush to go grab it off the desk to see who's messaged. I'm hoping it's the person I've been trying to get in touch with for some time now. Someone who may be able to answer questions I have about my dad. The other reason I've come to London. But it's not, it's only Jasper, asking how things are going and if I've settled in OK. My spirits sink as I wonder if I'll ever get the answers I seek. Perhaps not. Perhaps it's something I'll have to learn to live with. I text Jasper back saying everything's fine, and that we'll speak on Sunday. He says OK, and that Rochelle would love to see the place soon. Having mates over certainly wasn't on Adriana's forbidden list. Provided they don't stay overnight. Hopefully, she'll be fine with them coming round, despite Jasper's earlier probing.

I'm still feeling a little cross with him myself. Thank God he didn't mention the morphine Charles took; I would have died on the spot. Jasper can never leave things alone. Always thinks there's more to a situation than meets the eye. Still, I'd be lying if I said I didn't think it odd that someone as smart and successful as Charles Wentworth would go swimming after taking morphine. Also, that Adriana failed to mention it on Monday. She simply said he had a heart attack and left it at that. Then again, perhaps he'd been too high to know what he was doing. Just like Ethan. Plus, Adriana and I had only just met and maybe she felt embarrassed to tell me the truth, was simply looking to protect her husband's reputation.

I picture her face as we padded up the stairs together earlier. I'm sure I wasn't imagining the chemistry between us as we locked eyes and lingered there a while before she offered to cook for me. My head told me it was a bad idea – it still does, because I know it would be so easy to fall for a woman like her, as much as I denied it to Jasper. I'd never give him the benefit of being right because the bugger's head would grow even bigger. But the truth is, she's everything I look for in the opposite sex. Sure, she's beautiful, there's no denying it, but it's more than that. It's her intelligence, her life experience, the fact that I can see that she is broken, a bit like I am. Only, unlike me, she's not afraid to show her fragile side. There's an openness, an innate confidence about Adriana that draws me to her. It tells me I have nothing to fear from her, that Jasper's words of caution are misplaced. Really, the only thing I have to fear is me falling hard for her. That's the real danger I am placing myself in, moving here.

For this reason, I was tempted to turn down her offer of dinner. But when she made a point of saying it would be a one-off, what with it being my first night and me having had a long week, I told myself I was overthinking things. Giving myself too much credit. After all, why would a woman like her possibly be interested in someone like me? No job, no income to speak of, plus I'm fourteen years younger and a boy compared to her husband, one of the most successful businessmen of his generation. And clearly a man she had worshipped and with whom I could never compete.

It's just a harmless platonic dinner.

Nothing whatsoever to worry about.

Chapter Fourteen

Before

I'm still hiding out in Scarlett's house, on the first-floor landing, waiting for the bitch and her lapdog to go to bed. I've been here since her so-called mother sent her to her room. Two long hours I was forced to endure listening to Steph yack away, moaning about her daughter, blaming Brian for Scarlett's behaviour, her alleged lies, like the ignorant, vicious cow she is.

I couldn't leave Scarlett, and I'd so wanted to be able to comfort her. But I knew that I couldn't because of what I have planned. Things have gone too far; they've passed the point of no return and there is no turning back now. I know that Scarlett, being the good person she is, would be appalled by my intentions, despite hating her mum. But she'll thank me for it later. She'll be so much better off once I've done what's necessary.

I wait a few minutes longer, my heart beating so fast I think it might burst from my chest. I'm filled with both excitement and terror. I wait for the sound of the boiler to stop, a signal that both Steph and Brian have finished in the bathroom and are finally ready to slip under the covers of their super-king-size bed in the loft. Finally, there is silence. Only the faint sound of traffic outside, the natural stirrings of the house filling it. I know for a fact that Scarlett's sleep is restless. It's hardly surprising, given what she's been made to suffer. But after tonight, her sleep will improve. Maybe not immediately. But it will, after a time.

And fingers crossed I'll never be found out, because what I have planned is smart, watertight. I'm convinced of it.

I creep downstairs, praying that Steph and Brian won't wake. Nor Scarlett. Not yet, at least. I wince at the sound of the floorboards creaking, and inwardly breathe a sigh of relief when at last I reach the ground floor. The family cat, Molly, is there to greet me. I worry she might get scared, might go and alert her owners to my unfamiliar presence at this time of night, but to my delight she nestles her warm, furry head against my ankle. I've visited so many times now, she knows me well, almost like another member of the family, I think happily to myself. I bend down and give her a quick stroke, while at the same time I feel a twinge of guilt that poor Molly will most likely be blamed for the tragedy about to happen. That's the plan, at least. The only way I'll get away with it. But I'll make sure Molly escapes unscathed.

I tiptoe to the kitchen and hunt for a box of matches. I know Steph keeps a drawer full of them to light the hundreds of candles she gets through in a year and, to my delight, the first drawer I open happens to be the right one.

I pull out a box, imprinted with the logo of some fancy London restaurant I'm guessing Steph has been to with some of her airhead model friends, and then quietly close the drawer before stealthily moving to the living room. As well as countless over-the-top cushions reflecting Steph's brash taste, it's adorned with an array of candles of different shapes and sizes. Steph loves her candles. Every night she lights them, but always remembers to blow them all out. Tonight was no exception. Although no one will ever know that. They'll think that Steph forgot on this one occasion and that poor Molly must have knocked over the more discreet candle positioned in the far corner. Molly follows me to the candle I have in mind, a pink creation resting on a patterned dish, at which point I remove a match from the box I've been carrying, light it and ever so gently put it to the wick of the candle. It comes alight after a while, and I stand back for a few seconds admiring the beauty and simplicity of the flame. It almost feels like a religious moment, and I find myself saying a silent prayer that Scarlett will finally be liberated from the house of horrors she's forced to exist in. And then, with a gentle push, I tip the candle over, watch it fall to the ground, immediately setting alight the immaculate mink-coloured carpet beneath it. Molly senses danger and quickly scampers away, and then, having found myself briefly entranced by both the beauty and danger of the burgeoning flames, I rush out of the room and up the stairs to Scarlett's bedroom. I know that I need to alert her somehow, make sure she gets out safely.

While her parents perish in their bed, oblivious to the fact that they will never live to see another day.

Chapter Fifteen

Seb

'Hmm, smells good.'

I hover at the kitchen door watching Adriana stir something in a pan. An intoxicating aroma of lemon, salmon and red pepper fills the air, and it makes me realise how hungry I am, having not eaten much to speak of all day. She swivels around in surprise. 'Jesus, you scared me!'

'Sorry,' I hold my hands up, 'I didn't mean to.' There's a jitteriness about her. Noticeably different to how she was on Monday, and again I can't help wondering if something happened between then and now to rattle her. Possibly something she found out about me. Or perhaps connected with the strange man I saw loitering at the end of her road earlier.

She smiles. 'It's OK, I'm just tired. Not myself. The whole business with Ethan really unsettled me. I don't think I've had a full night's sleep in weeks. But it's not the only reason I'm a bit on edge. Truth is, I received some rather bad news yesterday. And it's got to me somewhat, despite me trying to put on a brave face.'

Perhaps a little selfishly, I feel relieved I'm not the cause of her anxiety. But at the same time, I feel bad for Adriana and all she's been through recently. 'I'm so sorry,' I say, 'what happened? Scratch that. You don't have to tell me, but if I can help in any way, don't hesitate to ask.'

She gives me a sad, yet grateful, smile. 'Thanks, that's very sweet of you. But I'm afraid there's nothing you can do. Unfortunately, I learned that someone I loved and respected, almost like a second father, died last Sunday. He was a psychologist who specialised in grief counselling. My aunt and uncle took me to see him after my parents died. I think I vaguely mentioned him during our meeting on Monday. He helped me deal with the pain and anger I felt at the time. Was the kindest, most genuine of men I've ever had the privilege of knowing. To think that I saw him only a few days before he died, it's kind of spooked me. He knew I was struggling after finding Ethan's body, and it was comforting to see him and chat through things. I had no idea he was sick. And I feel bad for being so wrapped up in my own problems that I failed to notice his.'

Adriana's eyes grow moist, and I instinctively edge closer, while resisting the urge to put my arm around her, having remembered Jasper's words of caution. I know he's right. That I need to keep my distance. But it's tricky all the same. There's just something about her. 'You can't blame yourself, you weren't to know,' I say, hoping my words of comfort will be enough. 'Besides, that was his job,' I add. 'To listen.'

'I guess,' she sighs, turning the heat down on the risotto and placing the lid over the pan. 'It's just hard, you know? To lose someone you love. And so soon after losing Ethan, who I came to care for very much.'

There's a pause in the conversation as her eyes settle on me, the silence once again unbearable and yet tantalising. 'Wine?' she says eventually.

'Love some.' I almost exhale out loud with relief.

I watch her fish out two elegant wine glasses from an overhead shelf, then remove a bottle of Sancerre from the wine fridge beneath it. 'Hope you're OK with white? It goes better with salmon.'

'Of course, I'm in your capable hands,' I say, while thinking how very grown-up this all feels. Only this time last week I was getting drunk on Corona with Jasper while waiting on a rogan josh from the local curry house.

She retrieves a bottle opener from a drawer, then begins to uncork the wine.

'Need any help?' I ask.

'It's fine, I can manage.' She smiles. 'I meant to say I've cleared a couple of shelves in both the fridge and freezer. So feel free to stock up. I'd happily share stuff with you, but you don't look like an almond milk and wheat-free bread kind of guy.'

Her eyes regain that unique twinkle I first noticed on Monday as she says this before she expertly draws the cork from the bottle in one fell swoop. It makes a loud popping sound that seems to echo around the room. A little background music wouldn't go amiss to break up the hush. I chuckle. 'Ah, you got that right, semi-skimmed and granary is about as fancy as I get.'

She laughs. 'Thought so.' Then pours us both a generous measure of wine. She hands mine to me, and we clink glasses. 'Here's to new beginnings,' she says. 'I hope you'll be happy living here.'

'Thank you,' I say. 'I'm sure I will be.'

As if reading my mind, she says, 'How about a little background music? Does Miles Davis suit, or are you too young and hip for traditional jazz?'

'Not at all, I love Miles Davis, love all kinds of jazz, in fact.'

She smiles. 'Great.' Then uses her phone to turn on the speakers built into the kitchen walls. Everything in this place is so sleek, so unlike what I've been used to. She keeps the music low, but just at the right pitch to break up any awkward silences. 'While the food's cooking, let's get your fingerprint set up for the front door,' she says, 'just in case I'm still not up when you get back from your run tomorrow morning. I'll also need to show you how the alarm works in the hallway.' She goes over to a drawer and pulls out a bunch of keys. 'And here's an extra set of keys to the other doors around the house. Except for my art studio, of course.'

I follow Adriana out of the kitchen and into the hallway where she opens the front door. We go outside and I instantly shiver with the sudden drop in temperature. It's dark but the porch light automatically comes on. I notice her eye her surroundings guardedly, the same way she did earlier, but I don't remark on this. She guides me through the process and in no time at all, I'm letting us both back inside with my fingerprint. It's pretty cool and I tell her this as she closes the door behind us and double-locks it once more.

'Thanks.' She smiles. 'The wonders of modern technology.' She then runs through the alarm system before we stroll back to the kitchen. 'Remind me to write down the code for you. The alarm should be switched on whenever both of us are out and at night by the last person to go to bed. And do make sure you double-lock the front door when you leave the house if I'm not here, and before going to bed if I'm already upstairs. Does that all sound

OK? I'm sorry it's all a bit OTT, but since Charles died, I've become rather security-conscious.'

'Fine by me,' I say. 'You can never be too careful.' I see this as a good moment to bring up the strange man I saw earlier. 'Speaking of being security-conscious, I don't mean to alarm you but this afternoon when Jasper and I first pulled up in front of the house, I noticed this guy hovering at the end of your road.'

Her eyes glimmer with concern. 'Really? What did he look like?'

'Well, he was some distance away, but he appeared to be dressed in dark clothing and a dark cap. Like he was trying to keep a low profile, but not really succeeding. I wouldn't have thought much of it had he not been standing there, watching me. I mean, he literally didn't move; it was clear he was interested in me and what I was doing.'

Adriana takes a sip of wine, her eyes still with that panicked look. 'It definitely wasn't a woman?'

'No,' I shake my head, 'I could tell by the build it was a man.'

'Did he leave when you looked his way? I mean, he must have realised you saw him.'

'No, he didn't, but I decided to ignore it. Told Jasper to drive on through the gates once you'd opened them.'

'Did you tell Jasper about the man?'

'No. Why do you ask?'

'No reason.'

I don't buy that, there clearly is a reason. 'Adriana, have you seen this man before? Do you know who he is?'

'I have my suspicions,' she says.

'Who is he then?'

She turns away. 'I'd rather not say, it's complicated.'

I take a tentative step closer, rest my hand on her shoulder. 'Adriana, please, I can see you're scared, I want to help you.'

She spins round so fast I almost jump in alarm. 'I said leave it.' Her eyes fix on me, her tone unusually sharp, almost threatening. It takes me aback, just because it's so unexpected, and it doesn't seem like her. But then, just like that, her eyes soften, perhaps noticing my wounded look. 'I'm sorry,' she says. 'I'm not sure where that came from, I'm just really wound up right now, what with Dr Adams's death. I shouldn't have snapped. Forgive me?'

I see the genuine remorse in her eyes and it's impossible not to forgive her. The poor woman has been through so much, plus we hardly know each other, why should she tell me everything? Perhaps in time, once we've built up a good level of trust between us, she'll tell me who she thinks the man is. 'Of course,' I say, 'we don't have to talk about it. Just know I'm here to help and listen, whenever you need a sounding board.'

'Thank you, that's kind, I really am grateful.' She smiles. 'Anyway, let's eat, I'm famished!'

I smile back, relieved I haven't soured the evening permanently. Yet somehow her swift shift in mood feels forced. Like she's trying too hard.

Because deep down, she's scared.

Chapter Sixteen

Before

'You're leaving me?'

Scarlett stared into Xavier's eyes as he said this, an overwhelming guilt consuming her.

When she first woke up that night and smelled the smoke, she thought perhaps she was dreaming. That the prodding she'd felt in her side for what seemed like some time was part of the same dream. But then instinct told her to get up, that this wasn't a dream, but rather a living, breathing nightmare and if she didn't get out as soon as possible she'd die.

All at once, she felt very much awake, the hideous events of the previous evening coming back to her, even though she'd found herself switching off part way through her mother's rant because it was the only way she felt able to deal with it. She couldn't believe the way her mother had defended her lover. Couldn't understand why she let him do the things he did to her, and even seemed to enjoy them. Or why she preferred him over her devoted husband, Brian, Scarlett's father. The scumbag babysitter knew Scarlett had seen them doing the disgusting things they did, but far worse was that he seemed to revel in this knowledge. He'd asked her if she enjoyed watching them go at it, said he'd be only too happy to do similar things to her when she was a bit older. She shivered just remembering his words. The creepy look in his eyes. He'd never touched her, thank God, but it was almost as if he had done.

He'd warned her that if she dared breathe a word of what they'd discussed to anyone, he'd make sure her father lost his job. And, quite possibly, his life. This had frightened the hell out of her. It was why she hadn't dared speak up until last night. When something in her just snapped. But none of that mattered now. Because her father was dead. Meaning her mother's bastard bit on the side's threats were immaterial. He couldn't hurt her any more.

Her mother had said some untrue stuff about Xavier too. She didn't know what she was talking about, didn't know him like Scarlett did. It had been convenient for her to blame someone else for her daughter's increasingly bad behaviour at school. Just like she had done last night. When she'd accused Scarlett of telling lies in front of her father, when deep down in what little soul she had left her mother must have known there was some truth to Scarlett's story. She was just too proud to admit it. Proud, but not ashamed. That was the really upsetting thing about it.

Scarlett had instinctively screamed out for her parents when she woke up, yelling out that the house was on fire and knowing that they were upstairs in the loft. She'd remembered the smoke alarm still wasn't fixed and cursed her father for not seeing to that yet. All this could have been avoided if he'd got the damn thing mended! As much as she hated her parents, her mother especially, she'd never have wished them dead. But she'd been too scared to try and save them. She knew if she tried to go upstairs and reach them, she'd perish up there with them. Her instinct had been to fight for her own survival. Was that selfish of her, she wondered.

'Yes, I have no choice,' Scarlett replied to Xavier's question.

'What do you mean?' Xavier asked. He looked angry.

'I'm a minor. Either I go into foster care, or my only other living relatives take me in. All my grandparents are dead. And my father was an only child. I don't much care for either option, *but my aunt and uncle aren't so bad and better the devil you know.'*

'But Guildford's miles away. How will we see each other? You don't have any friends there.'

'No, I don't,' she said. She felt the tears gather. 'I'll miss you, I'll never forget you. We can write to each other. I said the same to Eve.'

And that's when she saw something in Xavier's eyes she'd never seen before. A look of pure hatred. A look that frightened the hell out of her. Perhaps Eve had been right about Xavier all along. She'd said from the start that he wasn't quite right in the head, that he was volatile and obsessive and couldn't be trusted. Scarlett thought Eve had said those things because she was jealous. But perhaps Xavier wasn't as dependable as she thought he was. Perhaps Eve was the only one true friend she could count on.

'How can you be so ungrateful?' he said. 'All the months, years now, I've listened to you whine about your parents, and those bitches at school. All the shit they've put you through. And that's how you repay me? By abandoning me?'

'I don't have a choice, my parents are dead, don't you get it? What the hell am I supposed to do? I need to grow the hell up, make a sensible decision, make a new life for myself.'

He came at her, his face pressed up to her nose, his steely eyes boring through her. He was only just fifteen, but somehow at that moment he looked much older.

'I love you, you know that, and people in love go above and beyond for each other. They find a way. We are meant to be together. We're soulmates.'

She shook her head. 'I'll write, and as soon as I'm settled, I'll come visit. And you can visit me too.'

She held his gaze, willing him to understand, but he simply turned and walked away. Disappearing around the corner.

His failure to respond chilled her to the bone. She realised then that things would never be the same between them, and that she may have made herself an enemy for life.

Chapter Seventeen

Seb

'Another glass?'

Adriana holds up the second bottle of white we're midway through, having not long finished our food. The risotto was amazing, and I can tell my new landlady has a natural flair in the kitchen. It's gratifying to have eaten something home-cooked for once. I'm ashamed to say that ready meals and takeaways have been my staple diet these past few months. Even so, I tell myself not to get used to it, Jasper's warning about keeping things platonic between Adriana and me thrumming in my ears.

It's why I hesitate in response to her offer of more wine. Knowing I can't afford to lose my inhibitions around her. 'I shouldn't,' I say.

She grins, a glint in her eye. 'Go on, it's Friday. And we're celebrating your moving in.'

She holds my gaze, and it's hard to say no to her. Plus, thinking about what a rough few weeks she's had, I don't want to upset her. It's a big house, and I can tell she's enjoying having some company again.

'OK, sure,' I sigh. 'But I know I'm going to regret it in the morning. I'm supposed to be going for a run, remember?'

She grins again, the same glow lighting up her face. 'You're young, you'll brush it off in no time. Some water and a strong coffee and you'll be as right as rain. It's when you reach nearly forty like me that the hangovers are tougher to get over.' She tops up my glass as I hold the stem steady at its base, a little scared of how much I'm enjoying her company.

'Come on, you're still young yourself,' I say. 'Actually, I thought you were much younger.'

Shit, why did I say that? It sounds like I'm flirting with her. It's the wine talking. I'm usually so reserved around women, but the booze has loosened my tongue. Although perhaps that's just an excuse for what's really going on here. The fact that I have this innate desire to flatter her. Make her feel good about herself, just because she's so lovely. Plus, I feel a connection with her. Both of us orphans, having lost the people we loved most in this world, and yet finding solace in our creative pursuits. She's beautiful but she doesn't flaunt it the way some women do, and I can't help finding that incredibly attractive.

Adriana narrows her eyes, her lips curling up at the sides. 'Are you flirting with me? Because if you are, don't stop on my account. I need all the compliments I can get at my age. Keep them coming.'

Another smile and I feel my face flush. She may not flaunt her beauty, but she's not afraid of voicing out loud what she's thinking. Such a contrast to the girls I've dated casually in the past. Coy and reticent to speak their minds for fear of putting a step wrong. Her directness is refreshing. Sexy.

'Gosh, I hope I didn't embarrass you,' she says before sipping her wine. 'I meant it as a compliment.' She sits back in her chair, cocks her head to one side. 'How is it that a nice, handsome guy like you, well spoken and polite, doesn't have a girlfriend? You're twenty-five, right?'

I nod. 'Yep. And perhaps there's your answer, I'm too young to be tied down.'

Her gaze drills through me. 'Maybe. Or perhaps there's more to it than that?' She stops talking but her focus never leaves me. Brutal yet breathtaking. Again, it makes me wonder if she's been looking into my background. Or maybe she's just naturally perceptive? Just as I'm pondering this, she darts up from her chair, starts pirouetting around the room like a young girl, still holding her glass, if not a little precariously. It throws me a little. 'Oh, to be twenty-five again.' She swigs more wine. I can tell she's a bit tipsy. 'My twenties were the best years of my life.' She stops spinning, comes to a standstill, and yet still waves her glass around. 'University, meeting Charles, marrying him in the Seychelles in front of fifty friends and family. I'm not sure I'll ever have that kind of happiness again. Be that content.'

As I hear her reminisce about Charles and their idyllic wedding I feel a tug of jealousy, but I also have this delicious desire to get up and kiss her. Thankfully, I'm not that plastered and manage to restrain myself.

'Don't say that, you have plenty of time to find someone else and marry again,' I say.

'But that's just it, I don't want to marry again.' She sits back down. 'There'll never be another Charles. Whoever I meet will always be in his shadow, and that wouldn't be fair on them.'

I admire her devotion to her husband, and again can't help feeling slightly envious of the man she clearly put on a pedestal. He must have been one special bloke, and it tells me Jasper's wrong. That there's nothing iffy about the way Charles Wentworth died. It was an accident, pure and simple. Nothing more sinister to it.

'And what about you?' she says. 'Do you want marriage, kids, some day?'

'Maybe,' I say. 'One day. But I'm not in any hurry.' I don't tell her I'm too scared to have kids of my own. Knowing that I'd be forced to hide so much from them. My real name, for example, along with the ugly truth I carry around with me night and day.

There's that same intense stare. As if she's digesting my response, trying to decide if I'm being truthful with her. Whether she can trust me. *Why is that?* She can't have discovered my name change. Under UK law I was never obliged to register it with any official body. But then, just like that, it eases.

'And what about you?' I ask. 'You never wanted children?'

She sighs. 'I did, but Charles and I had trouble conceiving. I guess it might have happened eventually, but now we'll never know.'

I feel bad for asking the question. I should have known better considering what a sensitive topic having kids can be. 'I'm sorry, I shouldn't have pried.'

She shrugs her shoulders. 'It's fine. I'm not sure I'd have been any good at raising kids anyway. My own mother wasn't maternal at all, so there's every chance I'd have been just as bad.'

I hadn't expected that. Her revelation is laced with bitterness. I think back to when I asked her if she missed her parents. Her response had struck me as odd at the time, but now it makes more sense. Unlike my mum who showered me with love, it's clear from Adriana's remark that hers was a very different experience.

I shake my head. 'Not necessarily. I agree our childhoods can shape who we are as adults. But I also believe it can go either way. Sure, there are some who repeat their parents' mistakes, but there are others who learn from them, make a conscious choice not to replicate them, to do things better. I may not have known you for long, but I can tell you'd make a great mum.'

Fuck, I think I am drunk after all. And way too emotional. It's always been my problem, but Mum said it was what she loved about me. That I wasn't afraid to show my emotions. She said it was a rare quality in a man and something I should never feel ashamed of. Just thinking about her words, remembering the unconditional love in her eyes, makes my own well up. Shit, not in front of Adriana, I tell myself. I do my best to stifle my tears, briefly turn away and pretend to rub some imaginary dust from my eye in the hope that Adriana won't notice.

But she's not easily fooled. She reaches out and takes my hand, and I have no choice but to make eye contact with her. She edges closer, so close I can smell her perfume, my pulse accelerating. 'I think that's one of the nicest things anyone's ever said to me,' she says. 'Thank you.' She holds my gaze and this time I can't stop a tear from escaping.

'You're welcome,' I say.

She smiles. 'I can tell you were thinking of your own mother when you said that.' Before I have time to respond, she's wiped away my tear with her thumb, and there's a moment when I think something more is going to happen between us, that we might kiss, something I want so badly, and yet know what a terrible idea it would be. But then, just like that, she stands up and starts clearing the table, and I feel both relieved and deflated.

I help her clear then stack the dishwasher. 'I'll show you how to use the other appliances tomorrow,' Adriana says. 'Washing machine, oven, and so on.'

'That would be great.' I smile, slightly thrown by how we've gone from having such an intimate moment to talking about kitchen appliances. 'You mentioned you have a cleaner?' I say.

'Yes, Maria comes Mondays and Fridays, for four hours at a time. It's not easy keeping this place spotless, as you can imagine.'

'I can, not easy at all.'

'I like to keep things clean and tidy,' Adriana elaborates. 'Charles used to joke I had OCD, but I've always had a thing about cleanliness. My mother was the same, and I guess it became ingrained in me. Of course, I'm fortunate to be able to afford for Maria to come twice a week.'

'There's nothing wrong in keeping things tidy. I shall try my best to live up to your expectations.'

'Thank you.'

Another awkward moment. I glance at my watch. It's only ten but I'm not thinking straight having consumed nearly a bottle of wine and I desperately need to extract myself from this uncomfortable situation. 'Well, it's been a long day, a long week, in fact. I'll just grab some water, then hit the hay. Unless there's anything you need me to do?'

I pour myself a tall glass of water from the filter jug in the fridge while waiting for her to respond. She smiles. 'No, I'm fine, you go ahead. I'll lock up, set the alarm. Sleep well.'

'You too.'

I'm about to leave when she stops me in my tracks. 'Wait, let me write down the alarm code for you in case you decide to go for a run before I'm up.'

'Oh yes, good idea.'

She opens a drawer and pulls out a notepad, finds a clean page and jots down the code, rips the page out and hands it to me. 'Here you go.'

I thank her with a smile, then leave. Back upstairs in my room, I crash out on the bed and for a few minutes just lie there replaying the evening over in my mind. There's something so captivating about Adriana, and right now in my hazy alcohol-fuelled stupor all I can see is her face, the way she smiles, the way her hair falls in loose waves down her shoulders, the lost-soul look in her lovely eyes, a trait I recognise in myself. But I know I need to stop thinking about her that way. Truth is, we're worlds apart in ages and backgrounds and nothing could ever come of it. Plus, I've never been one for casual flings or one-night stands, that just isn't me, it never will be, and I'm guessing, from the way she talks about her late husband, it's not Adriana either. It's clear she's still in love with Charles. Besides, I have too many secrets of my own to make a meaningful relationship with anyone possible.

Within ten minutes, I fall fast asleep, but wake at three a.m., still in my clothes and desperately needing a pee. 'Fuck,' I say out loud, realising how cold I am, having been lying on top of the covers for the past five hours, while my head is throbbing from the wine. I knew I'd regret that extra glass. I lean over and grab my water, knock it back, wishing I'd brought two glasses up with me. I can't go downstairs and get a refill now as the damn alarm will go off and I might wake Adriana. I'll just have to accept feeling like shit when I go for my run. If, that is, I make it.

I hoist myself off the bed, head for the bathroom, pee then quickly brush my teeth and scramble into my pyjamas. I'm just clambering back into bed when my phone on the bedside table lights up. I half think about ignoring it, but then decide I'd better check, just in case the person I'm desperate to get in contact with about Dad has finally emailed me back. To my dismay they haven't. But there is one new message that catches my eye, because it's from an address I don't recognise. Protego@vistamail.com. I'm conscious it could be spam, but still click on it, intrigued. In retrospect, I wish I hadn't. Because once I've read it, I'm suddenly very much awake. And terrified.

> Hello Sebastian, I do hope you're settling in OK. You don't know me, but I'm an old friend of Adriana's. I quite like you, I think you're different to the last one, but I sense you're hiding something. Something you're ashamed of. I've tried to find out what it is, but you cover your tracks well, suspiciously well in fact, and so I've decided to give you the benefit of the doubt. For now, that is. But you need to know that if you hurt her like others have, you'll wish you'd never been born. You also need to tell your friend Jasper to stop meddling, because no good will come of it. Ethan meddled and we all know where that got him. Tell Jasper to back off, because if he doesn't, I'll have no choice but to intervene. She's been hurt too many times in the past. By people who didn't deserve her, who lied to her, betrayed her, took advantage of her sweet nature, and I just can't bear to see that happen again.

> One last thing – don't even think about showing this to your landlady or changing your mind about living

there. You'll be placing her in grave danger if you do, plus you'll upset her, and I feel sure, from the way you look at her, that's the last thing you want.

Sweet dreams, Sebastian. I'll be watching you. I hope your first night is a restful one.

I was cold before but now I'm chilled to the bone. How the fuck am I supposed to sleep now? I shoot up from the bed, start darting around the room, scanning the walls, the ceiling, the far corners, then underneath my bed, the desk, literally everywhere I can think of, looking for some kind of camera or listening device. Because it's obvious this place is bugged, and that someone is watching me. Is that why Adriana's been acting so nervy? Does she suspect she's being spied on? Is that why she clammed up when I mentioned the man I saw standing at the end of the street when Jasper and I arrived? Is he behind the email? Does he have some kind of hold over her? It would explain why she snapped at me when I asked her who she thought he might be?

The sender claims to be an old friend. But how do I know they're telling the truth? That they're not just some crazed stalker who's obsessed with Adriana, who fantasises about being her friend when, really, it's all just a figment of their imagination? It happens to celebrities all the time. And maybe because this person is infatuated with her, they're looking to scare her lodgers, yours truly being the next target. Even so, the reference to Ethan is beyond disturbing. Was his death really an accident, or at the instigation of whoever wrote the email? Whoever this person is, it's clear they've been delving into my background, but thankfully don't appear to have found anything. Yet. Just knowing there's someone out there who suspects I'm hiding something is freaking me out, though. Because the fact is, they're right, I am hiding something. Something big.

And how do I know they won't stop digging until they discover the truth?

Chapter Eighteen

Before

'So, tell me how you're feeling since we last met, Scarlett?'

I glare at the stranger sitting across from me. Pretending to be my friend, like he knows me, cares about me, understands me, despite this being only the second time we've set eyes on each other. Why are guys so full of themselves? Why do they always presume to know what a woman wants or feels? And why should this guy be any different from the rest of them just because he has the title 'Dr' at the beginning of his name? Is that supposed to make me feel more comfortable in his presence? Should it give me more reason to trust him?

How can I be sure he won't let me down too?

'It's not Scarlett.' I scowl. 'It's Adriana. I never liked Scarlett; it was my mother who insisted on calling me by my middle name. But now that she's dead, I'm free to use my first name. The name I prefer. Adriana.'

'Sorry, of course,' Dr Adams says. 'I know you told me that at our first meeting and I should have remembered. I apologise.'

I'm guessing Dr Adams got the low-down on me from my aunt and uncle who brought me here to Guildford around a month ago. I bet they told him I went from being a quiet, timid thing at primary school who wouldn't say boo to a goose, to a loud-mouthed trouble-stirrer at senior school, earning me a string of detentions and near expulsion. But what they don't know is what caused me to go off the rails. And I guess that's partly why I'm here. To find out what changed, whether it was just hormones, me falling in with the wrong crowd. Or something deeper. Darker. They also hope Dr Adams will help me deal with my grief. A grief no fourteen-year-old should have to endure.

' 'S OK,' I grunt. 'Just remember to call me Adriana from now on.'

He nods. 'Of course.'

'You asked me how I'm feeling? Well, my house burnt down, my parents are dead and I've been pulled away from my friends and the place I grew up in to start over in a new school where I don't know a soul. How do you fucking think I'm feeling?'

'I'm not your enemy, Adriana.' Despite my foul-mouthed outburst, Dr Adams remains calm. His voice steady. His gaze sincere. I hate to admit it, but secretly I'm starting to like him, and I'm gradually feeling more comfortable in his presence. And although I haven't told my aunt and uncle this, I secretly like living with them too. Find myself missing Eve and Xavier less and less. Although that could also be something to do with the fact that I'm slightly pissed they've not bothered to write back to me. Xavier I can understand, he's a hothead and tends to hold grudges, but I expected more of Eve. It saddens me that my friends appear to have abandoned me so quickly. Then again, I'm the one who's moved away. Perhaps Eve also feels I've let her down, even though, unlike Xavier, she gave me a big hug the day before I left. Said she understood and that she'd always be there for me if I needed her.

My aunt and uncle couldn't have kids of their own and I get the feeling they're starting to see me as the daughter they never had. Aunt Georgie is nothing like her sister, Steph, my mother. Neither in looks nor personality. She's quite plump, pleasant enough to look at but not a stunner like Mother was. She's super maternal too. Checks on me all the time, makes me cups of tea and is constantly asking if I need anything. We even watched a movie together the other night. She made popcorn, and after demolishing that, we shared a tub of Ben & Jerry's ice cream – cookie dough flavour, which she knew was my favourite. Afterwards, I felt sick, was quite disgusted with myself, and was almost tempted to go and vomit it up like Mother used to after a blowout, and like she encouraged me to do if I didn't want to get 'fat'. She'd always accentuate the word 'fat' as if the word was evil. If only she'd paid more attention to the real evil that contaminated our house.

It's clear Aunt Georgie and Uncle Philip have a good relationship too. They seem devoted to one another, no secrets between them. Secure and content in each other's company. Satisfied with the simple things in life. Such a contrast to how things were between my parents. Who barely talked, almost lived separate lives, hardly a kind word passing between them. It takes some getting used to, but I have to admit I like the change. But it's still too early to let my guard down completely.

'I'm not here to trick you or make you feel bad,' Dr Adams goes on. 'You've been through a traumatic experience and it's a lot to deal with. You're angry and you've every right to be.'

I study his expression. He has a kind, open face. There's nothing threatening about it whatsoever. But then again, appearances can be so deceptive, and I'll not be so easily fooled, no matter his credentials, or the fact that I find myself warming to him. I need to give it a bit more time before I truly open up, tell him what's on my mind, the things I've witnessed in my short life, even though I worry he'll think less of me if I do. I watch him adjust the thick black-framed glasses he's wearing, then sit back in his tan leather chair, a pad resting on his crossed knee, a pen poised in his right hand. I wonder what he's written down about me in those notes of his. He's not meant to discuss our conversations with anyone, not even my aunt and uncle. Nothing is supposed to go further than these four walls, and I so want to unburden myself, tell him everything, but how can I be certain he won't tell on me?

He's right, I just feel so angry with the world. With everything that's happened to me. It's like I can never seem to catch a break, that the world has for some reason conspired against me.

Can this really be my chance to start over, pretend that all the stuff I've seen and been forced to suffer never happened? Can it really be that easy to switch myself off from all that and simply forget? Make a fresh start.

I so want it to be the case, but I'm also smart enough to know that I can't turn my life around by curling up into a ball and shielding myself from my past. I need to be honest with Dr Adams, to be open to healing.

If I do that, it'll be half the battle won.

Chapter Nineteen

Seb

It's 6:30 a.m. and I'm wide awake, having barely slept a wink since reading the email. For a good three hours I tossed and turned, the words churning over in my brain, speculating who could be behind them.

Knowing I'm being watched is freaking the hell out of me. Adriana had the house remodelled in the last few years, and I guess it's possible that anyone who worked on the refurbishment could have installed a camera or listening device. It's probably not that hard if you know how. But how on earth do I find out who had access to the property without asking her? It's nigh on impossible.

I think of Max. Could it be him? He's had free rein to come and go as he pleases. He's only been working for Adriana since last month, but that doesn't mean he hasn't been watching her for some time. Playing her, playing me. He seems harmless enough, but the most innocuous of people can often turn out to be the most dangerous. Plus, he wasn't exactly shy about dishing the dirt on Ethan and his firm.

Even now, lying here, I keep seeing Mum's face, warning me to be careful, that I'm walking into a trap and need to get out before it's too late. And then there's Adriana's expression last night, when I asked her about the man I'd seen lurking on her street. She brushed me off but I saw the fear in her eyes and again it makes me wonder if she suspects she's being watched. Is that why she has a male lodger? For protection? Does she herself suspect Ethan's death wasn't an accident, which was what the email seemed to be implying?

My head is telling me to stand up to this creep, to not let them get to me. That I should warn Adriana right now and insist we call the police. But my heart is saying *run*, because I don't need this type of complication in my life, and the best thing I can do is get as far away as possible from my landlady. But I also know that the choice isn't that cut and dried. The sender made it clear that I'll be placing Adriana in danger if I mention the email, or even think about leaving.

I can't lie here a second longer. I crawl out of bed, go to the bathroom and splash my face with cold water, before hastily throwing on my running gear, grabbing my trainers, wallet and house keys and leaving the room. I creep downstairs, not a sound coming from Adriana's bedroom. My mouth is dry, so I stop off at the kitchen to grab some water. The house is eerily quiet, but as soon as I set foot in the hallway the alarm starts to beep, making me wince. I quickly punch in the code, having memorised it from the piece of paper Adriana gave me last night, and it turns off. I unlock the front door and step outside, being sure to double-lock it behind me. I pray I didn't wake Adriana, even though a part of me wants to check on her, just to make sure she's safe.

My head is screaming as I wait for the gates of Serenity House to open. It's not the wine that's causing a shooting pain to hammer away at my temples but rather the torrent of thoughts rushing around my brain, wondering if the person who sent the email is watching me this very second.

But more terrifying – whether my life could be in danger?

I cross over the road towards the Heath, my eyes darting left and right, half expecting to see the stranger in black hovering close by, again wondering if he's the mysterious 'watcher'. But I see no sign of him, or anyone, in fact. It's still early for a Saturday in London, and therefore hardly surprising that I should find myself alone. I'd be glad of the company right now, to be honest; safety in numbers and all that. Still, I need this run, need to run hard, release my stress, clear my thoughts in the open air and try to get my head around the nightmare I'm suddenly faced with.

I enter the edges of the Heath and see a few early morning dog walkers who give me a faint tilt of the head as I jog by, their lively companions chasing around them, not a care in the world. How I envy their uncomplicated lives at this moment. As I gather momentum, the steady echo of my Nike trainers pummelling the rough ground beneath me, my breathing accelerates in tandem, my legs starting to burn with a build-up of lactic acid, the sweat developing across my brow and slithering down my back. It's below zero degrees, but I don't feel it as I tread the uneven terrain, my breathing increasingly laboured until finally I come to a stop by a large oak tree. I bow my head, trying to get my breath back.

'Who are you running from?'

The voice comes out of nowhere and I look up with a start, my heart rate accelerating once more, only this time from fear rather than physical exertion. I see a woman, perhaps in her mid-forties, standing there, a beautiful golden retriever by her side. The woman's strawberry-blonde hair is unkempt, her skin blotchy, her eyes sunken, as if she hasn't slept well in days.

Having caught my breath, I stand up straight to meet her gaze. 'I'm not running from anyone. Why would you say that?'

'Most people jog around here for pleasure, but I didn't get that vibe from you.' She pauses, then says, 'You're the new lodger at Serenity House, aren't you?'

I frown. 'Yes, how do you know?'

'I live next door at number six. My name is Stella. Stella Jenkins. I saw you and your friend pull up in a van yesterday.'

My pulse quickens, and I instinctively look around. If Adriana finds out I've broken her rules by speaking to this woman, I'll be in deep shit. Although, when I think about the email, pissing Adriana off feels like the least of my troubles.

'She's banned you from speaking to me, hasn't she?' Stella says.

'What makes you say that?' My eyes scan the area like a sniper. I can't see anyone watching me, but that doesn't necessarily mean I am safe. I feel so tense, like I'm suffocating on fear despite being in the open air.

'It's just a guess.'

'And why would you guess such a thing?' I stammer.

'Because we don't exactly get along. Plus, she knows I saw something the night her last lodger died. Something she doesn't want getting out.'

My ears prick up. 'Ethan, you mean?'

She nods.

'What did you see?' I ask anxiously.

'I saw someone on the roof with Ethan that night.'

My heart jerks. 'Who? Who was with him?'

She shakes her head. 'I don't know, it was the middle of the night, and they were dressed in dark clothing. Presumably to avoid being seen. But I didn't imagine it, there was someone up there, I swear to God. There's a gap between the hedges in our houses and we can just about see out on to each other's rooftops.'

My thoughts again turn to the man I saw on the street yesterday.

'What were you doing on your roof at that time of the night?' I ask.

'I'm an insomniac. Sometimes I go up to the roof to clear my head, get some air. It relaxes me. The stranger came up behind Ethan. Ethan turned around and I think perhaps a few words were exchanged. And that's when whoever it was turned to look in the direction of my house.'

'And then?'

'I was afraid. Afraid they'd seen me, so I turned and ran back inside.' She bows her head. 'They may not have done, of course. Like I said, it's a small gap, but in that split second, I was scared, and I didn't want to risk it. But now I wish I had because I'm almost certain they had something to do with Ethan's death. Either the two of them fought and it was an accident. Or Ethan was pushed.'

Nausea grips me as I try to absorb what this woman is saying, the email's words of warning ringing in my ears.

Ethan meddled and we all know where that got him.

I can't help shivering as I join the dots in my mind and think about the possible connection between them.

It's perhaps why I then find myself trying to argue against it. 'The general thinking, so I've heard, is that

154

Ethan was high on drink and drugs when he went up there. That it was most probably an accident.'

Stella sighs heavily, as if she expected me to say this. 'I'm not disputing the fact that he was high, you can't argue with the post-mortem. Maybe he did go up there of his own accord. But then someone joined him. I'm not lying. I saw it with my own two eyes. Two figures were on that roof. Ethan and someone else.' She pauses. 'Look, I'm only telling you this because you're her new lodger. You have a right to know.'

Her gaze is steadfast, she seems so sure of herself, and yet I'm desperate to believe she's wrong about what she saw, despite what the email insinuated. 'Are you sure you weren't mistaken? It was late and dark, it's easy to imagine things at night. And the gap in the hedge is small, you said so yourself.'

Stella's expression goes from steadfast to steel-like, and I wonder if she's about to set her dog on me, she looks so mad, her eyes almost unhinged. 'I was NOT imagining things, no matter what Adriana told the police. OK, so the image was faint, but there were two figures on that roof. We all know Ethan was one of them, but the question is, who was the other?'

'What do you mean, no matter what Adriana told them? What did she say?' I ask.

She bows her head. 'That I might like a drink or two.'

The penny drops, and again I note the hollow eyes, the sallow skin, the unruly hair. On top of being an insomniac, she's a heavy drinker, meaning it's perfectly possible Stella didn't see what she thought she saw. That she hallucinated from too much booze coupled with sleep deprivation. Or perhaps had double vision. I've experienced the latter myself when I'm plastered. All told, it makes her a pretty unreliable witness. How can I possibly take anything she says seriously? Surely, Adriana was right to doubt Stella's testimony. Which explains why she never mentioned it to me when she talked about Ethan's death. Because it wasn't worth mentioning. Even so, there's still the damned email. In black and white.

'I explained to the police what I saw the next day,' she goes on. 'But Adriana told them that nothing I said could be trusted. Because I drank and I barely sleep. She discredited me. But the father believed me.'

'Who? Ethan's father?'

'Yes. Rick Savage. He came to see me. Didn't accept his son had thrown himself off the roof. He wanted the police to investigate further. But Adriana's a respected member of the community, a woman of influence, what with her husband being who he was. Neither Rick nor I had a chance against her. Especially with Ethan's firm wanting to brush the whole affair under the carpet.' She pauses. 'They offered to give a generous donation to a charity close to the family's heart and Rick didn't feel he could turn it down. Also, Ethan's mother was broken and begged him not to pursue things.' Another pause, then she says: 'I bet you also didn't know the firm happened to be Charles's lawyers.'

I shake my head. 'No, I didn't.'

'Ethan told me it was one of the reasons Adriana agreed to take him in as her lodger. When he mentioned he worked at Charles's former lawyers' firm, she told him it was as if her husband was speaking to her from the grave. Sending her a sign that she should take him on. I suppose there's nothing wrong in that, but her connection with Ethan's firm meant she had the means to manipulate its response to their employee's tragic death.'

Another moment of quiet as Stella lets me digest this, and now I'm suddenly not so sure who or what to believe.

I feel her eyes on me. 'Don't get me wrong, I'm not saying Adriana had anything to do with Ethan's death. She may well have been sleeping soundly in her bed, and I won't deny she seemed pretty cut up about the whole business. I mean, she looked shocked, really shocked, when I saw her the following day, when the police came round questioning everyone in the neighbourhood. White as a sheet, in fact. But what I can say with a hundred per cent certainty is that someone was on that roof with Ethan, and they may well have gone up there with the intention of pushing him off the edge. It wasn't sleep deprivation or the wine talking, I saw what I saw.' She places her hand on my arm, her bloodshot eyes boring through me. 'Look, it may be that Adriana doesn't want the police investigating further because she's scared for her own life. Plus there's been a spate of break-ins in the area recently. But whatever the truth is, people need to know it. Ethan's parents deserve that at the very least.'

She pauses to stroke her dog's silky head, her docile companion still panting away and sitting obediently by her side, while I try to process all she's told me.

'There's another reason Rick came to see me,' she says.

'Oh? What's that?'

'He knew that Ethan and I spoke shortly before he died.'

'What about?'

'He asked me what I thought of Adriana, whether she'd ever talked about her childhood, where she grew up.'

'Why would he do that?'

'I'm guessing he discovered something, but he never told me what. He simply said she never seemed willing to discuss her childhood, almost as if she was scared to talk about it, and that he believed there was something or someone in her past she was afraid of. Who'd done her harm.'

Again, the email flashes through my brain. The sender claimed they were an old friend of Adriana's and had been looking out for her for some time. Also, that she'd been let down in the past. Did they mean by her mother? Adriana let slip she hadn't been the best of mums last night while we were having dinner. But then again, if Adriana is afraid of someone in her past, could that be whoever sent me the email? Who possibly killed Ethan? But why kill him? Because they didn't want him uncovering things about Adriana's childhood? About them? That's what Stella seems to be implying.

'And what did you say? Did you agree with Ethan about Adriana being scared of someone from her past?' I ask.

Stella nods. 'Yes. I've been neighbours with Adriana since she and Charles moved in, and I've always had the feeling she's hiding something. Something she'd rather stay buried. When I asked her years ago about her child-hood, growing up, et cetera, she fobbed me off. Don't get me wrong, I sympathise that her parents died when she was young and therefore it was perhaps too painful to talk about. But somehow it felt like more than her being sad at their passing. There was a fear in her eyes that told me something bad had happened to her, and that she's spent every moment since trying to escape her past. When Charles died, she had the house refitted. OK, so she wanted to honour his legacy by going eco-friendly, but she also had all the windows redone, made the house virtually impenetrable. Why? It made me think she was scared of someone getting inside the house with Charles no longer around to protect her.' She sighs. 'I'm not Adriana's biggest fan, I don't think she's as innocent as she seems, for various reasons I won't go into now. But I don't think she's a bad person, or capable of murder.'

'So you think Ethan was murdered?' I ask.

'Yes. And you want to know what else I think?'

'What?'

'I'm betting Ethan discovered something big. I'm not sure what exactly, but big enough to cost him his life.'

Chapter Twenty

Adriana

I wake at nine a.m., my head a little thick from drinking the best part of a bottle of wine last night. I remember Seb grabbing himself some water before I wrote down the alarm code for him and we said a rather awkward good night. After he disappeared upstairs, I made sure all the doors on the lower and ground floors were shut, before switching on the alarm, killing the lights and retiring to my room. For some time I lay there, thinking about the evening, about how much I enjoyed Seb's company, how comfortable he made me feel. He has such a warmth about him, and I feel able to be myself with him, show him my vulnerable side. Because of this, I felt so guilty for snapping at him when he asked me who I thought the man he'd seen loitering on the street might be. I had a good idea, and I'm pretty certain it's unrelated to the email Dr Martin received, but if I told him it would mean getting into things I'd rather leave well alone, as well as defeat the whole purpose of me banning him from speaking to Stella next door.

Despite Seb's affability, I can tell he's haunted by some-thing. I don't for one minute believe it's anything bad he might have done, like the email to Dr Martin insinuated. But there's something troubling him. I wanted to ask him if everything was OK, but it's clear he holds his cards close to his chest, and I didn't want to risk offending him. Perhaps, with time, he'll confide in me. I'm guessing some kind of heartbreak lies at the root of his distress. Which explains why he clammed up when I asked him if he wanted to settle down some day.

I guess at some point I drifted off to sleep, but I don't feel rested. Given how much I drank it's hardly surprising, and I know I only have myself to blame. I shouldn't use alcohol as a crutch, but it helps take the edge off my anxiety. Anxiety which made a comeback in the years before Charles died, and recently only seems to have got worse what with all that's transpired lately. I just pray to God that all the precautions I took to keep this house secure and me safe are enough.

Last night was different as far as my drinking's concerned, in that I drank for pleasure, because I was enjoying Seb's company and it felt nice being able to chat with another human being over a bottle of wine. Just for a few hours I forgot about my worries, about my past, and it felt good, so freeing.

Before the night that changed everything – the night I saw *him* for the first time in years – I barely drank at all. I'd perhaps have the odd glass, but never more than that, because after I went to live with my aunt and uncle I pledged never to put myself in a situation where someone could take advantage of me. Particularly a man. And then later, when I met and married Charles, I was so happy, so in love, his company was all the stimulant I needed. But then my worst nightmare happened, on our six-year anniversary, and I couldn't help reaching for the bottle. Particularly when, just four days later, something else happened to scare the hell out of me. I drank not just to allay my anxiety, but to blot out the memories, if only fleetingly. Memories from long ago, but also, more recent ones. Memories that stoked the guilt and the shame in me. I went from barely touching alcohol to getting through nearly a bottle a night. Naturally, Charles noticed. But after I explained why, he understood. He wasn't angry I had kept my past from him. And that had been such a blessed relief.

But then the drinking got out of hand. The weeks turned into months, the months into years, and it took a toll on our relationship. I just couldn't stop myself. It was the only way to dull the crushing anxiety I felt. I could literally feel the blood pumping through my veins, my chest so tight I could barely breathe. Charles was a disciplined man himself. He only ever drank on weekends, which made my drinking more noticeable. It was hard fobbing him off when he asked me to seek help. I told him there was nothing to worry about, that I would get through it, that all I needed was time. But he wasn't stupid, he knew that no amount of time would help me get over what had happened in the restaurant the night of our anniversary. He couldn't have been kinder, more patient, more understanding. But the truth is, I was ashamed. Because I hadn't been entirely honest with him. Not by a long shot. I hadn't told him about the horrifying incident that happened four days later. And the deceit ate me up. To the point that, gradually, we drifted apart. It's my fault. And it's something I regret with all my heart.

We had a blazing row the day he died. He said I had a drinking problem, that he didn't recognise the person he'd married. He accused me of being moody, aggressive, but also withdrawn. As if I no longer found him attractive. It's true we went from having a good sex life, to barely touching one another. Something that put a strain on our marriage, because intimacy had always been a huge part of our relationship. I hadn't known sex could be as good and pure as it had been with Charles. But that night, when he said all that, I told him I'd been a fool to believe he was different, that he was just like other men, only after one thing. That he didn't really care about me, that all he cared about was getting laid. I remember the wounded look on his face. Something that stings even now, seven years on, when I think about it. I should have apologised, but instead I held my ground. And that's when he called me a heartless bitch. Said he was moving out because he couldn't take much more of my erratic behaviour. He'd never spoken that harshly towards me, and his words were like a knife through my heart. I'd stormed off to bed, calling him a callous bastard who could go fuck himself in the spare room.

Those were the last words I uttered to him. Words said in spite and which I regret with all my heart. Secretly, I wonder if they caused him to overdose on morphine, then take that swim, intending to kill himself. I knew severe stress made his knee pain worse, and the thought that I may have driven the love of my life to commit suicide is unbearable. It's tormented me ever since.

I stretch out my arms, then roll over onto my side and instinctively reach for my watch on the bedside table. Half asleep, I pick it up, slide it on to my wrist, then get out of bed and go to the bathroom, use the loo, before washing my face and pausing to examine the faint lines that are starting to form with age. I know I look good for thirty-nine, that I could pass for my early thirties, but sometimes I feel a lot older because of all I've endured over the years. The pain and loss I have suffered is enough to fill a lifetime. It's embedded in the dark shadows beneath my eyes. I go over to the door and remove my dressing gown from the hook before slipping it on and securing it tightly around my waist. Outside on the landing I am greeted with silence. I'm guessing Seb's gone for his run. I walk around to the top of the stairs, pausing by his room. I put my ear to the door but hear nothing. I'm tempted to go inside, check it out, but I restrain myself. As my lodger, Seb has far fewer rights than a tenant, and I'd have every right to inspect his room without giving him notice. But it would feel wrong to do so without him present. Even though a part of me wants to, just to prove to whoever sent Dr Martin that email that I have nothing to fear from Seb.

I go downstairs and head straight for the kitchen. Spend the next ten minutes or so making a cafetière of fresh real coffee before pouring myself a mug and taking it through to the study where I unplug my phone from the wall and check my messages. There are several but only one sends chills through me. Sent around 3:15 a.m. Via the same Protego@vistamail.com email address used to message Dr Martin.

> I'm watching you. And I'm watching your new lodger. I don't think he's as meddlesome as Ethan, but I still think he's hiding something, like I told Dr Martin, and I'm betting it has something to do with his mother's death. It's just a feeling I have from the way he talks about her. But clearly, he's hidden his tracks well, and for good reason, because I can't find any trace of him online. Which is suspicious in itself for a young man like him. I know you like him, but you'd be wise to fight your repellent urges; you know it never ends

well when you allow them to get too close. And don't even think about telling him or the police about this message because if you do, I'll reveal your secret and your life as you know it will be over. Don't be scared. I know you're upset about Dr Adams, but you need to move on, forget about him. You need to look out for number one.

Fear pulses through me as I practically throw the phone back down on the desk, as if it's laced with poison. I get up, rush around the room, scanning the ceiling, the walls, searching for some kind of camera or listening device, even though I only did that on Thursday, but again there's nothing obvious that I can see. It doesn't make sense. When I had the house remodelled, I made sure it was impregnable, so it's hard to imagine how anyone would be able to get inside. Unless it's an inside job, perhaps one of the workers at the company I hired? But why would any of them be interested in me? I can't even recall their names, let alone their faces. It's clear that whoever sent this message has been inside the house, though, because they know what I'm hiding. It's also obvious it's the same person who emailed Dr Martin. But why have they now chosen to contact me directly? And why, unlike the first message which seemed friendly, protective even, is this second one spiked with menace? Disgust, almost.

I wonder – was this creep listening in on my conversation with Seb last night? Or worse, watching? How else would they have known about the way Seb talked about his mother? And how upset I am about Dr Adams's death?

Not for the first time, I wonder if Stella could be behind the messages. It's true she's grown more hostile towards me since the whole business with Ethan. I think she was jealous from the moment I took him in as my lodger. What with him being young, handsome and smart. Ethan and I never went out on dates, to restaurants or bars or anything – the last thing I needed was people gossiping, plus we never professed to be a couple – but equally, we weren't always as discreet as we might have been. Perhaps she saw us kissing on the rooftop, the only place other than inside the house I felt sure we could be safe from prying eyes. Plus, I'm sure she's angry with me for telling the police she has a drinking problem, thereby discrediting her claim to have seen someone up on the roof with Ethan. Perhaps the letters are payback for this? Her wanting to scare me, seek revenge, by inventing stuff about Seb out of pure spite.

Then again, how could Stella know about my secret? That's what baffles me. Unless she found out in the brief period after Charles died when she used to come over and keep me company. I wasn't entirely with it, perhaps failed to keep things as secure as I might have done. But if that's the case, what's stopped her from going to the police? It makes no sense that she would have kept it to herself all this time.

And then there's Max. He has fingerprint access, knows the house inside out. But he only came on the scene a month ago, and he doesn't have keys to every room. Besides, I get the feeling we're dealing with someone much older here.

So, if Stella or Max aren't behind the emails, then who is? And how do they know what I've been hiding?

It's then that a startling realisation smacks me in the face. One that briefly crossed my mind when I first read the email Dr Martin received, remembering that hideous night years ago. When I was forced to do something that forever bound me to this house. A shocking truth I kept from Charles. I'd hoped they weren't connected but now that seems like a distinct possibility with this latest message and reference to my secret. Fact is, there is someone out there who knows the truth, but they promised I'd never hear from them again so long as I did what they asked. Which I did. But what's most terrifying is that I have no idea who they are or what they look like. All I received at the time was an anonymous note.

I can't know for sure if it's the same person, but it's a possibility I cannot ignore. I lay my head in my hands, my mind in turmoil, before once again picking up my phone and reading the message:

> you know it never ends well when you
> allow them to get too close.

The meaning of the words couldn't be clearer. And now, and as much as I can't bear to admit it, I can't help wondering if there is some truth to what Stella claimed she saw the night Ethan died.

I've been so desperate to believe Ethan's death was a tragic accident, but is it possible he was pushed after all?

If so, by whose hand? That's the question.

Chapter Twenty-One

Seb

I stand facing the gates of my new lodgings, the key fob in my hand, a sense of foreboding running through me as I try to work up the courage to go inside. Just twenty-four hours ago I was looking forward to a fresh start, to moving into Adriana's luxurious home and having the time, space and quiet to write. But now I dread going back inside knowing the house may be bugged, that possibly my every move is being watched. Jasper was right, the whole set-up was too perfect. I want to be able to pick up the phone to my best mate, tell him all that's happened, ask for his advice. But I can't. The person watching me made it clear that Jasper's life could be in danger if he continues to dig and, knowing how gung-ho Jasper can be, if I tell him about the email, it'll heighten his curiosity rather than dampen it. And that could prove fatal.

How is this even happening? It feels like I've fallen down the rabbit hole into some nightmare parallel world.

It's just after 9:30 a.m. and I'm guessing Adriana must be up by now, possibly having breakfast. How the hell am I going to be able to look her in the eye and act like everything's peachy, when things couldn't be further from the truth? I want to ask her about Ethan, why she was so quick to shoot down Stella's claim to have seen someone up on the roof with him the night he fell. Aside from the obvious, of course: that Stella is an insomniac who likes her drink. There was no mistaking the haunted look in Adriana's eyes when she talked about Ethan on Monday. I thought she was just upset about his death, about it being a tragic accident. But perhaps it runs deeper than that. Perhaps she suspects foul play, but is too afraid to speak out. Hence all the tight security, her vigilance about locking all the doors, her snapping at me when I asked about the man I saw hovering on her street.

Whoever sent the email clearly sees me as a potential 'threat', in the same way they appeared to have viewed Ethan after he asked questions about Adriana's childhood, based on what Stella said. It's a stark warning to me not to repeat his mistakes. They took extreme measures to stop Ethan from meddling and clearly won't hesitate to do the same with me. Still, if all Ethan did was ask questions, killing him seems extreme. It makes me certain he discovered something bad, as Stella suggested. Something that either implicates this person in whatever happened in Adriana's past, or something they fear might destroy the life Adriana's built for herself.

Are they protecting themselves or Adriana? That's the question. And if it's the latter, what is it they want to protect her from?

What secret is this person determined to keep buried?

It's going to be torture hiding the email from Adriana. Not being able to ask her if she has any inkling who might have sent it and why. I'm also desperate to get a professional in to check the house for spyware because I can't think how else they could have known about Jasper's digging unless they'd listened in on our conversation yesterday afternoon. But I know I'll be putting

Adriana's life in danger if I dare utter a word to anyone. I'm trapped in an impossible situation and it's like I can't breathe I'm so fucking terrified. I have to do something, though. I can't just ignore it, pretend everything's fine; my conscience couldn't live with that. I tell myself I must try and act normally, as tough as that's going to be, and in the meantime carry out some careful digging of my own.

Before parting ways with Stella, she insisted I take her mobile number. She said that if I ever needed to talk, I shouldn't hesitate to call her, despite this being on Adriana's forbidden list. She also gave me Ethan's father's number, in case I felt the urge to speak with him directly. I thanked her, then retraced my steps back through the Heath, trying to run off steam and my escalating anxiety levels. It was lighter by then, busier too, something that should have been a comfort to me, seeing other faces, knowing I was safe in the open air, that no one would dare try and make a move on me in public and in broad daylight. But I felt no more secure than I had done since setting out this morning. If anything, my conversation with Stella only served to heighten my nerves because it's now clear to me that something very sinister is going on, yet I have no idea how to get to the bottom of it.

I figure if I try and speak to someone close to Adriana, a friend or a family member, they might be able to shed light on her past, on anything bad she's been at pains to keep under wraps. It's unfortunate the doctor she remained close to in Guildford died; he'd have been a good place to start. Despite being bound by patient–doctor confidentiality, there's every chance he'd have broken his oath if he thought Adriana's life was in danger. Adriana's aunt and uncle in Guildford would be the other obvious choice. But how to approach them without raising their suspicions? I've only just moved in and they're bound to alert Adriana to my questions. For now, Ethan's father appears to be the only person I can credibly contact. Hopefully, Ethan told him something he didn't tell Stella that may prove useful.

One thing's for sure, though: I won't be making any calls from inside the house.

Feeling slightly clearer-headed, I'm about to press the key fob, when my phone buzzes. Another email. I shiver, fearing the worst, then feel calmer, buoyed even, once I see who it's from.

Dear Sebastian,

I hope you're well. Thank you for your message and I'm sorry for not responding sooner but I'm currently in Florida, on sabbatical. My wife and I bought a holiday home here last year and we decided to spend Christmas and most of January in Tampa. You're right, I did have dinner with your father back in July 2013. I know it wasn't long after that, that things took a horrible turn for you and your poor mother, for which I'm very sorry. I can't imagine how hard that must have been for you. I'd be happy to meet with you when I get back next week, although I'm not sure how much help I can be.

You mentioned you're staying in Hampstead. That's perfect for me, so how about we meet at The Spaniards Inn just by the Heath? Next Thursday, 26th at 1 p.m.

Looking forward to meeting you,

Very best wishes,

Trevor Carrington

Finally, it's the email I've been waiting for. From an old university friend of my dad's, and one of the last people to have seen him alive.

Before Mum received his suicide note.

Chapter Twenty-Two

Adriana

I'm in the gym, pounding the treadmill like there's no tomorrow, despite having promised myself I'd take it easier on the exercise front. I see no other way to deal with my stress, the email I woke up to hounding my mind and making it impossible to think about anything else. I crank up the speed so that I am sprinting, my arms and legs working at full capacity until the sweat pours off me, my lungs pushed to the limit, my heart rate dangerously high according to the monitor attached to my vest top.

I keep wondering how long my stalker has been watching me. Since Charles died? Longer? And if it's the latter, could it be the same person I thought of earlier? Someone who promised I'd never hear from them again so long as I abided by their conditions, but who may, in fact, have been watching me all this time. But why choose to make contact now? Is it because of what happened with Ethan? Are the emails designed to stop Seb asking questions the way Ethan did?

I can't believe I'm contemplating this because it sounds so outlandish, almost like something out of a movie, but I'm thinking I need to get someone in to check the house for spyware. How to explain this to Seb, though? He's only just moved in, for Christ's sake. Plus, being a writer, he's bound to be spending a lot of time here, meaning it's going to be tricky finding a window to carry out a search without him around. The only time I can be certain he'll be out for a few hours is when he's working his bar shifts. I'll get someone to do a sweep once I find out when he's next on duty. I'll not rest until I know if this whacko has actually infiltrated the premises or they're just toying with me to make me feel like my every move is under scrutiny.

So many unsettling things seem to have happened in quick succession lately, what with Ethan, Dr Adams and now these creepy emails, it's hard to think straight. I keep worrying what's next, whether this nightmare I've found myself in will ever end.

My chest is starting to hurt so I slow the machine down, conscious I've reached my limit, until it gradually comes to a stop. I bow my head, my knees a little shaky from pushing myself so hard, the sweat dripping off me and making unsightly puddles on the belt.

'Adriana, are you OK?'

Seb's voice makes me jump as I swivel around in surprise. He's standing just a few feet away.

'Seb, Christ, sorry I didn't hear you come in, just catching my breath here.'

'Sorry, I seem to be making a habit of scaring you,' he apologises.

'Don't worry, I've got so used to being alone in the house, it's made me a little jittery, I guess.'

The creepy emails don't help.

'How was your run?' I ask as I step off the machine and use the hand towel I brought down from upstairs to mop the sweat from my brow, chest and the back of my neck.

He hesitates, which strikes me as odd. After all, it's a simple question. His eyes seem harried, like something's happened to unsettle him. Although I could be imagining things, of course. Because of my own anxiety.

'Good, exactly what I needed,' he says. 'Hangover's practically gone.'

'Great.' I smile. Then glance at my watch. 'You didn't stop off at a cafe then? You seem back too early for that.'

'No, I didn't feel like it in the end. Bit too sweaty. I just wanted to check you were OK.' He bites his lip. 'Sorry, that sounds a little patronising. I mean, why wouldn't you be OK, you're a grown woman. I don't know why I said that.'

There's something wrong, I can tell. Has he received a message too? I badly want to ask him, but the email made it clear I'll be placing his life in danger if I mention it, which is the last thing I want. 'That's very sweet,' I say. 'And as you can see, I'm fine. Think I'll take a shower then grab some breakfast. I'm getting a Waitrose delivery tomorrow. Do you need anything?'

'Thanks, but I'll probably pop out and do a shop of my own, don't want to complicate things.'

I smile again, thinking how awkward things suddenly feel between us. 'It's really no bother, but I completely get where you're coming from.'

We leave the gym, then start walking up the stairs, my legs feeling heavier with every step. 'Thanks again for the lovely meal last night,' Seb says. 'You're an excellent cook.'

'My pleasure, my Aunt Georgie taught me well.'

'Do you still see a lot of her?'

'I try to see her and Uncle Philip at least twice a month. I usually get the train to Guildford, or they sometimes drive here and stay over.'

'That's nice.'

'Yes, I'm very fortunate. Actually, I spoke with Aunt Georgie yesterday and she said they might visit soon. They were naturally very upset to hear about Dr Adams. They knew how fond I was of him and wanted to make sure I'm OK. They were the same after Charles died.'

Seb gives me a warm smile. 'They sound like kind people. It's nice you still have family close by who you can talk to.'

He says this sincerely but there's no mistaking the sadness in his voice. 'It is,' I say. 'And I'm sorry your mother's family lives so far away. I'm guessing you don't have any relatives in the UK?'

'Yep. That's right. All Mum's family are in Nigeria while Dad was an only child. His parents died some years ago. When I was four or five, I think.'

'I'm so sorry. But I'll be glad to introduce Georgie and Philip to you. They were fond of Ethan and I'm sure they'll be equally fond of you.'

'Thanks.' Seb's face lights up with a smile. 'I'm very much looking forward to meeting them.'

By now we've reached the first floor and find ourselves hovering on the landing.

'Are you working tonight?' I ask casually. It's probably too late to get anyone in to check for spyware, but I see this as a good opportunity to check Seb's shift times for future reference.

'No, not tonight. I usually work Saturdays, but my boss knew I was moving house yesterday so I swapped shifts with a guy who works Sundays.'

'So you're working tomorrow?'

Shit, I hope that didn't sound too keen.

'Yes.'

Bingo. 'Well, you'd better make the most of your rare Saturday night off then. Any plans?'

'No, not really. I might try and get another couple of chapters written. Maybe watch a film. You don't mind me chilling out in the TV living room, do you?'

'Seb, don't be daft. *Mi casa, su casa*. I'm not a big TV person, as Max may have mentioned. I tend to read.'

He smiles. 'I heartily approve.'

I smile back. 'Maybe I can read your book once you've finished it?'

Seb looks a little alarmed and I laugh.

'It's fine, I don't have to. I just know authors have beta readers and if I can help in any way, give you my thoughts or advice, I'd be only too happy to. But no pressure.'

He grins. 'That's kind, I just worry you'll think it's crap.'

I laugh. 'I doubt that.'

We hold each other's gaze, a delicious tension filling the air around us, before we part company and I go to my room to take a shower, being sure to shut and lock the door behind me.

I think how nice it's been chatting to Seb, talking about normal stuff. So nice, that for a few minutes I'd forgotten about the email, about the fact that I am being watched. But then, as I glance up at the ceiling, thinking how easy it would be to hide a camera up there, a sense of dread floods my insides, while the guilt I feel at having not been honest with Seb fills me with self-loathing, simply because it's a feeling I'm all too familiar with.

Only in this instance I don't see that I have a choice but to hide the email from him.

Not if I want to keep Seb safe.

Chapter Twenty-Three

Seb

It's five p.m. and I've just ventured downstairs to the pool for a swim. After breakfast, I tried to write, but it was no good. I couldn't focus, my head spinning with a myriad of thoughts – my conversation with Stella, my upcoming meeting with Trevor Carrington, but most of all the email I received and the potential danger I'm placing myself in by remaining in this house. Unable to sit staring at the screen a moment longer, I decided to go food shopping. Something banal to take my mind off things. There's a Waitrose in West Hampstead but it's a bit pricey for me, so I ended up walking to the Finchley Road which has a large Sainsbury's halfway down. I spent a good forty-five minutes in there, aimlessly wandering the aisles, my mind not really focused on the groceries, shoving items I didn't really need into my trolley which meant I had to get an Uber back to the house because I couldn't carry it all.

Having unloaded everything in the kitchen, I found Adriana in her study just getting off the phone and asked if she was OK with me using the pool. I hadn't forgotten she'd already said I should feel free to use it whenever I wanted, but it's early days with me living here and I suppose I still feel more like her guest than a lodger. She seemed a little preoccupied, but said it was fine, that I shouldn't need to ask, and so, having gained her approval, I found myself padding back upstairs to change.

The rectangular twenty-five-metre pool is on the lower ground floor, and although I know I am safely tucked away inside where it's warm and secure and protected from the wintry elements, one side of the wall is glass and beyond that is the outdoor terrace where Max said Adriana sometimes entertains in the summer. Right now, it feels a little eerie, a little exposed, with it being pitch-black outside, although I suspect it's my imagination running wild because of all that's happened since I received the email.

The room is kept at a constant twenty degrees, and so I don't feel cold as I remove the white towelled bathrobe I found in the small interconnecting changing room and lay it across one of two cream cushioned loungers at the far end of the pool. It's almost like being at a spa – even though I've only been once to one of those when I treated Mum one Mother's Day – save for the absence of calming background music. Just now, I could do with some of that.

I slide my feet out of my flip-flops, tucking them neatly under the lounger, before standing at the edge of the pool, absorbing the serenity of my surroundings, the stillness of the water which is calling out to me. I'm itching to know what Trevor Carrington has to say about the last time he saw my dad, whether he had any inkling that he was depressed and planned to commit suicide. I still find it strange that he left us that week so full of life, as if he hadn't a care in the world. Granted, it seems he'd mastered the art of deception to a tee, but even so, could he really have been hiding that dark a depression so convincingly? Would he really have left Mum and me in such high spirits knowing he'd never set eyes on us again?

I swam a lot when Mum and I moved to Nigeria. In the warm freshwater lakes with my cousins. I found it helped with the anxiety attacks I started suffering from after the trauma I went through, the secure family life I'd taken for granted having been obliterated. Before that, I'd been a content sort. Not super confident, but not the nervous type either. My childhood had until then been a happy one, and so I guess when the shit hit the fan out of nowhere, it was a shock to my system, my ordered life thrown into disarray.

Back then, before we learned of Dad's suicide, and everything that ensued afterwards, I couldn't ever have imagined feeling like the air was being crushed out of me, the slightest thing setting me off and triggering periods of extreme light-headedness, my hands stone cold one moment, clammy and hot the next, my pulse rapid and erratic. It was just panic, the doctor would reassure Mum, after she got upset picking me up from school when the attacks started coming over me without warning, causing repeated disruption in class. My teachers were sympathetic but warned that something had to be done as I clearly couldn't go on like this. It didn't help that my friends abandoned me, probably at their parents' behest, and it was another reason why Mum decided to flee the UK.

I sit down and sink my feet and calves into the warm water, wait for a few seconds then slide the rest of my body in, the water caressing my skin like a comfort blanket. Then I start swimming back and forth, gently at first before picking up the pace. Faster and faster, I propel myself through the water. Breaststroke, front crawl, backstroke, I flip from stroke to stroke, a sense of calm filtering through me, despite all that's occurred these past twenty-four hours.

Having swum forty lengths straight, I rest against the wall of the pool, place my arms either side and pull my head back so that I am looking straight up at the glass ceiling, and again can't help wondering if there's a camera installed somewhere watching me. Catching my breath, I feel my heart rate slowly return to normal. After a few seconds I turn my head to one side. And that's when I see movement through the glass. Not an animal, I'm sure of it. But a human figure. I shut my eyes, tell myself I'm imagining things, my mind playing tricks on me. But when I open them again, I'm certain I see the outline of a person pressed up against the glass. From where I am it's impossible to decipher a face or if they're male or female.

But someone's out there. And before I have time to yell, they're gone.

Chapter Twenty-Four

Before

It's gone 2:30 a.m. and I've been hiding out in Adriana's house, waiting for Ethan to arrive home. I'm guessing he'll be high on drugs and booze, the way he normally is after a big night out. Perhaps more so after what happened recently. He told Adriana it was his firm's Christmas ball and that she shouldn't switch the alarm on because it was likely they'd move on to a club after and he'd therefore be back at some ungodly hour. He hadn't said it in a friendly manner. Rather, his tone had been terse. As had hers. Hardly surprising given their heated argument yesterday. Adriana told Ethan she wanted him out by the end of the month. I delighted in watching her do this on the recording I made, standing up for herself for once. He hadn't expected it, that much was clear from the shock on his face, once again proving his arrogance. Despite trying to make out that he was hurt. He's a good actor, I'll give him that.

I'm banking on him being off his face when he finally rolls in. Because if he's not, it'll derail my plan, and I'll then have to think up something else. It disgusts me the way he abuses his body, and I know it riles Adriana, but as usual she's too nice a person to say anything. Too forgiving. It's her biggest downfall. But I'm grateful for his lack of discipline on this occasion, because it will work to my advantage.

She was distraught when he admitted to speaking to Stella next door. That stupid lush had fed him lies about Adriana. She was sorely mistaken in what she thought she'd seen all those years ago, but there was no way of Adriana convincing Ethan otherwise short of telling him everything. A complete no-no what with him being a lawyer. She pleaded with him to let it go, but then he held up what he claimed was proof that she was far from the angelic widow she made out to be. I watched her freeze on the spot, horrified that he'd been snooping around in her study. He said he'd discovered it while she'd been out at a charity event. His actions motivated by her increasingly odd behaviour, by the way she'd become defensive when he asked her about her past. The bastard knew she'd be away for some time, and it gave him ample opportunity to poke around. How he had the nerve to throw it in her face and question her about it I'll never know. Like he was some hotshot lawyer cross-examining a poor defenceless witness in the box. Her eyes had been awash with alarm and hurt. Because it was the ultimate violation. She couldn't tell him the truth, of course. He'd never understand, and she'd be risking her freedom. It was careless of her to document what happened. Just as it was careless to allow herself to get close to Ethan. Intimacy comes with all sorts of risks. She should have known better by now.

As I played back the recording, I watched Adriana tell him that he'd killed their friendship, broken the trust between them, and that there was nothing he could say or do to repair the damage he had caused. I don't trust him either – I'm also cross with myself for missing the footage of him snooping around, it was slack of me – and that's why I have no choice but to take action of a drastic nature before things spiral out of control. Seeing the way Adriana manically paced the bedroom after he left, not knowing what to do, how to silence him, made things clear for me. I realised I cannot leave things to her. Once again, I must take matters into my own hands. Her kicking him out of the house isn't enough.

He won't stop, I know it. Ultimately, he'll discover the truth, and when that happens he'll go to the police and Adriana's life will be over.

I fish out my phone, type a WhatsApp.

> Hi Ethan,
> Sorry we fought (oh and by the way I lost my phone, so I'm using an old one in case you're wondering) I don't want you to move out. I can't sleep, I'm having a drink on the rooftop, do join me. I know it's a crazy hour, but the sky is so clear I can see the stars, and it's such a beautiful sight. I'm tired of lying. I'll tell you everything about me, my childhood, what happened that night all those years ago, if you come up and meet me.
> Love Adriana xxx

I nearly vomit on reading my own words back, they're so sickly-sweet. I press send, then start creeping up the stairs, certain Ethan will waste no time in staggering up to the roof. For one, he's trollied, and two, despite his inebriation, he'll be keen to know what Adriana has to say about her past. At least, I hope he will be. And that I haven't misjudged things and he'll decide to ignore her and bugger off to bed.

I reach the roof, then hide behind the wall, waiting for him to appear. Before long he does, and my stomach fizzes with excitement just thinking about what I am about to do. I feel no regret, because he pushed me to the limit. And when that happens, I can't be responsible for my actions. I simply do what must be done. He calls out Adriana's name, slurring his words, stumbling all over the place. I will him to stagger over to the east-facing wall, the best place to look out and admire the view. To my delight, he does, and that's when I get up from my crouching position, and start moving in his direction. The rooftop has garden sensor lights which automatically come on with movement. He hears my footsteps as I approach, turns around, and for a moment we lock eyes, exchange a few words. His glazed eyes are suddenly filled with alarm when I tell him who I am, and that's when I glance to my right for a split second and make out someone on the roof next door. I can't see a face, but there's no doubt it's her neighbour Stella – who else could it be? – spying on us. She spots me, although hopefully can't make out my face, just as I cannot decipher hers. Unlike her, I'm wearing a cap, dark loose-fitting joggers and a black anorak, making it that much harder to see me. Ethan starts to say something, but I don't give him time to finish his sentence. I spring on him with all the force I can muster. He's too pissed to react quickly and defend himself, allowing me to push him hard at which point he stumbles back and over the edge of the wall. I stand there stock-still. Watch his body crash to the ground below.

And then I wait a few seconds, just to check for any signs of life. But there are none. My mission is complete.

I breathe a sigh of relief, then steal away, remembering to delete my WhatsApp message to Ethan from both our accounts. That way it can never be traced.

Once again, I have done what I need to do to keep her safe.

Chapter Twenty-Five

Adriana

Someone's been in my study, I'm certain of it. After getting off the phone with Guy Collins, managing director at Homeguard security, who agreed to come over tomorrow evening to check for any hidden surveillance cameras or listening devices, I'd gone upstairs to put some washing away. A job that took longer than usual – I guess it's my anxiety getting the better of me, making me unable to focus on the simplest of tasks – and when I came back down later the study door was unlocked. It was unnerving to say the least because I'm a hundred per cent sure I locked it after leaving the room to go upstairs. But that's not what's most worrying. What's more unsettling is that some important items I keep locked away in a safe in my study were gone. Items that are hugely personal to me. The thought of them getting into the wrong hands terrifies me.

My mind automatically turns to Seb. Could it have been him? I'd been upstairs for some time, so it's possible he could have poked around, having pretended he was off for a swim. Perhaps that's why he checked with me first if it was OK for him to use the pool even though I already told him last night that he should feel free to use it whenever he wanted. Did he deliberately ask again so that I'd think that's what he'd been up to when the items went missing? Giving him an alibi? But what would have led him to do this? And how would he know where to look? Let alone figure out the code for the safe? We barely know each other. He has no reason to fish around. Unlike Ethan, who'd been living with me for some time when he decided to go snooping in my study, after I'd fobbed off his questions about my childhood. It's why I got a safe in the first place, because I couldn't risk a similar episode. Admittedly, I became a little short with Ethan when he said he believed I was hiding something. He was a lawyer, after all, naturally inquisitive. Seb, on the other hand, has only just moved in. Why on earth would he go sneaking around? Unless he's not quite as innocent as he appears. Just like whoever sent me the email insinuated.

No, stop it, I scold myself, it's just my paranoia talking. Which is perhaps the sender's intention. To get inside my head, turn me against Seb, for no other reason than the fact that they're crazy and obsessed with me. Fuck, I feel so tired, so stressed with it all. Like I'm losing my mind. There's something else unsettling me too, something that only seems to have got worse lately. But I can't think about that now. It's probably just the stress of the last month getting on top of me.

I tell myself to get a grip. That if I am being toyed with, I need to make sure my new lodger is safe, rather than waste energy on feeling needlessly suspicious of him. I turn on my heel, ready to dash downstairs to check Seb's OK but find myself almost colliding with him in the process.

'Seb, hi, I was just wondering how your swim went?' I rush my words, my voice slightly hysterical. He gives me a strange look.

'It was fine, thanks,' he says. He's dressed in one of the white towelling robes I keep for guests in the pool changing room. His damp hair reassures me he's only just finished his swim and so can't have been snooping in my study. He looks tense, though. Like something's happened to unnerve him.

'You OK?' I ask.

'Yes, I'm fine, it's just…'

'Just what?' I say.

'It's nothing.' He shakes his head.

'It's clearly not nothing. Tell me.'

I wait with bated breath, wondering what it is that's upset him. Finally, he says, 'It's just that while I was in the pool, I could have sworn I saw movement outside.'

'Movement?' I repeat twitchily. 'What, like an animal?'

'No, like a person was out there.' Alarm hurtles through me as he says this. And I'm guessing the fear must show on my face because he's quick to add: 'But it was dark, and very windy outside, so it was probably just my mind playing tricks on me.'

I nod. 'Probably, happens to me all the time. Being alone will do that to you.'

He smiles. 'Yes, I can imagine. Plus, this place is so secure, I can't see how anyone would be able to break in. I'll go take a shower, see you later.'

I watch him turn and leave, praying to God Seb's right, and that it was just his mind playing tricks, while trying to ignore my own instincts which are telling me that whoever stole something precious from me just tried to spook Seb too.

Chapter Twenty-Six

Adriana

Before

'So how have things been since we last met, Adriana? Are you getting on OK at your new school?'

This is my fourth session with Dr Adams, and I have to admit the atmosphere feels different to when I first came to see him. For one, *I* feel different. Less suspicious, less hostile, less angry with the world at large. The art therapy classes he suggested I take have helped calm my mind despite me being cynical about the whole idea at first. I've got so much joy out of them, literally cannot wait for the weekly session to come around. I'm still not sure I'm any good, but what matters is that they make me happy. Dr Adams said at the end of our first meeting that he understood how I might find it hard to express my emotions in words, was perhaps too afraid to, and therefore art would be a good alternative way for me to do this, deal with my grief and move forward in a positive fashion.

I've always loved to paint and draw, ever since I was a little girl. But my parents were never interested in my artistic pursuits. Even when my mother did spare a few seconds to look at what I'd proudly present to her, hoping and praying for a word of encouragement, any kind word at all really, she'd either sneer and say it was crap or tell me to get on with my chores. And so, after a time, I gave up.

'Yes, fine thank you,' I say. 'I've made some new friends. The teachers are very kind and supportive. But I think the main thing that's made a difference is Aunt Georgie and Uncle Philip. They've been amazing. And I love living with them. To be honest, I feel the happiest I've ever been. So safe and secure.'

I stop talking. Conscious I may have overshared. He's a shrink after all. It's his job to read between the lines. I'm not a baby, I'm nearly fifteen; I'm not stupid either, no matter what my mother used to say. I know what he's thinking.

'Did you not feel safe and secure before you came to live with your aunt and uncle, Adriana?'

And there it is. I let my guard down for two seconds and he's all over it like a rash. But perhaps that's a little unfair. After all, he's a nice person. What harm can there be in me confiding in him? It's not like he can tell anyone else what I say in confidence. Not even my aunt and uncle. Maybe I'll feel better getting it off my chest.

I bite my lip.

'You know whatever you tell me, Adriana, won't go beyond these four walls,' he says. 'All I want to do is help you. You've made a lot of progress in a short time; you seem a lot calmer, more stable. But I can't help thinking you won't be able to fully move on if you don't tell someone what's troubling you.'

I inhale deeply, summoning the courage to tell Dr Adams what I've never told any other adult. 'OK then. The truth is, no, I didn't feel safe before. To be honest, my parents weren't particularly great at the whole parenting thing.'

He cocks his head. 'In what way?'

'Father was always working, and Mother would…'

'She would what? Go on. Don't be afraid.'

'She would tell me off constantly, say I was a waste of space. She never did anything with me. Always too busy with her friends, or making sure she looked good, or…'

'Or?' he urges.

'Nothing,' I mumble.

He doesn't look convinced by my answer, but neither does he press the point. 'Did she hurt you, Adriana? Physically?'

His eyes are so kind, his voice so caring, I'm dying to tell him more. But I don't answer immediately. Instead, tears form in my eyes as I instinctively recoil in my chair, painful flashbacks appearing in my mind. But unlike the first time I saw him, I don't get angry or out of control. Rather, I keep my temper in check. Something I'm certain is down to Dr Adams's caring nature. The fact that I feel safe and calm with him. And then, finally, I give a tentative nod.

His expression remains impassive, his tone even. 'How did she hurt you?'

I swallow hard. 'She'd hit me, kick me, sometimes stub out cigarettes on my arms and legs. She'd say I deserved it after putting her through the pain of childbirth, ending her modelling career.'

The tears are falling hard and fast now as I recount such painful memories. But it feels good to finally let it out. After all, Xavier and Eve are the only ones I've ever told. I was too scared to tell my teachers, because I feared the consequences of doing so might be fatal. In fact, I was warned as much. But I knew my friends would never tell on me. That I could trust them never to put me in harm's way.

I explain how my mother made me feel so worthless, so unloved. How once I nearly took a razor to my wrists, partly because I was desperate for attention, some show of affection from her, but also because I didn't want to feel sad any more. But that a voice in my head told me not to go through with it. That I was stronger than I imagined.

'That voice was right, Adriana, you are stronger than you imagined. You've proved that these past few months. Look how far you've come. You're so different to the girl I first met.'

I smile. 'Thank you.'

'And are you still in touch with your friends, Xavier and Eve? I know they meant a lot to you.'

I shake my head. 'No, I'm not. I think it's for the best.'

'Why is that?'

I don't tell him that I wrote, but that they never wrote back. For ages I felt so angry with them, because it felt like they'd abandoned me. But then I realised I couldn't be mad, because really, I was the one who'd abandoned them. The look on Xavier's face had told me as much. In hindsight, it was probably best for all of us to make a clean break. I'm sure even Xavier feels that now. Eve too. 'Because I'm better moving on, leaving the past in the past. They're just a reminder of all the bad things that happened to me, even though it's in no way their fault. I need to put the dark times behind me, and that means leaving them behind too.'

Dr Adams smiles, seemingly pleased with my explanation. 'I think that's sensible, and I'm so glad you feel able to move forward, and that you've found new friends.

Although I get the feeling you haven't told me everything. I think you have more to get off your chest. Am I right?'

He is right. But I can't bear to get into that now, and I tell him this.

He nods, like he understands completely. 'You know, writing down a journal of your thoughts can also help with that. It can focus your mind, help you deal with your stress, your everyday worries. I do it myself. It's cathartic.'

I nod. Smile. My spirits lifted by his suggestion. 'OK, I'll try it.'

'Good. And you're sleeping better?'

'Much better,' I say. It's true. I can't remember ever having slept so well. Waking refreshed rather than tired and drained. I seem to see things so much clearer these days. Everything is brighter, more focused.

'That's good to hear. And there's nothing else you feel the need to tell me? Something that's perhaps been niggling away at you? Disorienting you?'

I look at him curiously, wondering what he's getting at. I tell myself not to get worked up about it. Things couldn't be better, really. For the first time in my life I feel happy.

'No, there's nothing else. It's all good.'

'OK, that's fine. But now, I have something to tell you. Something that's going to be hard for you to hear. But in the long run, it's for the best.'

My heart speeds up at his remark, wondering what it is he's about to say.

And then he drops a bombshell that makes me almost faint with shock.

Chapter Twenty-Seven

Seb

I'm in my bedroom throwing on some clothes, having just taken a long, hot shower. As I stood under the shower's powerful jets, no matter how hard I tried to banish the image from my brain, all I could see were two eyes staring at me through the glass. Did I imagine the whole thing, or was it real? Neither particularly appeals at this moment. The first suggests the email is sending me crazy, the latter that I am in terrible and imminent danger.

If I'm not going mad and my eyes didn't deceive me, then surely it has to be the same psycho who sent me the email? It's too much of a coincidence otherwise. But how the hell did they get in?

I purposely chose not to labour the point with Adriana. For one, I didn't want to make her overly anxious, and two, I thought it best to drop it in case whoever it was, was listening. As shit-scared as I am, I need to try and stay calm, not let this arsehole get to me. Something tells me that's what they want. That they're looking to unsettle me, the way I'm rapidly starting to believe they tried to unsettle Ethan before eventually killing him.

It's all a game with them, but I can't rise to the bait. Can't go asking too many questions of Adriana or Stella the way Ethan did. I need to be smarter than my predecessor.

I grab my phone off the bedside table and check for messages, relieved to find no more threatening emails or texts. There's a message from Jasper, though. Asking if he and Rochelle can swing by in the week sometime. Christ, I was hoping he'd have forgotten about bringing Rochelle over, but clearly she's been on at him to set something up. It's the last thing I need, but equally, if I say no, Jasper will sense something's not right and ask why. It's like he's got an inbuilt red-sensor alert or something. I tell myself that having them over for one drink won't hurt. Provided I'm able to steer Jasper off asking any more intrusive questions. Hopefully, he'll be more discreet with his girlfriend around. I tentatively suggest Wednesday, praying that Adriana won't mind, before tossing my phone back down on the bed beside me. No sooner have I done so, there's a knock on the door. It takes me by surprise. I know it can only be one person, but for obvious reasons I can't help feeling edgy.

I go to open it. Feel calmer on seeing Adriana standing there.

'Hi,' I say.

'Hi.' She smiles. 'Look, I know I said last night was a one-off, and it's a bit late notice, but I don't suppose you fancy grabbing dinner out locally?' Her gaze lingers on me, but there's a shyness about it I find almost irresistible. Also, a hint of trepidation, as if something's happened to scare her but she's too afraid to say what. I'm in a dilemma as to how to respond. On the one hand it seems like a bad idea for all sorts of reasons. Only yesterday I promised myself I wouldn't allow myself to get close to her. And knowing someone's watching me, someone who appears to be fiercely protective of Adriana, should surely only serve to strengthen my resolve. But on the flip side, the thought of escaping this house right now holds huge appeal. I also wonder if there's something Adriana needs to tell me. Something she doesn't feel comfortable broaching within the confines of these walls.

'It's OK if you don't want to, I understand,' she says rather hurriedly, doubtless prompted by my hesitation. 'Like I said, it's very short notice and you're probably feeling tired from the move and so on.' Her cheeks have reddened slightly, as if anticipating rejection.

'No, it's fine, I'd love to,' I say. 'As you said earlier, it's not often I get a Saturday night off, and it's a bit sad me sitting in front of Netflix by myself.' I grin and she grins back. At that moment, she looks so lovely, I have to fight off an impulse to pull her towards me and kiss her.

'Great,' she says, her face brightening. 'Shall we meet downstairs at eight? I'll try and get a table for eight thirty at this little bistro I know off Heath Street.'

'Sounds good, is it posh?'

'No, not especially.' She smiles. 'Smart casual is fine. See you downstairs in a bit then.'

She walks away and I close the door after her, hoping this won't turn out to be a colossal mistake. On the bright side, at least having dinner out will grant me a few hours' breathing space. And I can use the time to ask Adriana if there's something more than the sudden death of her former doctor troubling her. Perhaps I can even brave asking her about where she grew up, in a casual way of course.

There's one other thing I intend to do while I'm out. I'm going to message Rick Savage, Ethan's father. Ask him if he'll meet with me. It's too dangerous to call or even text him from the house for obvious reasons. But in public I'll hopefully be safe to do so.

I'm praying there's something Ethan told Rick that Stella's unaware of, something that could prove useful in getting to the bottom of this nightmare situation. And if that's the case, it's best I find out sooner rather than later.

Chapter Twenty-Eight

Seb

I'm waiting for Adriana in the TV sitting room, flicking through the channels aimlessly. Nothing sparks my interest, but it's an easy means of distraction to take my mind off the fact that I'm about to go out for dinner with my landlady, a prospect that makes me nervous for a multitude of reasons. Playing with the remote also briefly stops me thinking about whether every room in this house is bugged, including the one I'm in right now. The house is vast and there are any number of unobtrusive spots one might place a listening device if you have the means and the know-how. The very thought makes me shiver inside.

I glance at my watch. It's a little after eight. Hopefully, Adriana won't be too much longer, because I'm suddenly desperate to get out of here. Just as I'm thinking this, I hear movement from behind me. I turn my neck to see Adriana standing there. She looks like a million dollars, while I immediately feel distinctly average and underdressed.

'I thought you said it wasn't smart,' I say, unable to take my eyes off her. She's wearing a simple strappy black dress which falls just above the knee, diamante drop earrings completing the look, a pair of black peep-toe stilettos dangling in her right hand, and the effect is stunning.

'It's not,' she says. 'It's just that I seem to live in my jeans and gym gear these days, aside from the odd charity event, of course, and so it's nice to get a bit dolled up for once.' She pauses. 'But if it makes you feel uncomfortable, I can change.'

'No, no, of course not,' I say. 'Please don't change on my account. You look lovely.'

Her face breaks out into a smile. 'Thank you. Right, well, I've ordered an Uber.' She looks at her phone. 'And it's four minutes away, so shall we get moving?'

I nod and grab my phone before following Adriana out of the room. I notice her make a point of shutting the door after switching off the lights, then repeat the same routine with all the other ground floor rooms.

Having checked everything's secure, we grab our coats from the cupboard in the hallway, then slip on our shoes before Adriana kills the hall light and keys in the alarm code. Once it starts beeping, I follow her outside, slamming the heavy steel door behind me. We wait for the ringing to stop before Adriana secures each of the three locks, glancing left and right as she does so. I find myself doing the same, while wondering if she's acting purely on instinct, or because, like me, she has good reason to be watchful.

We start walking towards the gates. The air is still, not a hint of a breeze, making the chilly temperatures more bearable. 'Uber's here,' Adriana says, glancing at her phone. The gates open automatically as we approach and waiting beyond them is a silver Toyota Prius. But also, to my alarm, is Stella. What the hell? Did she see the Uber pull up then deliberately come outside just to cause a stir? She knows Adriana's banned me from speaking to her. What the hell is she up to?

I glance at Adriana. She'd seemed more relaxed as we left the house than she did earlier. But now she looks tense. I can't let on that I know Stella. Adriana will feel betrayed. She'll never trust me again. I just pray Stella will do the same and not drop me in it. I want to signal to her but I'm too afraid in case Adriana notices.

'Off anywhere nice?' Stella asks in a blasé fashion. She looks at me, and I find myself holding my breath. 'I don't think we've had the pleasure.'

Phew.

Her gaze switches to Adriana. 'Aren't you going to introduce us?'

I give a nervous cough, then extend my hand before Adriana, who's still looking uncomfortable, can respond. 'I'm Seb, Adriana's new lodger. And you are?'

'This is Stella,' Adriana interjects, her tone noticeably abrupt. 'Stella lives at number six.' She makes wide eyes at me.

'Oh, OK.' I feign surprise, making wide eyes of my own as if to emphasise my shock. 'It's nice to meet you, Stella.'

'Likewise.' Stella shakes my hand, thankfully continuing to play along.

'Well, as you can see, we have a taxi waiting so have a good evening,' Adriana says, barely making eye contact with Stella.

'I'm offended you haven't introduced us before now, Adriana,' Stella says. 'How long were you planning on keeping this lovely young man a secret from me? You made a point of bringing Ethan round when he first moved in. What's changed? It feels like you're avoiding me.'

Talk about awkward. She knows exactly why Adriana hasn't introduced us and yet she's choosing to play some juvenile game. Patently trying to wind Adriana up. It's a little cruel. Makes me question what she told me this morning. Whether she's desperate to discredit Adriana out of pure jealousy.

Adriana shoots daggers at Stella. 'There's not been any time to introduce you.' She doesn't raise her voice, but there's a definite edge to it. 'Seb only moved in yesterday. And you've been busy unpacking and finding your feet, haven't you, Seb?'

Adriana stares at me, her eyes unusually hard, willing me to comply.

The tension is stifling, and I'm desperate for this awkward situation to be over.

'Er, yes, absolutely, it's been non-stop.' I give a forced smile.

The Uber driver sighs impatiently. The customary tetchiness of cab drivers usually gets on my nerves, but at this precise moment I could kiss him. 'Well, I don't want to delay you any longer, wherever you might be off to. You both certainly look very smart. Almost like a couple.' Stella lets her gaze rest on me. I can't tell if she's cross or impressed. Perhaps she thinks I engineered this evening with the intention of plying information from Adriana over one too many glasses of wine. Or maybe she's just plain jealous.

'Thanks, have a nice evening, Stella,' Adriana says before we both scurry into the back of the cab, and the driver speeds off.

We sit in agonising silence en route to the restaurant. It's only a five-minute drive but it feels like longer. I can feel the tension radiating off Adriana as she stares straight ahead, seemingly lost in thought. I daren't say anything about what just happened, because I'm uncertain how she'll react if I do. I worry she's being cold with me because she somehow suspects this wasn't my first encounter with Stella. But perhaps I'm reading too much into things. Her rules forbade me from speaking to Stella, but there was nothing to stop Stella from accosting us both the way she did just now. I'm not sure Adriana planned for that.

Surely now she'll feel obliged to explain what she has against Stella, even though it obviously won't be news to me. I won't ask now, though. Hopefully, the moment will arrive naturally once we're sat down with a glass of wine.

Chapter Twenty-Nine

Seb

The driver pulls up in front of the entrance to a tiny alleyway off Heath Street, the main hubbub of Hampstead, whose quaint restaurants and bars are currently heaving with Saturday night punters, giving the area a lively, buoyant feel. We climb out of the cab and for the first time since we left Stella standing on the street outside the house Adriana looks at me. She seems a little spaced out, but I'm guessing it's just the stress of seeing Stella unexpectedly and our awkward three-way exchange. I ask her if she's OK, at which point she appears to emerge from her trance. She touches her head. 'Yes, I guess I just feel a little light-headed, I've not eaten much to speak of since breakfast. I need some food, that's all. Let's go, it's just a little way down.'

I follow her lead down the narrow, cobbled alleyway. It's lined on either side with several cafes, a florist's, a couple of boutiques and Malmaison, the restaurant she's booked for us. On entering we're greeted like long-lost friends, before being seated at a table for two against the wall. It's warm inside, the result of the restaurant's compact size and open kitchen. An inviting aroma of food infuses the air and I'm thankful when the waiter brings a basket of bread and some fresh olives along with the menus. He hands us both one, then asks what he can get us to drink, and we agree on a bottle of Barolo.

'Don't mind if I grab a piece, do you?' I ask, gesturing to the bread. 'I'm starving.'

Adriana smiles. 'Of course not.' She pops an olive into her mouth. Then looks at me with an amused expression. 'You're so polite. So proper. Ethan would never have asked the question, he'd have dived straight in. You remind me of Charles, he was always the perfect gentleman.'

I start to butter my bread. 'Mum always taught me to be polite and respectful,' I say. 'Especially towards women.'

'That's good to hear,' she says. 'And what about your father? Did he teach you the same?'

'Yes, always.' I nod, ignoring the sudden ache in my chest. There's a brief lull, in which I debate in my mind whether this is the right moment to bring up our awkward encounter with Stella. Whether Adriana trusts me enough to let me in on the truth behind their falling out. She seems more relaxed, so I decide to go for it.

'Listen, it felt a bit uncomfortable just now, running into your neighbour, Stella. And having met her, I don't blame you for wanting me to keep away from her. It was a bit creepy, wasn't it, seeing her standing by the cab, almost like she'd deliberately come out of her house to be nosy. Is that why you don't get on? She seemed like a bit of a trouble-stirrer. Stalkerish, even.' I stop talking, worried I've over-egged it. Hopefully, she won't twig what I'm up to.

The waiter returns with our Barolo. He uncorks it, then offers me a taste. I nod while he pours me a small measure. Adriana watches me intently as I put the glass to my lips and sip the wine. It's good and I tell him so, whereupon he fills both our glasses halfway and tells us he'll be back in a few minutes to take our order.

'Cheers.' Adriana offers up her glass. I return the gesture, wondering if she's going to ignore everything I just said about Stella, but to my relief she doesn't. She sets down her glass, having taken a generous sip. 'I'm sorry too. It's the last thing you needed: to be confronted by my slightly deranged neighbour on a Saturday night, and when you've only just moved in.'

'You think she's deranged?'

'Stella's an alcoholic. She's always liked a drink but when her husband left her for a younger woman, drink became her only friend. He was her world. It was obvious. She didn't have many female friends to speak of so when he left her, she turned to the bottle for comfort. I tried to console her, but she pushed me away. Truth is, she was envious of my and Charles's close relationship and being around me was just a reminder of what she didn't have. But then, when Charles died, she became friendlier. I think she saw us as being on a more even footing then, even though the circumstances in which we'd found ourselves alone were very different. And then, when Ethan moved in, she went all funny on me again. I think she was jealous.' *As I suspected.* 'She doesn't sleep either. It's not a good combination, lack of sleep and too much alcohol, and I fear it's skewered her ability to think rationally. To separate the real world from fantasy.'

At this point, I wonder if Adriana's about to tell me what Stella claimed to have seen the night Ethan died. I try not to appear overly anxious, though. Instead, I ask casually: 'What do you mean by that?'

Adriana's eyes linger on me, as if contemplating whether or not to say more. 'OK, so I wasn't going to mention this, but now that you've met her, I think I should, because although I can ask you not to speak to her, I realise there's nothing to stop her from putting ideas into your head. It was foolish of me to think I could control the situation like that. I guess I didn't want us starting off on the wrong foot.' She smiles. 'I like you, Seb, and I didn't want you to think any less of me. To think I'm a bad penny. I've always been a bit like that. I seem confident, but inside I worry a lot about what people think of me.'

I love how honest she's being with me right now. Showing me her vulnerable side. It's a side I feel sure Stella's never seen. 'Don't be daft, whatever it is you can tell me,' I try to reassure her. 'You're a lovely person and you've been through so much, I could never think any less of you.'

She gives me a grateful smile, her shoulders relaxing. Then tells me what I already know. 'Stella told the police she saw someone on the roof with Ethan the night he died.'

I act surprised, hoping to God it's convincing. 'Really? Who?'

'She claimed she couldn't make them out. But was adamant she'd seen them talking and that whoever it was caused Ethan to fall, whether by accident or deliberately.'

'Shit. But you didn't believe her?'

'No. I mean, for starters how the hell would they have accessed the house? You know how secure it is.'

'True. Although I suppose Ethan could have brought someone back with him?'

'Yes, I guess. But somehow, I doubt it. We had a bit of a row the night before and no matter how off his face he was, I don't think he'd have invited anyone back. Besides, he knew I didn't allow overnight guests.'

'What did you row about?' I ask, perhaps a fraction too eagerly.

Adriana sips more wine. 'Ahh, it was stupid really. I caught him snooping around my study.'

'Your study? Why would he do that?'

I think back to what Stella told me this morning. That Ethan found something of Adriana's that got him into trouble. Possibly killed. I'm on tenterhooks wondering if Adriana's about to tell me what it was.

'I don't know,' she replies.

My spirits immediately sink. I'm certain she's lying. That she knows exactly what Ethan found, but for some reason is too afraid to tell me.

'It pissed me off,' she goes on, 'and I told him I wanted him out of the house by the end of the month. I didn't feel like I could trust him any more.'

'That's understandable,' I say.

In my mind, I'm more convinced than ever that whatever Ethan came across in Adriana's study shed light on her past, on something she's desperate to keep buried. Something that whoever sent me the email was prepared to kill Ethan for to stop him exposing it.

'Thanks for being so understanding,' she says. 'I liked Ethan, I really did, and it broke my heart to have to kick him out.' She stops talking, her eyes anxious. She looks like she has more to say, possibly confess whatever it is that's preying on her mind, the words seemingly on the tip of her tongue, but then the waiter appears and asks if we're ready to order.

I inwardly sigh with irritation, while Adriana looks relieved. We both give our orders, the waiter topping up our wine before leaving us be. I pray she'll reconsider opening up to me, but she doesn't. Instead, she excuses herself to the ladies, telling me she'll be back soon.

Feeling a little deflated, I take the opportunity to message Ethan's father. Texting isn't ideal, but there's no time to make a call. Besides, I don't want anyone overhearing. God only knows who's watching.

> Hi Rick, my name is Seb Walker and I'm Adriana Wentworth's new lodger. I hope you don't mind me messaging you out of the blue, but Stella Jenkins passed on your number. I'd like to speak to you about what happened to Ethan. It goes without saying I'm very sorry for your loss. Perhaps we could meet this week? Somewhere busy. I was thinking Soho if that's not too much trouble. Look forward to hearing from you. Seb. ps please keep this between us. I don't want Adriana finding out. She's scared, I can tell, and I think it might be related to your son's death.

I press send just as Adriana returns to the table.

'All OK?' she asks, her eyes a little anxious.

'Yep, just Jasper,' I lie. Although I use this as an opportunity to raise the subject of Jasper bringing Rochelle round to the house. 'He wants to bring his girlfriend over on Wednesday to see my "new pad".' I do the air quotes thing. 'You don't mind, do you? I can tell him no.'

She smiles sweetly, although it's sometimes hard to read what's going on inside Adriana's mind. Plus, I get the feeling Jasper's not exactly her favourite person since he gave her the third degree yesterday. 'It's fine. I'll make sure I'm home. Be lovely to meet her.'

'Great.' I pretend to text Jasper, then sit back in my chair. But no sooner have I done so, I get a reply from Rick. I quickly scan the message, glancing up at Adriana as I do. 'It's Jasper again.'

'Ah.' She smiles.

> Hello Ethan, I can meet you. How about Monday lunchtime? Cafe Barista on Brewer Street, 1pm. Rick.

Result. Once again, I pretend to text Jasper back.

> Great, thanks Rick. See you then.

I press send just as the waiter arrives with our starters. His timing on this occasion couldn't be better.

I put my phone away in my pocket, conscious of Adriana watching me as I do. I try to appear unfazed. Instead I look up at the friendly waiter as he places the food in front of us.

'Ah, it looks divine.' I grin broadly at Adriana. 'Can't wait to dive in.'

Chapter Thirty

Adriana

I'm trying to focus on what Seb is saying as we tuck into our starters but it's a struggle. I didn't really need to use the loo when I excused myself to the ladies. I heard my phone buzz in my handbag which was hanging by its strap on the side of my chair and wanted to check who the message was from. Every time my phone beeps I worry it might be the person who's watching me. Trying to scare me. The same creep who quite possibly stole something valuable from me, and may well have been the face Seb saw while he was swimming earlier. And so, in case it was them, I didn't want Seb to see my frightened reaction.

It wasn't, thank God. It was a message from Dr Martin, updating me with some news about Dr Adams. But to my alarm, it was just as disturbing. He informed me that Dr Adams didn't die of complications arising from pulmonary edema. Rather, the post-mortem detected cyanide in his system. Meaning he was poisoned, and the police are now treating his death as a murder investigation. They also confirmed he died on Sunday afternoon, around four p.m., and not later that same night as we'd previously assumed. In which case, who the hell emailed me at eleven p.m., and how did they know about my meeting with Dr Adams on the Monday? Because they checked his calendar? Or because they know me and have been tracking my every move?

Shock ripped through me when I read the message. I couldn't for the life of me think who'd want Dr Adams dead. It seemed inconceivable.

His ex-wife, Jeanette, with whom he remained on good terms, and his daughter, Melissa, are both understandably in bits. Dr Martin said he was going up to Guildford on Monday morning to express his condolences in person. I messaged back, offering to accompany him, but he immediately replied saying it was best he went alone on this occasion. He added that the police would be looking to speak to all of Dr Adams's patients, and I should therefore be prepared for a phone call.

'Are you OK?' Seb asks. I realise I've been staring at him vacantly as he's been talking and haven't a clue what he said. My head is banging, so many thoughts swirling around in it, I can barely hear myself think. I'm not even sure why I asked Seb out for dinner. As much as I want to tell him about the emails, about the fact that he and I are being watched, I know that I can't, because the sender made it clear that I'd be placing his life in danger were I to do so. But it's not just that. It's also the fact that they know my secret. And I daren't do anything to anger them, lest they expose it.

I suppose I asked Seb out because I was desperate to escape the house. To feel free, if only for a few hours. But Seb's not stupid. He must suspect something's up, while our awkward run-in with Stella earlier won't have helped his suspicions. I told him that Stella can't be trusted simply because I don't want him mixed up in all this. But now, having learned how Dr Adams really died, I can't help wondering if there is some truth to her claims. Whether Ethan was, in fact, pushed?

Is it possible that whoever sent the emails to me and Dr Martin killed both Ethan and Dr Adams? But why? That's what I don't understand. Because they were jealous of my close relationships with both men? Perhaps, I guess. Although that's more understandable in Ethan's case. After all, we were sleeping together. But my relationship with Dr Adams was only ever platonic. He was like a father to me.

None of this makes any sense, and I feel so stressed I can hardly catch my breath.

Yet, I try to appear calm. 'Sorry, yes, I'm fine.' Do I tell Seb how Dr Adams really died? I can't think what harm it could do, there's no reason why he'd make any connection between his death and Ethan's. On the face of it, they're completely unrelated. Plus, I worry he'll read about it in the newspapers or my aunt and uncle might say something when they visit and then he'll wonder why I failed to mention it.

I decide to tell him. 'Actually, I'm not fine.'

He looks concerned. 'Why, what happened?'

'I received a message while I was in the ladies.'

Concerns morphs into alarm. 'What message?' he asks anxiously. 'From who?'

'From Dr Martin,' I say, while wondering why he suddenly seems so jumpy.

But just like that, with my response, his features relax. Why is he behaving so erratically?

'Who's Dr Martin?' he asks.

'An old friend of Dr Adams. I've been seeing him on Dr Adams's recommendation since Charles died.'

'Ah, OK. And what did he say?'

'The post-mortem came back on Dr Adams.'

'And?'

'And it seems he was poisoned. With cyanide.'

Seb instantly drops his cutlery. It makes a bit of a crash and I spy a couple on a nearby table glance our way. Seb notices it too. 'Sorry,' he mouths in their direction, then leans forward. 'Poisoned? Who the hell would want him dead?'

'I, I just don't know,' I whisper, even though the couple have resumed their conversation. 'I mean, obviously he had a lot of patients. Some more mentally unstable than others. I suppose any one of them could have had it in for him, blamed him for something.'

'Or possibly someone connected with one of his patients? Like an angry relative or romantic partner who felt he'd given them the wrong advice,' Seb offers. 'Someone who perhaps wanted to put a stop to them seeing him. I mean, it's a pretty drastic way of going about it, but even so, it's possible, I guess.'

It is possible, and I acknowledge this with a faint nod. 'I can't quite take it in. He was such a good man and he didn't deserve this. His poor daughter, she doted on him and he on her. She'll be devastated. I'll always be grateful to him for helping me. I still wish I knew what it was he wanted to talk to me about last Monday. Dr Martin and I presumed he cancelled because he wasn't feeling well and needed to see a doctor.'

'I guess he genuinely might have been ill and cancelled before the murderer got to him.'

'No.' I shake my head. 'We now know that can't be the case.'

'How?'

'Because the post-mortem concluded he died around four p.m. on Sunday. I received his email seven hours later, around eleven.'

I stop talking, but Seb reads my mind.

His eyes narrow. 'Are you thinking that whoever murdered him emailed you cancelling your appointment?'

I nod. 'Yes, that's exactly what I'm thinking. What worries me more is how they knew about my appointment with Dr Adams, not to mention why they'd have been bothered about emailing me to cancel. I mean, why would they care? It's like…'

'Like they knew you,' he interjects. 'Personally.'

'Yes.'

I'm treading dangerous waters here in discussing all this with Seb. But I still can't think how he'd make the connection between Ethan's and Dr Adams's deaths. The waiter appears and collects our plates. Informs us that our mains will follow in a few minutes. We say thanks and wait for him to leave before resuming the conversation.

Seb sits back in his chair, the look in his eyes telling me something just occurred to him. 'I suppose they could have killed him, then hacked into his calendar, seen what his upcoming appointments were then pretended to be him and cancelled them all. Perhaps it was the killer's intention to delay the time between Dr Adams's death and his body being discovered. Maybe under some false apprehension that time reduces the chances of the cyanide being discovered.'

It's a thought, and I'd love for Seb's theory to be correct. But my sixth sense tells me otherwise, last night's email turning over in my brain:

I know you're upset about Dr Adams, but you need to
move on, forget about him. You need to look out for
number one.

'Perhaps,' I say with a weak smile.

Our main courses arrive. I look down at my food, not feeling in the least bit hungry, but put on an act all the same. 'Looks great, thank you,' I tell the waiter.

He tells us to enjoy then leaves us be.

'Thanks for being such a good listener,' I say. 'I'm not sure I'd have coped very well hearing the news had I been alone in the house at the time. I mean, I'd probably have called Aunt Georgie, but there's nothing like being able to talk to someone in person.'

Seb reaches across the table, takes my hand in his, his fingertips softly caressing mine. Warm and soothing. It's strange, I've only known him a few days, and usually I'm so cautious, but there's just something about him that makes me feel safe. Something in his touch that reassures me that whoever's trying to paint him in a bad light, is doing so out of malice. 'My pleasure, any time. You can tell me anything.'

Just hearing him say this, I'm sorely tempted to tell him about the emails Dr Martin and I received, but I manage to restrain myself. It's not that I don't trust him. I just can't risk Seb's life. If whoever emailed me killed Dr Adams, and possibly Ethan, what's to stop them from killing Seb?

I just can't take the chance. For now, I need to try and figure this out alone. But with each hour that passes, I find myself more and more convinced as to who's behind it all.

The same person who infiltrated my house on that terrifying night a decade ago.

Chapter Thirty-One

Seb

'How about we walk home? I could do with a stroll after all that food.'

Adriana and I have just left the restaurant. She insisted on paying even though it made me feel like a kept man. I offered to go halves, but she wouldn't have it. Said she'd be upset if I didn't agree so I reluctantly gave in, but made her promise she'd allow me to return the favour another time.

All the while we were eating, I couldn't stop thinking about the fact that Dr Adams was poisoned. Couldn't help wondering if the killer was the same person who emailed me. Who possibly killed Ethan. I wouldn't neces-sarily have made the connection had it not been for Adriana's revelation that Dr Adams's murderer emailed her, cancelling their appointment. It indicated to me that they knew Adriana and was aware of the appointment. But why murder Dr Adams? That I don't follow. Unless he discovered something about Adriana or her past, and the killer feared him exposing it? In the same way he feared Ethan would do the same.

Or am I looking at this the wrong way? Perhaps Dr Adams discovered the killer's identity and was on the brink of exposing them? Perhaps it's someone from Adriana's past, someone she's scared of, who she's spent her life running from, as Stella had intimated. No matter what Adriana says about Stella, what she said is swiftly making more and more sense. Hopefully, Rick can fill in some gaps.

After Adriana told me her shocking news, we moved on to lighter topics. Music, restaurants, theatre, books. I'd wanted to somehow broach the subject of her upbringing, but I could see how stressed she was and decided against it. If anything, she might have grown suspicious. I'm nervous, though. Nervous about too many bad things having happened in such a short space of time. Right now, my head is telling me I should run for the hills, get as far away as possible from Adriana. After all, I've only just met her, and I don't owe her anything. But my heart is saying otherwise. Just because when I look at her, she seems so fragile, so afraid and alone, and I can't bring it upon myself to abandon her.

'Sure,' Adriana says to my suggestion of a walk. 'I love Malmaison but it was rather stuffy in there. I could do with some fresh air.'

'Great, hope you know the way, though, because my sense of direction is pretty shit.'

She laughs. 'Don't worry, I know this area like the back of my hand.'

We start walking. 'So, plans for tomorrow?' I ask.

'Well, I've got a couple of meetings lined up for next week I need to prep for.'

'For your charities?'

'Yes.'

'Remind me which ones you help out with?'

'There's Sisters Together, also the Elizabeth Clemency Foundation and Female Aid. And I do a bit of campaigning for Safe House UK.'

All for abused women and children. Coincidence or not?

'I guess you've only heard of the last one. The others aren't so well known.'

'Actually, I know them all,' I say. 'Mum donated to three of them.'

'She did? That's wonderful. Your mother sounds like a really good person.'

'She was,' I say. 'The thought of children and women being abused made her sick to her stomach.' I look directly at Adriana. 'It does me too.'

She holds my gaze and there's a gratefulness in her eyes that touches my heart, making me wonder if she too was abused as a child. Is that what she's so afraid to talk about? It would make sense. If so, did Ethan find out who abused her? I glance down to my right, and realise there's barely an inch separating our hands as we walk alongside each other. I badly want to reach out and grab hers, yearning for the touch of this beautiful, kind woman who, as much as I don't want to admit it, has drawn me under her spell. But I don't need to, because just like that I feel her fingers slip into mine, and the feeling is so electric it scares me. Right from the first moment I saw her I felt it. And as I look up to meet her gaze once more, I know she feels it too. That connection. Both physical and spiritual. And it's at this point that I don't hesitate. I stop dead in my tracks, and pull her towards me, her lips within touching distance of mine. I know I shouldn't be doing this, that it's an insane idea for so many reasons, but I just can't help myself.

We lean in simultaneously and kiss, softly at first, and then more passionately, my body and soul having never wanted a person as much as I want her at that moment.

Chapter Thirty-Two

Adriana

Every step of our walk home I knew what Seb and I were about to do was a mistake. That we were crossing a line that couldn't be undone. That it was selfish of me to put my own desires first, when I knew I could be placing him – an innocent in whatever game my stalker is playing – in danger. Jesus, it's why I haven't told him about the emails. But when he kissed me, it was as if all logic went out the window. My rational side no match for that part of me that yearned to be loved. All I've ever craved is love from another human being. To be cared for, valued. Respected. And I guess, whenever that chance comes along, and with someone I'm attracted to, it's impossible for me to resist.

I tell myself it's not as if I'm forcing Seb into doing anything he doesn't want to do. He's a grown man after all. And I'm not blind. I knew from the first moment our eyes met that he was as attracted to me as I was to him. That magical moment when you look into another person's eyes and everything and everyone around you becomes peripheral.

And that's why, as we enter the house in silence, I know I am powerless to stop what's about to happen. Even though the email's words of warning are lodged firmly at the back of my mind:

I know you like him, but you'd be wise to fight your repellent urges; you know it never ends well when you allow them to get too close.

I watch Seb turn off the alarm then lock the door. We remove our shoes and coats and then I take his hand and carefully lead him up the stairs, leaving the lights off. I guide him to my bedroom and open the door, the desire in me swelling to new heights with sweet anticipation.

A faint light filters through the blinds which are not quite closed, so I can see the silhouette of his handsome face. He shuts the door gently then takes my hand in his, draws me near so that our bodies meet, then softly caresses my cheek, his gaze never leaving me, the hunger in his eyes burning through me. And then he brings his lips to mine and kisses me with a tenderness that takes my breath away.

All thoughts of the animal who might be watching us fade into the background as we succumb to the feelings we've been harbouring for one another since we first met. Wordlessly, gently, Seb lays me down on the mattress, then starts kissing every inch of my body. And suddenly I have never felt more alive or more desirable. Or more content in my own skin.

–

Seb and I lie in each other's arms in the near darkness, having made love. There was nothing stilted or forced about it. The sex with Ethan had been wild and exciting but with Seb it was passionate and tender, the way it had been with Charles. I could lie here forever, but I know I cannot and that the darkness that's suddenly enveloping my life hasn't faded away. It's something I'll need to face the moment I leave this bed.

Seb raises himself up on his elbow, lays his head in his hand while looking down at me. He grins. 'I've never been a toy boy before.'

I grin back. 'So that makes me a cougar, right?'

Another cheeky smile. 'I guess so.'

I pull a face. 'That makes me feel old.'

He leans in and kisses me. 'You most certainly aren't old.' His expression becomes serious. 'You're the most beautiful thing I've ever seen. And right now, I feel like I must be dreaming.'

It's such a romantic thing to say, and I feel the tears collect in my eyes.

Seb looks alarmed. 'Sorry, I didn't mean to upset you, I...'

I press my index finger to his lips. 'Shush, I'm not upset, I'm just overwhelmed by how lovely you are. But also, a little afraid.'

'Afraid of what?'

'Of falling for you.'

Seb lowers his gaze. Then looks back up to meet my own. 'Me too. I never meant for this to happen. Never meant to develop feelings for you. I told myself it was a bad idea, but I just feel this...'

'Connection?' I interrupt. 'I know, I feel it too.'

I hesitate.

'What is it?' he asks.

I take a deep breath, hoping he won't react badly to what I'm about to ask. But it's precisely because of the connection we've this minute acknowledged, along with what's just happened between us, that I feel able to.

'It's OK, you can ask me anything.' He grins. 'I won't bite.'

I smile as he says this, feeling somewhat bolstered by his blithe encouragement. 'OK, well, it's just that I get the feeling you're carrying something painful. And I wanted you to know that if you ever need to talk about it, I'm here. I want to help if I can.'

All at once his face grows sombre. No trace of the cheeky grin in sight. He seems taken aback by my comment. And it tells me my observation wasn't far off the mark.

'Sorry, I didn't mean to make you feel uncomfortable,' I say. 'It's just that I care about you, and I wanted you to know that I'm here to listen if you need a sounding board, the way you listened to me just now in the restaurant.' I don't mention that my question is largely prompted by the emails Dr Martin and I received. Not because they've made me suspect Seb's hiding something terrible – that's what the twisted fuck who's playing with me wants me to think. Rather, it's because they've caused me to really look at Seb, deep into his soul, and I can tell there's something weighing him down. Like Max said, it's odd for someone his age not to be on any social media. I'm not, and there's a reason for that, which makes me think Seb must have his reasons too. 'You're not on any social media…' I start to say.

I don't get the chance to finish my sentence. Before I can say another word Seb springs off the bed as quick as lightning. Shit, I've gone too far. He turns around, his face twisted into an angry grimace. An expression I never imagined seeing on him. One that scares me.

'You've been looking me up online?' he says, disbelief engulfing his face. 'Max ran a credit check. Wasn't that enough? Why do you care what social media I may or may not be on? It's not a crime not to have my life on display for all and sundry, you know. Maybe I like keeping my private life private. What's wrong with that?'

It kills me to see the wounded look in his eyes. Only a few minutes ago I was lying in his arms, his fingertips caressing my skin. Now he's looking at me like I'm the enemy. It's a feeling that makes me sick to my stomach.

But I also find his reaction a little over the top. Why so defensive? I'm now more certain than ever that he's keeping something buried. 'Seb, I...'

'And what about you, Adriana?' All at once he turns the tables. 'What are you hiding? Because I'm pretty sure there's something. Something you're too afraid to talk about, and which I'm guessing might be related to Dr Adams's death. Possibly Ethan's too.'

What the fuck? Anger rises up in me. Where is all this suddenly coming from? I shouldn't have brought up the social media thing, granted, but I hadn't expected what feels like a vicious and utterly unfair counter-attack.

'How dare you!' I exclaim. 'Why would you even say that?' I narrow my eyes as something occurs to me. 'Tell me, was that the first time you met Stella earlier? Or had she already got to you? You did rather go on about our "chance" meeting when we talked about it in the restaurant.'

The look on his face tells me everything, and all at once I feel like the biggest fool. Lied to, betrayed. Like so many times in my life. How could he keep that from me, act as if it was the first time he'd crossed paths with Stella? I ask him this very question.

'I didn't want to upset you,' he replies. 'I knew you didn't want me speaking to her, but it wasn't my fault.

She followed me to the Heath when I went for my run this morning. Told me about seeing someone on the roof that night with Ethan. How she didn't think his death was an accident, and that Ethan's father believed her. She said Ethan spoke to her shortly before he died, asking questions about you and your childhood, about what you might be hiding or running away from. He told her he'd found something, but didn't elaborate what. I'm guessing that was when he went looking in your study, like you mentioned earlier. Stella said you'd always been reticent to talk about your childhood but that she sensed there was something or someone in your past you were scared of.' Seb edges closer, his expression no longer angry but sympathetic. 'Tell me, Adriana, what is it you're afraid of? I want to help. Could it be connected to Dr Adams's and Ethan's deaths?'

I look at Seb, and I want to believe him, confide in him, but I'm too angry. Too hurt by his deceit. How can I possibly be honest with him when he's failed to be honest with me? He's kept this to himself all day, having had plenty of time to own up. Why couldn't he just have been honest from the start? Why play these games? I can't even look at him right now, I feel so wronged. So deflated.

'Please leave me,' I say.

He comes over, tries to grab my hand. 'Adriana, I...'

I feel the stress rise up in me, so much so I feel dizzy as we lock eyes, my heart wanting him to stay, my head warning me I can't trust him. 'Leave, now. I need to be alone.'

He does as I say, and I feel shaky as I watch him leave without saying another word.

I lie flat on the bed and shut my eyes, hoping that sleep will come but far from convinced that it will. Knowing

Seb's now given whoever's watching us more reason than ever to do him harm.

Chapter Thirty-Three

I was right to suspect you, Sebastian. I knew in my heart you were bad news even though I tried to give you the benefit of the doubt, see the good in you. You hurt her, betrayed her. Lied to her. Just like the rest of them. Even Charles let her down in the end. His was the ultimate betrayal and one she's never truly recovered from. It's why she needs me, even though she doesn't know it. No one can take care of her the way I do. More than anything I want us to be able to talk, to connect like old friends might. But I know how temperamental she can be, so I've not yet dared show myself to her after all these years of hiding in the shadows. It's a risk I can't take just yet. Particularly given how she reacted when Dr Adams told her something at the end of a session all those years ago. Not long after she started seeing him. An incident I later read about in the journal he urged her to keep. Something that shocked her to her core and took her some time to recover from. It's why I had to shut the good doctor up recently. Because he found out about me. My cover finally blown. He planned on telling her everything last Monday. That's why he arranged their meeting. I had nothing against the man per se. And I'm sorry for the loved ones he's left behind. But I didn't have a choice. She always comes first.

Thankfully, I am not like her. Emotional, impetuous. I am disciplined, guarded. I choose my moments wisely. I know when it's safe to come out of the shadows and when I must stay well-concealed. And for now, I must stay hidden.

I press play on the recording saved to my phone and watch her screwing you. I cannot believe you had the nerve to sleep with her in her own house, Sebastian, after the message I sent you. I was wrong to believe you were different to Ethan. To think that you went ahead and fucked her when you knew only too well I might be watching, listening, is breathtakingly arrogant, sick even, and it's something that deserves to be punished. She also knew I could be watching, but I forgive her because I know how needy she is, despite my warning. She yearns for affection the way I yearn to keep her safe, and it's an urge she can't repel, just as I am powerless against my desire to protect her.

I'd like to think she'll kick you out for talking to Stella behind her back, knowing it was against the rules. But I'm not sure she will. With Ethan having only just met a nasty end, it might look suspicious to others that you couldn't even last a week as her new lodger. It's why I can't take matters into my own hands either. Reluctantly, I will leave things be a while longer. As much as I want to punish you, to put a stop to your snooping.

She shouldn't have told you that Dr Adams was murdered, that was a mistake, and I worry it'll only give you cause to fish some more. Then again, she wasn't to know you'd talked to Stella. Found out things you should have steered clear of.

I will watch and wait. I will follow you and find out what it is you're hiding. For I feel sure it's something juicy. Something that will make her see sense.

Make her rue the day she ever met you.

Chapter Thirty-Four

Seb

It's eight a.m. on Sunday and I'm in the kitchen making myself some breakfast. Adriana hasn't appeared yet. When I walked past her bedroom door I couldn't hear movement, and so I assumed she must still be asleep.

I barely slept myself. And what little I had was fretful. I kept seeing the hurt in Adriana's eyes when I admitted to speaking to Stella yesterday morning. I felt like such a charlatan for having kept the truth from her. For feigning surprise in the restaurant when she told me what Stella claimed to have seen the night Ethan died. Particularly after she'd unburdened herself to me about Dr Adams. She placed her trust in me, opened up to me, gave her body to me, and yet I deceived her at every turn. Even though, in my defence, my actions were prompted purely by my desire not to hurt her.

The guilt for lying, for having caused her more pain, made me toss and turn. I kept thinking how one moment we'd been lying in each other's arms, the next she was ordering me to leave. I should have listened to Jasper, should never have allowed myself to fall for Adriana. Let alone sleep with her. But it's too late, the damage has been done, and I wouldn't be surprised if she kicks me out. It's something I need to prepare myself for when she appears.

I pour myself a second mug of coffee then start spreading margarine on the toast I just made, my mind still racing with thoughts. I was thrown when Adriana asked if there was something troubling me, and I fear my reaction has only made her more suspicious. I just hadn't expected her to put me on the spot like that, and it made me wonder if she knew more about my background than she was letting on. I can't think how she could, unless someone's been putting ideas into her head. But perhaps I'm wrong. Perhaps she's just an insightful person and I need to stop overthinking things. Mistaking harmless concern for something more sinister.

I pull out a stool and sit at the countertop, my toast and coffee in front of me. I don't feel particularly hungry, but we drank a fair bit last night and I need something to mop up the booze. I pick up a piece and take a bite, all the time speculating what Adriana's going to say when she appears. Perhaps I should be rejoicing at the possibility she'll ask me to pack my bags. That I've unwittingly drafted my get-out clause, allowing me to be on the first train out of King's Cross back up to Edinburgh. OK, so I've been warned to not even think about leaving, but if Adriana's the one to kick me out then surely I cannot be held accountable for that? Unless every word of our conversation last night was being listened to and whoever was listening will look to punish me for betraying her. Hurting her. I tremble at the thought, and once again find myself staring up at the ceiling, at the crevices in the walls, wondering if there's a tiny device concealed somewhere that's invisible to the naked eye.

Just then, I hear faint footsteps approaching. I set down my toast, my pulse quickening as I watch the door handle slowly turn. Each second feels like hours.

'Hi.' It's Adriana. I inwardly sigh with relief, while asking myself who else it would be. Aside from the arsehole who's threatening me, of course.

'Hi,' I say, jumping up from my stool. 'Can I get you some coffee?'

She gives me a weary smile. 'Sure.'

She's in her dressing gown, her hair messy and falling loose around her shoulders. No make-up. But she still looks lovely. If not tired. Markedly so. As she makes her way towards me, I see the dark shadows beneath her eyes, which are slightly bloodshot. Has she been crying? Am I the cause of that? Fuck, I feel like such a bastard.

Adriana sits down at another stool and waits for me to bring her coffee. The silence is excruciating. Once I'm seated again, she's the first to speak. 'Look, I'm sorry we fought last night. I should never have pried into your life…'

'Adriana, I…'

'Please, Seb, let me finish.'

'Sorry.'

'I shouldn't have pried like I said. It's just that after what we did, I felt so close to you and I wanted you to know I'm here to listen if you need me.'

I *was* overthinking. All she was doing was trying to help. To be kind. Unlike me.

'But equally, it wasn't your place to interfere in my life either. You should have been upfront about talking to Stella, you knew my position on that. It felt like I was being conspired against, but now, looking back in the light of day I realise you were scared. Scared to tell me she approached you after I banned you from talking to her. OK, so you could have walked away, but you're only human, and I get that it's not that simple.'

231

'Thank you,' I say.

'And please don't concern yourself with how Dr Adams died, or Ethan. It's got nothing to do with you, and I mean that in the nicest possible way. Focus on your writing, not my problems, OK? I'm telling you as a friend, it's for the best.'

She's scared, I know she is. And I can tell she's trying to protect me from whoever it is she's frightened of. Not for the first time I can't help wondering if she's also received a threatening email. I'm desperate to ask her, but it's too risky. For one, because I've been warned not to, and two, if I'm wrong, it's only going to scare her more.

'OK,' I say.

'So,' she smiles, 'what do you say we start afresh? No more questions. A clean slate.'

I smile back. Amazed and thankful she's being so forgiving. 'I like the sound of that.' I hesitate. 'And what about us? Was last night just a one-off? I mean, I'm fine with that, I understand if you want to keep things platonic.'

'I like you, Seb. But as much as I enjoyed it, I think last night was a mistake. I think it will be simpler to just be friends. That way we can avoid complications like this.'

I feel a huge stab of disappointment as she says this. But I know in my heart it's for the best.

I take her hand. Give it a squeeze. 'Sure, I agree it makes sense.'

At the same time, I think about my meeting with Rick tomorrow, and am instantly filled with shame at the thought of going behind Adriana's back yet again. And yet, I'm desperate to get to the bottom of what feels like something really bad. A mystery that needs solving, even if it means betraying Adriana once more.

I need to know what the connection is, if any, between Ethan's and Dr Adams's deaths. More importantly, whether someone in Adriana's past played a part in them.

And knowing we're going to keep things platonic between us from now on makes my guilt easier to bear.

Chapter Thirty-Five

Adriana

I enter my art studio and shut the door behind me. I haven't been in here for over a week, what with all that's gone on. But it's one of the few places I feel able to close myself off from the world and think. Something I need to do more than ever right now. It was torture acting like everything was fine with Seb just now in the kitchen; looking him in the eye and telling him it was best we keep things platonic between us when all I could visualise in my mind at that moment was him holding me, kissing me, making love to me. When I woke up this morning, I planned on saying I'd overreacted last night and that, before we argued, I'd felt the happiest I had done in weeks. That I didn't want us to just be friends, that more than anything I wanted us to repeat last night. To feel the closeness and warmth of his skin against mine. But all that changed when I checked my phone for messages and saw that I had another email from the bastard who's been watching me and this house.

> Haven't you learnt anything by now, Adriana? After all that happened with Ethan? How can you be so gullible, so needy? So pathetically desperate? If you allow yourself to get close to Sebastian, he's going to

find out your secret, you mark my words. He's already asking questions, talking to others behind your back. He'll wheedle it out of you and then even I won't be able to help you. You need to finish things with Sebastian, because otherwise you'll end up telling him something you shouldn't, and then it'll be too late.

End things, or I'll have to deal with him like I dealt with Ethan. I don't want to do that. Two lodgers meeting a tragic end under your roof in such a short time frame is going to look suspicious, you must realise that. And so I'm hoping you'll see sense and do the right thing. And don't even think about checking your house for listening devices or cameras. If you do, you'll be putting Sebastian's life in danger, and knowing the way you feel about him, I'm guessing that's not what you want. The fact is, you need me to keep an eye on you, even if you don't realise or appreciate it. Plus, don't forget, I know your secret.

End things this morning. Or else…

I wanted to be sick when I read the message. As Seb and I made love last night I knew at the back of my mind that there was every chance we were being watched. But I'd wanted Seb so badly I purposely blotted the thought out. Just as I had this morning when I resolved to tell him that I didn't want whatever we'd started to end. It was dumb of me to accuse him of talking to Stella behind my back knowing someone might be listening at the time. In doing so, I've made this creep angry and potentially put Seb's life in danger. But I was livid that he'd betrayed me. Couldn't help myself, my emotions getting the better of me. Seb is not the enemy, I know that. It's the psycho who's controlling my every move I need to be watchful of. It angers me that he's able to do this and get away with it, but right now I don't see that I have a choice. He has the upper hand while I remain as defenceless as a kitten lost in the wild.

One thing's clear from this latest message: Stella was right – Ethan's death wasn't an accident. He died because of me. I should have told him everything that day he confronted me, but I was scared. Scared about it all coming out. Scared that Ethan wouldn't understand why I did what I did.

I walk over to the far-right corner of the room, come to a standstill next to a large wooden chest containing various art implements, rolls of canvas and my paint-stained overalls. I open the lid and hover there a while. Looking down at its contents.

Knowing that buried at the bottom of the chest lies evidence that could put me behind bars for life.

Chapter Thirty-Six

Adriana

Before

It's a scorcher of an evening in mid-July and I cannot wait to be in the cool of the air-conditioned restaurant Charles has booked for our wedding anniversary. I don't know where we're going, but as he held open the door of the cab he told me I wouldn't be disappointed. I smiled when he said this. I didn't doubt it. It's rare that Charles disappoints me. In fact, I don't think he ever has. Not in a meaningful way, that is. He always seems to get things spot on when it comes to making me happy. It's not like I demand things, I've never been that way inclined. If anything, I always feel a little embarrassed when he buys me expensive gifts or sends me flowers, or books somewhere posh for my birthday because, even after all this time we've been together, I don't truly believe I deserve those things. To be spoiled. When you are brought up to believe you aren't worthy of someone's love and attention, when you are made to feel utterly worthless and unloved from when you are a small child, it's hard to believe otherwise. If only my mother could see me now, I think to myself.

Charles told me to wear something fancy for the occasion, so I decided on the dress he always says I look lovely in. A chiffon sea-green one-shoulder floaty number which falls just above my knee. I never wear anything too short, because I don't feel comfortable doing so, but this feels just the right length, plus it's nice and cool and therefore perfect for a sultry evening like tonight. I'm wearing my hair up, a few loose tendrils framing my face, silver backless shoes completing the look. I feel good, on top of the world, in fact, and as the cab meanders its way through Hampstead en route to wherever Charles is taking me, I almost have to pinch myself because it's hard to believe I am the same girl I was fifteen or so years ago when life barely held any joy or meaning for me, and I sometimes wondered if I'd be better off dead.

'Happy?' Charles looks at me with adoring eyes, squeezing my hand. He knows my childhood wasn't the happiest. That my parents had been neglectful and that I struggled with depression and panic attacks. That from the ages of eleven to fourteen all I felt was angry, going off the rails, lashing out at teachers, at other pupils at my school, playing truant and getting into all sorts of trouble. That this continued for a while after my parents died, but that seeing Dr Adams helped me temper my anger, reinvent myself.

But Charles doesn't know everything, because as much as he loves me, and as much as I know he's a good, kind and understanding man, I'm not sure he'd look at me in the same way were he to learn the extent of what went on in my childhood home; the treatment I was forced to endure, the terrible things I saw. I sometimes feel so guilty for not being entirely honest with him, but then I tell myself: every couple has secrets they keep from each other, and I am sure there are things from Charles's own childhood he hasn't told me about. The point is, we are happy, and I don't want to jeopardise our happiness. I would crumble without him.

'Very,' I reply, planting a soft kiss on his lips. 'You look tired, though, darling. I think we should take a holiday soon, you've been working so hard and everyone needs a break.'

He smiles warmly, his eyes creasing up at the sides as he does so. Revealing prominent crow's feet which would be deemed unsightly on a woman, but somehow look dignified on a man of Charles's age. 'Don't worry, we will. Next month, I promise.'

'OK,' I say, 'but you had better keep to your promise.' I raise my eyebrows, then give him a long drawn-out stare as if to emphasise I'm deadly serious.

He laughs. 'Ha-ha, don't worry, I will, I wouldn't dare break my promise to you, my love.'

Feeling slightly relieved, just because I am genuinely concerned about how hard Charles has been working and can't bear the thought of him running himself into the ground, I say OK and turn to look through the cab window, noticing that we're already in Central London, the traffic having been lighter than usual for a Saturday evening. I adore London at night, seeing all the lights in their full glory. It's magical, and there's such a buzz about the place, so different to where I grew up. I love the vastness of the capital, its cosmopolitan nature, no two areas the same, but mostly I love it because I know I can get lost here. I realise that's precisely what frightens a lot of people about London – its size and anonymity, how easy it would be to find yourself in danger and no one would know. But for me that's its draw. Because I know that here, I am so much safer than I was as a child at home in my tiny village. Where everyone knew each other. Where there was nowhere to run. But, most of all, where *he* could find me.

Finally, the cab turns on to a tiny side street in the heart of Mayfair, and my heart skips a beat because I think I know where we are going. Around six months ago I was flicking through the latest issue of *Vogue* one Sunday afternoon and there was a piece on a new Asian fusion restaurant that had just opened off Dover Street. I had casually mentioned this to Charles but he was busy on his laptop and I wasn't sure if he'd heard me. But clearly, he had. He knows how much I love East Asian food, Japanese being my favourite.

Sure enough, before long, we've pulled up in front of Umai, which has two bouncers on the door, indicative of its exclusivity. Having hopped out first, Charles takes my hand and helps me step elegantly onto the pavement. I am so excited, like a child in a sweet shop, and my heart is almost bursting with love for my husband.

Once inside, the restaurant is everything I hoped it would be. Beautifully decorated with low-level lighting and striking East Asian paintings and sculptures, exquisite bridges link various parts of the restaurant to the other, while tables for two lie adjacent to mini pools of water adorned with brightly coloured exotic fish and gently lapping fountains. I am in heaven. Until, that is, we sit down, and I glance to my right and spot him.

A snake in human form.

The room is suddenly closing in on me. I can't breathe, my throat constricted, my chest tight. It's as if I am a frightened child again.

'Adriana, what's wrong?' Charles asks, his eyes full of concern. 'Don't you feel well?'

The last thing I want is to spoil our special night, but how the hell can I get through this evening while *he's* sitting less than twenty feet away from me? I had hoped never to set eyes on him again.

Or maybe I can get through it? Maybe I just need to compose myself. After all, I've not seen him in years. I'm a different person now. Stronger. Plus, I'm with Charles. He can't hurt me, manipulate me, the way he used to.

'I, I think it's the heat. Not in here, obviously. But today in general. It took it out of me. I just need some water.' I say all this as calmly as possible, even though I'm not sure how convincing I'm being. 'Can you order me some sparkling water? I'll just go and use the ladies, don't worry, I'll be fine, back in a sec.'

My knees are shaking as I get up and fast walk to the ladies. I'd run if I could, but I don't want to draw attention to myself. Frustratingly, the loos are upstairs, and I find myself holding on to the banister tightly to stop myself from tripping up or falling backwards and making the scene I am so desperate to avoid. I reach the entrance, feel a semblance of relief and achievement that I have got this far, but that's when I hear his voice call out from behind. Unchanged. Unmistakeable.

'Scarlett? Is that you? It is, isn't it?'

I haven't been called that name in fifteen years and I want the ground to swallow me up. Want to get as far away as possible from here. But I know that's not an option. I need to be strong, even though I catch myself trembling. Slowly, I turn around, and our eyes meet. His as dark and disturbing as ever.

'Hello,' I say. 'It's not Scarlett. I'm Adriana now.'

'Is that right?' His gaze penetrates mine, as dirty as his tone of voice.

'Yes, Adriana's my middle name. I always preferred it. Mother was the one who liked Scarlett, not me.'

He grins. 'Yes, I remember. Like Scarlett O'Hara. Remember I used to call you that? My ideal woman, feisty and beautiful. And yet in need of a strong man to put her in her place. Tell me, is that how you've grown up to be? I always envisioned you would.'

A shiver runs through me. 'I do remember you calling me that,' I say, even though it's something I've tried so hard to purge from my mind. I ignore his second question.

'So, who are you with?'

'My husband.' I say this firmly, as if to make a point.

He doesn't seem to care. Doesn't bat an eyelid. I should have known it wouldn't put him off. It never deterred him from screwing my mother. 'Ah, how lovely, congratulations.' He couldn't sound more insincere.

'Thank you. And what about you? Are you here with your wife?'

Quite clearly he isn't, but I ask the question all the same.

'No, just some old friends. I'm not married.'

Can't say I'm surprised. He certainly isn't husband material.

'Well, I must use the bathroom,' I say. 'My husband is waiting. It's our anniversary.' A voice in my head is saying hold on a little longer, you've got this, you're doing OK and you can't let him get to you.

'Of course,' he says with a smile. I turn to leave, but just as I do he grabs my bare arm, catching me unawares. My pulse quickens with fear at his touch, although I try not to flinch. It's what he wants.

I turn around. 'What?' I say as calmly as possible.

'It was terrible, what happened to your parents.' His eyes laser through me. 'Tragic. And nothing short of a miracle that you survived. Almost like you had some kind of guardian angel watching over you. Very fortunate indeed.'

What is he insinuating?

'Yes, I'm very lucky,' I say.

'Steph was always so painstaking when it came to blowing out her candles.'

'Yes, she was. But she was only human' – *although that's debatable* – 'and mistakes happen.' I feel like I'm going to throw up any second. I need to get away.

'True, mistakes *do* happen.' He pulls out a card from his jacket pocket. Hands it to me. 'Listen, I'm in town for a few days. If you fancy a drink, just for old times' sake, let me know. It would be good to catch up properly. You're looking good, *really* good, Scar... sorry, Adriana.' There's a pause as his eyes travel over me, making me nauseous. 'Like mother like daughter. I always knew you'd grow up to be beautiful like Steph. But really, she's not a patch on you. I can't help thinking she'd have been very jealous.'

It's meant to sound like a compliment, but the way he says it makes me feel cheap. Dirty. The way he enjoyed making my mother feel cheap. Dirty. Only she seemed to get some perverted kick out of it. I look down at the card in my hand. See that he's now an accountant. Such a normal, respectable job. No one would ever suspect what he got up to in his spare time.

'Thank you.' The words just about escape my lips.

I turn around and make for the washrooms, realising to my dismay that they're unisex. A fad of many modern restaurants these days. I wish it wasn't the case. I'd feel safer in a ladies-only bathroom. Even he wouldn't follow me in

243

there. I find the first available cubicle, bolt the door then sit down on the closed lid and start rocking back and forth. I'm still clutching the business card, feel like ripping it into a million pieces and flushing it down the toilet, where it and he belongs.

But something tells me to hold on to it, a little part of me saying don't do anything rash, it may yet be of some use, even though I can't for the life of me think how at this moment in time.

Chapter Thirty-Seven

Seb

It's Monday and I'm in a small coffee house on Brewer Street in the heart of Soho, waiting for Rick Savage to turn up. I know what he looks like because I found his profile on LinkedIn. Rick is head of risk at some high-flying US insurance company near Liverpool Street station, and so I'm fully expecting him to be as sharp, and as tough, as nails.

I'm glad he agreed on Soho. I can't help feeling it's safer to meet in Central London, where I can get lost in the crowds. Leaving the house earlier, I felt like a fugitive on the run. Looking over my shoulder every few minutes, taking three Tubes even though I didn't need to change lines, doing a circuit of Leicester Square after I'd reached there around midday, then strolling through Chinatown and up Charing Cross Road, occasionally ducking in and out of music shops and bookstores just to make sure that no one was following me. I didn't get the impression they were. And even if I'm wrong, I'm certain I'd have lost them eventually. Then again, who knows? I don't have a clue who I'm supposed to be hiding from. That's what's most frightening. What's really screwing with my head.

The cafe is packed, a heady combination of coffee and delicious-smelling pastries permeating the air. But

I'm not hungry. My stomach is churning at the thought of questioning a grieving father even though I know he wouldn't have agreed to meet with me if he hadn't been curious to hear what I had to say. I'm also dog-tired. Although my bar shift last night was shorter than my usual Saturday stint, mentally I'm feeling drained, from both worry and insomnia. Lying in bed, I kept hearing strange noises, my mind playing tricks on me, mistaking every natural creak and moan for an intruder roaming the house. I also can't get Adriana out of my mind. I keep thinking about our night together, about how things might have been different had I kept my big mouth shut. She left the house before me today. Around eleven. Saying she had a couple of charity-related engagements then was seeing a friend for lunch. I wished her a good day and she returned the sentiment. But it still felt awkward between us. And I hate that.

I sit nursing a large cappuccino at a corner table, my gaze fixed on the door waiting for Rick to appear, hoping I don't look suspicious sitting here alone with nothing but my phone to occupy me. Finally, at five past one he walks in, his eyes cagily scanning the tables.

I raise my hand as subtly as possible, my own eyes doing a circuit of the cafe to check if any customers are looking my way but they're all engrossed in their own conversations which reassures me they're harmless. Rick sees me – I sent him a photo earlier to confirm my identity at his request. He gives a brief nod, then heads in my direction.

'Seb?' he says, plonking his large frame across from me. He's dressed in a suit and is sturdily built. Looks like someone who'd have spent much of his youth on the rugby field.

'Yes, thanks for coming, Rick,' I say.

A waitress comes over and Rick orders an Americano before she leaves us be.

'So, you're her new lodger?' He's a handsome man, but his drawn, sullen expression suggests he's not slept in weeks. Hardly surprising given what he's been through.

'Yes, I moved in last Friday. I'm sorry for your loss.'

'Thank you. It's been hell. For me and my wife. And my daughter, Sara, of course, who was very close to her older brother. Do you work at Ethan's firm too?'

'No. I'm a writer. I saw the ad on a private landlord website. I have no connection to Adriana whatsoever. I understand your son was a trainee at the law firm that represented Charles Wentworth?'

Rick's about to respond when the waitress returns with his Americano. He gives a clipped thanks as she sets it down before leaving us alone again.

'Yes, that's right.'

'I take it you live in London?'

'No. Although I work in the City, the family home is in Guildford.'

'Guildford?'

'Yes. I've commuted to London for work for over fifteen years. Ethan went to Durham University, but his closest friends found jobs up north, so he didn't really know anyone to share accommodation with when he first started at the firm. Neither did he fancy commuting with his old man, which is understandable. He was looking for a room to rent in London before starting his training contract. It was only meant to be until he found his feet and had enough saved to put down a deposit on a flat of his own. He was a stubborn lad. I offered to lend him the money, but he wouldn't take it from me. Was determined to do it on his own. He heard about the room from his partner mentor.' Rick shakes his head. 'I told him not to take it. Sure, he didn't know anyone in London, but I advised him he'd be best finding people his own age to share with. You know, one of those properties where the landlord lets out rooms to various tenants. Safety in numbers and all that.'

'Why wouldn't he feel safe with Adriana?' I ask.

Another shake of the head. 'OK, perhaps *safe* isn't the right word. I just felt it was a bit weird. Living with a widow in her vast house. No offence.'

I hold up my hands. 'None taken. I'm also pushed for money, and the house is so incredible I'll admit it was hard to resist.'

He sighs. 'I get that. It was the same for Ethan. I've been inside the property, and it's stunning. I don't blame you for being tempted. Ethan had an eye for the finer things in life, and when presented with the chance to live in luxury it was something of a no-brainer for him. Sadly.' He pauses. 'So why exactly did you want to meet with me? You mentioned it concerned Ethan.'

'Yes, that's right. I spoke with Adriana's neighbour, Stella Jenkins, who I know you also had a conversation with. She said she was certain she'd seen someone up on the roof with Ethan the night he fell, and that you believed her. Why? I take it you know Stella's an alcoholic as well as a chronic insomniac; something Adriana pointed out to the police.'

'Yes.'

'So what makes you think she's telling the truth?'

'Because I know my son. He wouldn't have gone up to that roof for no good reason in the middle of the night having just come back from a party.'

'But you know he'd taken drugs.'

'So? He'd taken drugs before.'

'People do strange things when they're high. There's always a first time.'

Rick fires me an angry look, then makes to get up. 'I didn't come here to be interrogated. Or have my son's name dishonoured.'

Guilt shoots through me. I see the anguish in the poor man's eyes and immediately hold up my palms. 'I'm sorry, I didn't mean to offend you or your son, please sit down.'

He holds my gaze, then his own softens as he slowly sits back down. He scans the room once more, then says in a low voice: 'Ethan was having an affair with Adriana.'

His revelation hits me like a bullet, jealousy enveloping me. I feel irritated with myself because Adriana's sex life shouldn't be my focus here. I will myself to get a grip even though I feel cross with her for not telling me she had a sexual relationship with Ethan. I mean, why wouldn't she? It feels sly, manipulative even. 'He was? For how long? Did Stella know?'

'Yes, she knew, but I made her promise not to tell a soul. I didn't want word getting around. It's bad enough that my son is dead without adding a sex scandal into the equation.'

Understandable. Maybe that explains the 'look' Stella gave Adriana and me on Saturday evening, seeing us dressed up and on our way out together.

'Anyway,' he goes on, 'I'm not sure they were that discreet about it. I think it started a year or so after he moved in. My son had a way with women. He was good-looking, smart, charming, had everything going for him really. But a bit too much of a roving eye. Adriana's a beautiful woman as I'm sure you've noticed, and I guess it was inevitable they'd succumb eventually. Particularly given her history and them both being attractive people living under the same roof.'

I frown. 'Her history?'

'Yes. Stella didn't tell you?'

'Tell me what?'

'Adriana cheated on her husband.'

I'm gobsmacked by this revelation. And I find it hard to believe. Whenever Adriana talks about Charles it's with nothing but unbridled devotion. It's clear how much she adored him, worshipped him, in fact. I can't imagine she'd be unfaithful.

'How on earth would you know that?'

'Stella saw a man come to the house one time when Charles was away on business. She said he arrived around eight p.m. Let himself in with a key. She waited until gone midnight to see if he left, but he never did.'

'Were there other times?'

'She didn't say so. But perhaps.'

I give an unimpressed look. 'Stella seems like a bit of a troublemaker to me. It's weird, don't you think? Her constantly watching her neighbour's house. A bit *Rear Window*. Have you ever thought perhaps Stella's jealous of Adriana? Or obsessed with her?'

Rick's eyes narrow. 'You're quick to defend your new landlady. Have you fallen under her spell too?'

His steely gaze drills through me. 'No, of course not,' I say defensively.

Rick leans in. 'Look, the way I see it, Adriana pretends to be this innocent grieving widow, but I don't think she's as goody-goody as she appears. And that's something I said to her face. She seduced my son, and was quite possibly unfaithful to her husband.'

I still can't believe Adriana cheated. But the fact that Stella saw a man let himself in with a key is baffling.

'What did Adriana say when you confronted her?'

'She denied it, of course, said Stella had got the wrong end of the stick, and that if I didn't back off she'd file a restraining order against me.' He sits back, gives a heavy sigh. Then drains the last of his Americano. 'But having said all that, I don't think she's to blame for Ethan's death. Well, not directly, that is. She seemed genuinely upset. I can tell it really shook her up.'

I frown. 'What do you mean by "not directly"?'

'There's something I've not told Stella about, because I'll admit she likes a drink and I didn't want word getting back to Adriana before I have proof.'

'Proof? Are you having her followed?'

'Maybe.'

The penny drops. 'There was a man watching me when I moved in last Saturday. I take it that was whoever you've hired?'

He remains poker-faced. Then says, 'Maybe.'

I lean in, almost hiss: 'You can't bloody do that, I could report you. He scared the shit out of me.'

Before I have time to think, Rick grabs my wrist, his eyes ablaze. 'My only son is dead. Do you know what that feels like, to lose a child? No father should have to bury their own son. Something strange is going on in that house and I'll be damned if I let you stop me discovering the truth about what happened to my boy.'

He loosens his grip, his eyes now wet with tears. I glance around the cafe, and notice that we've attracted the attention of two women on a neighbouring table. I smile at them and they immediately look away, realising they've been caught out. 'OK, OK, I understand, I get it,' I say. 'I can't imagine what you're going through. Or your wife and daughter. But what kind of proof are you looking for? What have you not told Stella about? If you don't think Ethan's death was an accident, and Adriana's not directly responsible, then who is to blame?'

He doesn't answer immediately, just looks at me as if he's trying to decide if he can trust me.

I assure him that he can, and at this, he relents. 'Ethan started receiving disturbing emails in the month or so before he died.'

My heart almost stops. 'Who from? And how do you mean *disturbing*?'

'They were from someone claiming to have known Adriana for some time. It was a weird email address: Protego@vistamail.com.'

Fuck.

'They said they were watching him. Warned him that if he hurt her, or asked too many questions, he'd regret it.'

'Ethan told you this? When?'

'The week before he died. He'd been too scared to tell me before. The sender told him he'd be placing both himself and Adriana in danger if he mentioned the emails to anyone.' This is all sounding frighteningly close to the bone. 'But despite being scared, my son was too curious, too much of a risk-taker,' Rick goes on. 'He nosed around and found something in Adriana's study two days before he died. While she was out.'

Christ. I immediately think back to dinner with Adriana on Saturday night. When she told me she found Ethan snooping in her study, and that this led to them rowing and her telling him she wanted him out by the end of the month. But from what Rick just said, it seems Ethan was on his own when he found whatever he did.

Does that mean Ethan confronted Adriana about it, and not the other way around?

Why did she lie to me? Hopefully, that will become clear when Rick tells me what Ethan found.

'He came across her journals. Stacks of them.'

'Journals? That's pretty personal stuff. I guess you can't blame Adriana for being upset.'

Rick leans forward. Whispers: 'Ethan didn't care by this point. He was receiving crazy messages from some lunatic, was at his wits' end trying to find out who could be sending them, and by any means possible. My son was also smart, naturally inquisitive. He was fond of Adriana, didn't want to scare her, alert her to the fact they were being watched. And, like I said, he'd been warned to keep the emails to himself. So it's not like he could ask her outright, he had no choice.'

'I understand,' I say. 'So, what was in the journals?'

'Various ramblings, everyday stuff you might find in a diary. But also, more specific entries. Dating back to when she was a teenager. She talked about her parents' deaths, how she wished she'd had the chance to say goodbye to them despite everything.'

'Despite everything?'

'Yes. Ethan said it read like she'd had a tough childhood. She talked about bad stuff having happened to her, about her mother beating her, and there being someone else in league with her mother who made her life hell, but how going to live with her aunt and uncle was like a new beginning, and that someone called Dr Adams changed her life for the better, opened her eyes to the truth so she was finally free. She mentioned missing her two childhood friends, how one of them made her feel so bad for deserting him, but that leaving Devon was the best thing that ever happened to her.'

'Devon?' I say. 'That's where she's from?'

As I ask the question, I can't help wondering what Adriana meant when she referred to Dr Adams changing her life for the better, to opening her eyes to the truth so she was finally free. It seems like pretty heavy stuff for a teenage girl.

'Seems so. But there was one thing that stood out.'

'What?'

'She wrote in a later entry how she wished she could have told Charles everything, that she hated lying to him, but that she'd had no choice but to keep the truth about what she'd done buried.'

'What she'd done? What did she mean by that?'

Rick shrugs. 'I'm guessing cheat on her husband.'

I frown. 'But *buried*'s a weird choice of word, isn't it?'

Rick shrugs again. 'I guess. It was clearly something bad. Something she's not proud of. She went on to say how she couldn't believe *he'd* hunted her down, having thought she'd never set eyes on him again.'

I frown. 'Who's he? Again, "hunted" seems like a strange word for a lover.'

Rick appears to think on this. 'You have a point.'

'So maybe it wasn't a lover. Maybe it was the same person in league with her mother, as she put it?'

'I don't know. But I do wonder if it's the same person who sent Ethan the messages.'

And me, I think to myself.

'Although when I asked Ethan about this,' Rick continues, 'he became vague.'

'Vague?'

'Yes, like he knew something else but wanted to speak to Adriana first before telling me.'

'So, based on the emails Ethan received, you think someone's stalking Adriana? Someone potentially dangerous from her past, who was jealous of Ethan's relationship with her?'

Rick nods. 'I'm sure that's a large part of it. Things were OK before they started sleeping together. I know Ethan tried to ask Adriana about her childhood before he found the journals, but she told him it was none of his business. It only made him more curious. And then, when he later confronted her about what she'd said in her journals, including the stuff about her childhood, she went berserk. Told him he had no right to read her private thoughts. That she wanted him out.'

'Ethan didn't think to tell Adriana about the emails at this point? She might have been more forgiving, more willing to open up about her past if she knew he was receiving threatening messages.'

'No. He was too afraid of what the sender might do to Adriana if he did. It was clear their every move was being watched. He thought the house was bugged, because the sender knew stuff, intimate things he and Adriana had done. Poor boy was being blackmailed into keeping his mouth shut.'

As am I.

Rick stops talking, pain etched across his face. 'There's one other thing Ethan said to me the last time we spoke. The night of the party.'

'Oh, what's that?'

'He said he believed the key to everything was in Adriana's art studio, but that he couldn't get access to it because she keeps it locked up.'

I frown. 'Her art studio?' I think about how Adriana always maintains it's her private workspace, which is why she doesn't allow anyone inside without her express permission. But perhaps there's more to it than that. As Rick seems to be suggesting.

'Why would Ethan think that?' I ask.

Rick shakes his head. 'I don't know. Ethan didn't elaborate. Again, I think he must have found something in the journals and wanted Adriana to tell him of her own accord before he told anyone else. Poor boy wanted to give her a chance. They'd been sleeping together, for God's sake, and I genuinely think he'd come to care for her. It's why he didn't move out instantly, after she went crazy at him. I think the morning after the party he was going to try and reason with her. Possibly even tell her about the emails. But, of course, someone saw to it that he never got the chance.'

Rick pauses to wipe a stray tear from his eye. I can't begin to imagine what the poor guy is going through. We've only just met, but it breaks my heart to see him broken like this.

'The really sad thing is,' Rick carries on, 'that keeping quiet got Ethan nowhere. Perhaps, as you say, if he'd told Adriana about the emails she'd have understood. She might have let him into her past and they could have gone to the police together if she knew who was watching her. But he didn't. And all she saw was a massive betrayal of her trust. I know she blames herself for telling Ethan she wanted him gone, possibly even thinks it might have tipped him over the edge. But I don't accept that; my son was stronger than that. He genuinely wanted to help Adriana, to find out who it was she was so afraid of. It's why he went to see Stella. He knew she'd lived next door for a long time, and thought she might have some answers. But, like I said, Adriana had been just as reticent to talk about her childhood with Stella as she had been with Ethan. Which tells me something truly awful must have happened. Well, we know it did, because the journals imply as much.'

Just then something occurs to me.

'Did Ethan ever think about talking to her therapist?' I ask. 'Dr Martin?'

'I'm not sure. Perhaps. But doctors are bound by confidentiality, as I'm sure you know.'

I nod. 'The night I moved in, Adriana told me a child psychologist she used to see in her teens after her parents died had recently passed away. He was based in Guildford. Like you.'

'That must be the Dr Adams she refers to in her journals. I think I read about his death in the local paper.'

'Yes, probably. Her aunt and uncle took her to see him when she went to live with them. Mainly to help her deal with her grief. I get the feeling she told him a lot about what went on in her childhood. More than she's perhaps confided in Dr Martin.'

'Yes, I sense that too, from the little Ethan recounted to me from her journals. Such a shame the man died.' Rick sighs. 'He would have been a good person to speak to.'

I hesitate, realising the police haven't yet made Dr Adams's true cause of death public. Then I whisper: 'It turns out he didn't die of natural causes. He was poisoned.'

'What the hell?' Rick's face is aghast.

'Yep. Adriana told me on Saturday night. It really shook her up. She'd only seen him the Thursday before last.'

'Christ.'

'There's more. The day before he died, Dr Adams called Adriana saying he urgently needed to see her again and they agreed on the Monday afternoon. But on Sunday evening, around eleven, she got an email from him cancelling. He said something had come up and he'd be in touch to rearrange. But the thing is, we now know it can't have been him who emailed Adriana because he was already dead. The post-mortem suggested he died around four p.m. on the Sunday.'

'Jesus. So you think the person who was threatening my son, who might have killed him, possibly killed this Dr Adams too?'

'Yes, I mean it's a definite possibility,' I say. 'And I wouldn't be surprised if the same thought's crossed Adriana's mind. But unlike Ethan, Dr Adams would have been privy to details Adriana told him in confidence about her childhood. I'm wondering if he found out some new information recently. Something that either paints Adriana in a bad light or exposed who killed Ethan. Perhaps his killer got wind of this and murdered Dr Adams to put a stop to him talking before he had the chance.'

Rick rubs his forehead. 'Shit. It's possible, I guess.'

'Do you think it's worth speaking to someone Dr Adams worked with, his secretary perhaps, see if they can help? You live in Guildford, maybe you can pay her a visit? If you're up to it, that is.'

'Yes, sure, no problem, leave it with me,' Rick says, 'I'll see what I can find out. This may be my best chance to discover what really happened to my boy.' Just then, he frowns. 'There's one thing that's bothering me.'

'What?'

'You've just moved in with Adriana, and you're suddenly asking me all these questions. Forming all these theories. Why? Why not stay out of it?'

'I already explained, Stella approached me. She told me about seeing Ethan on the roof with someone.'

'But you said yourself you're not sure her testimony can be trusted.' He squints, as if trying to gain the measure of things. Then I see a flash of recognition in his eyes. 'You've received an email too, haven't you?'

I feel my cheeks burn. I try not to fidget in my seat but my awkwardness is telling.

Rick leans in. 'It's OK, you don't have to say anything. You're being blackmailed by the same arsehole. My advice, get out now. Don't get involved. It's not your battle to fight.'

'I can't,' I whisper. 'The email warned me I'll be placing Adriana's life in danger if I leave.'

I don't mention that I'm also worried that whoever this nutjob is, they might dig deeper into my past if I don't comply.

He sighs. 'Same dilemma Ethan had. But look where that got him, you need to look out for number one.'

'I can't do that, my conscience won't allow it.'

He sighs again, only more heavily. 'And that could be the death of you.' There's a pause, before he says: 'What I don't understand is why this psycho doesn't just let you leave. They're clearly obsessed with Adriana, so driving you out should be what they want, surely?'

I shrug my shoulders. 'I don't understand it either. Perhaps it's all part of some sick, twisted game they're playing. Perhaps they know it'll look suspicious me leaving so soon having just moved in. Also, what's to stop me from going to the police and telling them about the email once I leave? This way I'm trapped, at their beck and call.'

'True,' Rick acknowledges. We sit in silence for a moment.

'So you've hired someone to monitor Serenity House?' I say eventually. 'To see if whoever this creep is shows their face?' I wonder if Adriana suspects Rick hired a private investigator to watch the house? Or maybe she thinks it was Rick himself? Perhaps that's why she was so snappy with me last Friday evening when I asked her who she thought the strange man might be. That was before I'd spoken to Stella, of course, when Adriana was trying her level best to keep the ugly possibility about how Ethan really died from me, along with her altercation with Rick.

And before either of us knew Dr Adams had been poisoned.

'Yep, but so far he's found nothing,' Rick says. 'It's only been a couple of weeks and I'm guessing the bastard's lying low.'

'What I don't get is how he gained access to the house.'

Rick shakes his head. 'I can't answer that, but it's not impossible these days. If you know the right people and have the means, it's possible to infiltrate the most secure of buildings. And there're a lot more places to hide in big houses.' He leans in, gives me a stern look. 'Which is why I'm warning you to keep your distance from your landlady. Don't get involved with her the way Ethan did. Because if you do, I'm almost certain things won't end well for you.'

Chapter Thirty-Eight

Adriana

Before

It's been two days since I saw him, and I've hardly slept in all that time. Barely eaten either, my stomach heaving at the thought of the way his eyes wandered over me, remembering the touch of his hand when he reached out and grabbed my arm. Just thinking about it, I feel so dirty, so reviled. Lying in bed now, I play back the encounter, wishing to God that Charles and I had never set foot in that restaurant. Why did he have to be dining there of all the thousands of restaurants in London, and on that day of all days? It's as if fate has conspired against me. Punishing me even though I am the least deserving of punishment. I wanted to call Dr Adams, tell him everything. After all, he knows what happened to me as a child. Back then, he urged me to go to the police, but I told him no. My parents were dead and there was no way of proving what went on. It was my word against *his*, plus the last thing I wanted was to draw attention to myself. I yearned for a fresh start, to get away from my past, not dredge it up in public. And now, with so many years having passed, and Dr Adams being so proud of me for conquering my demons and making something of myself after I never thought I'd amount to much, I guess I don't want him to think that I've regressed. That I can't handle a little adversity. After all, it's not as if the bastard can hurt me the way he used to.

Poor Charles has no idea what I'm going through, of course. When I eventually returned to the table that night, he looked worried. Commented that I didn't seem like myself. That I appeared troubled, distant. I could hardly blame him for being concerned. For one, I'd been away nearly half an hour. And two, having attempted to compose myself in the washroom, I was aware of how pale my skin looked, my eyes having lost their earlier sparkle. Really, I wanted to get the hell out of there, especially as *he* was still sitting less than twenty feet away from me, occasionally stealing sly glances our way. But I also couldn't bear to give *him* the satisfaction of watching me squirm, of seeing that I was frightened, and that he still exercised a power over me from which I would never be free.

I told Charles that I was fine and repeated my earlier excuse that the extreme heat we'd been having had got to me and that once I had something to drink, I'd feel better. He thought I meant water, but I didn't. I meant something far stronger. And after three glasses of champagne, I managed to calm down, although my appetite remained poor. In all honesty the rest of the evening passed in a blur, and I can barely recall what I said, even being there at all. All I wanted was to be able to get through it without having to face him again. The strongest part of me willing me on. And I thought I was almost there. But then the thing that I had dreaded most happened.

He got up and walked over to our table. Stood there looming over us like the Grim Reaper.

'It was so nice to see you again, Adriana.'

I almost died on the spot when he said this, a voice in my head telling me to keep it together, that this hideous moment would pass, that I wasn't a child any more, and that he couldn't hurt me. Even so, the little food I'd had repeated on me, while the champagne burned my gullet.

I saw the confusion on Charles's face as he looked from me to *him* and then back to me again. Naturally, Charles had no idea who he was, no inkling of the history between us.

Swallowing down my fear, along with the vomit creeping up my throat, I managed a smile. 'You too, I hope you have a lovely rest of your stay in London.'

He returned the gesture. Only his was the smile of a monster. 'Thank you. I intend to.' The way he reinforced those last three words disturbed me. And then there was an unsettling pause, in which I prayed he'd leave us alone or, better still, keel over with a heart attack.

I also prayed that Charles wouldn't ask the one question I knew must be going over in his mind. But he did.

'So how do you two know each other?'

It caused another uneasy silence, my mind trying to think up something, anything, but the ghastly truth.

'I'm an old friend of the family's,' he said. 'After Adriana's parents died, we lost touch, sadly. Tell me, did you lose contact with your other friends too? Your school ones, I mean. I remember there being a really troublesome one. Got you into all sorts of mischief. Which was so unlike you.'

I knew full well what he was getting at, but I wasn't going to rise to the bait, even though something inside me was itching to tell him to fuck off and die. In fact, at that moment my mind was in a state of flux, torn between wanting to lash out at the bastard and keeping silent for Charles's sake.

'What a coincidence bumping into each other here,' Charles said cheerily. Completely oblivious like the darling, trusting man he is.

'Yes, coincidences happen, I guess,' I said.

'Are you here for work?' Charles then asked him.

'A university reunion actually,' came the reply as he looked back over his shoulder.

'Ah, how nice. I love meeting up with my old mates.'

A painful silence ensued, and it was all I could do to stop myself from screaming at the top of my lungs: 'Fuck off!'

'Are you OK, darling?' Charles then said. 'You look a little flushed.'

'Just the champagne,' I lied.

'Anyway, I understand it's your anniversary,' the arsehole said, 'so I won't disturb you lovebirds any longer.' His gaze flitted between the both of us, before it rested on Charles. 'Nice to have met you.'

'Likewise,' Charles replied, before the demon's eyes reverted back to me.

'Great to see you looking so well and content, Sc… sorry, Adriana. You deserve it after all you went through.'

Again, something inside me was saying *I want to rip your cold heart out and burn it*, but instead I managed a faint thank you and then, just like that, he returned to his table.

I prayed to God it was the last time I would ever set eyes on him, ignoring that little part of me which said my prayers might be in vain.

Chapter Thirty-Nine

Seb

It's four p.m. and I'm on a Northern line Tube back to Hampstead, my mind replaying my conversation with Rick. The carriage is packed. So many faces of different colours, ages, genders, faiths. I view them all suspiciously, the way people tend to eye strangers on the Tube. Only in my case, it's because I can't help wondering if one of them might be the psychopath making my life a living hell.

I grasp one of the handholds tightly as the carriage careers from side to side, nearly missing my stop because all I can think about are Rick's revelations about Ethan and Adriana and the fact that Ethan too received threatening emails. I'm annoyed with myself for still feeling jealous of their relationship. Can't help wondering if this is some kind of fixation of Adriana's – picking up younger men, making them her lodgers and sleeping with them. Is it a power thing? Does she get off on luring young, single men into her bed? Then again, I'm sure I wasn't imagining the easy chemistry between us, or the warmth of her touch. It didn't feel like she was just using me for sex. Our lovemaking had been tender, intimate. She had let me take control, not the other way around. And afterwards we had lain in each other's arms, happy and content. Before I blew things.

I get off the carriage and battle my way through the crowds to the lifts which will take me up to the exit. As I stand impatiently with a load of other commuters waiting for one to arrive, I realise Rick is right. If I don't watch out, I'll end up like Ethan. He was warned not to go snooping, but he went and did it anyway and it cost him his life. I understand him being frustrated, desperate to know who was behind the emails, but I have to be craftier than him. That aside, I'm more convinced than ever that Ethan should have confided in Adriana. She saw his actions as disloyal, but she may have been more under-standing had Ethan been truthful about what motivated him to read her journals.

For this reason, I make up my mind to tell Adriana about the email I received. Along with my suspicions that whoever wrote it may have killed both Ethan and Dr Adams. I hate the fact that I'm going to be laying more stress on her, but I don't see that I have a choice. Hopefully, once I tell her, she'll open up to me. Tell me about her childhood, her journals, who the person was she referred to as having hunted her down. And, crucially, what it is she wished she'd been honest with Charles about, having felt she had no choice but to keep it buried? I'd be lying if I said I wasn't scared, but I'm also determined to find out who this monster is and bring them to justice, for Rick and his family's sake, as well as my own. They cannot be allowed to get away with their crimes.

Obviously, I can't talk to Adriana in the house, though. Somehow, I need to get her to meet me elsewhere. Some-where neutral, preferably noisy, where there's no chance of us being overheard. But how to engineer that now she's made it clear we need to keep things platonic between us? It's not like I can suggest dinner or drinks somewhere, which would smack of a date.

There's nothing else for it. I need to be blunt. I'll send her a text making it clear there's something urgent I need to speak to her about, but that it's too dangerous to discuss inside the house. I don't want to frighten her, but neither can I see another way. Besides, I have my suspicions she knows more than she's letting on.

Time is ticking, and I'll be damned if I live my life to the tune of the arsehole who's watching me a second longer.

Together, Adriana and I might just be able to nail the bastard.

Chapter Forty

Adriana

Before

It's gone eight on Wednesday evening when the doorbell rings. I jolt in fright. Wonder who it is. I'm not expecting anyone. Charles is away overnight in France on business, and I am all alone in the house. He was still concerned about me before he left. Said I hadn't seemed like myself since our anniversary dinner last Saturday. That I was acting aloof, troubled. Depressed, even. Disappearing for hours without a word, failing to answer my phone when he called from work to check I was OK. He said he didn't mind postponing his trip, that he could send his brother, Stuart, instead. I was half tempted to take him up on his offer, because the fact is, he's right. I haven't felt like myself at all, far from it if truth be told. I don't even know what I'm doing half the time, I feel in such a daze, still unable to believe what happened in the restaurant. But in the end, I felt too guilty. Ellen, Stu's wife, is heavily pregnant, and I'd never forgive myself if she went into labour while he was away and he missed the birth. So, despite still feeling unnerved by my unwelcome blast from the past, I told Charles I'd be fine. After all, it's just one evening. I can cope with that. Even if it means staying awake all night because I feel too afraid to close my eyes.

I've only just finished eating. After working out in the gym for an hour, I showered then made myself a healthy prawn stir-fry. As I stirred the food, I sipped a cold glass of Chardonnay, and it relaxed me a little. I know I shouldn't rely on alcohol to relieve my stress. And I don't normally. But in the last few days it's helped take the edge off. And what with me being alone in the house overnight I'll do whatever it takes to get me through to daylight hours.

The bell goes again. Only this time it's a grating, protracted ring. Signs of an impatient caller. Aggressive, even. I wipe my mouth with a napkin, then gingerly get up from the kitchen table. My heart is pounding as I move to the hallway, and then I nearly collapse in shock when I see on the video cam who's standing at the door.

Then again, perhaps it's stupid of me to feel surprised, to wonder how he found me. After all, I'm married to one of London's most prominent businessmen. It wouldn't have taken too much detective work, despite my concerted efforts to avoid being photographed and lack of social media. Especially for a devious lowlife like him. But what the fuck does he want? Why has he turned up on my doorstep at this late hour out of the blue? I'm a grown woman now. I'm married, with money and connections. He knows that he'd be foolish to try anything. Surely, he's not that arrogant?

More ringing.

Don't answer the door.

My throat is suddenly bone dry. It's a struggle to swallow, but I manage somehow. I press the intercom, then say, trying to hide the crack in my voice: 'Why are you here? What do you want?'

'You invited me.'

'What? Don't be ridiculous, you're the last person I'd invite.'

'Look, I need to speak with you.'

'About what?'

'It's easier if I come inside.'

'You must be joking. How do I explain that to Charles?'

'Charles isn't here.'

Terror shoots through me. He knows I'm alone. 'How do you know that?'

'Because I watched him leave earlier with an overnight bag.'

'You've been stalking our house? You sicko. I'm calling the police.'

'I don't think that's wise.'

'And why's that? I'll tell them what you did to my mother. The sick things you made her do. Forced me to watch on those repulsive recordings you made.'

'And you think they'll believe you after all these years? How are you even going to prove it?'

He has me there. There is no way I can prove it. But he is harassing me right now. And I have every right to tell him to leave.

'Whatever,' I say. 'The fact remains that you're harassing me now. And if you don't leave, I'll have no option but to call the police.'

'And if you do that, I'll have no choice but to tell them what I know about you. Stuff your mother told me about the company you kept as a child. You know what else I think? I don't think your parents' deaths were an accident.'

I've no idea what he's talking about. He's speaking in riddles. Trying anything to unsettle me, break me. The way he used to. It's just a game with him. It always has been. He's sick in the head, gets off on controlling women. Particularly attractive women.

'I'm not kidding, I will call the police. Now fuck off, you complete and utter shit.'

I stride away from the hallway, having checked the door is locked, tempted to phone the police, but then hold back. If I do, it will all come out. My grim past. I can't bear for Charles to know what my mother was really like. The things I saw her do. The things *he* made me watch. The scandal could ruin everything he's worked so hard to achieve. I couldn't do that to him.

Despite bolting all the doors, I go to the kitchen and grab the largest knife I can find, keep it close to my side as I make my way downstairs to my art studio. It's the one room in the house I feel safest, particularly when I am alone. I will go there, stay all night in there painting if I must. Just to take my mind off things. To wait for this night to pass and the morning sun to appear.

I open the door to my safe space, shut it behind me. But I don't lock it, on the off-chance I need to make a quick escape, even though I know I am being irrational, because nothing and no one is getting inside this house.

I tell myself to stay calm even though adrenalin is coursing through my veins. I badly want to call Charles. Just to hear the sound of his voice. For him to soothe me. But what would I say? How would I explain my fears? *The person I've spent years hiding from is standing outside our front door. The nice chap and old friend of the family you met last weekend. Who I said nothing about afterwards. Even when you asked me repeatedly what was up because I looked like I'd seen a ghost.*

The same arsehole who's responsible for me not seeming like myself these past few days. For my appearing down and depressed. For not answering my phone.

I will myself to get a grip, and instead turn my mind to my latest project. A portrait of Charles. A surprise for his birthday next month. I'm nearly there, and perhaps if I work through the night, I can finish it.

I put on my overall and feel my heartbeat slowing, then go over to my workbench and mix up some colours, feeling more confident that he's finally got the message and has disappeared, this time for good. My back is facing the door, so I don't see the handle turn. Don't see him walk in. 'Hello, Scarlett.' Fear races through me, and I almost can't get enough oxygen into my lungs.

How the hell did he get inside the house? It's all I can think as I turn around slowly and see him standing there. I curse myself for not setting the alarm. It's triggered by any movement in the hallway and lower ground floor, meaning I wouldn't have been able to come down here to my studio. In hindsight I should have switched it on and gone upstairs, locked myself in my bedroom. But it's too late now. From the corner of my eye I spy the knife lying tantalisingly within my reach on the workbench to my right. If only I could somehow get hold of it.

'There's no need to be afraid, I just had to see you again. You've become such a beautiful woman. I knew you would. Plus, I think behind that butter-wouldn't-melt exterior, you're a bad girl, who's done bad things. And I can't tell you how much of a turn-on that is for me. Are you not a little bit pleased to see me?'

My stomach flips, and I want to hurl. Is he serious? If only I could reach the damn knife.

'How did you get in?'

'A friend of yours gave me the code to your spare key box. I must say, I found that a bit of a turn-on too.'

I frown. 'What? Who? What are you saying? You're talking rubbish. No friend would betray me like that. You need to leave now.'

Besides, the only people who have the code are Charles, Stuart and my aunt and uncle. There's no way any of them would give it out to a total stranger.

Closer still. And then he grabs me. Not like before, all those years ago. When he grasped me by my hair and threatened me. Told me if I dared breathe a word he'd make sure my father lost his job. No, this time he does so around my waist, a lecherous look in his eyes. I shut my own tight.

Tell myself that soon this nightmare will be over.

Chapter Forty-One

Seb

When I get back to the house the cleaner's been and gone, and I find Adriana alone in the kitchen cradling a mug of tea.

'Hi,' she says, glancing up at me. 'Good day?'

She doesn't look well. Her lovely face is drawn and pasty, but given our row on Saturday night I'm too afraid to remark on this for fear of upsetting her. I also can't risk giving whoever's watching us further reason to attack me, the way they attacked Ethan. Speaking to Rick has strengthened my resolve to beat this bastard, but I'm also fully aware I can't be gung-ho about it. These walls have ears. It's why, although I'm desperate to tell Adriana everything, for now I know I must hold back and wait for my chance to get her out of this house where we can speak freely. So, in response to her question, I simply smile and tell her I've had a great day. Lie about meeting up with a friend for lunch, then visiting an exhibition at the National Portrait Gallery before coming straight home. She smiles, appears to believe me, even though it feels like the deception is written all over my face.

'And how was your day?' I ask her.

'It was fine,' she says wearily. 'I went into town for a meeting with the head of one of the charities I support.

We're organising a fundraising walk to coincide with the death of Chelsey Donavan, the little girl who was abused and killed by her stepfather six months ago. You may have read about it in the newspapers?'

'Yes, I remember it being quite a high-profile case. Absolutely tragic.'

Adriana sighs, her eyes glassy. 'Words can't express just how tragic. Even now, campaigning all this time for various charities, hearing the numerous stories of abuse and child cruelty that goes on, I can't fathom the evil done to children.'

I nod, give a sad smile, not for the first time wondering if Adriana is speaking from personal experience.

'Just so you know,' she continues as I go to grab some juice from the fridge, 'I'm having some impromptu drinks here tomorrow evening. In aid of the fundraiser. I know it's a bit of a pain, but it's really important to me. You're welcome to join, it won't be a late one. I'll be busy getting the house in order during the day, so I apologise in advance for the disruption.'

My heart sinks. What she's doing is admirable, but it also couldn't be any worse timing because now she won't have time to meet with me. Plus, the last thing I want is to upset her before the drinks; they're important to her, like she said. She's so fragile and stressed with all that's happened, she needs this in her life right now. Something positive. I can see that. I resign myself to the fact that it'll have to wait until Wednesday morning.

'Sure. No problem.' I force a smile. 'Not sure I'd be comfortable joining, though. I don't know anyone.'

'Why don't you invite Jasper and his girlfriend? Instead of them coming over on Wednesday. That way you'll know someone, and it'll kill two birds with one stone.

Stuart, my brother-in-law, is coming. And Aunt Georgie and Uncle Philip. I'm sure they'd all love to meet you. I think my aunt and uncle will stay the night. You don't mind, do you?'

All at once my spirits rise on hearing Adriana's aunt and uncle will be at the drinks. This is my chance to chat with them, and perhaps gain some insight into their niece's childhood. I'll obviously have to phrase my words carefully. I can't have them growing suspicious and reporting back to Adriana. She'll never agree to meet with me outside the house then; she may even kick me out.

'Of course not, it's your house,' I say. 'It will be lovely to meet them.'

Adriana smiles, then gets up from the kitchen stool. 'Well, I'm going to take a bath. I'll see you later.'

She walks away and I feel a slight ache in my chest, remembering how less than forty-eight hours ago we made love. But then I tell myself to snap out of it, that I need to focus and keep my wits about me if I am to defeat the person who's watching me.

There can be no room for error.

Chapter Forty-Two

Adriana

It's Tuesday evening, and I'm looking forward to hosting the drinks tonight, if only to feel a little normal for a few hours. It's been two days since I received a third message and I've not heard anything more since. The wishful part of me hopes that whoever's behind the emails has had their fill of tormenting me. That they've decided to leave me alone, now I've made it clear to Seb that I just want us to be friends. It's hard being around him, not being able to reach out and touch him. I should never have given in to my feelings, but what with the wine we drank that evening, the way he'd listened so patiently to me, the longing I'd seen in his eyes that matched my own, it had been impossible to resist. I'm praying that, with time, things will get easier between us. We'll just have to ride things out until July when our agreement is up and then I'll ask him to leave. Hopefully, whoever's watching me won't have a problem with that, even though July feels like a lifetime away, and I still have no idea what they plan on doing with the items they stole from the safe in my study on Saturday. My journals. It has to be the same person who took them. Although perhaps they won't do anything. Perhaps taking them was just another trick to unsettle me, keep me under their control. Make me suspect Seb, turn me against him. Come July, I'm determined to find out for certain who the hell this tyrant is, though, even if it means risking my secret coming out. I won't act now, because I can't bear the thought of another person I care for getting hurt. But the moment Seb's lease is up all that will change, because I've come to realise this is no way to live. I just hope I'm strong enough to get through the next six months without going insane. Then again, maybe I won't have to wait that long or act of my own accord. Perhaps the police officers looking into Dr Adams's death will find something to nail the murderous son of a bitch. I spoke to one of them earlier. Told him about my recent visit to Dr Adams, and the fact that I was supposed to be meeting him again last Monday but that someone pretending to be him – presumably, his killer – had emailed cancelling our appointment late Sunday evening. The officer was grateful, said I'd been most helpful and would keep me informed of any developments going forward.

Dr Martin also rang, to ask how I was doing. I haven't told him about the emails. I lied and said all was well, and thankfully he seemed content to leave it at that. Relieved that the email he received appeared to be a one-off. I felt bad for lying to him, and I do wonder if he secretly suspects all's not as rosy as I made it out to be, but again, I don't want to bring him any deeper into this mess. I can't have him meeting the same fate as Dr Adams. I asked him how things went with Dr Adams's ex-wife and daughter. He said they were understandably still in shock, but determined to bring the killer to justice. Apparently, forensics have been all over Dr Adams's house and office, scouring every nook and cranny for any possible clue. I just hope and pray they find something soon. For all our sakes.

It's seven p.m. and I'm in my bedroom getting ready. I'm wearing a deep blue Bardot-style knee-length dress. I've straightened my hair, the sapphire earrings Charles bought me for my thirtieth birthday completing the look. Aunt Georgie and Uncle Philip arrived around five. It was so good to see their friendly faces, feel their warm embraces. They'd reiterated how sorry they were about Dr Adams, and hoped I was doing OK. I saw the worry in their eyes, the fear that I might regress to a dark place, but I assured them that I was better for seeing them, despite the child in me bursting to confess that I was far from OK, that my every move was being watched and that whoever's stalking me may well have killed Dr Adams.

At that point Seb appeared. They exchanged pleasantries and Aunt Georgie later took me aside when we'd gone to make some tea in the kitchen to say what a lovely young man he seemed. I said I couldn't agree more and left it at that. I couldn't begin to imagine what she'd think of me if I admitted to sleeping with Seb the day after he moved in. Like mother, like daughter perhaps. She knew what her sister had been like, and although we never discussed it in detail, she was also aware my mother had cheated on my father. I would never want her to know the hideous ins and outs of all that went on in our house, and I'd begged Dr Adams long ago to keep the truth to himself. Something I feel sure he did to his last breath. Aunt Georgie never knew about Ethan and me either. At least, I don't think she did. The less people who know the better. If she knew, she might suspect his death may not have been an accident; that maybe someone disapproved of our relationship, and that might put her at risk from whoever is watching this house. I can't have Aunt Georgie asking questions and end up being this maniac's next target.

Just then, there's a knock on the door. I go to answer it and see Aunt Georgie standing there. 'Darling, you look beautiful,' she says. 'Just to say the first of your guests have arrived, so you might want to come downstairs. The catering team have things under control, so don't worry about that side of things.'

'Thanks, Aunt Georgie, you look lovely yourself.'

She does, dressed in a velvet green A-line dress with short sleeves. I notice she's lost some weight, presumably the result of her starting up Zumba classes at her local gym.

'Thank you.' She hesitates, then says: 'Are you sure you're OK? I can't help worrying, because I know you, and although you always look wonderful, my intuition tells me you're not coping as well as you let on. I can see it in your eyes, can tell you've not been sleeping great.' She takes my hand. 'Come on, pet, a problem shared is a problem halved. Isn't that what Dr Adams used to say?'

He did, and it's then that I can't stop the tears from amassing and rolling down my cheeks.

'Come here,' Aunt Georgie says, taking me in her arms and pulling me close.

'I'm just so tired of it all, Aunt Georgie,' I say. 'Ever since Charles died, things have never been the same.' It's a lie. Really, things have never been the same since that godawful night. But I can't tell her that. Too much time has passed, and she'd be appalled if she knew my secret. Plus, like I said, I can't risk placing her in danger.

'I know,' she says soothingly, stroking my hair. 'It's been tough, I just wish you could find someone new to share your life with. I can't help thinking that would help. I know you're lonely and it's why you have a lodger, but you need some romance in your life, someone who can fulfil your every need. And I think selling up and moving away from here would do you wonders.'

I could have moved a long time ago, I suppose. Destroyed the one piece of evidence that implicated me. But in truth, I was scared of being caught in the act. Particularly when Charles was alive. I couldn't risk bringing his name into disrepute. And then, after he died, with time it just got harder. Keeping the evidence inside this house always felt like the safest option. Even if it was the most cowardly.

I break free from Aunt Georgie's embrace, wipe my eyes with the backs of my hands, realising I'll have to retouch my make-up before I go downstairs. 'Maybe,' I say, just to appease my well-meaning aunt. 'I'll think about it. Anyway, give me five minutes to sort out my face, and then I'll come down if you can keep my guests entertained until then.'

'No problem, darling,' she says before turning away and leaving the room.

I go over to my dressing table and sit down. Stare at my reflection in the mirror, unsightly streaks of foundation and black mascara staining my cheeks. And that's when my phone lying to my right buzzes. A text. I pick it up tentatively. Fear choking me.

It's from Dr Martin.

Adriana, I need to speak with you urgently.
Can you come and see me this Friday
morning? I'm in Bristol today and tomorrow
at a conference, but it's imperative we
speak. Let me know if 10 a.m. suits?

I wonder at the urgency of Dr Martin's request. Perhaps
the police discovered something? They went public with
Dr Adams's murder last night. Then again, why not pick
up the phone and tell me? Why the need to see me in
person?

I trust that he must have his reasons, and text him back.

Yes, of course, I'll be there at 10. Hope
everything's OK. See you then. Adriana.

I see to my make-up, then get up and make for the door.
Ready to put on my best face for my guests and play the
part of perfect hostess.

Chapter Forty-Three

Seb

I'm standing in the lower ground floor function room chatting to Jasper and Rochelle when Adriana appears. As usual she lights up the room, donning a smile that could launch a thousand ships and make the most anxious of people feel at ease. No one would suspect that behind that radiant visage lies a woman damaged by loss and harbouring a fragility only a few of us are alive to. I long to take her hand, to ask her if she's OK, if she's aware she's being watched and has any idea who might be behind it all. But for now, that will have to wait. Tonight, I must play along, pretend all is well, not just for her sake, but for Jasper's. I can't let him into my turmoil, can't risk his life.

Rick texted earlier to say he'd spoken to Dr Adams's secretary but that she hadn't been able to offer any helpful insight into her boss's murder. The poor woman was devastated and, like most people, couldn't think who would want him dead. It's disappointing, but at the same time fortifies my belief that the same person who's watching me killed both Dr Adams and Ethan.

Right now, the room is only a quarter full, but I expect it won't be long before the remaining guests arrive. The catering staff Adriana's hired seamlessly circle the space offering mouth-watering canapés served on silver platters, along with crystal flutes of Moët & Chandon and non-alcoholic options. Considering the cause, it seems a little decadent, but I'm guessing most of the guests are loaded and used to only the good things in life. If this is the way to get them to sign a cheque, then so be it.

I'm captivated by Adriana as she circulates the room with ease, meaning I fail miserably to take in what Jasper's just said. 'Hey, Earth calling Seb, come in, Seb. Take your eyes off your landlady for one second will you and shut your mouth, it's not polite.'

'Jaz, don't embarrass the poor guy.' Rochelle softly nudges Jasper in his side as I come back to reality and feel my cheeks grow hot at being caught out.

'Jesus, Jasper, could you be any more indiscreet, keep it down, will you?' I say through gritted teeth, conscious that Adriana's aunt and uncle are standing only a few feet away from us talking to a couple of guests. Even so, I'm glad Jasper and Rochelle are here. I'd have felt incredibly awkward if they weren't.

'Sorry,' he apologises.

'Don't mind him,' Rochelle says with a smile. 'And I can't say I blame you, Seb, I can hardly take my eyes off her myself.'

I don't always see eye to eye with Rochelle but right now I'm grateful for her show of solidarity.

'So, you like the place?' I ask her, changing the subject.

'It's amazing, exactly how Jaz described,' Rochelle says. 'And you're happy, so far? I mean, I know it's been less than a week, but you're finding your feet around the area? It must feel a whole lot safer than where you were before.' She giggles as she says this, giving Jasper an impish look with no clue as to how far off the mark she is. How could she? Looking around, I'm in the seemingly perfect home, in one of the most prestigious areas of London. How could anyone guess that these last few days it's felt like I've been living in a closed box, where the air is gradually getting thinner? Suffocating the life out of me.

'Yeah, I couldn't be happier.' I hear the slight catch in my voice as I say this. So subtle that Rochelle doesn't notice. Unlike Jasper. He glares at me, an expression of *what the fuck?* I return the gesture in the split second Rochelle looks away, as if to say *not now*, although as far as Jasper's concerned, I don't want there to be an ever. At least, not while we're in this house.

I wonder if we're being watched this very second. It's noisy in here, animated chatter and laughter filling the air around us, so I imagine it's next to impossible to make out individual conversations. Still, I can't take a chance and say anything too provoking. It's too dangerous.

'I think I'll go and introduce myself to Adriana, let you guys catch up,' Rochelle says, much to my dismay. There's no avoiding Jasper's questions now. But just as she moves away, Adriana's aunt and uncle come over, rescuing me from his line of fire. He gives me a look that tells me I'm not getting off that easily.

Uncle Philip is the first to speak. He's a tall, wiry man, with a soft voice and neatly trimmed white beard. 'Seb, how are you finding the evening, a bit overwhelming, I expect? I don't know most of these people myself. I usually spend much of the time chatting to Stuart, Adriana's brother-in-law, but he couldn't make it in the end. Still, we like to support Adriana's charitable endeavours whenever we can.'

'It is a little overwhelming, I guess,' I reply, 'but all in a good cause, as you say. I'm sure Adriana really appreciates your support.'

'Yes, it's very kind of you,' Jasper chips in. 'I expect it's been a difficult time for you all, what with Ethan's death.'

For God's sake, Jaz, was that necessary?

Thankfully, Uncle Philip interprets Jasper's comment as one of mere concern, rather than fishing. 'Yes, it's been extremely tough on Adriana. She's been through so much in recent years and now this latest blow has really hit her hard.'

'She was that close to Ethan?' Jasper says.

Oh God.

'No, not Ethan,' Aunt Georgie interjects, 'although she was fond of him, granted. Philip meant Dr Adams.' She narrows her eyes at her husband, as if to get him in line with her train of thought. 'Our *family* doctor.'

'Ah, I see, I'm so sorry,' Jasper says. 'What happened, did he die?'

'Yes,' Uncle Philip says. 'But it's more than that.' He looks around the room warily, says in a low voice, 'I shouldn't be saying this, but if you read about it in the papers you'll wonder why I failed to mention it. The police did go public last night.'

Shit.

'Mention what?' Jasper says, cutting me one of his looks.

'Apparently, Dr Adams was murdered.'

At this, Jasper's jaw practically drops. I dare not look him in the eye.

'Adriana was very close to him, so it was quite a shock,' Aunt Georgie goes on.

'Yes, I can imagine,' Jasper says. I feel his gaze boring through me but I still don't make eye contact. 'I'm so sorry, it can't be an easy time for any of you. Have they caught his killer?'

'No, not yet,' Aunt Georgie says with a heavy sigh. 'I can't for the life of me think who'd want him dead. No money was taken, nothing obvious was out of place in his house, so I hear. Although the police are still looking. I know his ex-wife quite well and we spoke just yesterday on the phone. They were still close, and she said he'd never mentioned falling out with anyone, or having trouble with any of his patients. He had no money issues either, so it's something of a mystery. When Adriana's parents died she went through a really tough patch. So much anger inside her. So much grief. But Dr Adams was a godsend. He helped her turn over a new leaf and feel good about life again.'

'I really am very sorry,' I say.

'Thank you.' Aunt Georgie smiles. 'Anyway, onwards and upwards as they say. I'm glad you've moved in, Seb. I hate to think of my little girl being alone in this big house with no companionship. I keep telling her to move, but she won't have it.'

'Why's that, do you suppose?' Jasper asks.

'I think it allows her to still feel close to Charles.' She sighs. 'Another tragic waste. My poor girl, she's had so much sadness in her life.'

I glance at Jasper, and can tell what he's thinking. That Adriana is a curse on anyone who gets close to her. I want to tell him he's wrong, that it's not her fault. But I can't get into that now.

Just then Adriana taps the side of her champagne flute to call for everyone's attention, before thanking her guests for coming and talking a bit about the fundraising walk and several other initiatives in the pipeline. She speaks so eloquently, her voice animated, her mood seemingly elevated by the evening's success.

It makes me nervous for the conversation I plan on having with her tomorrow, presuming she agrees to meet with me. A conversation I know is going to be difficult for both of us, but which could help zero in on who's watching this house.

Chapter Forty-Four

It was impossible to discern from the recording I made all that you were discussing with her aunt and uncle last night, Sebastian. So much noise, chatter and commotion. Despite zooming in, my lip-reading skills still leave a lot to be desired. Having said that, I got the feeling from your friend's facial expressions – he really doesn't know the meaning of discreet, does he? – that Dr Adams's unfortunate passing may have come up in the conversation. I saw the way he looked at you, the way you avoided his gaze after listening to what her aunt and uncle, whose mouths are a little too big, had to say. It clearly made you feel uncomfortable, Sebastian, and I can't say I blame you, because it's none of his fucking business. I'm pleased you appeared to have followed my instructions and not told him about my messages. Nor Adriana. You'd be wise to keep this up if you wish to stay alive. I can just about cope with you staying with Adriana for a short while so long as you follow her rules and refrain from asking meddlesome questions. And then, when you do eventually leave, which I'm hoping will be in July when the tenancy ends and a decent amount of time will have passed so as not to make your leaving look suspicious, I'm confident you won't blab to anyone, simply because I see the way you look at her and feel sure you'll do anything to keep her safe. Especially when I make the stakes clear to you.

He really is trouble, that friend of yours. Doubtless he believes Adriana to be cursed; finds it suspicious that so many of her loved ones end up dead. He has no idea how clueless she is about the whole thing, that I'm the mastermind behind it all. That I take care of things on her behalf, because if I don't, she'll fall to pieces. It's been that way since we were kids.

And it's how it's going to be with Dr Martin. I know she's agreed to meet with him on Friday. She wrote it down on her calendar. She won't be there, though. I'll make sure of it.

I will be, though. My first and last encounter with the good doctor. One that will hopefully be swift.

And close the lid on any possibility of the truth coming out.

Chapter Forty-Five

Seb

'Thanks for meeting me.'

It's two p.m. on Wednesday and I've been sitting at a snug table inside the Punch & Judy pub in Covent Garden for less than ten minutes waiting for Adriana to arrive. She looks harried as she sits down across from me, her eyes full of suspicion given the cryptic text message I sent her first thing this morning.

After everyone left last night, we sat in the kitchen with Adriana's aunt and uncle, drinking cocoa and nibbling on the last of the canapés, while reflecting on how well the evening had gone. Adriana seemed relaxed and in good spirits, partly the result of a successful event but also, I think, having her uncle and aunt there for support. They left at lunchtime today, although I said my goodbyes around eleven. In hindsight it was unrealistic of me to have imagined I'd get the chance to ask them about Adriana's past. Even casually. Not only would it have been a strange question to ask on the basis I've been living with her all of five minutes, there was also never an opportune moment.

Writing is also proving to be an impossible feat for me right now, and with my imminent conversation with Adriana weighing heavy on my mind this morning I've found it hard to sit still. That being so, I went into town early, stopping off at Regent's Park for a long walk to clear my head, before hopping on the Bakerloo line to Piccadilly, then strolling to Covent Garden where I find myself now.

Adriana orders a Diet Coke, while I plump for a beer, in need of some Dutch courage.

'Any more news on Dr Adams?' I ask, just to break the ice, even though I know it's not the most cheerful of topics.

'No,' she says. 'Nothing since I told the police about my meeting with him that Thursday. Apparently, forensics are still combing his house and office – his laptop, phone and so on – for any evidence as to who's behind it all.' She pauses. Then says: 'What's all this about, Seb? What could you possibly need to talk to me about that we couldn't discuss at home?'

This is it. I do my best to pluck up the courage to tell her why I've asked her here. 'I'm sorry to have dragged you all the way into town, but I had to be sure we could talk freely.'

Adriana's eyes zip around the pub, while I notice her fiddle with her wedding band. She looks at me anxiously. 'You're scaring me, Seb. Please, no more games, whatever it is you have to say, please say it.'

I take a deep breath, then just come out with it. 'The night I moved in, well, in the middle of the night really, after we'd had dinner, I received a threatening email.'

Adriana gasps.

I plough on. 'Whoever sent it, told me they were watching me. They warned me not to hurt you, and made it clear that something bad would happen to Jasper if he asked any more questions. And by that, I'm presuming they meant about Charles's and Ethan's deaths. They also hinted at being behind what happened to Ethan.'

Adriana's face is suddenly drained of colour.

'Whoever it is, it's clear they're watching us both. That somehow, they've infiltrated your house. They also claimed to have known you for a long time. I'm taking a big risk in telling you this, because they said if I tried to leave or alert you to their threats I could be putting your life in danger. But I'm also hoping that's a bluff and all part of this sicko's game in wanting to control me. Control you.'

'Seb, you promised me there'd be no more secrets between us! You bloody well said it to my face on Sunday morning, and yet you've kept something so huge from me. That's why you were so keen to know if I was hiding something, wasn't it? Why you asked about my upbringing, whether there was someone in my past I was scared of while we were in bed. It wasn't just about your conversation with Stella.'

I reach out and grab her hand, but she snatches it away just as the waitress returns with our drinks. There's an awkward moment of silence as she places them down, before leaving.

'Look, I just explained why.' I can't help thinking how unreasonable she's being, but she's probably just scared, her emotions getting the better of her. I keep talking. 'They said I'd be endangering your life if I told you. I wanted to, believe me I did. But I was too scared. You must understand that, surely? If this person killed Ethan and Dr Adams, they're not to be fucked with, they mean business.'

She narrows her eyes. 'So why tell me now? What's changed?'

Shit, she seems so mad, do I tell her about my meeting with Rick? Yet another instance of me going behind her back. She may even see it as me conspiring against her, may never trust me again. But then, if I don't tell her and she finds out later, it'll only make things worse. I'm damned if I do and damned if I don't!

On balance, I decide it's best to be honest, which also includes telling her about the emails Ethan received. I won't mention I know about the journals for now, though. It's a risk, but hopefully she'll open up to me about those after she hears what I have to say.

'Look, don't get mad, but getting the email scared the hell out of me. And then when Stella approached me and explained her theory, I was even more scared. I knew I couldn't put you at risk. And it's why I decided the best person to talk to might be…'

'Ethan's father.' Adriana finishes the sentence for me.

I lower my eyes. Give a meek: 'Yes.'

'How could you go behind my back like that? You know he hates me.'

'I'm sorry, I was going crazy, and I was desperate for some answers. And he doesn't hate you. He thinks you're hiding something, though. That you're scared.'

'And what else did he tell you? Anything useful?'

'Yes.'

'Like what?'

'He told me Ethan received threatening emails too. It's why he spoke to Stella, and went looking in your study.'

'What?' Adriana looks visibly shocked. Her face having regained some of its colour turning pale once more. 'Why the hell didn't he tell me?'

'Same reason I didn't. Whoever sent the emails made it clear he'd be putting your life in danger. He was trying to protect you. But like me, he couldn't bear to be at this psycho's beck and call any longer. He needed answers, to find a way to put a stop to it.'

Adriana puts her head in her hands. Presses her fingers against her temples. 'Fuck, I feel so guilty. If I'd known he was asking questions because he was being threatened, it could all have turned out so differently. I'd never have spoken to him like that, never have kicked him out.' She looks up and I see tears streaming down her face. I want to reach across and take her hand but I'm not sure how she'll react.

'I know how upset you must be. Rick told me that you and Ethan were *close*.'

She looks up. Seemingly embarrassed. 'Ethan and I were a mistake.'

'Like we were a mistake?'

She leans in. 'Look, I'm not some sex maniac, if that's what you're thinking. I don't go luring young men into being my lodgers for sex. You have to believe me. Things just happened after a time with Ethan. He wasn't exactly shy about coming forward. But with you...'

'With me what?' My heart accelerates as I wait for Adriana to finish her sentence.

'With you I felt this instant connection.' She stares deeply into my eyes. 'Not just physical but emotional. You're kind and gentle like Charles, but you also seem slightly broken, like me. And it's why I asked if there was anything you needed to get off your chest.'

Hearing her say this, I feel bad for having even contemplated that sleeping with her lodgers is some kind of fetish for Adriana. I smile, as if to reassure her. 'Look, you don't have to explain or try to defend yourself. I'm a grown man and so was Ethan. It takes two to tango. And I know what you mean about the connection between us. I feel it too.'

For the first time since she got here, Adriana looks at me with a softness in her eyes. We don't speak for a moment, but it's not awkward. Rather, it's comforting. But then she breaks the silence.

'Seb, there's something I need to tell you, now that you've been so honest with me.'

I lean in, take her hand. She doesn't rebuff my touch, which gives me a glow inside. 'What is it?'

'I've also been getting emails.' *Shit. Emails?* Not just the one like me. And there was her accusing me of keeping secrets. Still, I tell myself to rise above it. 'They warned me to be on my guard with you. To not get close to you. Said they believed you were hiding something, but that if I told you about the messages, I'd be placing your life in danger. I was going to get the house checked for spyware but I was warned against that too. I've felt so scared, so trapped. Knowing my every move is being watched. It's why I told you I wanted to keep things platonic between us. Because whoever this sicko is, they said if I didn't, I'd be putting your life at risk. But that's not everything.'

'No?'

'Dr Martin was the first to receive a message.'

'Dr Martin?'

'Yes. The day before you moved in I went to see him and he showed it to me. It was sent to him on the Tuesday, the day after we first met. Telling him to warn me to be on my guard with you because they were sure you were hiding something. It felt like friendly concern. But the ones after, the ones sent to me, were more vicious. Threatening. As if they didn't like how you and I seemed to be getting on, almost as if they were jealous. I think that's why they contacted us. Because they wanted to put a stop to it.'

I sit there, stunned. I always sensed something had shaken Adriana from the day I moved in. Only because she seemed less relaxed than the first time we met. I thought it was perhaps just the shock of Dr Adams's death. But now I know different. That, like me, she's being terrorised.

'I'm sorry I didn't tell you,' she says. 'You must think me a bit of a hypocrite.'

'It's OK, it's understandable. Have you told Dr Martin about the other emails?'

'No, I haven't. I was too scared. Plus, I didn't want to put him in danger.'

'But what about the one he received? He must have been concerned? Even if it was friendly.'

'Yes, he was. He wanted me to go to the police.'

'Why didn't you? At that point, there was no threat to my life.'

She hesitates. 'I thought it might be a one-off. Charles got crazy messages all the time. I hoped it would go away.'

I look into her eyes and can tell she's keeping something from me. Something she's too afraid to talk about. But I don't press the issue for now.

'Have you any idea who it might be?'

'No.' She shakes her head firmly. A little too firmly, perhaps. 'At first, I thought maybe it was Rick or Stella. Wanting to get back at me. For not taking Stella seriously. I even thought that perhaps the man you saw on the street was Rick. Watching me. But now I don't think so, based on what you've told me. Poor Rick. Why didn't he go to the police with this? Or tell me, at least?'

'I'm not sure. I guess maybe he lost faith in them after they dismissed Stella's claims. And perhaps he thought you might accuse him of making it up. I also think he wanted to get more proof.'

She frowns. 'More proof? How?'

'He's got an investigator watching the house.'

'What?' She twigs. 'So that was the man dressed in black you saw?'

'Yes. But so far, he's not come up with anything helpful. Tell me again, the night Ethan died, you heard nothing?'

'No. I remember taking ages to drop off because I was still cross with Ethan. Well, more like really upset. But once I was asleep, I was dead to the world. Didn't hear a thing.'

'Think again. Think hard. Any old boyfriends, or someone in your past who might be jealous? Or was perhaps a little controlling, a little unhinged, even back then?'

I watch her think on this for a second or two. A nervous glint in her eye. But then she shakes her head. 'No.'

Again, I'm far from convinced she's being honest with me. And no mention of Ethan looking at her journals either. Why? There must be something in them she's petrified of coming out. And it's possibly why she didn't want Dr Martin alerting the police. Her failure to open up to me is frustrating, but I don't want to lose her trust by pressing the issue. I try a different angle. 'It's looking more and more like whoever this psycho is, killed Dr Adams. Wouldn't you agree?'

She nods. 'Yes.'

'Who knew he was your doctor back then? When you were a teenager, I mean?'

'Just my aunt and uncle. Some people at my school. My teachers, close friends. They all knew he was helping me deal with my grief.'

'What about later?'

'Well, there was Charles. I'm not sure if he told Stuart. He may have done, they were very close, and I wouldn't have been cross with him for doing so. And Dr Martin, of course.'

'Ethan? Stella?'

'No, I never told either of them about Dr Adams. It was private. I only told you because he died.'

I feel deflated. I had so hoped asking the question might have sparked something. 'Perhaps ask your aunt and uncle if they ever told anyone?'

'I can't imagine they would.'

'Just in case.' I hesitate.

'What?'

'Can you think why this person would want to hurt Dr Adams? Anything you might have told him? You said you went to see him the other Thursday because you were still feeling fragile after Ethan's death.'

'Yes, that's right. I just needed to see a friendly face.'

'Did you tell him that you and Ethan argued the night before he died? That he'd been asking questions about your past.'

She hesitates. 'Yes, I did. But even so, it's confidential. Dr Adams would never have told a soul. Not even my aunt and uncle. I trusted him implicitly.'

She seems so sure of herself, and again, I'm stumped. There must be some reason, though. Clearly, this person viewed Dr Adams as a threat. 'There's nothing else you told him? A secret perhaps?'

Adriana looks taken aback. 'A secret? Why would you think that?' she asks defensively.

It's clear from her reaction that I've hit a nerve. And that she's hiding something. But what?

'Sorry, I didn't mean to imply anything. I'm just trying to think of a reason why this person killed Dr Adams, and him knowing something they didn't want getting out seems like the logical conclusion.'

She nods. 'Sorry, yes, you're right. It is logical, but honestly, I can't think what.'

'It's OK. Whoever this person is, they're clearly obsessed with you, and jealous of you getting close to anyone.'

'But what about Charles? I lived many happy years with him.'

It's a good point. One that baffles me. 'That's true,' I say.

'I'm scared, Seb. I don't know what to do. Don't know how we get ourselves out of this.'

I reach across the table and take her hand once more. 'I think we need to bring the police in. It's the only way.'

'What? Are you crazy? We'll be putting our lives in danger.'

'True. But how can you live like this? It's no way to exist, our every move being watched. And who's to say they'll make good on their threats? It could be a bluff.'

'And what if it isn't?'

I frown. Frustration getting the better of me. I can't hold back any longer. 'There's something else, isn't there? Something you're not telling me.'

It's obvious from Adriana's guilty expression that I'm right. 'Yes. I'm sorry, I lied when I said I've no idea who might be sending the emails. It's complicated, though. They have something on me.'

Finally. 'What?'

'I can't say. But you're right about me having a secret. It's something that could destroy me. Put me away for a long time. But please know I did what I did because I had no choice. They're using it to blackmail me into keeping quiet. That's why we can't go to the police.'

Her explanation is something of a relief. It at least allows me to make sense of her behaviour. 'Is that why you were so keen to shut down Stella's claim to have seen someone on the roof with Ethan?'

'No, that happened before the emails started. But you're sort of right. I wanted as little contact as possible with the police. The last thing I need is to draw attention to myself or the house.'

'The house?'

She shakes her head. 'I, I didn't mean the house per se, I just meant me and my life. Look, I did something I'm not proud of, but I had my reasons like I said. And I'm not a bad person. You believe me, right?'

As I look into her eyes, I do believe her. I wish she'd trust me enough to tell me what it is, but I'm not one to talk. I've not been honest with her about who I am, about my past. How or why should I expect any different from her?

I sit back, let out a sigh. 'So what the fuck do we do? I'm all out of options.'

'I don't know,' she sighs. There's a pause. Then she says: 'I'm seeing Dr Martin on Friday.'

'Oh?'

'Yes, I normally see him every fortnight, but he texted me yesterday saying he needed to speak to me urgently about something.'

'Really? I wonder what it could be?'

'No idea. Although I do wonder if he received another email. But then why not say so over the phone? I know he's been helping the police with their enquiries. Perhaps he discovered something important. Something he felt the need to share in complete confidence.'

'Yes, perhaps. What time are you meeting him?'

'Ten a.m.'

'OK. Well, let me know if he says anything helpful.'

She gives me a bleak smile. 'Will do. Look, Seb, I know this is hard, but for now I think we need to lay low, ride it out, and not do anything to aggravate this monster. I can't bear the thought of any harm coming to you, or anyone else I care about.'

Her expression is so sincere, it warms my insides. I hate that we're both at the mercy of this arsehole, and it bugs me that she's not being upfront about who she thinks it might be. But at least now I know why.

Hopefully, the police investigating Dr Adams's death will find something. For now, I focus on my meeting with Trevor Carrington tomorrow, and pray that I finally get some answers about my dad.

Chapter Forty-Six

Adriana

I can't believe Ethan didn't tell me about the emails. It breaks my heart to think he was suffering in silence all that time, being terrorised, blackmailed. All because he was trying to protect me. No wonder his father was spitting mad, he had every right to be. And now the same thing is happening to Seb.

For five years I lived a quiet, admittedly lonely life. Losing Charles crushed me, but at least there were no emails, no sinister goings-on. My life was relatively stable. Peaceful. But it seems as soon as I took in a lodger, things started to take a disturbing turn. The way it did after that night. The night that led to the near breakdown of my marriage and left me tied to this house. Whoever this person is, it's clear they'd rather I live a solitary existence than be intimate with a man. They say they want to protect me, but really, they want to control me. It's a possessive kind of love, rather than unconditional.

I wish I could talk to Dr Adams about it. But I can't. I told Seb to leave things for now, that we needed to ride things out and hope the police investigating Dr Adams's murder find something to nail the bastard who killed him. But with each day that passes I'm slowly losing hope.

So, I've made up my mind. I'm going to confess my secret to Dr Martin when I see him on Friday. The guilt and the shame are eating me up and I can't live like this any more. Neither can I continue to be a puppet to the monster who's pulling my strings.

At least then my conscience will be free, and no more harm can be done to the people I care about.

Chapter Forty-Seven

Seb

It's one p.m. on Thursday, and I'm sitting at a table in The Spaniards Inn, waiting for Trevor Carrington to arrive. I know what he looks like from his Facebook page. Plus, there are numerous photos of him on Google Images from his job working at a top chartered accountant's firm in the City. He seems like a good guy, a family man with three daughters and a wife who used to be a GP. But then again you never can tell what people are really like behind closed doors. He could be a psychopath for all I know.

Things felt awkward between Adriana and me before I left to come here. I guess it's understandable given what we discussed yesterday. It's hard to act naturally, have a normal conversation, and I only hope whoever's watching doesn't suspect we've confided in one another. After we talked in the pub, we left separately. We thought it safest. As I watched Adriana walk off, I felt a mixture of relief and disappointment. Although it's good to have got things out in the open about the emails we've both been receiving, it's not like I'm any closer to discovering who's behind them. A task made more impossible now I know the sender has leverage over her. I'm desperate to know what that leverage is, but right now I don't hold out much hope of her telling me. She's clearly scared out of her wits, but being kept in the dark grates on me all the same.

I can't think about that now, though. For now, my focus must be my dad. But as I wait for Trevor to arrive, my hand clasped around a pint of beer, I'm not sure what to expect from our meeting. Obviously, I'm hoping Trevor can provide me with some answers. Then again, Dad turned out to be such a secretive man, I wonder if it'll prove to be yet another fruitless exercise.

The pub is packed, and I was lucky to get a seat. But it's also a good thing. Less chance of us being overheard. Finally, he appears and spots me instantly. He comes over and I immediately stand up and shake his hand. He's a tall, well-built man, his face tanned from the Florida sunshine. 'Seb, it's good to meet you, son. I'm sorry for all you've been through.'

'Thanks,' I say. 'What can I get you?'

'Ah, well, if you're sure, I'll have a Guinness.' He smiles. 'As much as I love Florida, that's one thing I found hard to come by in the States.'

'Coming right up.'

After a bit of a fight to get to the bar, it's another ten minutes before I'm back sitting across the table from Trevor.

'Thanks for agreeing to meet.'

'It's not a problem. So, what is it you wanted to ask me?'

'I know you and Dad's other university friends were the last people to see him before he sent Mum his suicide note. Aside from the staff at the hotel where he was staying, of course.'

He nods. 'Yes, I believe that's true. That's what the police said. Bill and Paul, who your dad studied maths with at uni, organised the reunion. It had been twenty years since we all first met.'

'Yes, I remember the morning Dad left. He was so excited to see you guys, said it had been ages, and that he was looking forward to catching up. No suggestion whatsoever of him being depressed or troubled by something. But did he seem different to you? Did he show any signs at all he might end his life?'

Trevor shakes his head. 'Absolutely not. He seemed in the best of spirits. That's why his suicide came as such a shock. He told us how well he was getting on at work, having just been made a senior partner. Said Yvonne was thriving with her charity work, as were you at school.'

I frown. As odd as it might sound, I was hoping Trevor's response would be different. That perhaps, after one beer too many, Dad had let him into the darkness clouding his life, given some insight, some hint, of what he was about to do. Owing to the demons he felt unable to fight off.

'I'm sorry I can't be of more help, I was just as shocked as you when I heard the news,' Trevor says. 'I couldn't believe it, if I'm being honest. None of us could.'

'Thank you,' I say. 'Do you remember much about the restaurant you went to? I'm just trying to paint a picture of Dad's movements while he was here in London.'

Trevor takes a long slug of his pint. 'It was an Asian fusion place in Mayfair. It was Mike's – one of the other guy's – suggestion. He was into that kind of food, said he'd read rave reviews, and we all liked the sound of it.'

'Do you remember the name?'

'Umai. Yes, that was it. I believe it's still there, although not quite as happening as it was back then.'

'And nothing out of the ordinary occurred while you were there? Dad didn't seem bothered or distracted?

He didn't speak about meeting anyone else in London? Someone he'd perhaps lost touch with?'

'Why would you say that?'

'Because of this.' I pull my wallet out from my jeans pocket and retrieve a business card that's been tucked inside since it first slipped out of one of Dad's crime fiction books that Mum kept after he died. She hadn't kept them all, just the ones I was keen on, and which I inherited following her death. I hand the card to Trevor who takes it from me, looking somewhat perplexed. 'Does the name mean anything to you?'

He reads the front of the card. 'Frederica Bailey, CEO of Female Aid.' Then looks up at me, his expression still quizzical. 'No, I don't know the lady.'

'Look on the back. At the scribbled name. It's Dad's handwriting. Ring any bells?'

'Scarlett Monroe. No, I'm sorry, I don't know either name.'

I slump back in my chair. Another dead end. Trevor was my last hope. None of Dad's other friends scattered all over the country were able to shed light on the name when I asked them.

'Again, I'm sorry I can't be of more help,' Trevor says. 'I realise how hard this must be for you.'

'Thanks, it is,' I say. 'I mean, a part of me gets it. Dad was so ashamed of what he'd done, what he was, that he didn't feel able to live with himself. That's what he said in his suicide email, at any rate. But the thing is, he never gave off any signs of being suicidal. And that makes me suspicious. Makes me think there's more to it than meets the eye.'

'How do you mean?'

'It's hard to explain. I just get the sense that something happened here in London to rattle him. He travelled here specifically to meet you guys but for some reason extended his stay at the hotel. He told Mum it was work-related but we all know that's not true. And crucially, they never found his body. Something feels off.' I pause. 'Is there anything else you can think of, anything at all that might help?'

Trevor seems to consider this for a while. 'Well, there was one thing.'

'What?'

'We'd just finished our starters, when your dad excused himself to the gents. We thought nothing of it, of course, but he was away for perhaps fifteen minutes, and I remember we all took the mick when he got back. Asked him if the chilli prawns he'd had had perhaps disagreed with him. He said he'd bumped into an old friend. Then pointed to a couple sitting at a table perhaps twenty feet away. I'd noticed her when she came in, just because she was stunning.'

'Who was she?'

'At the time I didn't know, he didn't elaborate. But towards the end of the evening he went over to talk to them.'

'And then?'

'And then he came back and we asked him how he knew them.'

'What did he say?'

'He said he knew the wife from a long time ago. Said his father had been her father's boss.'

'In Devon, you mean? Where my dad grew up?'

'Yes. He said it was a bit of a tragic story as the wife's parents died in a fire when she was a young teenager.'

I freeze. 'A fire?' I repeat.

Trevor nods. 'He said he hadn't seen her in years, because when her parents died her aunt and uncle became her guardians and she moved away.'

No, this can't be. 'What was her name?' I ask, so quietly I can barely hear my voice.

'Are you OK? You've gone quite pale.'

'I'm fine. Please, tell me her name.'

'I can't recall the wife's name. But I do remember the husband's only because he was well known in business circles. Charles Wentworth. Poor man died of a heart attack a few years back, I remember reading in the paper. Such a shame, I heard he was a nice fellow. I feel sorry for the wife, they seemed like a lovely couple.'

I feel like time has stopped. I came here seeking answers and now it seems that the truth may have been staring me in the face.

'Gosh, I wish I could remember her name. Lovely-looking woman as I said, now what was it?' Trevor drums the table with his fingers, but I fear I already know the answer.

'Adriana,' I say. 'Adriana Wentworth.'

Trevor raises his eyebrows in surprise. 'You're right. But how the devil did you know that?'

'Because she's my landlady.'

Chapter Forty-Eight

Adriana

Before

I wake up on the cold stone floor of my art studio. I'm lying on my side, shivery and hungry, and still in the clothes I was wearing last night. For one blissful moment I forget that he was here in my house, that he'd grabbed me by the waist and tried to assault me. But then, just like that, it all comes back to me with startling clarity. And I wonder to myself how many other women he violated back then? How many children he tormented.

How many more since?

What happened? And how the hell did he get in? Clearly, he was lying about a friend of mine giving him the code to the spare key box because only family members have it. I suppose, if he's been watching me it's possible he figured out a way to get inside. He may be a scumbag, but he's a clever scumbag. After all, he's managed to pull the wool over everyone's eyes until now.

I slowly raise myself up, feeling groggy and a little unsteady on my feet, almost like I've been drugged. I glance to my right, and that's when I see him. Lying spreadeagled on the floor. My heart pounds. I automatically look around for the knife I brought down from the kitchen, thinking maybe I killed him in self-defence, but it's still lying on the workbench in the exact same place I found it, plus I see no sign of blood.

Is he actually dead or has he passed out? Slowly, I stand up, go over to the workbench and grab the knife, just in case. Nausea grips me like barbed wire around my insides and it's a struggle not to vomit as I creep over to where he's lying to take a closer look. There's definitely no blood. But he's lying so still he must be dead. I bend down on my knees, lean over and put my ear to his chest. Hear nothing. See no sign of it moving. No indication that his ugly heart is beating inside it. He is dead, that much is clear. But how? A heart attack perhaps? Did we struggle, and in that struggle, he went into cardiac arrest? It's all such a blur. The last thing I remember is him grabbing me by my waist.

But it's then, as I look up to my right, in the direction of the door, that I see something pinned to it. A piece of paper that wasn't there last night. Gingerly, my heart beating so fast I almost can't breathe, I get up and go over to the door. Read the note.

> *You're welcome. He won't hurt you any more. You're free. Report this, and you will go to prison and Charles will be ruined. I'll see to that. Keep it a secret, hide the evidence, and you'll never hear from me again. Your choice. I hope you choose wisely.*

Fear pulses through me as I realise what this means. That the man I hated with every inch of my being didn't have a heart attack, but was murdered. But how, and by whom? Someone else he abused? A victim's loved one seeking revenge? Perhaps they followed him here, hell-bent on revenge? I've not been upstairs yet. They may have smashed a window for all I know. I never switched on the alarm. Or perhaps it's someone from my past who knows what I suffered at his hands? Could it have been the same person who gave him the code to the key box? Did *they* drug me? Is that why I feel so woozy?

I won't lie. I'm glad the bastard is dead. I'm not sorry one bit about that. But it doesn't change the fact that his corpse is lying in my studio and I need to think quickly. I can't go to the police, tell them what happened, that much is clear from the note. There's also every chance they won't believe me and will think I killed him. Neither can I risk Charles's good name being dragged through the mud by allowing the truth to come out. I know it's a risk, that someone may have seen him enter the premises last night, Stella at number 6, for example. But even if she was watching, like I know she often does because she has nothing better to do than spy on her neighbours, I have to hope she was plastered as usual. No one will believe her fantasy stories then.

I frantically look around the room, my mind working overtime, desperately trying to think of a way out of this. I mean, it's a dead body, it's going to stink to high heaven before long, so what the fuck am I going to do? But that's when, as blind panic shoots through me, I spy my drying cabinet in the far-left corner, where I store and protect my ceramic pieces during the drying period. Yes, yes, that's it, I'll hide him in there. With the high humidity it's my best option to mask the smell. I'll cover the cabinet with a weighted blanket, and pray for a miracle. Pray that the heat will shrivel his body to bones before long.

I'm too nervous about trying to get the body out of the house. I'd have to bury it in the woods or throw it out to sea, but what if I'm caught in the act? Or the police find it – they're bound to conduct a widespread search – and discover traces of my DNA despite me taking precautions. Or worse, I'm spotted on CCTV. No, it's safest keeping the evidence in my studio. Charles never comes in here without asking me, he knows it's my sanctuary.

This is the safest place. No one will ever know the man who made my life a misery lies within these four walls.

I will tell no one. My secret will be safe. And, with any luck, I'll never hear from Jason Stevens's killer again.

Chapter Forty-Nine

Seb

Dad knew Adriana?

It's 3:30 p.m. on Thursday and I'm still trying to get my head around this bombshell, having recently got back to the house after my meeting with Trevor. When Adriana told me she came from Devon, I didn't think much of it. Just because she and Dad grew up in the same place, there was no reason to think they'd known each other. Particularly given their age difference. But it appears they did, and that her dad worked for my grandfather. At nineteen, Dad moved to London for university, returning to Devon for the holidays and later to train for three years at a local chartered accountants, before transferring to Brighton where he met Mum. He loved the sea but said he grew bored of Devon. Told me it was too provincial, and that he craved the excitement and diversity of big cities. But now I wonder if there's more to it than that. Whether something else spurred his move.

I'm desperate to discuss all this with Adriana, to ask her what she and Dad chatted about that night in the restaurant and, more importantly, if she saw him again that week, before he died.

But I also know that if I do that, she'll realise I've been lying to her all this time. Lying about who I really am, about my past. To say nothing of proving the person who's been watching us right – that I am hiding something. Something dark. Something I'm deeply ashamed of.

Like Trevor, like all Dad's friends and acquaintances, she'll doubtless be aware of the scandal that erupted soon after Mum received Dad's suicide email. She'll know that the very next day, after she showed it to the police, they raided our house and found indecent images of older teenage girls and women on his laptop. Discovered that he enjoyed watching women being beaten and abused during sex, and that he belonged to a group of similar sick-minded individuals who indulged their fantasises via the dark web. Not only had he enjoyed watching women being tortured during sex online, he'd practised this in real life courtesy of online sites that exploited mainly young, vulnerable foreign women who'd been smuggled into the country against their will or in the belief they'd be given honest work.

I can still recall the shock on Mum's face when she learned the truth. I remember her collapsing on the spot, and me screaming for help, barely able to comprehend that our perfect world was suddenly crashing down around us. One of the officers had been kind. He'd called for an ambulance, and they'd checked her over, sedated her. All I could do was sit by her side and watch, feeling helpless, still not fully able to take on board that my dad, the man I worshipped, had this whole other side to him behind the kindly façade he presented to the world. A side we never had any notion of. I was only fifteen after all, and it was as if someone was playing a horrific trick on us, and any minute now Dad was going to walk back through the door and assure us it was all a big misunderstanding and everything was going to be fine. But he didn't, of course.

It was all too frighteningly real, and nothing was ever the same again. Including my darling mum.

His suicide email hadn't explicitly stated what he had done. I guess he was too chicken for that. All it said was that he wasn't the man Mum believed him to be, that he had done some terrible things in his life, committed crimes he was so ashamed of he no longer felt able to live with himself. He said there was something wrong with him, a defect he was born with that was impossible to tame. He said he was sorry. That he loved her, and hoped she'd find happiness again. That she'd be so much better off without him.

The police were never able to trace Dad's email. They said it was likely he'd sent it using a virtual private network, because he hadn't wanted to be found. On reflection, I thought this odd. After all, if he was dead, what did it matter? They'd wasted no time in searching our house, in confiscating Dad's laptop and other electronic devices. They did the same at his office. The humiliation for Mum had been too much to bear, the effect on my mental health huge, which is why we sought refuge in Nigeria. Where we could lose ourselves and escape the looks, the stares, the constant whispering behind our backs.

My name was Lucas Stevens back then. But before returning to the UK I changed it. I no longer wished to be associated with the name Stevens. I became Sebastian Walker from the moment I stepped back on English soil. But the worry that someone would unearth my real identity was always there, despite me doing everything possible to ensure that never happened.

It still niggles me that Dad went away that weekend giving no hint of being suicidal. And why send Mum an email? Why not a handwritten note? A typed note even. And how has his body never been found? The police orchestrated a nationwide search, but to no avail. Their only conclusion was that he must have gone out to sea somewhere, but why bother going to London for a reunion at all if he was planning to end his life? Unless he saw it as his final hurrah.

I think about the name Dad wrote on the back of the business card: *Scarlett*. Who is this woman and what is her relation to Dad? Is it just a coincidence that her name is written down, or is she connected somehow with the charity which, I note, is one of Adriana's? Perhaps Adriana knows her?

My head tells me there's little point in my pursuing this path. It's not going to change what Dad did or bring him back. But my heart is saying otherwise. That I need answers, because the way Dad chose to end his life, the timing of it all, the email, makes no sense to me.

It's going to be a deeply uncomfortable conversation, I know that. And I almost can't bear to see the look on Adriana's face when she realises I've been lying to her. But I don't see that I have a choice.

I have to confront her about Dad. About what he said to her that night in the restaurant. Whether she had any insight at all into his state of mind. Along with the kind of person he was back in Devon.

If I don't ask her, it will gnaw away at me, and I'll never have peace.

Who is Scarlett? Hopefully, Adriana can tell me.

Chapter Fifty

Adriana

Before

It's been two days since I found Jason dead in my art studio and in those forty-eight hours it's been a struggle to behave normally around Charles. I'm stressed beyond belief, my peaceful life thrown into chaos. I'm petrified at the thought of being found out and haunted by the fact that, somehow, someone's gained access to the house, and I haven't a clue who. This morning I had a full-on panic attack after Charles went to work, similar to the attacks I suffered as a child. I kept thinking about the way I'd stripped Jason naked, before dragging his corpse to my drying cabinet and locking him inside. I'm not sure how I did it, to be honest, and there were moments when I thought I might not make it. But I guess it's true that a person can find superhuman strength when put under extreme pressure, and where the alternative is unthinkable. I was sweating profusely by the end, my entire body aching with exhaustion. I've not set foot in my studio since. I nearly called for an ambulance earlier I was so convinced I was going into cardiac arrest. I ended up fainting the way I used to, coming around a couple of hours later. The panic has had me reaching for the wine a little too often, but also to blot out my guilt. The guilt I feel for lying to Charles, the man I love with all my heart, not for concealing the body of the monster who, together with my mother, ruined my childhood. For that, I feel no shame whatsoever.

I keep checking the news, to see if he's been reported missing but I've not seen or heard anything yet. There'll be something at some point, though. He's a professional, high up in his team, according to his firm's website, so it won't be long before his absence is missed. Plus, surely the hotel where he was staying will wonder why he never returned to his room or checked out?

Other than him being an accountant in Brighton, I can't find out much about him online. I wonder if he lied about being single. It's hard to imagine him being a family man, but then again you hear stories all the time of seemingly upstanding members of society who lead double lives. Who on the surface appear to be the perfect husband and father, but serial cheat on their poor unsuspecting wives. I'm betting he frequents all sorts of horrific websites using a different name, but perhaps avoids regular social media in case someone linked to those sites recognises him.

What if he was spotted entering the premises that night? I can't stop the possibility from going round in my head. I'm less concerned about our chance meeting in the restaurant. The police will be more interested in speaking to the group he was with, I expect. But someone may have seen him walk up the pathway. Stella, for example. She's got nothing better to do than pry into other people's lives. And what about the person Jason claimed gave him the code to the key box? What if it wasn't Jason's killer, but someone else entirely? Might they say something? Report him missing?

It's nearly six and I go to the kitchen and pour myself a glass of wine before taking it through to the living room. I pick up the remote control and switch on the TV, a sucker for punishment knowing that BBC News is about to start. I have butterflies in my stomach as the headlines are read out, but there's nothing in the top stories or the rest of the programme related to his disappearance. Half an hour later I'm back in the kitchen when Charles walks through the door. He looks tense, his face wan, almost like he's seen a ghost. He finds me nursing a second glass of wine and I notice the flash of concern in his eyes, what with me having never been a big drinker. I don't comment on it, and neither does he, although I'm sure he's tempted. I ask him if he's had a good day, while at the same time picturing my tormentor's shoes and clothes lying in the wooden chest I keep in my art studio, concealed beneath various rolls of canvas and art implements. I've turned the heating up full blast in there, in the hope that this, coupled with the drying cabinet's high humidity, will accelerate the mummification process, thereby making it easier to conceal. Perhaps then I can move it, bury it in the woods or something. But the truth is, I'm terrified of being caught out. And as time goes on, I know that's only going to get harder.

Charles doesn't say anything. And his silence panics me. He opens his briefcase, and removes a copy of *The Times*.

'Page four.'

'What?' I say, a lump suddenly wedged in my throat.

'Go to page four.' His eyes are missing their usual vibrancy. His complexion still pasty.

I tentatively pick up the paper, go to page four and that's when my heart almost stops. Because in the bottom left corner there's a photo of Jason, the headline reading:

Brighton accountant exposed as a violent sex predator

In something of a trance, I read the article, learning to my horror that he had a wife and son who couldn't be named for legal reasons, and who, unsurprisingly, knew nothing of the dark secret he was hiding. It goes on to state that police had carried out a search of the family home, uncovering hundreds of indecent images of women and older teenage girls, on his private computer.

According to the report, the devastated wife received an email from her husband late Wednesday evening telling her he had done some terrible things and couldn't live with himself. When she didn't hear from him the next morning following repeated calls and text messages she reported his email to the police.

I'm so confused, I hardly notice Charles staring at me. My mind flits back to the smarmy way Jason spoke to me on Wednesday night, the way he leered at and tried to force himself on me. I saw no signs of regret or remorse. What the hell is going on? Unless his killer wrote the email?

'Adriana, this is the man who came up to us in the restaurant, isn't it?'

I look at him blankly. How can I deny it?

I nod. 'Yes.'

His gaze softens, and he takes me in his arms. 'Did he hurt you? Is that why your mood changed so suddenly? Why you've been drinking so much? Did something happen in your childhood?'

I can't keep it in any longer. Just looking into Charles's eyes, seeing the concern in them, his love for me, it's killing me not to be honest with him.

'Not in here,' I say, 'let's go to the living room.'

Minutes later, we're seated on a sofa, my body shaking because I'm so frightened of what I'm about to tell him irreversibly changing things between us.

Charles takes my hand in his, strokes it gently, but it's no use. There's no way I can keep still or look him in the eye as I explain. So I get up and start pacing the room. 'Jason, who you met in the restaurant, and who appears to have committed suicide according to this article' – I make a point of reinforcing the way he died – 'was my babysitter on and off for around five years. He was seventeen when he first started coming to the house. I was six. He was my father's boss's son. He claimed he needed the cash for college, then university, even though his parents were loaded. He was charming and intelligent, and extremely good-looking. My mother fancied him big time. And he flirted with her from the outset. It made her feel good, desirable, being fancied by a younger man. They started up an affair, and one night I caught them at it. Only it wasn't normal sex, it… it was violent, extremely so, and he was always the one dominating.' I take a breath, will myself to continue, to fight off the sickening images raiding my brain. 'My mother appeared to enjoy it. Despite the bruises she had to show for it. How she managed to fob my father off I'll never know. Although, to be honest, he was a weak man and I suspect he always knew something was going on but was terrified of upsetting his boss and losing both his job and Mother.' I pause again, knowing the worst is yet to come. 'Jason caught me watching through the slit of the bedroom door one night, when my father

323

was away at a work conference. I heard noises and was curious, like most children would be. I ran away, terrified over what I'd seen, but later he came to my room and said…'

'He said what?' Charles urges.

I swallow hard, in an effort to steady my breathing. 'That he'd kill me and my father if I told anyone.'

'Jesus Christ.' Charles makes to get up but I gesture for him to remain seated. I'm on a roll now and if he tries to hug me, I'll lose my nerve. He seems to understand and stays put.

'I told you my parents weren't great at raising me. But it was more than that. My mother was a nasty woman. Didn't have a maternal bone in her body. She never wanted me. Never said a kind word to me, never encouraged me. She'd put me down at any available opportunity. Weak, stupid, clumsy, fat, ugly, the list of words she'd throw at me was endless, and it got to the point where I started to believe I was all those things and good for nothing.'

'Adriana, I'm so sorry, I can't even express how heartbroken I am for you. She didn't deserve a daughter as wonderful as you.'

'She'd stub her cigarettes out on my chest, hit me, make me go without dinner sometimes as punishment.'

'Punishment for what?'

'Oh, nothing in particular. Because I was a drain on her resources, or I'd bothered her, or looked at her the wrong way. But to be honest the emotional abuse was worse. The constant put-downs.' I take a breather. 'But nothing terrified me more than Jason's threats to both my and my father's lives. That scared the shit out of me. So much so I'd wet the bed.'

'You didn't think to tell your teachers? Or your aunt and uncle?'

I shake my head. 'I was a child, and I'd seen what Jason did to my mother. He frightened the life out of me, and I couldn't even imagine what the consequences would be if I told someone, and nothing came of it. I was so happy when he went to university and stayed away for weeks at a time. But I dreaded the holidays, when I knew he'd be back. After he graduated, he came back permanently to train as an accountant. He didn't babysit me any more, but he'd still come over when Father was at work or away. He knew Mother was an easy lay, I guess. She was obsessed with him, and it drove her mad thinking about all the women he'd no doubt slept with at university. And being the egomaniac he was, he enjoyed having that power over her.'

I can see it's torture for Charles to hear all this and it reassures me how much he loves me, that we can get through this.

'Did Jason ever touch you?' Charles's voice is so faint I can barely hear him. It's like he needs to know the answer but is too afraid of my response.

'No,' I say. 'But like Mother, he'd talk down to me. Say nasty things. Tell me I was the bane of her life. And when I got a bit older, he'd make me watch videos of them doing it. Instead of watching kids' TV, that's what I had to look forward to. He asked me if I liked it. That I should take notes and pay attention for when I turned sixteen and he could legally do the same to me. I dreaded those nights when he babysat. I wanted to run away, tell Father, but Jason threatened me. Said he'd find me, track me down and kill me. Kill Father. He continued making threats even when he stopped babysitting, when he'd come round for a quick shag with Mother and catch me on my own. I hardly slept for those three years. Because everything I'd seen, those dreadful images, would go round and round in my head, driving me crazy. I was desperate to escape them, for someone to come and rescue me. But they never did. And so one night, I told my parents about Jason's threats. I couldn't take it any more. But my mother accused me of lying, and Father was too weak to stand up to her. I was distraught. Felt utterly helpless. Abandoned. And then the fire happened. And as much as I never wished such a thing on my parents, their dying in that fire saved my life, I'm sure of it. I can't help thinking it was the work of some higher being saying *this child has suffered enough.*'

I go back over to Charles, tears streaming down my face, and kneel by his side. He kisses the top of my head, his own eyes filling. 'Oh, my poor darling, I'm so sorry, so very sorry. You should have told me sooner, I would have understood.'

I look up at him, wipe my nose with the back of my hand. 'I was too scared of how you'd react. I felt so ashamed. Didn't want you to think I was damaged goods.'

'Don't be daft, I could never think that. Does Dr Adams know?'

'Yes,' I admit. 'I told him everything that went on. But I begged him not to report it. Because I didn't want all the grim details becoming public. Couldn't bear to have to face Jason again. In a courtroom where there were no guarantees I would be believed. Even though I think Jason was worried I might say something, because soon after the fire he left Devon. Instead, I wrote it all down in my journals. Like Dr Adams encouraged me to. It was cathartic, and it helped. It has done for years. Until now.'

Charles rests his fingertip beneath my chin and tilts it upwards so that I am staring into his eyes.

'Dr Adams is a good man. You need to talk to him. Tell him what happened. I feel sure he can help you get through this, the way he did before. And don't stop with the journals, keep writing, it will help you to heal.'

There's a momentary lull as I lay my head on Charles's lap. I luxuriate in his tender touch as he softly strokes my hair.

'And now you know this bastard is dead,' he continues, 'you can finally move on. He can't hurt you any more. You are free.'

Oh, how I wish that were true. But with his body rotting on the floor below us, I know I am far from free.

I'll be haunted by his presence for the rest of my days. But that's something I can never tell anyone. Not Charles. Not Dr Adams.

Not anyone.

But who gave Jason access to our house? That's what scares me. Was it the same person who killed him? Or someone entirely separate? I'm hoping it's his killer, because the note made it clear I can trust them to keep my secret safe so long as I did what they asked.

But what if it's not? What if there's someone else out there who knows how to get inside?

Someone who knows this was the last place Jason was seen alive?

Chapter Fifty-One

Seb

It's six p.m. and I'm sitting upright on my bed, my head resting against the wall, my laptop laid across my knees as I contemplate a way to establish the connection between Adriana and my dad. Adriana isn't back yet, so I'm using the time to gather any information I can before I confront her. If only I knew what Adriana's surname was back then. But just as I'm pondering this, an idea hits me. One I had entertained when she first told me about her parents dying in a fire but had pushed to the back of my mind out of respect to Adriana. I go to Google and search for 'fire, Devon, parents killed, 1998'. I'm desperate for answers and this might be my only hope. There are several results, but the top one catches my eye immediately:

> Daughter of respected Devon property developer orphaned in tragic fire.

I waste no time in clicking on it. There's a photo of the charred remains of Adriana's house, but also one of her with her parents: Stephanie and Brian Monroe. She's standing between them, and they're all wearing broad smiles for the camera. Smiles that somehow feel forced. But that's not what I find myself focusing on. Neither do I pay much attention to their appearance or what the article says.

Rather, my eyes remain glued to the caption at the foot of the photo:

Scarlett Monroe with her parents Brian and Stephanie.

I swallow hard. Say out loud: '*Adriana is Scarlett?*'

The fact that my dad wrote her name on the back of the business card would imply he knew she worked with the charity. Had he been trailing her for some time, I wonder. Had he gone to London not only to see his friends, but also to reconnect with Adriana? But why? Why would he have been so interested in tracking her down after all these years? What was she to him? She can only have been fourteen when Dad, then aged twenty-five left Devon permanently for Brighton having qualified as an accountant. The same time Adriana moved to Guildford. Maybe I'm making too much of a leap here.

I look back at the article and a little way down there's a quote from my grandfather calling it a tragic waste and saying that he'd lost a great friend and loyal employee with Brian's passing. There's also reference to the family cat most probably having knocked over a candle – as Adriana mentioned to me the first time we met – and then, oh fuck, a quote from Jason Stevens, son of Toby Stevens, who had frequently babysat for the Monroes, and had just completed his chartered accountancy training at a local firm. He mentions how the Monroes were like family to him and how devastated he was by Steph and Brian's deaths, especially as Steph was usually so careful to blow out her candles every night. He said it was a miracle of

God that Scarlett survived. That he'd babysat her for five years since she was six. There was no suggestion of arson, while the article went on to explain how the orphaned Scarlett was being cared for by her aunt and uncle.

'Dad was Adriana's babysitter?' Again, I can't help saying the words out loud, I'm just so dumbstruck. And then I remember what Ethan told his father. About the things Adriana wrote in her journals. That her mother had been in league with someone, and that *she couldn't believe he'd hunted her down, having thought she'd never set eyes on him again*.

Was she talking about my dad? I feel sick at the thought. Stella, Ethan, Rick, they all believed something bad had happened to Adriana in her childhood, something she was too afraid to talk about.

God help me if that something was my dad.

It can't be true. He was never a paedophile as far as the police could tell, he only ever targeted older teenage girls and women. Even so, I have an uneasy feeling about this. And now, knowing what I do, I'm not quite sure how I'm going to look Adriana in the eye when she walks through the door. Or how she's going to react when she finds out who I really am.

Still, I can't bottle out now. I'm desperate to discover what happened to my dad. And instinct tells me that's something Adriana can help me with.

Did he really commit suicide?

Or is there more to it than that?

Chapter Fifty-Two

I knew all along you were a meddler, Sebastian. Just like Ethan, just like Dr Adams. And once again I've been proved right.

I followed you earlier to the pub, curious to know who it was you were meeting. I watched an older man join you at the table you bagged in the far corner, your eyes anxious, as if this wasn't a social meeting. I have no idea who the man was or what you talked about, but the shock on your face when he told you something towards the end of your conversation was plain for all to see. I had no clue if what you discussed concerned Adriana, but I wasn't taking any chances. So I followed you home. Watched you enter the house on the live feed on my phone, before grabbing a drink in the kitchen and going up to your room. I then quietly slipped in and went to my secret hiding place where I keep a laptop. I watched you open your own laptop, desperate to know what it was you were up to. I didn't think it was research for your book, you looked too tense. Something told me it concerned Adriana, despite you promising her you would let things be.

And then, as I watched you read whatever it was, you looked up, your eyes agog and you made a big mistake. You blurted out the words:

'Adriana is Scarlett?'

And then, a short time after that:

'Dad was Adriana's babysitter?'

I could hardly believe my ears when you said the word 'Dad'. Learning that you are Jason Stevens's son is a bombshell I never

331

in a million years expected. I'm guessing you found the article about the fire, in which Jason, Adriana's babysitter, your father, who tormented her, made her watch things no child should ever see, commented. He, who years later came to London for the sole purpose of finding her, having seen an article in the newspaper about one of the charities she worked for, her photo alongside it. That's what he told me before I killed him. After I put Adriana to sleep. Adriana had been meticulous about ensuring her photo was never in the press because she was afraid of Jason tracking her down. It's why she'd told Charles she yearned for a quiet wedding abroad, because the last thing she wanted was it being featured in Tatler *or* Hello! *which had both approached him. But this one photo had slipped through, and the pervert had seen and seized upon it. Now she was a grown woman he couldn't resist. Her being married wouldn't stop him. It hadn't stopped him fucking Adriana's mother in her own house.*

The way you emphasised the name 'Scarlett' made me certain this wasn't the first time you'd come across it. I'm guessing you also discovered something back home, Sebastian. Something that referred to a mysterious 'Scarlett' and, like your father, you came to London to track her down. I know you wanted to find her for a different reason. Because you're desperate to know what happened to your father. Why his body has never been found. Why he emailed his suicide note. Why he showed no signs of being suicidal before he left you and your mother. You perhaps thought this 'Scarlett' could help you answer those questions. But I don't care if your intentions were pure, that's not going to save you. Like father like son, so the saying goes, and I wouldn't be surprised if the same tendencies that ran through his veins run through yours. After all, you fucked her the day after you moved in, despite the shy persona you adopt. Maybe it's all just an act.

Whatever the case, it won't be long before you find out what happened to your father, once you question her, put her on the spot. She's not strong enough to lie to you. And when you do, you'll want her punished, because the fact is, blood is thicker than water.

And so I have to act before that happens. Before it's too late. Although I won't go straight for the kill. I'll indulge in a few little mind games first, send something fun to Adriana for her to ponder. Something that will make her see that I was right, and that despite your promises, you could never be trusted. That way, when you die, she'll miss you a little less.

Dr Martin will have to wait for now. Dealing with you takes precedence, Sebastian.

The way I deal with all the men who harm her. Dr Adams. Ethan. Even her own husband, Charles.

But first, like I said, I'm going to have a little fun.

It was me who removed Adriana's journals from the safe in her study last Saturday. I thought it best, because I couldn't risk you finding them the way Ethan had. Even though, since that happened, she's kept them locked away. It also had the added bonus of making her suspicious of you, wondering if you had taken them while pretending to be off having a swim.

But now, instead of keeping them from you, I'm going to lead you straight to them. You know too much now, and anyway, you deserve to suffer her anger, being the son of that monster.

I pick up my phone and type a WhatsApp message to you.

And then I press send and wait for that little blue tick to appear.

Chapter Fifty-Three

Seb

Where the hell is Adriana? It's nearly seven and there's still no sign of her. I've sent her several texts, but she hasn't responded. I worry something bad's happened to her.

I feel like I'm going stir-crazy. I can't sit in my bedroom a second longer. I need a drink, something strong to calm my nerves, even though I'm not usually one for the hard stuff. I leave the room and bolt downstairs to the larger sitting room, where I know Adriana keeps various spirits in a cabinet set against the wall behind the sofa. There's a set of decorative crystal tumblers along with a decanter resting on top of it. I grab one tumbler, then fish out a half-full bottle of Glenfiddich from the cabinet and pour myself a generous measure. I'm about to sit down when my phone vibrates in my pocket. Finally, I think to myself, it's Adriana texting me back. But when I pull it out and see that I have a WhatsApp from a number I don't recognise I flinch. I'm too curious, though. I ignore the option to block, then read the message.

The journals will tell you everything you need to know. Look on the bookshelf in the study, behind the biography of Winston Churchill, second shelf. There's a safe, code 2964. Go on. You know you want to.

I look around and up to the ceiling, wondering if I'm being watched this very second. I know it's more than likely that I am, while the timing of the message chills me. It's almost as if the sender knows what I found, who I really am. Knows I'm desperate to discover the nature of the relationship between Adriana and my dad. It has to be a trap. But I don't care. I'm past the point of caring. The urge to discover what Adriana wrote in her journals is too great.

I place my tumbler down on the coffee table and race to the study, open the door and immediately make a beeline for the bookshelf. I scan my eyes across it for the bio of Churchill, remove it and instantly spot the inbuilt safe. My fingers are twitching as I type in the code, so much so I make a mistake and an error code comes up. 'Shit,' I say out loud, willing myself to calm down, at the same time aware that Adriana's going to walk through the door any minute now and catch me red-handed. I try again and this time I'm in. The safe is deep and, on reaching inside, I'm shocked to find around two dozen journals hidden there.

My heart is beating so fast I can hardly breathe as I shift them, six at a time, to Adriana's desk.

I sit down and start leafing through each one. They seem to date from when Adriana first started seeing Dr Adams and it's clear from what she says that it was him who encouraged her to use a journal as part of her therapy.

There's so much here and there's no way I'm going to be able to get through them all before Adriana gets back. They're not diaries as such, more ramblings of Adriana's thoughts, as Rick explained, and seem to jump forwards and back in time making it harder to know where I might find stuff relevant to my dad, if at all. She speaks fondly of Dr Adams throughout, how she regrets being harsh on him initially, how patient he was with her when she told him off for not calling her by the name she preferred – Adriana. How she'd always hated the name her mother had given her: Scarlett.

In one of the earlier journals, she explains how her mother made her life hell, how she had both emotionally and physically abused her since she was a little girl. My heart bleeds for Adriana as I read this, wondering how a mother could possibly do that to her own child, the contrast between my darling mum and hers never starker. And then comes the section I dreaded finding. Having hoped that Rick had been wrong in recounting what Ethan had told him. The passage where she talks about the person in league with her mother. I can't be certain it's my dad, but all the evidence is pointing towards this.

I flick through more of the earlier entries, and that's when my worst fears are realised. Adriana talks about it being a relief to tell Dr Adams about her babysitter, Jason. Who'd been sleeping with her mother on and off for eight years and did unspeakable things to her. She describes how she told her parents the night before the fire that Jason had threatened to kill both her and Brian if she dared breathe a word about what she'd seen him and her mother do, but that her mother accused her of lying, while her father was too weak to stand up to her. I didn't think I could hate my dad more for being the person he was behind closed doors, but I was wrong. Knowing what he put Adriana through as a child is nigh on unbearable, and as much as it sickens me to even contemplate it, I'm now certain he came to London to seek her out, with the intention of making Adriana another one of his conquests.

I glance at my watch and see that it's gone half-seven. I shouldn't risk looking at more entries in case Adriana walks in on me, but I can't help myself. I frantically leaf through the pages of her later journals, and then eventually find what I'm looking for. An entry where she mentions coming face to face with my dad on her and Charles's wedding anniversary in the same restaurant where he met with Trevor Carrington – the night of his university reunion. How he leered at her, made her feel uncomfortable, made strange comments about it being a miracle she survived the fire her parents perished in. How she was desperate to leave but had to put on a brave face for Charles's sake. I keep leafing through and then my heart almost stops when I come to an entry where she talks about my dad coming to see her at the house a few days after, when Charles was away in France. How he somehow gained entry, claiming a friend of hers had given him the code to their spare key box, something that both puzzled her and scared her witless. Once again I think back to my conversation with Rick and an entry Ethan read, where Adriana said she wished she could have told Charles everything, that she hated lying to him, but that she couldn't believe he'd hunted her down, and that she'd had no choice but to keep the truth about what she'd done buried.

My heart is galloping as I wonder what she meant by this, and I literally can't turn the pages fast enough, desperate to know how things panned out that night. But then I hear movement outside, and before I have time to put the journals away, the door opens and Adriana is standing there.

Chapter Fifty-Four

Adriana

'How could you, Seb? How could you go sneaking around my things when you promised me you wouldn't?' There are tears in my eyes as I vent my frustration, and I almost can't speak properly, I'm so choked with rage. How could Seb betray me again after I was so open with him yesterday when we met in Covent Garden? We made a pact to wait, to ride things out, to see if the police investigating Dr Adams's death come up with anything that might lead us to catching the person tormenting us. But clearly, he lied, is just the same as all the men in my life who have ultimately let me down. It *was* him who took my journals last Saturday after all. But how the hell did he access the safe? That's what puzzles me.

'Adriana, let me...'

I hold up my hand. 'Save it. I don't want to hear it. There's no justification for this. These are my private thoughts, Seb. Nobody's business but mine. How could you betray my trust like that? I know you're hiding some-thing too, I can sense it, but I agreed to respect your privacy. I haven't gone snooping in your room, as much as I've been tempted to. You're a bastard, just like the rest of your sex.'

Seb looks at me imploringly. 'I'm sorry, Adriana, but if you could just let me explain—'

'Explain what? There's nothing to explain as far as I can tell. I caught you red-handed. Tell me, did Rick put you up to this? Was this a set-up from the start? Maybe you're working for him? Maybe he's paying you to dish up dirt on me, because he's obsessed with the notion that his son was murdered, and he'll stop at nothing to uncover the truth. Maybe Seb isn't even your real name and you're not a writer. Maybe you're some undercover private investigator he's hired who's a pro at cracking safes, who the fuck knows, I don't know what the hell to believe any more.'

I stop talking, shattered. My head is banging, my body literally twitching with anxiety. Not just because of Seb and everything that's transpired these past few days, but because of something else that happened today. Something that freaked the hell out of me. It's happened before, and I've ignored it. But I really don't feel well, and the exhaustion only seems to have got worse. So much so I've booked myself in for a blood test tomorrow, before I go and see Dr Martin. I need to know what's wrong with me, because I feel certain something's not right.

Seb comes over to where I'm standing in the open doorway, my gaze still focused on my journals spread all over Charles's desk. His eyes are fearful, his movements tentative, as if he expects me to lash out and tell him to get the fuck away from me. But I don't. For one, I'm too worn out. And secondly, I can't help being curious to hear his explanation. I guess it's because I see a goodness in him, a vulnerability I recognise in myself, and a part of me is still desperate to believe he's not like all the rest.

'Adriana, I'm not here to spy on you, and Rick didn't hire me. I really am a struggling writer, and I did grow up in Brighton and lose both my parents. But you are right about one thing. Seb isn't my real name. It's something I should have told you yesterday, but at that moment I had no idea it was relevant to what we were discussing.'

My heart judders at this last confession. 'What do you mean?'

'My real name is Lucas Stevens, but I changed it to Sebastian Walker before I came back to the UK from Nigeria. Three years after Mum received my dad's suicide note. Well, when I say note, it was sent by email.'

Stevens? Suicide note? All of a sudden my legs are like jelly, a queasy sensation filling my insides.

'Suicide note?' I repeat, my voice frail. 'So you lied to me when you said he had cancer?'

'Yes, but with good reason. I was too ashamed to tell you the truth. A truth I've fought to keep concealed these past ten years. Plus I didn't think you'd take me on as your lodger if you knew about my past.'

'Knew what about your past?' I again echo Seb's words, the fear in my voice palpable. 'Why did you change your name?'

I'm almost certain I know the answer, but I need to hear him say it.

He holds my gaze firm. 'It's a question I could ask of you. *Scarlett.*'

I feel my stomach lurch. But I can't get sidetracked. Of course he knows my real name. He read my journals. 'Don't change the subject. Carry on.'

'Dad wasn't the person Mum and I believed him to be,' he says. 'He had a dark side, a separate life we were

341

completely oblivious to. As were so many people close to him.'

Hearing the pain in his voice, for the first time since I caught Seb with my journals, I feel a pang of pity for him. 'How do you mean?'

'He did some bad stuff. Truly awful, unthinkable things that made me so ashamed. It broke Mum. Nearly broke me. It's why we upped and left for Nigeria for a few years. Because of the backlash we faced at home.'

I say nothing. Walk to the chair opposite Charles's desk and sit down. Because if I don't sit right now, I will collapse.

'I met an old friend of Dad's today,' Seb says. 'A man named Trevor Carrington. He was one of the last people to see Dad alive.'

I frown. The name not ringing any bells. 'And?'

'Dad had dinner with Trevor and some old uni friends the Saturday before he emailed Mum his suicide note.'

I swallow hard. Ask faintly, 'Where?'

'An Asian fusion restaurant in Mayfair. Trevor said Dad went over to speak to you and Charles at one point. He remembered Charles, what with him being such a renowned businessman.'

The room is suddenly spinning and I want to be sick.

'Dad told Trevor that his father was your father's boss and that he knew you and your parents from when you lived in Devon.'

It's all too horrifying. Seb moves closer and I instantly recoil.

'I think you know who I'm talking about?' he says. 'And I'm guessing you heard in the news what happened shortly after? What the police found on Dad's laptop in our house?' Seb lowers his gaze, then slowly looks up again, his expression etched with guilt and shame as a tear escapes his left lower lid and starts to trickle down his cheek. 'Dad said he couldn't live with himself in his email to Mum. He never told her exactly what he'd done, but explained it would all come out before long. It puzzled her why he chose to email, rather than send her a written note or even leave her a voicemail. It puzzled me too. Still does. The police had no luck tracing the email. Neither did they ever find a body. It's something that's troubled me to this day.'

I sit here rigid, unable to believe what I'm hearing. Unable to comprehend that the son of the man who abused me as a child is standing right in front of me. Has been staying in my house. Has made love to me. I'm in so much shock, I can't even speak.

'I realise this is a lot to take in, and you must hate me for lying to you,' Seb goes on. 'But you have to know, I'm as sickened by what my dad did as you must have been. And everyone else who knew him. Or thought they did, at any rate. Mum and I couldn't leave the house for a time. Her friends turned on her, I got bullied at school and my mental health suffered. It helped Mum going back to Nigeria, where she could be with family in a safe place, and where Dad's crimes couldn't follow us. Not a day goes by when I don't feel guilty for persuading her to return to England. Because coming back just brought home what he'd done, the fact that Dad wasn't the person she thought she'd married. That he had this evil side he hid so masterfully. The classic Jekyll and Hyde.'

I study Seb's face and realise that despite there being more of his mother in him than Jason, he has the same jawline as his father, the same shaped eyes, although there's a sincerity about Seb's that Jason's lacked. But when it

343

comes down to it, he's the child of the man who, together with my mother, ruined my childhood. He's the reason Charles and I argued. The reason I suffered from depression and a lack of self-confidence for so many years. The reason I crave attention, crave sex, and yet at the same time, have moments when all I want to be is alone, the thought of being touched by a man repulsing me. It's hard to look at Seb and not feel disgusted. Because now I know the truth, all I see is Jason.

'What is it you want to know, Seb? You've been reading my journals so I'm guessing you know that Jason, together with my mother, abused me as a child. Well, not sexually, but in many ways, it was as good as. I hated him, like I hated her, and when I left Devon for Guildford I prayed I'd never see his face again. It's why I made a point of never looking him up. I wanted a clean break. But then, as you correctly pointed out, I saw him that night in the restaurant. It was my and Charles's wedding anniversary. A night that was supposed to be special for the both of us, but which, thanks to your father, drove us apart.' I pause, as something occurs to me. 'You didn't just come to London to pursue your writing, or because you wanted a change of scene, did you?'

'No.' Seb shakes his head. 'Around six months ago I found a business card for the then CEO of Female Aid, Frederica Bailey. It slipped out of one of Dad's books that I inherited after Mum died. The name Scarlett was written on the back of it.'

So now I know for sure that Jason didn't just come to London to see his friends and happened to bump into me. He came here seeking me out too. Perhaps having seen my photo in the newspaper. I always shied away from press photos, tried my best to keep my name and face as private as possible, hence my lack of social media. But I couldn't stop that one photo from slipping through and it was enough to whet Jason's appetite. Perhaps meeting me in the restaurant was a coincidence, but now I'm certain he was determined to find me that week, and if it hadn't been that day, it would have been another.

Seb says what I'm thinking. 'I think Dad looked you up, that he perhaps intended to get in contact while he was in London, but then ran into you anyway. But like I said, what I don't understand is why he sent Mum that email and killed himself. He showed no suicidal tendencies when he left, but now I'm wondering if perhaps seeing you sparked something in him?'

I wince inside when he says this. Knowing how close to the truth he is. But I can't let him see my fear. 'Are you blaming me for your father's death?' I say angrily.

He doesn't answer my question. Something that unnerves me further. His gaze drills through me. 'I saw an entry in your diary. Where you talked about not being able to believe "he hunted you down". I'm guessing by that you meant my dad?'

I say nothing.

'In the same entry you said you hated lying to Charles, but had no choice but to keep the truth about what you'd done buried.' Seb pauses, then says: 'What did you mean by this, Adriana? Did you meet with my dad again? After that night in the restaurant?'

I don't regret Jason's death. Right to the last he was as narcissistic as ever. The consummate misogynist. A serial abuser. And I don't for a moment believe he repented for his sins. But as I look into Seb's eyes, I can't help pitying him and his mother for all they have suffered. I hate that I am partly responsible for their suffering. That all these years Seb's never been able to bury his father. And it's for this reason that I know I must come clean and tell him the truth.

'Adriana, please answer me.' His tone becomes sharper, impatient even. 'Did you meet with him? What did you mean in your journal when you said you had no choice but to keep the truth buried?'

I get up, with the intention of going over to Seb and confessing everything to him. But suddenly I feel so overwrought, so overwhelmed with stress, it's like I can't get enough oxygen into my lungs. I feel light-headed, my eyelids twitching. Like I'm overcome with an indescribable exhaustion. I start pulling at the neck of my sweater, in an attempt to ingest some air.

'Adriana, are you OK, can I get you some water?' I hear Seb say.

I vaguely see his face, his look of concern. Similar to the look Dr Adams gave me the last time I saw him, after I poured out my heart and soul to him. Told him everything I was frightened of.

But before I can say another word, everything goes black.

Chapter Fifty-Five

Before

I don't take much pleasure in what I'm about to do, not the way I did with my other kills. But really, I can see no other way. Charles went too far when he called her a heartless bitch this afternoon. And for that he must pay. All he seems to do these days is cause her unhappiness. Accusing her of being moody, depressed, seeking solace in the bottle instead of getting help. Neglecting 'his needs'. So typical. In the end it all boils down to sex.

I mean, of course she feels angry and depressed! She was emotionally abused for most of her childhood, made to suffer things no child should have to endure, and having thought she'd seen the back of that time, that dirtbag came back into her life. Charles knows all this, for God's sake, because she told him. She laid herself bare to him. So, you'd think he'd cut her a little slack instead of telling her he'd had enough and that perhaps they needed some space. I mean, it's not like she could tell him the truth. That her tormentor's leathery carcass lies in a wooden chest in her art studio. Where she moved it to after a time, joining his clothes and shoes. I have to say I was impressed with her ingenuity that night. Her thinking outside the box. That drying cabinet idea was a stroke of genius. Charles may profess to love her, he may claim he'd do anything for her, but there's no way he'd be comfortable with harbouring a secret like that. Even though she wasn't the one who killed Jason. The reality is, I made her an unwitting accomplice that night, and so I need to step in now, stop the worst from happening. Because I fear that it's only a matter of time before Charles discovers the truth.

Adriana has no idea that I exist in her, that I am a part of her, because I am smart. I hide out in her consciousness, and I listen and wait for the right moment to show myself. Not to her, but to others. She created me to help her in moments like these; moments that make her incredibly stressed and trigger my coming out. I am always on standby to help her when she needs me, the way I helped her escape her parents. The way I helped her deal with Jason when he was about to molest her. She has no recollection of either, of course. She thinks the former was an accident caused by Molly the cat, while the latter remains something of a mystery.

Adriana loved her two imaginary friends, Xavier and Eve. They were a comfort to her, as imaginary friends often can be to children. But she secretly idolised one of them more than the other, wished she could be more like them, have the life they did. Perfect in every way. And that's why, over time, they went from being an imaginary playmate, the kind of playmate so many kids have but grow out of, to becoming a part of her. Her guardian angel.

I am that guardian angel. Her alter ego. The stronger side of her, who deals with the hard stuff. The side that came out when finally it all got too much, and she just couldn't take any more abuse from her filthy whore of a mother. I am the cocoon she built around herself, the one who wasn't forced to endure her mother's beatings and vicious comments, the one who hadn't witnessed the violent sex she and Jason Stevens partook in and which he made her watch recordings of. I come out when she needs an escape. And then, when things are more settled, I disappear. Until she needs me again.

Although I exist in Adriana's head, and can often hear her conversations, remain alive to where she goes, I don't always hear or see everything I need to be aware of. That's why I planted cameras everywhere in the house so I can play back the day's events, observe all that's gone on, what might be troubling her, just as I was able to watch Charles break her heart earlier.

Charles is currently in the larger sitting room having a whisky, trying to cool down after their heated argument. I'm still dressed in the clothes Adriana was wearing, because I'm going to pretend to be her. It's the only way my plan will work. I've perfected her voice, of course, so it won't be a problem. She stormed up to their room an hour ago, sobbing uncontrollably on the bed. The stress triggered my emergence and, as I played back the footage of her and Charles arguing from my secret lair, it angered me. I made the decision there and then to take matters into my own hands.

And so here I am standing at the sitting room door, Charles's back to me as he slouches on the sofa, a crystal tumbler in his right hand.

I take a deep breath, my insides tingling with excitement. Then I walk over to him and put on my best Adriana smile. 'I'm sorry for our argument, I really am. I know I've not been myself for a long time, and that my drinking's got out of hand. I want to stop, and I'll go and get help like you suggested. I can't bear the thought of losing you.' I drop to my knees and place my head on his lap in a dramatic show of remorse. And he falls for it. Rises to the bait like a lamb to the slaughter. I feel his fingertips stroke my hair, a sensation that repulses me, but I don't let on.

'I'm sorry too, darling. I love you so much and I want to help,' he says. 'But I think you're right. You need professional help. Why not talk to Dr Adams again? Are you sure you told him everything about Jason Stevens, like you said you would?'

That useless meddler. He's the last person Adriana needs to see. He doesn't know about me, at least I don't think he does, because thankfully Adriana's never become so upset in front of him that she's forced me out. He did know about Xavier and Eve, though. He realised quite early on into their sessions that

349

she suffered from child psychosis, and that Xavier and Eve were a product of that, rather than being innocent imaginary playmates so many kids invent. It was more than that with Adriana, or Scarlett as I knew her better then. It always has been. She had an illness. Because of all she was made to suffer. And when Dr Adams told her this towards the end of her fourth session, it was a real bombshell. But it also liberated her. Helped her make sense of things. For example, why her friends never wrote back, why Xavier never got into trouble when they caused mischief at school. Why her mother referred to her as weird in having her 'freakish' friends, and that she was incapable of finding any real friends. Something she told Jason too.

But the truth is, I was already a part of her by then. As is often the case with children who have imaginary friends but go on to develop dissociative disorder in their teens. And even though she repressed me for years after coming to terms with her anger, her grief, going to those wretched art classes at Dr Adams's behest, I never really left her. In some ways I should thank that bastard, Jason. Because seeing him again after all those years triggered my return.

I was the one who gave him the code to the key box the day after she saw him in the restaurant. I dialled the number on the business card he gave her – using one of my many unregistered phones – and which she kept in her dresser drawer, and I told him I liked playing hard to get, that I had two sides to me and I wanted him to see the other naughtier side. He fell for it, was turned on by the whole scenario, in fact, like the sleazy fucker he was. Poor Adriana was so confused when he mentioned a friend of hers had given him the code. He thought it was part of a sex game she was playing with him, but he was wrong. So wrong.

Just now, I agree with Charles's suggestion that I get in touch with good old Dr Adams. Solely to get him on side. 'Yes, that's a great idea, I will. But first, there's something I want to show you, something I think will help you understand why I've not been myself.'

'Of course,' he says affably, making me experience a fleeting pang of regret at my deception. But only fleeting, because I know I have to be practical about things and that once he realises what lies in Adriana's art studio there'll be no comeback for him.

I take his hand and lead him down the stairs. Then I open the door to Adriana's studio while he looks at me quizzically because she rarely allows him inside her most precious space any more.

'What is it, darling?' he asks.

'You'll soon see. This way.'

I guide him to the far corner where a large, heavy wooden chest sits.

'Have a look inside,' I say.

He looks at me like I'm coming across a bit weird. Which I am, I suppose.

'Please, Charles, you'll understand once you do.'

He tentatively lifts the lid, as I slip my hand in Adriana's jeans pocket, primed and ready to strike. 'It's just your art materials, darling,' he says, looking back over his shoulder.

'You're not looking properly,' I say. 'Have a good rummage around.'

He must really think I'm mad now, but I guess he doesn't want to antagonise me, so plays along. I watch him sink his hand inside the box and lift up the canvases and various art materials, and then, when he quickly retrieves it and looks back up at me in horror, I know that he's struck gold. I don't give him time to ask any questions, though. I pull out the needle from my pocket containing enough morphine to kill an elephant and plunge it into his shoulder. It worked with Jason so I know it will work with Charles. He looks at me in horror. 'Adriana, tell me why?'

At this point I'm not quite sure if he's referring to the skeleton he's discovered or me injecting morphine into his arm. Maybe both, but I feel the need to set him straight before he dies. It's the least I can do. After all, he's not a bad person. But this wasn't working for him and Adriana any more. His fate was sealed when that arsehole came back into her life.

I tell him who I am. The one who protects her. The one who protected her when she was just a little girl. The one who protected her from that slimeball, Jason Stevens. Whose bones he just touched.

'And now, I'm protecting her against you,' I say.

He looks at me with a puzzled expression, and then I see recognition in his eyes, like he might have finally grasped the implications of what I just said and who I really am. I hope it brings him some peace as I watch his eyelids grow heavy and he slumps to the floor. I lie him gently on his side, his breathing becoming increasingly laboured, and then, before I know it, it's stopped altogether. I know this is going to be painful for Adriana, that it's going to hit her hard. But that's what I'm hoping. Because with Charles dead, she'll be so distraught she's going to need me even more. There'll be no getting rid of me now. I'll just have to make sure I hide myself well when she starts speaking to her shrinks, which I've no doubt she will. I can't have them find out about me. If they do, she's the one who'll suffer. Because all they'll see is her. Not me. She'll go to prison for something I did, not her. All because I wanted to protect her.

Charles is a dead weight, but I am strong, stronger than Adriana. I work out a lot, sometimes pumping iron in the middle of the night when Adriana is asleep. I always make sure Charles is out for the count when I do, but of course I won't have that problem now.

When I am certain he is dead, I drag him across the floor by his feet. At the open door I have a rest, then repeat the process from the art studio to the pool, although it's a bit easier hauling him across the parquet flooring. He glides much better. I am sweating, though, by the time I get him alongside the pool. I strip him naked, then fetch the trunks I quickly placed in the changing room before I went to apologise to Charles, and pull them on him. And then I waste no time in rolling him into the water. He's a big man, like I said, so it makes one almighty splash, and I pray it doesn't trigger Adriana's return.

He drifts away, face down. A less painful, less frightening death than that of Adriana's parents. Because Charles wasn't a bad person, after all, and he didn't deserve to suffer. Not like how I made Jason suffer.

I grab Charles's clothes, leave them on a bench in the changing room, to make it seem like he had intentionally come down here for a swim.

At least, that's what I hope and pray everyone will believe. That, having taken morphine for the pain in his knee, Charles thought a relaxing swim might also help ease his discomfort. Either that or he took too much by accident and wasn't thinking straight as a result.

All I need to do now is wipe my prints from the needle and leave it for Adriana to find. Along with her husband's floating corpse.

Chapter Fifty-Six

'Adriana, are you OK? You blacked out.'

It's the first time I've studied you in real time, Sebastian, rather than via a recording. There've been occasions when I've tried to view you with my naked eye, just so I could take a proper look at you. But she wouldn't let me. Being around you has generally had a calming influence on her. But tonight has changed things. Your revelation that you are Jason's son and your suspicions that Adriana knows a lot more than she's letting on about your wretched father's death have proved far too stressful for her to handle, thereby triggering my emergence. But in the same way I fooled Charles, I won't let on for now that she's gone away, and that in her place stands her stronger half. I fooled Dr Adams the same way the other Sunday, when I went to his house pretending I was her and saying that I couldn't wait until Monday to see him because I was scared that there was something wrong with me. I offered to make him a cup of tea by way of thanks. With just a dash of cyanide in it. It's amazing what you can get off the dark web. Thankfully, his house doesn't have CCTV, and when I boarded the train to Guildford, I made sure I wore a cap and dark glasses. So far, so good. No one's spotted me yet.

I adopt my most harrowed expression. 'Yes, I, I think so. I just felt faint all of a sudden. It's all the stress, plus you know I don't sleep well.'

'Yes, yes of course,' you say, your eyes full of concern.

You're not a bad guy, Sebastian, I truly believe that, despite having my doubts on learning your true identity. You're not like your father. You're kind and caring, and would never do the terrible things he did. It's not your fault you share his DNA. But I cannot allow any sympathy I might have for you to cloud my judgement. Her sentimentality is her downfall, it always has been, and that's why she has me to shield her. The fact is, you are on the cusp of breaking her, of figuring out what happened to your father, and when that happens, she'll be locked away. And so will I.

'Can I get you some water?' you ask.

'Yes, yes, that would be good.' I nod.

You go off to fetch me some water, and before long are back with a tall glass I don't really need but drink down all the same. Just to please you. To play the game. I get a fizzing in my stomach as I do, not because of the liquid cooling my guts, but because the game always excites me. Being bad, devious, outwitting someone who's caused her pain excites me.

'Better?' you ask.

'Much,' I say with a grateful smile.

This is it.

'Seb, you asked me just now if I met with your father again, after I saw him in the restaurant that night.'

You nod nervously.

'Well, the answer to that is yes, I did.'

There's a sudden spark in your eyes. 'And, what happened?'

I will my own eyes to moisten. It's amazing how the human body responds to willpower. Being disciplined, mentally focused, has the capacity to force it to do so much more than we give it credit for.

'Give me a second,' I say. 'I'll be right back.'

You look confused but say OK, evidently relieved I'm about to give you information on your father and therefore you are prepared to wait a little longer if that's what it takes.

I rush up to the sixth bedroom, where Adriana never goes. Here, I keep a laptop and various unregistered phones hidden away which allow me to monitor this house and its inhabitants' movements when I emerge. Along with several items of dark clothing and caps I use to disguise myself when I need to. The night-time is typically when Adriana's mind dwells on all the dark episodes masking her life, when the stress of shouldering them gets too much and she finds herself needing me. I'm lucky in that sense, because it's the safest time for me to emerge. Even though I know it means poor Adriana doesn't get enough sleep.

I go over to the wardrobe, open it and reach up high for a box I keep on the top shelf containing various items including a stash of needles and vials of morphine I stole from Charles all those years ago. Just in case they came in handy.

Conscious you might be growing impatient and could follow me upstairs to check I'm OK, I quickly and expertly fill a needle with enough morphine to cause your heart to stop. I plan on stabbing you with it at the most opportune moment.

'Adriana, are you OK?' I hear you call up. My heart racing, I slip the needle into my trouser pocket, shut the wardrobe and leave the room. I will my pulse to slow down by taking deep lungfuls of air, then calmly descend the stairs.

You are hovering at the foot, looking anxious.

'Are you OK?' you repeat.

'Yes.' I nod. 'I had to use the bathroom and splash my face. You may have read in my journals that I suffered from severe panic attacks as a child. I always found cool water on my skin helped calm me down.'

'Of course,' you say. 'I hope you feel better now.'

So naïve. So trusting.

'I do, thank you.' I inhale deeply again. 'Anyway, I want to show you something.'

'What?' you ask.

'Downstairs, in my art studio.'

There's a glimmer of apprehension in your eyes. 'Your art studio? What's that got to do with my dad?'

I reach for your hand, place it in mine. 'Please, trust me.'

'OK,' you say, although there's no mistaking the tremble in your voice. I can hardly blame you.

'Great, let me get the key, wait here.'

I go and retrieve the key then lead us downstairs to the lower ground floor. I hope I won't have to wait too long to make my move. I want your death to be swift, Sebastian, unlike your father's. I revelled in making his as long and drawn-out as possible. Also, unlike your father, I realise I am going to have to dispose of your body elsewhere. Another death of a loved one under her roof will break Adriana. Even if it is for the best. I will tell you the truth first, though. I owe you that.

We're at the art studio door now. I insert the key and turn the lock and then you follow me inside, whereupon I slam the door shut. The sound seems to reverberate through the air as I do, my heart beating double time.

'Adriana, why are we here? What is it you want to show me and how does it concern my dad?'

I don't reply, but continue to guide you to the end of the room, so that we're standing just a few feet away from the wooden chest that holds the key to the answers you seek.

I stop and turn to face you. 'Seb, your father broke into this house and confronted me in this very room one night when Charles was away on business. He attacked me.'

I watch your eyes fill with horror. I think, deep down, you knew something like that might have happened, but were desperate not to believe it.

357

'I, I'm so sorry,' you say.

'It's OK, it's not your fault.' I lower my eyes, as if I'm too ashamed to make eye contact with you.

And then you ask the one question I'd hoped you would.

'Adriana, did you kill my dad?'

I pretend to look ashamed. Then nod. 'Yes. But in self-defence.'

For a moment I wonder if you're going to explode and attack me in a fit of rage. But you don't. You simply ask: 'Where is he? Is he buried in this room? Is that why you brought me down here?'

I don't respond. I simply walk over to the wooden chest, open it, then say: 'Take a look inside.'

I watch you gingerly make your way to the open chest. You eye me questioningly as you hover over it.

'Put your hand inside,' I say.

Hesitantly, you do as I command, reaching down into the chest, beneath the art materials and overalls, my insides prickling with anticipation as I see a look of horror sweep over your face the moment you find what I know you must have suspected was buried there. Your father's remains. You look like you're on the verge of vomiting. You bow your head, and it's at this point that I slyly reach into my pocket and wrap my fingers around the syringe, primed and ready to plunge it into your neck. I edge closer, your head still bowed, and I'm on the brink of whipping the needle out and doing what needs to be done when the door crashes open and I see Dr Martin and three men I don't recognise standing there. I drop the needle in shock, caught off guard.

And that's when you stand up straight and look me dead in the eye. 'Hello, Xavier, what have you done with Adriana?'

Chapter Fifty-Seven

Seb

I want to be able to vent my rage at Adriana. But I know that wouldn't be fair. Because she's not the one who killed my dad. It was a part of her she didn't know existed, but perhaps had always sensed deep down was there. A part which, together with her mother, my dad helped trigger. Creating Xavier was a form of self-defence, a stronger part of her that emerged to shield her when the pain and stress she suffered repeatedly got too much. A side Dr Adams missed all the years he'd been treating her, because when she was with him, she felt safe. Calm. And when Adriana felt calm, there was no reason for Xavier to come out. It was like that for years. Until the last time she went to see him, when she told him her fears; fears that were starting to cripple her. He had pushed her, really pushed her. Something he'd never done before. And that's when it all got too much, and he finally realised what he was dealing with.

While Xavier was upstairs fetching the vial of morphine he planned on injecting me with, I received a text from a number I didn't recognise. I hesitated to read it, for obvious reasons. But then succumbed. And thank God I did. Because Dr Martin's message most likely saved my life.

Seb, this is Dr Martin, Adriana's therapist. If you're with Adriana in the house you could be in danger. Adriana's not well. She has dissociative disorder, with a violent alter ego named Xavier. We believe he's killed before and he may mean you harm. I'm currently en route to the house with the police. Hang tight.

I froze when I read the message. Realising what this meant. That all this time it was Adriana who was behind the emails, who had been watching me from when Max first showed me round the house. Hers was the silhouette in the window I saw when I went for my swim. I wanted to run, knowing how dangerous she was, that she had most likely killed Ethan and Dr Adams, possibly even Charles. All three later confirmed when I spoke at length with Dr Martin after Adriana was taken away.

After she blacked out in the study and came to, I knew, looking into her eyes, that there was something different about her. That I wasn't looking at my landlady any more. But rather, Xavier. A cunning, clever and ruthless personality who hid in the shadows and fooled so many of us for so long.

Even the man Adriana loved like a father. Dr Adams.

Chapter Fifty-Eight

Adriana

Before

'How are things, Adriana? I know all this business with Ethan can't have been easy. But what else is troubling you? Because I get the feeling that something is.'

I look at Dr Adams and wonder if I can trust him with what's really preying on my mind, almost driving me to distraction. I think that I can. He's never let me down to this day. Whenever I come to see him, he always makes me feel so calm, and I invariably leave feeling clearer-headed. He's had that effect on me since the first time I stepped inside his office, and I'm hoping that will be the case today.

'I, I just don't understand why Ethan went up to the roof when he got home from the party.'

'He was high, like the post-mortem confirmed. People do strange things when they're under the influence of drink and drugs.'

'Yes, yes, I get all that. The thing is…'

'The thing is what?'

'We argued the night before.'

He frowns. 'You did?'

'Yes.'

'What about?'

'For some time, he'd been asking questions about my childhood. Specifically, if something bad happened.'

'Why would he do that?'

'At the time I had no idea. He'd been behaving oddly in general, like he was spooked by something. And then, the day before he died, he confessed to reading some of my journals. The things I wrote down about my childhood, all the bad stuff that happened to me. Like you told me to. I was so angry with him, it felt like a huge betrayal of my trust, and I told him I wanted him out by the end of the month. But now I worry I might have driven him to throw himself off the roof.'

'That doesn't seem likely, Adriana. I know you were in an intimate relationship, and you cared for him. But for starters it was wrong of him to read your private thoughts, and secondly, from what you told me he didn't seem like the depressive type. Am I right?'

'Yes.' I nod. 'If anything, he was overconfident. The thing is, though, he got high before, but never went up to the roof at such a ridiculous hour. Even in summer.' I pause. 'I've not told Dr Martin this, but Stella, my next-door neighbour, claims she saw someone on the roof with Ethan. She thinks he was pushed.'

All at once, Dr Adams leans forward in his chair.

'Really? But you didn't hear anything?'

'No, I was asleep. But I don't understand how this person got in. You know how tight my security is.'

'I do. And you found no evidence of an intruder?'

'No, except...'

'Except what?'

'It's just that, I don't feel safe in the house. I haven't for a long time now. It's why I got a lodger in the first place.'

'How do you mean?'

'I don't know, it's a feeling, I guess. A feeling like I'm being watched. Again, I've not told anyone but you. Not even Dr Martin.'

'Watched?'

'Yes. Like when I'm walking home, even in the house sometimes. I know it sounds crazy, but things aren't always in the same place I left them. I close the door when I leave a room, and sometimes later I find it open again. I worry someone's been inside and moved things. Like they're playing some kind of game with me.'

'Can you think of anyone who'd want to do that?'

'No, that's the thing, I can't.'

'Do you think that perhaps it's your imagination running wild, after the whole business with Ethan, after all you've been through generally?'

'I thought of that, and yes, maybe. I mean, I'm not sleeping well. I go to bed, wake up hours later, but I don't feel rested. I'm guessing lack of sleep can make you hallucinate, imagine things? Become paranoid. Dr Martin's said that in the past. Ethan used to comment I never seemed rested, that I appeared morose, vacant sometimes. Charles said the same, before he died.'

'It's true, lack of sleep can have all sorts of detrimental effects. But is there something else? Because I'm sensing there is, I've known you too long.'

'Yes,' I admit. 'There are occasions when I seem to... lose time.'

Dr Adams straightens. 'Lose time?'

'Yes, it's like I have these gaps in my memory. I've been trying not to worry, but recently, it's starting to get a bit much and I wondered if it's low blood sugar or something.'

'How long has this been going on for?'

Since I saw Jason. Since the night he came to the house. Since the morning I woke up to find him lying dead on my art studio floor.

But how can I tell him this? I can't.

'What is it, Adriana? What aren't you telling me? Tell me, I know there's something you're keeping from me. Is it to do with Jason? You need to speak up, else we can never resolve this and you'll never have peace. Did you do something bad, Adriana? Something you can't remember doing? Adriana, are you listening?'

There's a steeliness to Dr Adams's gaze, a harshness to his voice I've not seen or heard before, and it scares me. Looking into his eyes, I think he suspects why I'm feeling this way. But if I tell him the truth about Jason, that will be it. He'll never agree to keep my secret, no matter how sorry he feels for me. I suddenly can't breathe, I feel so confused, so dizzy, like the walls are closing in on me. I need to get out of here now, need someone to rescue me from this uncomfortable situation. It's how I felt the first time I saw Jason in the restaurant. How I felt the night before my parents died in the fire, when my mother had ranted at me. Stressed me out. And then suddenly, just like that, everything goes black.

-

'Adriana, are you OK?'

My eyes motor through you. I'm so cross you let her down like this, Dr Adams. Pushed her to her limit. Why now? After all the years you've been so gentle with her, why did you have to go and ruin things?

There's nothing for it. I'm out now.

'I'm not Adriana. I'm her smarter half.'

364

Your face all at once twigs, and I feel a smug sense of satisfaction that I've managed to evade you, the great Dr Adams, all these years.

'I see,' you say calmly. 'Do you know why Adriana hasn't been sleeping well? Are you the reason?'

A rage burns through me. 'Don't you dare go blaming me for that! If it wasn't for me, she'd most probably have slit her wrists years ago. I'm the one who's protected her since she was a child. I've saved her so many times from those who've wanted to hurt her.'

'Saved her? How do you mean?' You pause. 'Were you the one on the roof with Ethan? Did you push him?'

'You think I'm going to go into details? I'm not stupid. Just lay off, OK? Don't go working her up any more. She's fine. She'll be fine. So long as she has me.' I pause, sensing what's running through your mind. 'And don't you dare tell her about me. You'll ruin her life if you do. It's not her fault. She's been mistreated since she was born and she doesn't deserve to be punished. They'll put her away and I know you don't want that. I'm giving you a chance, Dr Adams. But this is the only one you'll get. Don't disappoint me, don't you dare say a word to anyone. Because you won't live to regret it if you do.'

Chapter Fifty-Nine

Seb

I'm sitting in a courtroom in the Old Bailey, watching Dr Martin give evidence for the defence during Adriana's trial for multiple murders. Her barrister is pleading not guilty by reason of insanity, on the basis that she wasn't 'Adriana' when those murders occurred. But rather, someone entirely different: Xavier, her alter ego. A ruthless persona, who takes advantage of Adriana's placid nature. Who revels in causing those who try to get close to her, or hurt her, even inadvertently, immeasurable pain. Charles being the prime, most shocking, example of this.

The police investigating Dr Adams's death discovered hundreds of handwritten journals he kept locked away in the basement of his house. According to Dr Martin he was a traditional man, and always favoured writing things down on paper, and therefore Dr Martin wasn't surprised he'd advised Adriana to do the same. In one of his last entries, he described his encounter with Xavier, one that frightened him, but which he'd also found surreal when Adriana reappeared and asked him what had happened, because the last thing she remembered was telling him how she had gaps in her memory and wondered if low blood sugar might be to blame. He said he hadn't wanted to unsettle her further that day, so made no mention of Xavier's emergence. But it was the reason he called her two days later, to arrange another meeting the following Monday. He planned on telling her then what occurred, when she was hopefully calmer. He feared she'd committed terrible crimes without realising, but felt he owed her this last meeting, to help her understand her condition, before voicing his suspicions to the police.

'But Xavier is smart,' Dr Martin says. 'It is my belief that he regularly checks Adriana's texts and emails, and that on reading Dr Adams's somewhat anxious email to Adriana that Saturday, he realised what Dr Adams planned on doing, and knew that he had to be stopped.'

'And how does the condition normally come about?' the defence barrister asks.

'From a previous trauma experienced by the sufferer,' Dr Martin replies. Everyone is silent, the entire courtroom transfixed, as he explains. 'In Adriana's case, I believe it was triggered by the extreme and repeated emotional and physical abuse she endured from as young as two at the hands of her mother, Steph Monroe, and then later, her babysitter, Jason Stevens.'

I shudder at the mention of my dad's name. I know most people here feel sympathy for me. But suddenly, I feel their eyes on me. The son of a vile abuser of women. Someone who tormented an innocent child – the woman now on trial for his murder.

'Since her arrest, Adriana has told me intimate details about her childhood, including the terrible things that happened to her,' Dr Martin continues, 'the things she witnessed and which she feels ashamed of, despite it being no fault of her own. Traumatised beyond repair, I believe, and having now had the chance to read Dr Adams's journals in detail, that she at first found solace in two imaginary friends – Eve Jacobs and Xavier Barton – before her mind shattered into fragments, forming two separate identities: her own, Scarlett, as she was then known, and Xavier, the stronger of her two friends. Xavier is fearless. He became her protector when things became intolerable at home. Dr Adams believed that he was the one who set Adriana's parents' house on fire, something Adriana has no recollection of. When she became him, she was untainted by her mother's abuse. Only Adriana bore those scars, while Xavier remained undamaged. A far stronger alter ego but also fiercely protective of her and jealous of those who got close to her. It is my belief that when she went to live with her aunt and uncle in Guildford and started seeing Dr Adams, things took a turn for the better, and Adriana experienced years of stability. For the first time in her life, she felt happy and valued. Free of her past, it had been a rebirth of sorts. And, in turn, Xavier had disappeared. Pushed to the far recesses of her troubled mind. A phenomenon that can happen in cases such as Adriana's because multiple-personality sufferers often hold down regular jobs and relationships, managing to live relatively normal lives and, in this way, unwittingly fool their friends, colleagues and family into believing they are just like everyone else.

'But then, one day, something happened to upset that balance. Something that caused Adriana to become severely stressed and trigger Xavier's return. Adriana told me she came face to face with Jason Stevens. Who days later turned up at her house and tried to molest her. I believe at this point Xavier emerged and killed Jason, and that he later went on to kill Charles Wentworth, Ethan Savage and Dr Adams, because he believed they were on to Adriana and her secret and would before long out her to the world and lead the police to the remains of Jason Stevens hidden in her art studio.'

Dr Martin briefly looks my way as he says this, and I feel the tears gather in my eyes. Not for Dad, but for Adriana, for Mum, for all the women my wretched dad hurt and abused.

'Thank you, Dr Martin,' the defence barrister says. 'No further questions.'

At that moment, Adriana glances at me, and I see the apology in her eyes. Along with the fear. She doesn't deserve to be locked up. She needs care, understanding. Treatment. I just hope the jury feels the same way.

'Your witness,' the judge says.

I watch the prosecution barrister stand up. Can tell by his confident strut, the eager anticipation in his eyes, that he's about to tear Dr Martin to shreds.

'Dr Martin, do you really expect us to believe Mrs Wentworth has no recollection of murdering four men in cold blood? It seems like a very tall story to blame it all on some "other personality" we have yet to see any evidence of, despite putting Mrs Wentworth on the stand twice. Have you yourself met this Xavier in your sessions with her?'

'No, I have not.'

'I see. Is it not the case that the defence of dissociative disorder is a highly controversial one and has been proven to have doubtful validity?'

'I disagree,' Dr Martin says. 'There have been many proven cases, the most famous being Billy Milligan who was found not guilty of kidnapping, robbing and raping three women in 1977 owing to a diagnosis of dissociative disorder. Furthermore, Dr Adams's final entries prove that Mrs Wentworth is a sufferer. He had not witnessed such behaviour before, but having pushed her – to the point she became extremely agitated – Xavier emerged. I believe Mrs Wentworth's shift at that moment was a genuine one.'

'And yet, as you say, in eighteen years of treating her Dr Adams had not observed this "switch". Despite being a highly regarded psychiatrist and someone who knew Mrs Wentworth perhaps better than her own husband.'

'As I said, sufferers can go for years undiagnosed living normal lives.'

I look up at Adriana. Notice that she's started fidgeting in her seat. She looks uncomfortable. Really uncomfortable.

'I put it to you that Mrs Wentworth is faking. The fact is, she lured Jason Stevens to her house when her husband was away with the intention of murdering him to avenge years of abuse she suffered at his hands as a child. She hid his remains and then when her husband started asking questions, perhaps grew suspicious, she killed him too. Seven years later, she killed her lodger and Dr Adams for the same reason. Mrs Wentworth is nothing but a cold-blooded killer.'

'But how do we explain the laptops, the unregistered mobile phones and vials of morphine found in Mrs Wentworth's spare room? The threatening messages sent to Ethan Savage and Sebastian Walker? Messages sent to her own email account, including one from Dr Adams professing to cancel their meeting, but which we now know her alter ego sent having hacked into Dr Adams's email? Why would Mrs Wentworth have needed to go to such lengths? I believe she had, and continues to have, no recollection of doing any of these things because it was Xavier who did them. Mrs Wentworth lacked intent to murder, but she needs help. She needs psychiatric care, not punishment.'

The prosecution barrister shakes his head. 'There is no Xavier. And as sorry as I am for her traumatic childhood, Mrs Wentworth cannot be allowed to get away with her crimes. She knew exactly what she was doing. Xavier is but a convenient scapegoat for her own ruthless intent.'

'You men need to shut the fuck up!'

The entire courtroom looks up to where Adriana is sitting. Her eyes have that same look I saw the night she blacked out.

'It's so typical of your kind to think you know what's best, to label a woman as sick in the mind, in need of care or punishment.'

'Mrs Wentworth!' The judge bangs his gavel. 'You will be quiet or I will have you restrained.'

Adriana glares at him. 'And you can shut the fuck up too, sitting there in your poncy chair.'

I watch the stunned look on the judge's face. Everyone in the room, including him and both barristers, is speechless.

'She's been willing me to appear this whole time, begging me to come to her rescue, tell the truth, and finally you bastards have pushed things too far. So here I am, the person who did all those things you just described.' She glares at Dr Martin. 'But you and Dr Adams were wrong about it being Xavier. Again, it's so clichéd of your kind to believe that only a man could come to her rescue, be the stronger one.'

I watch Dr Martin's expression switch from one of puzzlement to a slow realisation. And then he says, almost inaudibly: 'Eve.'

Adriana smiles. 'Yes, that's right, Eve. You know it means "life". Well, that's what I am to Adriana. Her means to breathe. Her source of life.'

Chapter Sixty

Eve

Before

'Hey, big boy, I was just teasing. Just playing hard to get. It's me, Eve. The one who called you on Sunday. Who gave you the code for the key box.'

The sleazeball's eyes light up as I run my painted fingernails up and down his shirt. I'd been wondering when Adriana was going to call for me. Being a part of her, I could sense her stress, could hear her and Jason's muffled voices. And then, when he grabbed her and she screamed out for him to back off, that's when the switch happened. And so here I am. As cool as a cucumber. Primed and ready for something I wish I'd done years ago.

I can see how turned on he is by my sudden shift. He doesn't know I am the last person he'll ever set eyes on again. He thinks I'm playing some kind of naughty sex game, pretending to have this risqué other side. With a different name. A different personality. The way a prostitute might. Plus, of course, 'Eve' is the oldest temptress in the book. The original fallen woman.

He grins. 'Like mother, like daughter, I see.'

He's right. Adriana's mother would have delighted in such a game. The bitch would dress up in bondage gear and allow him to whip her. Hard. He thinks Adriana's into that sort of thing too. Has inherited her mother's sick tendencies. He has no idea things couldn't be further from the truth.

I push myself up against him, and at the same time try not to be sick. 'I always knew you'd find me one day,' I say. 'I was hoping you would. But you must understand, a girl like me enjoys playing hard to get. And what is life, if we can't have a little fun?'

'I agree.' He grins. 'I wouldn't have it any other way.' I feel him go hard and realise I need to make my move now, else I'll end up fucking the arsehole, and that would really make me puke.

I force myself to kiss him on the lips. Just to make him believe I mean business. And then I whisper into his ear, 'Let me get some wine. Be back in a sec, don't go anywhere.'

He pulls me closer still. Shit. 'But can't we go up to your living room, drink it there?'

I give a suggestive smile. 'I like it in here, it's more risqué. The living room is so boring, plus I don't want to be thinking of Charles when you screw me. He never comes in here. And by "come" I think you know what I mean. You'll be the first.'

This does the trick. 'OK then, you go, but don't keep me waiting too long.' He slaps my bottom as I scuttle off, and I resist the urge to grab the knife Adriana brought down and thrust it into the side of his sick brain.

I quickly leave the room, then sprint up to the kitchen where I retrieve a bottle of red – unlike Adriana, I prefer it to white – from the rack and pour two glasses, then find the strip of Diazepam Adriana keeps in a tall cupboard. I pluck one out, crush it to a powder with the back of a teaspoon then sprinkle the contents into one of the glasses which is slightly chipped and therefore easily identifiable. I give the liquid a good stir. Fingers crossed he won't be able to taste it.

Within two minutes I am back downstairs. I push the door to, find him still standing where I left him.

'Let's sit,' I say.

I hand him the chipped glass.

'Cheers,' I say, before sipping my wine, my eyes peeping over the rim suggestively. I then knock it all back. He seems to think it's all part of the game and follows suit.

While I wait for the sedative to kick in I try to stall him making any moves by engaging in banal chit-chat.

'So, did you know I was in London before we met in the restaurant?'

'I did,' he says. 'I saw your photo in the newspaper. Taken at a charity dinner.' He looks around. 'You've done very well for yourself, marrying someone like Charles Wentworth. When I think about the little girl I knew. The little girl whose mother said she had to invent friends because she couldn't find any real friends of her own.' His words sting, and I despise him more. But I have to be patient.

'Imaginary friends never let you down,' I say. 'Not like real people.'

He's on the cusp of replying but then I see his eyelids grow droopy. 'What the fuck was in this wine?' he slurs. He gabbles some other shit, and then before long, he's drifted off.

I slide his phone out from his trouser pocket, place it to one side, then waste no time in tying his wrists behind his back, his legs to the chair, before darting up to one of the spare rooms where I keep a vial of morphine I stole from Charles at the top of the wardrobe. I draw enough to do the job before going back downstairs to Adriana's studio.

He's still away with the fairies but it won't be long before he comes around, it wasn't that strong a dose of Diazepam, just enough to make him drowsy. Within the hour his eyes start to open. I'm sitting on a chair opposite him. He blinks a few times as if trying to make sense of his surroundings, and then finally his eyes open wide and he looks down at his feet, starts writhing around.

'What the hell is this? Did you drug me?'

'What's the problem? Don't you like being tied up? That's what you like doing to women, right? Tying them up? Hurting them.'

'Look, Scarlett, this isn't funny, untie me.'

'Who's Scarlett? Never heard of her. I'm Eve, remember.'

He gives an uneasy laugh. 'Seriously, you've had your fun, but this isn't what I expected. Just untie me and I'll be gone. I think this was a mistake, after all.'

I raise my eyebrow. 'Your mistake, maybe. But it most definitely wasn't mine.'

I pick up his phone. I wasn't able to get into it unfortunately, because it's locked with a PIN.

'What are you doing with that?' he says.

'It's not what I'm going to do, it's what you're going to do. Tell me, Jason, did you lie to me when you said you weren't married? Because I have a feeling you did. And if you don't tell me the truth, you might just never get out of here.'

He looks fit to burst with anger. 'Untie me, you crazy bitch. Your mother was right about you, you're nuts.' I shake my head, make a tutting sound as if I am far from impressed, then go over to the worktable and grab the knife Adriana brought down.

I go back over to him, put it to his throat. 'PIN. Now.'

'OK, OK,' he stammers. 'Three two nine four.'

I put down the knife, type the code. I'm in. I refrain from looking at his photos. I don't want to know who his friends or family are. Don't want it to weaken my resolve when I see their smiling faces. I go to CyberGhost, the same site I use on my own phone and laptop, then log in, so the police won't be able to trace the email I'm about to send. Then I go to Jason's inbox, scroll through scores of emails, and very soon it becomes clear to me that he does have a wife, whose name is Yvonne.

'Yvonne is your wife?' I demand.

'Yes,' he says faintly.

'Do you have children?'

'One.'

'I pity them,' I say.

I copy and paste Yvonne's email address into a new email. Then start typing.

'Who are you messaging?' he asks nervously.

'Your wife.'

'Please, no. She's a good person, this will break her.'

I pause typing momentarily. 'If she's a good person, like you said, then it's even more imperative she knows the truth about the monster she married. The same goes for your child.'

It's not that I want to cause Yvonne pain, but killing Jason isn't enough. His crimes need to be exposed. Finally, I stop typing. I go back over to Jason, and thrust the phone in his face.

'Read it.'

I watch his eyes scan the text, and judging by his reaction I wonder if he's going to be sick.

He looks up. 'You bitch. How can you be so fucking heart-less?'

I ignore him. I can't stand the sound of his voice a second longer, it's really starting to piss me off. It is time. I press send on the email, then place the phone down on the table, before reaching inside my pocket for the syringe. I whip it out, and then, before he can utter another word from his miserable mouth, I plunge it deep into his neck. Catching him completely unawares.

'What the fuck?' he cries out.

I bend over, whisper into his ear, 'That was for Adriana. For all the women whose lives you've helped ruin.'

He starts struggling frantically, in a pathetic attempt to free himself. But it's no use. Within five minutes, he goes into cardiac arrest before his heart stops permanently and he is dead.

I don't have time to celebrate the moment. I check the email has gone then remove the SIM from the phone and race upstairs with it to Adriana's study. I go over to her desk and place the SIM in the paper shredder lying to its left. I turn the shredder on, then listen to the grating sound of it pulverising the SIM to nothing. I grin to myself, knowing the police will never be able to trace Jason's phone, or where he sent the email from. I go back downstairs, and hastily untie Jason's wrists and ankles, before grabbing him under the armpits from behind and lowering him down onto the floor. I lie him flat on his back. Ready for Adriana to find him.

Then I fish out some paper from a drawer, grab a pen lying on the table and write a note to Adriana. In my handwriting, of course. Not hers. I can't have her thinking she killed him. Because she didn't. But I also need to ensure she doesn't go to the police and fuck up both our lives. As ever, she needs my guidance. Needs to follow a plan. A foolproof one. I could take Jason's body off the premises. Bury it somewhere. But it's safer to make her an accessory. It's a tad risky, but I will give her no option but to hide it herself. That way, she remains under my control even though I will lie and promise she'll never hear from me again provided she follows my instructions.

I am glad she chose me to be a part of her and not Xavier. Like a typical man, he was all mouth and no trousers. Going in all guns blazing. But Eve was the quietly self-assured one. Quiet yet shrewd. Always on hand to give sage advice. To follow her head and not her heart.

I will continue to guide Adriana for the rest of her life. We are two halves of the same coin. She cannot exist without me, nor I without her. We are women, after all. We need to stick together.

Because when it boils down to it, the female of the species is stronger than the male.

It's always been that way. And it will be until the end of time.

A Letter from Alex

I started writing *Under Her Roof* in March 2023, two months before *The Final Party was* published, and finished the first draft in July of the same year. It's quite different to my previous books, focusing mainly on a two-person narrative, rather than the multiple voices that feature in my other psychological thrillers, but I really enjoyed the challenge of developing the characters of Seb and Adriana who, for me, are probably the most sympathetic and emotionally fragile of all my characters to date.

What makes the psychological thriller so compelling is the way it focuses on ordinary people in everyday situations/relationships we can all relate to in our own lives, but which necessarily take a darker turn – this being a thriller after all! The landlord–tenant relationship is a perfect example of this, and one I was keen to explore. Many of us will have been tenants at some point in our lives, some of us may even be landlords, and in fiction this set-up has the potential to take a particularly ominous turn because in the majority of cases each party will be a total stranger to the other, thereby conjuring up all sorts of ideas in the devious minds of thriller authors like myself!

Likewise, living in the digital age, a world where we freely expose our lives to perfect strangers on social media, along with the idea of 'Big Brother' watching us, I thought it would be intriguing to weave this into a landlord–tenant story – the idea of being watched, every aspect of our lives under surveillance, and the sheer feeling of helplessness, claustrophobia and terror it induces on the part of the victim. I, for one, find this a terrifying concept, and one I hope never to experience.

I chose to base the book in Hampstead for several reasons. For one, having lived in the North West London area for the best part of thirteen years, it's an area I'm very familiar with, but one I couldn't in my wildest dreams afford to buy a place of my own in! I remember going for long winter walks around Hampstead Heath as a student, gawping at the area's mansions with their stately gates, wondering who lived in them, and then in later years pushing my son around in his buggy in the summer months with my NCT friends. It's a very pretty, picturesque, affluent part of London, and one where a person should feel incredibly safe. But, of course, Seb and Adriana feel anything but safe with their lives being monitored, despite living in a veritable palace, and therein lies the dramatic irony I wanted to convey.

One other important thing to mention is that in *Under Her Roof* I explore various difficult and painful real-life issues I won't reveal here should you, the reader, happen to read this letter before the book itself, in respect of which I did a considerable amount of research, including via on-line chat forums and reading scientific papers and studies. I hope I have addressed these delicately and with empathy. It was certainly my intention that this be the case.

I hope you found *Under Her Roof* an exciting, twisty and compelling read that kept you turning the pages and guessing until the end. I've loved every minute of writing it, and I'm so grateful to you for taking the time to read it. After many months of hard graft and editing, it really means the world. If you enjoyed the book, I would be thrilled to hear your thoughts via a review, which I hope might also encourage other readers to read it. It's so uplifting seeing positive reader reviews; they are hugely inspiring and greatly appreciated. Incidentally, if you enjoyed this book and haven't yet read my other books with Hera, *She's Mine*, published in August 2021, *The Loyal Friend*, published in June 2022, and *The Final Party*, published in May 2023, I'd love for you to look them up. They're available at Amazon, Waterstones and all good online book retailers.

Again, thank you for your support on my writing journey and I hope you'll continue to follow me as I work on new releases.

You can get in touch on my social media pages: Twitter, Facebook. Instagram, LinkedIn and TikTok. Also, please visit my website for further information on my books, and latest news/blog posts. I'd love to hear from you if you'd like to talk about any of my books or anything else for that matter.

Much love,

Alex x

https://www.facebook.com/AAChaudhuri/
https://twitter.com/AAChaudhuri/
https://www.instagram.com/A.A.Chaudhuri/
https://www.instagram.com/AAChaudhuri/
TikTok Handle: @alexchaudhuri0923
https://www.linkedin.com/in/a-a-chaudhuri-55a83524/
Website: http://aachaudhuri.com/

Acknowledgements

There are a whole host of wonderful people I'd like to thank for helping me bring this book to the shelves. And, more generally, for being an immense source of friendship and support through the ups and downs of my writing journey.

My agent, Annette Crossland. Thank you for reading the first draft so quickly and, more importantly, for loving it!! There's no better feeling for an author than hearing they kept their agent up until two a.m. reading a new book! One of those 'sorry, not sorry' moments! Your boundless enthusiasm for the book was so uplifting, while your unflinching support, patience and faith in me over the years have been such a blessing. I can't thank you enough for always spurring me on and urging me to believe in myself.

Jennie Ayres, Keshini Naidoo and Iain Millar of Hera Books. Thank you so much for your support, encouragement and faith in me and my books. Jennie, your insightful comments and passion for this book from the outset were so inspiring, along with your tireless commitment to getting it into the best shape possible. Huge thanks also to Kate Shepherd, Thanhmai Bui-Van and Dan O'Brien for all your hard work and help on the publicity and marketing/production side of things.

Ross Dickinson, for being such a brilliant copyeditor and saying such lovely things about the book. Your eagle eye and intuitive observations were invaluable! Also, to the proof-reader, Vicki Vrint, for helping to make it as error-free as possible.

Chris Shamwana at Ghost Design for creating such an eye-catching cover. I love how different it is to my previous covers, particularly the striking colour palette but, like the others, it captures the essence of the book perfectly. I'm so grateful for the time and immense effort invested by Chris, Keshini and Jennie in the cover design – it was certainly worth it!

Kirstie Long and Caroline Raeburn. Thank you for reading an early draft. Your comments are always so on point, and I'm so grateful for your support, encouragement, and wonderful friendship.

The kind and brilliant, Graham Bartlett, for your expert advice on a particularly tricky issue! Thank you for giving up your time so generously, for listening so patiently, and for working so hard to help me crack the problem! Thank you also for enlisting the help of the wonderful Dr Julie Roberts for her expert forensic advice on the same issue. It was a privilege to meet you, Julie. I learned so much from you both on that fascinating Zoom call, and I would never have solved that very sticky problem without you!

All the lovely, kind and talented authors who read an early copy of *Under Her Roof.* I am immensely grateful to you for taking time out from your busy schedules to read the book and for saying such lovely things about it.

The kind and talented Awais Khan, for being such a wonderful friend, and the ultimate social media guru! Since we launched our debuts back in 2019, you've always been there to advise me and boost my spirits, but most of all make me laugh so hard sometimes it hurts! I am eternally thankful. A special thanks also to Jacqueline Sutherland (my awesome library tour partner-in-crime!), Emma Scullion, Sarah Clarke, Lucy Martin, Christie Newport and Joy Kluver for being such kind, lovely and supportive writer friends.

Sabine Edwards for being such a kind, generous and supportive friend over the last five years. I am forever in awe of what you do – you make it look so easy, when I know it's not!

The amazing book blogger and reading community on Twitter, Facebook and Instagram. I wish I had the space to list out all your names (!) but I hope you know how grateful I am to you for constantly championing my books. A special mention to Danielle Price (you are so wonderful and kind and an absolute superstar!), Vik Wakeham and all The Squad Pod ladies, Karen Huxtable of UK Crime Book Club, Kelly Lacey of Love Books Tours who organised the most brilliant books tours for me, Donna Morfett, Melissa Allen, Shay Griffiths and Surjit Parekh. Also, Elizabeth Beverley of Surrey Libraries and all the amazing libraries who've invited me to speak this past year with my lovely author friend, Jacqueline Sutherland.

Friends and family who've supported me and my books over the last few years. It's such a tough, competitive industry, so I can't begin to express how much I appreciate you sharing my posts, buying and reading my books and just generally spreading the word.

Dr Jacky Collins (Dr Noir) for all your help, advice and selfless support with my books. I love being interviewed by you, it's always such a pleasure, your kindness and enthusiasm is so inspiring, and I'm so grateful for the opportunity.

Ayo Onatade for your kind and generous support, guidance and friendship over the last five years, and telling me to believe in myself! I'm so grateful for all the help you've given me.

Harrogate Festivals/Theakston Old Peculier Crime Festival, Capital Crime, Bloody Scotland, Newcastle Noir, The Dark Side of Brighton, CrimeFest and The CWA for your fantastic support over the last few years and for giving me such brilliant opportunities to promote my books and help them to reach wider audiences.

My very special girlfriends – Chika Ripley, Priya Pillai, Jessica West and Dawn Ford – for always supporting me and my books, and for always being there to listen and advise and cheer me up when I'm having a bad day. I hope you know how wonderful you all are, and I'm so grateful for your friendship.

My parents, Mukul and Diane. I'm so grateful for your love and support with my writing. Thanks for always believing in me.

My husband, Chris, for being so patient and supportive of my writing, through all the ups and downs, and for giving me space and time to write. To my wonderful boys, Adam and Henry. I'm so proud of you. Thank you for making me smile when I'm having a bad day. Love you SO much.